C000165491

ABOUT THE AUTHOR

The youngest son of a Lieutenant-Colonel in the Cameronians (Scottish Rifles) and a Faroese mother, Richard Young – aka 'Siggy' – has spent much of his working life with the Scottish Court and Tribunal Service. During this time he has also forged a fine reputation as an accomplished amateur cricketer and also as a cricket administrator.

Young's extensive cricketing background and passion for sport, allied to his long career in the processes of the law and an innate capacity for forensic probing, combined to produce in 2014, the acclaimed 'As the Willow Vanishes', a remarkable work of scholarship and myth-busting revisionist history that has made a significant contribution to the sizeable canon of Scottish sporting and social literature.

But while he was conducting in-depth research for 'As the Willow Vanishes', Young began to discover connections and coincidences that became personal in that, perhaps, his own family history itself had a fascinating story or two to tell.

The result is 'The Stream', a first time novel with a plot-line that will make you, the reader, reconsider established history.

Written in an engagingly descriptive and informative style, you are about to be drawn into a story of intrigue starting in pre-war Germany and how a chain of events stream through time and link with each other in the present day.

The
Stream

Richard S Young

This novel is entirely a work of fiction.

The names, characters and incidents portrayed in it are the work of the author's vivid imagination. Any resemblance to actual persons, living or dead, events or localities is entirely coincidental.

Acknowledgements

I have many people to thank for their help and assistance in enabling me to write this book, but in the first instance, special praise has to be given to John McGraw for providing me with the original inspiration for the embryonics of the story. Of course I have to thank all of my Nordic relatives, especially Johan and his family, and Simona, for all their help and advice, but I also have to thank the Faroe Islands themselves for providing such a dramatic back-drop landscape to most of the tale.

Special thanks must be given to Kieran Hatton of Diving in Depth for the provision of all the detailed technical specifications, and to Eric, Derek, Fiona, Paul and Frank for their continued welcome support and guidance. To my many school chums and work colleagues - you know who you are – thanks again.

Finally, I have to thank my wife, Lesley, and my daughter, Freya, for their patience, and their support, in allowing me to finalise the completion of this project.

The Stream

Foreword

A number of years ago, a work colleague, John McGraw, delivered an entertaining presentation about genealogy and the painstaking research he had undertaken while compiling his own family tree. It was certainly impressive and interesting stuff and also evident that his work was clearly a labour of love. Time passed, and my siblings and I were sadly tasked with taking our late mother's remains back to her native Faroe Islands for burial.

While we were up there, a cousin passed over copies of our own family tree, going back a thousand years. As a subsequent result of this gesture, my brothers and I embarked on the periodical population of an on-line family tree, and over the years, it expanded with other 'connected' relations around the world inserting their various branches, lineages and details and adding to our own information.

Matches and connections to differing ancestors began to appear in regular e-mail communications and alerts, and my passing interest in my Nordic roots, and its history, certainly increased. I had being doing research for some other projects, and purely by coincidence, I started to identify names, events and circumstances in history that some of my ancestors had been involved with. I collated all these links together and set them aside to study at a later date.

The Stream

It was only while I was watching a television documentary about genealogy and familial discoveries, I suddenly had the idea of revisiting the previously collected information and perhaps writing a work of faction based around my own mother's hidden story, and using her wartime experiences to concoct the backdrop to a plausible yarn set in a modern day context.

The result is 'The Stream' and while over 85% of the historical information contained within it is factually correct, with the rest coming from my vivid imagination, it is probably possible or even closer to the actual truth of historical events than we will ever know.

From Berlin to Glasgow to Switzerland to Denmark to the Faroe Islands to Afghanistan to London and back to Glasgow, be prepared to embark on a continuous flow of a story that surges to a climactic finale.

Whatever you may finally surmise or conclude, I hope you enjoy the book.

There is a lot more of this to come....

Richard S Young

8.00pm – Friday 1st July 1938
Quedlinburg Abbey, Saxony-Anhalt, Germany

A bespectacled figure steps forward from the line of dark uniformed figures and dignitaries and slowly approaches the tomb of King Henry I. The occasion is the 702nd anniversary of the death of the first Saxon ruler of Germany, Henry I, who was the founder of the Ottonian dynasty of German rulers who would rule a unified Germany, and later the Holy Roman Empire, from 919 until 1024. Every other king of Germany for the next thousand years would be a descendant of King Henry I.

The bespectacled figure is none other than the Reichsführer SS Himmler himself, who bows solemnly and lays a wreath on the tomb of the king. Behind him, SS group leader Karl Wolf and Gauleiter and Reich Governor Rudolf Jordan, SS General Heydrich and SS Obergruppenführer Heissmeyer watch on as Himmler stands to attention, extends his right arm in the air as a salute and shouts *"Sieg heil!"*. The assembled darkly uniformed figures and invited dignitaries follow suit in a deafening crescendo of acclaim…..

The Stream

It's the middle of September and the city of Glasgow is experiencing unusually warm weather for the time of year. Instead of the expected smir of horizontal rain that completely soaks you with unrelenting waves of inescapable wetness, the urban sprawl is bathed in warm unseasonal sunshine, it is 22 degrees and the local populace is mainly dressed as if they are, perhaps, on their holidays in the Mediterranean in the middle of July and not the early onset of autumn on the west coast of Scotland.

Freyja Fulton, a pretty 17 year old girl with thick, long brown hair, alights from the bus and starts making her way up Hope Street as she heads for St. Kentigern's College to start her life as a student of Nordic Studies for the next four years. She spots other teenagers heading in the same direction and is relieved that she has got off the bus at the right stop. The fellow teenagers seem to be struggling with their back-packs of books as well.

Her mother had fussed with her earlier that morning about where she was going and when to get off the bus and did she want a lift in on her first day? Freyja, being a strong-willed individual had refused and said that she would prefer to be able to make her first day at college her own experience. Groups of older students go past her as she slows in her approach to the college. The blonde sandstone frontage of the college creates an imposing edifice with its entrance marked with neo-classical Doric pillars and she stops as she studies a signpost with the layout of the college in front of her. The other students seem to know where they are going and Freyja thinks to herself that "She's a dooley and should have listened to her mother".

Freyja takes off her back-pack and reaches inside to get her mobile phone out to call her mother for advice and directions. Her search is interrupted by a pair of floral-patterned Doc Martin boots stopping beside her and a voice says "Are you lost as well? Me too! What you studying?"

Freyja stops retrieving her phone, stands upright and looks at the owner of the voice and the floral-patterned boots. It's a girl about the same age as Freyja, the same height, 5 foot 6, with a round, kindly and pretty face surrounded by a shock of raven-black curly hair that finishes halfway down her back.

"I'm Wendy Russell, by the way" and sticks out her right hand for a hand-shake.

"I'm Freyja Fulton. Pleased to meet you Wendy. I'm doing Nordic Studies. Well. I hope to be if I can work out where I have to go".

"Snap" says Wendy. "Let's go inside and find out where we have to go" and trots off to the entrance. Freyja picks up her bag and follows. Wendy is inside and talking to a clerical officer who points to her left and seems to be given directions as Freyja joins her.

"We've to go up those stairs and head for the Mary Johnstone wing. Apparently that's where the Nordic Studies department is" says Wendy. As they are going up the stairs, Wendy asks "Freyja? That's a Nordic name? Is there a reason you are called that and is it coincidence you're doing Nordic Studies?"

Freyja goes on to explain that her grandmother was from the Faroe Islands and that she was named after the Viking goddess, who in Norse mythology, is the protector deity of the islands and the goddess of the month of February, the same month that she was born in. Freyja also explains that one of the rewards of completing the Nordic Studies course is the high possibility of getting an interesting job with one of the college's private finance investment partners, and with one of the perks of the course being the various and frequent private investor sponsored field trips to Iceland, Norway, Sweden, Denmark, Greenland and the Faroes, and as she has relatives in Denmark and the Faroes, she could possibly use these trips as opportunities to catch up with them.

"Cool" replies Wendy. "To be honest, I only changed my mind last week and signed up for the course because of those trips away and that the prospect of archaeology and brushing dirt off some unearthed rocks in a bog somewhere doesn't have the same appeal as visiting volcanoes, glaciers and bathing in hot springs in Iceland and maybe seeing the Northern Lights in Norway".

The two girls arrive at the top of the stairs and see the sign-post pointing to the Mary Johnstone wing and push through a set of swing doors to start their lives as Nordic Studies students.

The Stream

7.00pm – Friday 17th February 1939
Grand Opening of the Reich Chancellery, Voßstraße 6, Berlin, Germany

The new constructed Reich Chancellery had the Berlin address of Voßstraße 6, and was to be found just around the corner from the old Reich Chancellery, located at Wilhelmstraße 77.

In 1938, the German leader, Adolf Hitler directed the architect, Albert Speer, to build a new Reich Chancellery befitting his aspirations of a thousand year Reich and had given Speer a blank cheque to deliver a new building. Hitler had stated that the cost of the project was immaterial with the condition that this new building had to be of solid construction and it was to be completed by January 1939 in time for the next annual diplomatic reception to be held in Berlin. This immense construction project was finished 48 hours ahead of schedule and cost over 90 Million Reichsmark, well over one billion dollars today.

Speer had kept to the timescale and the Fuhrer was pleased. Speer had been lucky in that he had industrialists at his disposal who could deliver on time. One such industrialist was Peter Bressler. Peter was 34 years old, married to a Danish national, Mille Lauridsen, and was the proud father of two children, a girl called Petra, aged 6, and a boy called Albert, aged 4. It was no coincidence that young Albert was so called. Peter's childhood friend in Mannheim, Baden, Germany had been Albert Speer and on leaving school, they had gone to study together at the Karlsruhe Institute of Technology. Peter had inherited the family steel stockholding business and had financially benefitted from the fact that his childhood friend,

Albert Speer, had commissioned his company to produce the thousands of lengths of steel required to hold the many granite and red marble blocks that decorated the internal façade of the new Reich Chancellery.

The silver Horch 853A Erdmann automobile's engine purred as the driver down-geared and turned into the entrance to the Reich Chancellery. The driver, and his two backseat passengers, stare open-mouthed at they view a long avenue, the Ehrenhof, a court of honour, lined with Schutzstaffel (SS) paramilitaries on either side of the avenue. A SS officer steps out and stops the car, asks the driver for papers who duly hands over a hand-written card invitation. The SS officer reads the contents and realises that it is written by Reichsführer SS Himmler himself and directs the driver towards the end of the avenue. The driver, Ralf, almost stalls the car.

From the back of the car, Peter Bressler calmly tells Ralf to relax and concentrate on getting to the end of the avenue and to ignore the SS and turns to the woman beside him and says to her re-assuringly.

"We are almost there Dagny. You are going to be very impressed with what you will see and even more so with the people that I am going to introduce you to tonight."

The woman, Dagny, is Dagny Poulsen, a 19 year old Danish woman originally from the Faroe Islands, an archipelago of 18 islands in the middle of the North Atlantic, 200 miles south of Iceland and 200 miles north of Scotland. Dagny is the nanny to Peter's children. She had been in Copenhagen in 1938 and was staying with her Uncle Paul when she had met Mille

Lauridsen, the daughter of his next door neighbour, and the two women had quickly become friends.

Mille had gone home to Copenhagen for a short holiday and had taken the children with her to see their grand-parents. She wanted them to grow up appreciating their Danish roots. Inwardly, Mille knew that Germany was changing and she wished her children to have somewhere to go when things went awry, and while Mille had been home, she had noticed that the children adored Dagny.

Every night at bedtime, they pleaded with her for Dagny to be able to go home with them to Berlin. Mille had tried to explain to her children that it would not be as simple as they would like and that Dagny might not be able to go to Berlin. But the children persisted with their mother and eventually, after telephoning her husband in Berlin, her mind was set and she asked Dagny if she would like to come with her back to Berlin with the children and become their nanny. For Dagny, leaving the Faroe Islands for the first time and going to Copenhagen had been an adventure in itself, but going to Berlin and Germany and to have a job as well, there was no second asking and immediately accepted the offer.

Ralf stops the vehicle at the end of the Ehrenhof and opens the rear passenger door for the occupants to exit the vehicle. Dagny takes the hand of Peter and they walk into the Reich Chancellery from an outside staircase. They enter a medium-sized reception room with double doors almost seventeen feet high opening into a large reception hall clad in mosaic. They ascend several steps, pass through a round room with a domed ceiling and enter a gallery that is 480 feet long. The gallery is thronged with people. A chambermaid appears and takes Peter's overcoat and Dagny's long shawl that reveals her to be wearing an azure blue evening dress made by the Anglo-American couturier Charles James, one of the great talents of haute couture. His complication of sculptural shapes through masterful cutting and seaming with short sleeves spiralling under the arm, over the shoulder and then forming cross-over drapery cut with a bodice front certainly draws the attention of other guests. Mille had been most insistent that Dagny wore her best evening dress to this occasion and had even adorned the dress by affixing a small pewter and silver brooch of a sailing ship on the left shoulder.

"Just to signify where you are from Dagny" Mille told her as she fastened the clasp through the fabric.

Mille had been feeling unwell in recent days and had suggested that Peter took Dagny instead. It would be good for her to meet some of Berlin's social elite and it would certainly make the gossip tongues start to wag about who was this attractive young brunette with Peter Bressler. Dagny blushes as she realises that everyone is staring at her. Peter pats her hand, pulls her gently towards a group of guests admiring the red marble decoration of the gallery, takes two glasses of Champagne from the tray of a passing waiter, hands one to Dagny, and introduces himself and Dagny to the group.

A discussion on steel supports for red marble is interrupted with shouts of "Peter". "Peter". "Is that really you?" as Albert Speer approaches. Peter and Albert shake hands and Peter introduces Dagny to him.

"I am delighted to meet you Fraulein Poulsen. I am so glad you have come this evening. Please come with me. I would like to introduce you to some friends of mine".

Peter and Dagny follow Albert to a group a few feet away. Dagny cannot believe who she is about to meet. Albert Speer introduces her briefly to Adolf Hitler, the Fuhrer himself, then the Deputy Fuhrer, Rudolf Hess, then Martin Bormann, his personal secretary, then Joseph Goebbels, the Minister of Public Enlightenment and Propaganda and finally to Reichsführer SS Himmler. Himmler adjusts his spectacles and shakes Dagny by the hand.

"Ah. Fraulein Poulsen. It is a real pleasure to meet you. I believe you are from the Faroe Islands. Correct? The islands are one of the last settlement colonies of the Vikings?"

"Yes Sir" replies Dagny.

Himmler turns to the man beside him and introduces him to Dagny.

"This is my colleague Dr. Pelle Lindemann, the Director of the Ahnenerbe. He has just recently returned from his third expedition to Iceland where he has been researching Viking heritage and local church records".

"Good evening Fraulein Poulsen. We have much to discuss."

9.30am – 17th September, present day
St. Kentigern's College, Glasgow, Scotland

The curriculum for Nordic Studies at St. Kentigern's College was fairly diverse. The enrolled students, over a four year period, are exposed to a vast raft of topics and subjects to explore. Critical evaluation on historical, social and economic development within the Viking world was a key analytic to the global course and the significance of the cultural history upon Europe and beyond, both in isolation and in temporal and geographic terms were major aspects for study.

Obviously the understanding of linguistics, literature, history and the development of language in the main Nordic settlement areas of Denmark, Norway, Sweden, the Faroe Islands, Iceland and Greenland, from times of settlement to the present day, were crucial to interpret the multi-layered issues that these Nordic territories are responsible for, and accordingly, the main topics were palaeography, runology, old Norse and North Atlantic rim studies. Various field trips to Nordic territories were a major feature of the course, where the class-room research and study could be utilised for physical and tangible investigations in situ. Other features of the course centred on settlement geography, archaeology, landscape history and urban morphology. A further feature was sustainable development which focused on economics, politics, ecology and culture but investigated human genetic variation in a Scandinavian and Nordic context such as genetic drift, population genetics and adaptive evolution of the human genome.

A fairly in-depth course such as this was an expensive exercise to deliver and St. Kentigern's College used partnership private finance initiatives to fund many of its courses. Multi-national companies in the late 1990s had discovered that entering into partnership funding arrangements to deliver specific courses within colleges, universities and areas of learning created opportunities for these companies to have the pick of bespoke applicants for the many differing fields of employment that they had to offer. It was a profitable relationship that St. Kentigern's College enjoyed with its various private finance partners. The college had had extensive refurbishment and redevelopment in recent years as a result of its various associations, attracted students from all over the world and provided a curriculum that was fairly unique in comparison to more established and respected colleges and universities.

One such multi-national company that utilised a partnership private finance initiative with St. Kentigern's College was Das Volker Syndicate, a world renowned and respected pharmaceutical and medicinal supplies manufacturer and research establishment from Switzerland. Das Volker Syndicate had originally been a collection of independent pharmacists who had shared materials, ideas, knowledge, experience and contacts with each other in rural and remote parts of the various cantons of Switzerland before the Second World War. It was a type of supply and demand initiative that was of mutual benefit to a group of independent pharmacists operating small businesses. When hostilities broke out, and owing to the neutrality of the country and the isolation that it endured, the syndicate, or co-operative union of independent pharmacists for the benefit of the people, had become extremely capitalist in its workings. With war all around them, the syndicate quickly realised that it could supply the various warring factions with the pharmaceutical and medicinal supplies that they desperately required, had short or limited supplies of and as the war continued, there would always be a constant demand for replenishment. Conjoined with the Swiss banking rules and regulations, the original members of the Das Volker Syndicate had very rapidly become extremely rich but also anonymously at the same time.

Such had been this unexpected, opportune and constant demand for pharmaceutical and medicinal supplies, the syndicate invested vast sums of money into research and development projects and had created clinics and test centres throughout Switzerland. At the war's end, the syndicate had been the recipient of a number of scientists and medics who were escaping from the collapse of Germany, fleeing from the probability of Russian internment or assisting the Allies. The company didn't ask questions of their new staff but did demand loyalty as the Das Volker Syndicate realised that a brave new world was upon them and that they could continue to use their isolation and neutrality to their financial advantage and become expansionist.

Slowly, but efficiently, the syndicate had built clinics, research facilities and production factories throughout what had been the European theatre of war, and by creating employment for thousands living in post-war austerity and coupled with advancements in science and technology, the company had become a world leader in research and development.

The Stream

The company had been fortunate to provide valuable assistance through its many research and development facilities from the late 1960s onwards to the on-going global search for the cure for cancer.

In 1967, two scientists working in the United States of America as part of a National Cancer Institute screening programme, isolated a natural substance from the bark of a Pacific yew tree, *Taxus brevifolia*, analysed the structure and components of this substance and labelled it as 'taxol' and arranged for biological testing.

The two scientists, Monroe E. Wall and Mansukh C. Wani, had identified that this substance 'taxol' had an efficacy as an anti-cancer agent and their discovery has now gone on to become a vital ingredient in many of the treatments for ovarian, breast and lung, bladder, prostate, melanoma, esophageal, and other types of solid tumor cancers as well as Kaposi's sarcoma.

However, the extraction of 'taxol' from the bark of the Pacific yew, usually meant the death of the tree, and owing to the fact that the tree is a slow-growing and long-living plant (it can live well over 500 years), it was ascertained fairly quickly that commercial propagation, growth and harvesting for medicinal development was not a viable concept and that a total synthesis of 'taxol' had to be commenced. By the 1990s, over thirty different research companies around the world were working together to discover a total synthesis.

The Das Volker Syndicate, having fully joined the global search to develop a total synthesis of 'taxol', had thrown a considerable amount of finance and resources as a commitment to assist with the chemical compound analysis and synthesis of a possible wonder drug. The company's research and development section had been looking at the records of ancient medicines and folklore concerning the healing properties of plants from territories such as Brazil to Greenland to China to Australia.

A Das Volker Syndicate researcher based in St. Albans, England, going by the name of Phil Harris, had been studying Norse mythology, and had chanced upon some ancient writings and the story of *Yggdrasill*, the tree of life, an immense tree that is central to Norse cosmology and how it connects the nine worlds that exist within it. The writings referred to *vetgrønster vida* which means "evergreen tree" and *barraskr* or needle ash, the Old Norse name for the European yew tree *Taxus baccata*. Phil had passed on a suggestion that the European yew tree might provide the answer, and it transpired that "taxol" can be easily synthesised from extracts of its leaves and is a more renewable source than the bark of the Pacific yew.

Through Phil's initiative, the Das Volker Syndicate had received many plaudits for its contribution and had been rewarded with the contract for the development, production and supply of its own variation of 'taxol', the current market leader drug, Philotaxel™.

Flushed with his inspiration, Phil had suggested in a memo to the Das Volker Syndicate management that they should consider assisting the human genome project, and in doing so, by using direct DNA analysis of mitochondrial DNA (mtDNA), certain illnesses and diseases could be possibly cured or treated in the future by examining the genetic structure and eliminating the defect at the source now.

The Stream

In genetic anthropology, by looking at the properties of direct, unaltered inheritance of mtDNA from mother to offspring without the 'scrambling' effects of genetic recombination, it was possible to look backwards in time and assess the racial groups and their variations most likely to be affected by certain afflictions, such as hereditary haemochromatosis, an overload of iron in the metabolism of the body that can present sufferers with diabetes, cirrhosis, arthritis, testicular failure, cardiomyopathy and hepatocellular carcinoma, the most common type of liver cancer.

Geneticists, through DNA research, identified that a particular mutated gene, C282Y, the gene mutation most commonly associated with the hereditary condition of haemochromatosis, was to be found amongst people of Celtic and Scandinavian origin with studies establishing that 10% of the demographic are carriers.

Population studies had revealed a very distinct distribution pattern for the C282Y marker in Europe. The highest frequencies of this mutation are found along the coastline of Europe. DNA studies revealed that the C282Y mutation first appeared in Europe about 70 generations ago. If each generation is classified as a period of 25 years, the traceable origin of this mutation can be placed to about 1600 years ago, spreading rapidly along the coastline of Europe and disseminating from Northern and Western Europe.

The timing and pattern of the spread of the C282Y mutation has a very close correlation to the migration of Vikings and the locations of their settlements throughout Europe, resulting in the suggestion of the "Viking hypothesis" and that the C282Y mutation is associated with the Vikings and their descendants.

Further investigation of the "Viking Hypothesis" found that C282Y is found in greatest frequencies in regions that are known to be Viking colonial settlements in the Scandinavian countries including Iceland and the Faroe Islands. Further support of the Viking Hypothesis was indicated by studies which showed that the lowest frequencies of C282Y were found in regions of Europe that were not affected by Vikings such as Central Europe, the Balkans, the Mediterranean countries and the many Russian territories.

Phil Harris had submitted his suggestion internally to management to consider and review, and hadn't expected to get a response. As what appears to be a fairly common practice in most large companies, suggestions coming from the coal face, from those who are working daily with the many issues and obstacles that have to be overcome by the frontline staff, these tend to be buried as they expose a management failing or get assimilated into someone else's agenda as they climb the corporate ladder.

To Phil's surprise, he received an e-mail thanking him for his suggestion and that he was to design a template on how to recover as many DNA samples in northern Europe as possible to obtain definitive proof of the origins of the C282Y mutations and solidifying a Viking link to this prominent European genetic disease.

Three weeks had passed since he had originally submitted his suggestion and receiving a response. The response had come directly from the Director General of the Das Volker Syndicate himself, one Torstein Lindemann. Phil was even more shocked to discover that he was being promoted to the title of 'Project Manager', being given a ridiculous salary, a corporate expense account and was being mandated to establish a fast-track DNA sample processing laboratory at the St. Albans site with an unlimited budget to deliver a state-of-the-art testing programme by any means possible. He was to use his initiative, think outside of the box and produce a definitive library of DNA samples that could be added to the human genome project database as well as assisting the Das Volker Syndicate's ongoing epigenetic research activities.

Phil had really struggled coming to terms with the enormity of what he had been tasked with. He was just a humble researcher who had, as a result of the success of one suggestion and the presentation of another, been accelerated far beyond his managerial capabilities and entrusted with the responsibility of delivering a data collection project on a scale that had never been attempted before.

Then he had a brainwave. His son was in Sixth Form and sitting his A-Levels. The topic of conversation at home had been about which university he should go to and what to study. Various university prospectuses had littered the house and Phil had noticed that many of them used partnership funding arrangements to deliver specific courses. There were nearly 2.5 million students in the United Kingdom, either as under-graduates or post graduates, attending higher and further education courses at colleges and universities. The Das Volker Syndicate could pilot a DNA sample collection initiative in the colleges and universities that it already had an association with via partnership funding initiatives, and could roll out a collection service throughout all the colleges and universities in the country. The data collection would be able to provide the company with a fairly extensive demographic to work from to collate a working and realistic assessment of the threat of hereditary haemochromatosis throughout a diverse population and a welcome opportunity to develop medical advancements in how to treat it, cure it or even remove it.

However, while solving one problem, that of data collection and how to go about it, Phil also realised that he had a vast range of other problems arising from the introduction of a data analysis collection programme on such a scale. The main problem would be the justified concerns of the individual in respect of confidentiality, the sharing of identities and information with governmental agencies, and conforming to the eight principles of the United Kingdom's Data Protection Act 2010. These eight principles control how an individual's personal information can be used by whatever organisations, businesses or the government that have access to it. Those responsible for using such data are duty bound to follow strict rules called 'data protection principles', whereby, they must make sure that the information that they have is:

- used fairly and lawfully
- used for limited, specifically stated purposes
- used in a way that is adequate, relevant and not excessive
- accurate
- kept for no longer than is absolutely necessary
- handled according to people's data protection rights
- kept safe and secure
- not transferred outside the UK without adequate protection

Phil thought long and hard on how to coerce a student population and get them to sign up to provide DNA samples for analysis. He had to think of some sort of enticement or inducement that would convince an individual to provide a sample. The answer was relatively simple and was one that had befallen mankind since time began, and that was greed.

Float out the DNA sample collection service with specific dates and times at the various colleges and universities throughout the United Kingdom when the new educational year started in September. Collections could be managed on set dates throughout October and November with the samples express delivered to St. Albans for processing, collation and extrapolation purposes. With the collections being held early in the educational calendar and with most students being financially restricted, lure them into providing a sample with the promise of a payment of £30.00 in cash, there and then, for basically 5 minutes of their time for filling in a form and allowing a mouth swab to be taken from them.

Most of them would sell their grandmother for £10.00, so increase the chance of collecting a sample by paying a handsome amount for doing so. Phil had been told that money was no object and the Das Volker Syndicate had mandated him to get the results.

As Phil was leaving the entrance of St. Kentigern's College, he looked back and watched the pretty clerical officer at the reception desk. She had just taken delivery from him a sizeable amount of promotional flyers, posters, information disks and memory sticks, as well as t-shirts and stickers with the slogan 'Re-programming the Code' to advertise that the

DNA sample collection initiative would be held within the college on the 7th and 8th November.

She opened one of the boxes, took some posters out and started to put them up on information boards around the entrance foyer.

Phil smiled as he jogged down the steps and got into the black BMW X5 that was waiting patiently for him. Another institute sorted he thinks to himself as he straps on his seat belt, ticks off St. Kentigern's College in his 'to deliver to' list and speaks to his driver.

"Pollokshields Community College please. We've only got four more places to deliver to today and that's all of the Glasgow area completed. We can do the Edinburgh colleges tomorrow. What do you guys do for entertainment up here?"

The driver, a local man called Stuart McGregor, stares straight ahead, starts the engine and replies.

"What are you looking to do, Chief?" and pulls away from the kerb.

The Stream

8.14am - Tuesday 23rd May 1939
The Rudolf Virchow Hospital, Augustenburger Square,
Berlin, Germany.

The utilitarian starkness of the hospital room was evident. A
net-curtained window to the right threw diffused daylight into
a white walled room that had a solitary bed occupying the
middle of it. Thrust hard up against the far wall, the bed has
sterile white sheets that are covered with a pale blue blanket.
Beside the bed there are two chairs and a bedside table with an
Emesis basin, a jug of water and a single glass.

In the bed lies Dagny Poulsen. She has been there for four
days as she recovers from Scarlet fever, a common enough
disease among children but a dangerous ailment for adults.
Dagny has been quarantined, but undeterred, two men sit in
the chairs beside the bed and scrutinise the contents of her
handbag that they have unceremoniously upturned on the
bed.

The two men are Kriminalassistents from the Geheime
Staatspolizei, the Gestapo, the abbreviated name for the Secret
State Police under the administration of Heinrich Himmler.
They are there because an informant had told them there was
a foreign woman talking in strange languages in her sleep and
that it was unacceptable that a non-German was receiving
medical attention.

A nurse enters the room and the two men turn and look at
her. The taller of the two, a brute of a man called Ernst Muller,
shouts at the nurse.

"Get out bitch!"

She quickly leaves. The other Gestapo officer, Kurt Obergmann, laughs and leans over the bed and shakes Dagny by the shoulder. Dagny comes round and is immediately frightened by the presence of two strange men standing over her and speaking to her menacingly in languages she didn't understand.

Obergmann snarls at Dagny "Honnan jöttél?" No response. He barks "Prej nga jeni?" at her and there is still no response. He screams "Odkiaľ ste?" at her and she does not reply.
A voice booms out from behind the men.

"If either of you two imbeciles could read, you might find from her papers that Fraulein Poulsen is Danish and she does not speak Hungarian, Albanian or Slovakian".

Muller, red-faced with anger at being spoken to in such a manner, wheels around and is met by the figure of a Doctor, replete with white coat and stethoscope draped around his shoulders, standing in the doorway of the room. The doctor instructs the nurse behind him to carry on with her duties. The nurse approaches the bed, takes Dagny's right arm, inserts a needle into a vein and begins to draw blood into a syringe.

"That'll do for now, nurse" and the nurse removes the syringe, places it in a kidney dish, swabs the insert point on Dagny's arm and hurriedly leaves the room.

"Who the hell do you think you are talking to?" shouts Muller at the Doctor.

"I am Dr. Pelle Lindemann, Director of the Ahnenerbe and Senior Doctor of this hospital and Fraulein Poulsen is under my direct care. Show me your identity papers as I will be mentioning your behaviour to Reichsführer SS Himmler himself over dinner this evening. Now get out of my hospital, bitches!"

The two Gestapo Kriminalassistents are ashen-faced as they salute Dr. Lindemann and hurriedly rush past him into the corridor and make for the exit.

Dr. Lindemann approaches the bed, sits on the pale blue blanket and starts to put Dagny's effects back into her handbag.

"I am sorry that you have had to experience that, Fraulein Poulsen. I will make sure they are disciplined for their actions and that they are made to apologise to you in due course. It has been a worrying few days for you and it is important that you recover fully from this illness. I will get the nurse to bring you something to eat and drink. You need to get some rest so I will leave you alone for now. It is important that you get better quickly."

As Dr. Lindemann sits up from the bed and leaves the room, Dagny begins to wonder why she seems to be so important.

The Stream

The Bressler Residence was a red clinker brick villa in Kreuzberg, south-west Berlin. The house itself was in the middle of the Kreuzbergstraße, directly across the road from the Viktoriapark, a delightful urban park that commanded excellent views over the central and southern portions of the city.

Dagny had taken the children, Petra and Albert, over to the park to its vivarium to see the animals such as birds, badgers, foxes and reptiles that were kept in viewing areas. Having left the vivarium, Dagny had walked the children past the Schinkel Monument, dedicated to King William III of Prussia and his victory against France in the Napoleonic Wars, and the children were playing and chasing each other beside the many cascades of an artificial waterfall originating at the foot of the monument and continuing down a wooded hillside to the road junction of Großbeerenstraße and Kreuzbergstraße and the main entrance to the park. Dagny had promised to have the children home for 1.15pm and lunch, but if they had time, she would let them play in the playground near the park gates. It was just a short distance from there to the house.

She had looked at her watch and had gathered the children beside her on a bench.

"Yes Moster?" says Petra.

Dagny smiles at how both the children affectionately called her "Moster", the Danish for a maternal aunt. It was a confirmation of the bond that she had developed with the children and how close her friendship with their mother, Mille, really was. When Dagny had returned from her stay in the Rudolf Virchow Hospital, the children had been so excited, and Mille had remarked that they were both never that pleased to see their own mother when she had been away on one of the many business trips with their father, Peter. Dagny is about to explain to the children what she planned to do with them before lunch when she sees Mille entering the park at the bottom of the cascades. Mille is shouting "Dagny? Dagny? Hvor er du?" in Danish.

Dagny realises that something must be seriously wrong for Mille has come into the park looking for her and is calling for her in Danish. She stands up and waves in Mille's direction and catches her attention. Mille waves back and runs toward her. As she gets closer to Dagny, Mille is speaking in Danish at a very rapid rate and it isn't making any sense. As Mille approaches Dagny and the children, she asks the children to go to the playground and that they will collect them to go home for lunch. The children run off down the hill and enter the playground.

"What's wrong?" asks Dagny of Mille, who is clearly distressed.

"Germany invaded Poland this morning and there is now going to be a war. You cannot stay in Berlin, Dagny. You are a foreign national and you must get out of Germany while you can. I'm safe because I am married to a German and have German-born children, but you are not safe here and there are far too many strange people interested in you for some reason. You have to go. You have to leave now!"

The Stream

Mille takes a hold of Dagny by the arm and starts briskly walking down the path towards the playground and the children. Dagny tried to protest with Mille that she'll be safe and that there was nothing to worry about, but Mille was not in the mood for entertaining any of her pleadings.

"You are leaving now. Today. I have telephoned your Uncle Paul in Copenhagen and he will meet you at Københavns Hovedbanegård, the main railway station, and will take you to the port. There is a new ferry and postal ship, the Hans Broge, leaving for the Faroe Islands tomorrow. You have to be on it".

The two women collect the children and walk along Kreuzbergstraße and No. 48. Ralf, the driver, is standing beside the silver Horch 853A Erdmann automobile outside the house.

"I have packed your things into two suitcases. Ralf has put them in the trunk. While I get the children back into the house, get in the car. I will be back in a minute".

Ralf opens the back passenger door and Dagny enters inside. Mille returns soon after, opens the car door and hands Dagny an envelope. She kisses Dagny on both cheeks and hugs her. With tears running down her face, she says to her friend.

"Good luck Dagny. Thank you for friendship and I will see you again when this war is over", shuts the car door and pats the door panel to indicate to Ralf to drive off.

As the car turns into Großbeerenstraße, Dagny opens the envelope that Mille had given her and examines the contents. Inside was Dagny's Danish passport, a signed letter of transit authorising her travel status as a foreign national within Germany and another smaller envelope. This smaller envelope contained a substantial amount of Reichmarks together with a hand-written note saying 'to ensure you get home - Mille' There was a final surprise at the bottom of the larger envelope. A small cloth bundle.

Dagny was perplexed by the cloth bundle. There was no reason for it to be there and Mille must have put it in by mistake. She reaches inside and lifts the bundle out.

"There's something inside it" says Dagny to herself and begins to unravel the cloth folds. The folded cloth contains the ornate pewter and silver brooch of a sailing ship that Mille had attached to the dress Dagny had worn to the Reich Chancellery earlier in the year.

There is note attached, also in Mille's handwriting. 'To keep you safe from danger.'

The Stream

2.30pm - Thursday 10th August 1944
Maison Rouge Hotel, Strasbourg, German Occupied France.

The Maison Rouge Hotel had been an important meeting place in Strasbourg for centuries. Facing onto the cobbles of the Kleber Square, it was an integral part of the centre of the city, but today, it was the venue for a secret meeting to discuss the future of Germany in anticipation of defeat by the advancing Allies and to put in place a plan for that eventuality. At this secretly convened meeting, many of Germany's leading industrialists, scientists and bankers had been covertly gathered together and tasked with establishing a secure future for the resources and wealth of the nation that would be freely available to fund those prepared to build a new Reich. But the building of a new Reich, these resources, whether it be men, supplies, materials or finance, all had to be safely secured outside of Germany and be readily accessible in the future. This was the planning meeting to continue the dream of a thousand year Reich and it was to be delivered by any means possible. The recorded minute of the meeting read:

'The party leadership is aware that, following the defeat of Germany, some of her best-known leaders may have to face trial as war criminals. Steps have therefore been taken to lodge the less prominent party leaders as "technical experts" in various German enterprises. The party is prepared to lend large sums of money to industrialists to enable every one of them to set up a secret post-war organisation abroad, but as collateral it demands that the industrialists make available to it existing resources abroad, so that a strong German Reich may re-emerge after the defeat.....'

The outcome of this meeting was the creation of a well-financed entity that was named the "Organisation Der Ehemaligen SS-Angehörigen" ("The Organisation of former SS members), better known as ODESSA, that gave its members new identities, smuggled them out of Germany during the chaotic end of hostilities, and to freedom through an underground network called "Die Spinne" (The Spider) across the un-patrolled Swiss borders.

Doctor Pelle Lindemann, as the Director of the Ahnenerbe, leaned back in his chair in the meeting room and drew deeply on his cigar. He exhaled the smoke in a long and drawn out fashion, as if whistling, as he realised that he now had the financial backing and wherewithal to relocate his relatively small section of the SS into neighbouring Switzerland, lay low and rebuild for the future. The mission, to re-create the pure Nordic blood of the forefathers of Germany, was secure as long as it maintained secrecy, and for that, it was time to be assimilated under the umbrella of an extant company in Switzerland, Das Volker Syndicate. He extinguished the cigar in a nearby ashtray, smoothed back his hair and got up from the meeting table. The other attendees were leaving by the front door, but Pelle reckoned now was the time for discretion, walked to the back of the hotel and exited by a side door into a cobbled street.

He walked quickly away from the Kleber Square and made for the car he had left parked, out of sight, some hours earlier. It was time to get his family out of Berlin and into Switzerland and the safe house in La Chaux-de-Fonds. Once settled, the relocation of the Ahnenerbe could then be achieved discreetly.

The Stream

The Swiss city of La Chaux-de-Fonds lies in the canton of Neuchâtel, a few miles from the French border and is located in the Jura Mountains at an altitude of 1000 metres. The local area is heavily forested, and because of the altitude and various geological reasons, very little farming can take place and the landscape is largely unspoiled. However, because of its strategic position for trade with neighbouring countries, the city has enjoyed economic importance for manufacturing and the watch-making industry and with many of the latter's leading brand names having their operations based there.

Unique as a Swiss city, in that it has been built following a grid street plan layout, the planning and the buildings reflecting the watch-makers need for rational organisation, Karl Marx, the German revolutionary socialist, had been a great admirer of the city and its unique urban design and referred to it as a 'city-factory'.

It welcomed investment in its city and had supported the creation of a central storage facility for medicines and pharmaceutical products by the Das Volker Syndicate just before the Second World War. With the city being served with a railway station since 1857, it was the junction of three separate railway lines serving Morteau in France, Neuchâtel and Biel, the city on the invisible language boundary between the French and German speaking parts of Switzerland. The syndicate had been able to shuttle supplies along the railway lines from its centralised store. Pelle Lindemann's father had been a storeman at the facility but had died as a result of fire breaking out in a building in October 1939. The then members of the syndicate had tried to brush any issues of negligence on their part under the carpet, but had not reckoned on the return of a vengeful son whose ruthlessness in discussion had seen the syndicate offer up a 51% share of their business to Lindemann by way of reparation for their liability in causing his father's untimely demise.

Lindemann had unexpectedly been the recipient of property with inheriting the family home and had, at the same time, procured a financially viable shareholding that could be developed over time. With Lindemann now being the major shareholder of the syndicate's concerns, he quickly developed a business stratagem that became extremely profitable for all involved. The compliance and assistance of the other shareholders was assured as they enjoyed the financial rewards, and although they no longer controlled the syndicate, the monetary returns were far beyond their wildest dreams.

The meeting at the Maison Rouge Hotel in Strasbourg had provided Lindemann with a further opportunity to expand the business, both personally and for his mission objective with the Ahnenerbe. He now had the perfect cover company to relocate all of the Ahnenerbe's assets to, and as a Swiss national, he had the extenuation of being a neutral citizen practicing medicine in Berlin and had become involved in Nazi research projects under duress. He could always justifiably claim that he had made his escape out of Germany and back to Switzerland in late 1944 when the first opportunity arose for him to do so safely.

70 years had passed and the relocation of the Ahnenerbe, and its subsequent assimilation into the Das Volker Syndicate had gone un-noticed. Lindemann had been fortunate with his timing and the subsequent chain of events in the final months of the Second World War that had conspired in his favour. The firebombing of Hamburg by the Royal Air Force on the 29th July 1943 had caused Himmler to order the immediate evacuation of the Ahnenerbe headquarters and its archives from Berlin.

The extensive Ahnenerbe library was moved to the Schloss Oberkirchberg, Illerkirchberg, near to the city of Ulm in Baden-Württemberg, the birthplace of Albert Einstein, while the majority of the administrational staff and resources became based within the 17th century Steinhaus in the tiny village of Waischenfeld near Bayreuth, Bavaria. The Ahnenerbe remained in both venues until captured by advancing American forces in April 1945, and on inspection, it appeared that a great number of the stored documents and records had been destroyed before their arrival. They hadn't been destroyed though; they had just been simply relocated.

Pelle Lindemann had been investigated during the Nuremberg trials in 1946 but had not faced any war criminal charges. Having effectively destroyed any incriminating evidence and removed the various and questionable paper trails that could associate him with the Ahnenerbe's activities and its dissolution and disappearance, he had gone on to enjoy life as the Director General of the Das Volker Syndicate and its global development. He never set foot outside of Switzerland again, and conscious of repeated investigations made by many countries, intelligence agencies and privateers over the years, the sins of his secret past died with him in 1978 at the age of 71.

But the Ahnenerbe's secret mission did not die with him. Pelle had entrusted all of the knowledge, information, history, documentation and importantly, its research archive, to his son, Torstein. Pelle had had constructed in the 1950s a subterranean storage bunker in the sandstone below the Das Volker Syndicate's headquarters in La Chaux-de-Fonds. The bunker contained all of the Ahnenerbe's data, but it also held the personal papers, manuscripts, books, documents and artefacts belonging to Pelle Lindemann. There was even a small research laboratory within and where Pelle had spent many hours trying to find the answer to the original mission priority - to re-create the pure Nordic blood of the forefathers of Germany.

Torstein had spent a number of years since his father's death researching the Ahnenerbe archive and had meticulously studied all of his late father's case-notes and findings. Torstein had launched various expeditions to a number of the places that his father had visited and had followed up many of the embryonic avenues of investigations that had been started but not completed as a result of hostilities. In the mid 1990s, with computerisation and more and more information becoming freely available on the world-wide-web, Torstein had embarked on the creation of a digital database of the archive. Money was no object and Torstein reckoned that its creation would accelerate the process of recreating the pure Nordic blood by being able to extrapolate answers from all of the information it contained. But the major factor for its creation was the result of Torstein's discovery of a file that Pelle had become fixated upon and had seemingly spent thousands of hours researching and investigating. The manila file cover simply said 'DAGNY', but what was inside the folder wasn't simple. The contents changed everything and caused Torstein to become fixated also.

The manila file called 'DAGNY' was about 4 inches thick and was full of medical charts, analysis reports, blood group definitions and other such data. At the front of the folder, on the inside cover, was a sepia photograph of a young woman called Dagny Poulsen. She is looking up towards the camera in a natural looking and relaxed pose. She is smiling genuinely for the photograph. The back of the photograph has a date written on it 'April 21st 1939, Berlin'.

On the front page of the folder is an admission sheet for the Rudolf Virchow Hospital in Berlin dated 19th May 1939. The admission sheet gives Dagny's details such as that she is a Danish national, aged 19, living care of the Bressler family at 48 Kreuzbergstraße, Berlin, and that she has been diagnosed as suffering from scarlet fever. The admission sheet has 'Scharlach – Ansteckende', (Scarlet fever – Contagious) stamped in bold red ink diagonally across the middle of it.

The following few pages detail her stay in hospital, x-rays, body dimensions, distinguishing features, the treatment and medication that she is given and her subsequent release. There are handwritten notes in Pelle's writing in the margins of the medical records and all sorts of notations and mathematical equations on a page concerning her blood samples.

The first two inches of the folder are records concerning Dagny's known medical history to June 1939, her stay in Germany and surprisingly, a record of Pelle's various meetings with this woman. They all seemed to be at various functions but in July 1939, the two had had dinner with each other at Berlin's top restaurants of the time, the M. Kempinski & Co. establishment to be found at No. 27 Kurfürstendamm in Charlottenburg-Wilmersdorf and Kempinski's legendary Haus Vaterland on Potsdamer Platz. These two evening dinner arrangements were the subject of very detailed notes that not only relayed the events of the evening, such as the times of picking Dagny up and returning her home, where the two of them had been and what they had both eaten and drunk, but what the topic of conversation had been about on both occasions. The majority of these conversations had been about her upbringing in the Faroe Islands, how she had arrived in Berlin, Dagny's family members, their names and history, Viking lineage and settlement and general enquiries about her ancestors and what she knew of them.

A following page had a note dated Wednesday 2nd August 1939 from Reichsführer SS Himmler to Pelle asking him to desist from having contact with Dagny Poulsen with immediate effect. The note went on to say *"Frau Bressler, the wife of the important industrialist, Herr Bressler, has expressed her concerns to none other than Albert Speer about the true intent of your relationship with her Danish friend and companion, Fraulein Poulsen, and is suggesting that you have an unhealthy interest in her and that you may be harbouring un-natural desires bordering on the realms of moral turpitude."*.

A copy of the reply to Himmler's note states that Pelle was only attempting to assist Fraulein Poulsen in her recuperation from her recent illness and was only showing compassion and friendship towards her, but that he would respect the wishes of the Reichsführer and refrain from all further contact with immediate effect for the greater good of the Reich.

The remaining two inches of the folder mainly related to various blood analysis reports, test results, newspaper cuttings and articles from around the world concerning blood groups. One of the articles was a feature about Conrad Waddington, a man often credited with coining the term epigenetics in 1942 as "the branch of biology which studies the causal interactions between genes and their products, which bring the phenotype into being".

Waddington, through research, theorised that although inheritance occurs through the DNA code from parent to offspring, epigenetic inheritance, hidden influences upon the genes and that genes have a memory, suggested that a parent's experiences could be passed through to future generations in the form of epigenetic tags.

The supposition of this theory suggested that the experiences of ancestors, such as the air that they breathed, the food that they ate, even the things that they saw, directly affect descendants, decades later, and what you do in your lifetime could in turn affect your grandchildren and their grandchildren. If science could control the genetic make-up of the DNA sequence, it would be possible to 'switch' genes on or off and that ancestral experiences could be re-lived through a modern descendant.

And this was the crux of Pelle's research. To re-create the pure Nordic blood of the forefathers of Germany, he needed to find someone that was directly descended from a traceable blood-line going back to the time of King Henry I, the first Saxon ruler of Germany. He had been introduced to a young

Danish woman from the Faroe Islands, a population of 27,000 in 1939, and being the descendants of Viking settlers of a thousand years ago, their genetic code and DNA had been relatively untouched and not interfered with for a millennium. He had a fresh palette to work from to paint a new landscape.

This Danish woman had taken unwell and had given Pelle the chance to procure blood samples from her to then use for study and research. He had been afforded an opportunity to combine his medical expertise with his Ahnenerbe directive and was confident, that given time, he would be able to prove that the mythology of the Aryan race was indeed true. But the outbreak of war had curtailed the research. His target specimen, Dagny Poulsen, had disappeared in September 1939, the blood samples that he had procured and stored, had become degraded over time, and post-war, Pelle had attempted to continue his research, but privately, and in complete isolation in Switzerland.

However, the discovery of DNA, deoxyribonucleic acid, by François Jacob and Jacques Monod in 1961 had re-invigorated Pelle. A scientific journal of the time quoted both men during an interview with them at the Institut Pasteur in Paris, France: "...the genome contains not only a series of blueprints, but a coordinated program...and a means of controlling its execution." François Jacob and Jacques Monod were awarded The Nobel Prize in Physiology or Medicine 1965 and the prize motivation was *"for their discoveries concerning genetic control of enzyme and virus synthesis"*.

Through contacts in 1976, Pelle had been able to have a sample of Dagny's blood DNA tested by the Institut Pasteur and had kept the results within the folder. He had extensive written notes explaining that the answer to his quest lay within these results but he needed more analysis, and time, to discover it.

A final report in the folder was a document written in 1977 by the Swedish anthropologist, Bertil Lundman. He had written a very comprehensive work called *'The Races and Peoples of Europe'* and had introduced the term "Nordid" to describe the Nordic race as follows:

"The Nordid race is light-eyed, mostly rather light-haired, low-skulled and long-skulled (dolichocephalic), tall and slender, with more or less narrow face and narrow nose, and low frequency of blood type gene q. The Nordid race has several subraces. The most divergent is the Faelish subrace in western Germany and also in the interior of southwestern Norway. The Faelish subrace is broader of face and form. So is the North-Atlantid subrace (the North-Occidental race of Deniker), which is like the primary type, but has much darker hair. Above all in the oceanic parts of Great Britain the North-Atlantic subrace is also very high in blood type gene r and low in blood type gene p. The major type with distribution particularly in Scandinavia is here termed the Scandid or Scando-Nordid subrace."

Pelle had died in February 1978 and had not been able to realise his dream. He had been very close to discovering the answer to his search but a combination of factors, such as a lack of sufficiently advanced scientific technology of the time, had prevented him from doing so. His son, Torstein, however, on discovering the 'DAGNY' folder and understanding the importance of what was contained within it, had moved heaven and earth to be able to finally achieve his late father's quest.

Torstein had sent a degraded sample of Dagny's blood for a full DNA analysis, and on its return, had spent huge amounts of money and resources on the profile being thoroughly investigated by the Genetic Inheritance Research and Development department of the Das Volker Syndicate. But a major breakthrough came in 2004 when the collation of the genetic history of Europe was proposed as a scientific research venture to complement the compilation of the human genome. Torstein could use Dagny's DNA profile to search for similar matches in the collected human genome database, and if a close allele marker match could be traced, he could use that match to finish his father's work. Dagny's DNA profile had been uploaded into the database and a search was under way when a close allele marker match caused a result to be pinged back.

There was a match, but it was separated by a millennia. A total of 1068 years existed between Dagny's DNA sample and the match found within the human genome database. Torstein, was at first incredulous when he got a message through by e-mail telling him that a match had been found, but there was a thousand year difference between the two samples. He clicked open the attached report and read its contents. His right hand gripped the computer mouse so hard his fingers turned white with the pressure. His heartbeat slowed to almost no pulse at all. His eyes had dilated in shock at what he was reading.

The close allele marker match with Dagny Poulsen was none other than King Henry I, the first Saxon ruler of Germany. There had to be a mistake. If this was true, the answer to the original search had been standing in front of Reichsführer SS Himmler in Berlin in 1939 all along and he didn't know it, but Pelle had had his suspicions at the time and had been trying to confirm them, one way or another. Did this Dagny Poulsen have children, or grandchildren, and if so, were they alive and where were they?

The Stream

11.41pm – 9th November, present day
Das Volker Syndicate Research Clinic, St. Albans, England.

Harry Shalestrick had a great job. Well paid, hours of his choosing and time on his hands to do what he wanted. A laboratory technician for the Das Volker Syndicate didn't sound interesting, but Harry really enjoyed his work. He chose to work the night shift which meant there were less people to interact with, less distractions, he could get on with his work and while waiting for results to come through, he could play his computer fantasy game on-line with his 'virtual' friends all over the world.

Harry was 5' 10", had disheveled curly titian hair, a pasty face and was very thin. He was so thin, his work colleagues that did know him, often referred to him as a skeleton with a skin graft, but Harry didn't care. Yes, he worked his long shifts supplied with a diet of high energy caffeine drinks and sugary sweets to help him through the hours and yes, this unhealthy diet of drinks and sweets may have altered his appearance over time, but to Harry, his looks weren't important as long as he got his job done.

His job was the processing of the thousand of DNA samples that the Das Volker Syndicate was collecting for an on-line database of genetic fingerprints.

He had once asked why the company was collecting the samples and was told it was all part of a multi-agency initiative to collate sufficient data for the human genome project that a number of leading universities were researching. If the human genome profile was accurately completed, then medical research could begin on how to remove certain afflictions and illnesses from the genetic codes. "Re-programming the code" was the buzz-word phrase he remembered from his induction course and the Das Volker Syndicate's Research and Development department's speciality was epigenetic inheritance, where some of the experiences of the parents may pass to future generations through genes. Das Volker Syndicate's main interest in this field was to ensure that the epigenome remains flexible as environmental conditions continue to change but the epigenetic inheritance could be adjusted without changing the original DNA code. Continue the lineage but remove all the varying health issues such as diabetes and you save the human race.

The courier arrived with yet more boxes of samples to be tested. Harry signed for the delivery, got himself a trolley and transported the four boxes through to the laboratory. He stopped at a worktop and placed the four boxes on its surface, picked up a bar-code scanner and zapped the labels on each of the boxes. The computer screen beside him on the worktop came to life as the scanned data from the labels generated fields for additional information to be added. Each box had five hundred DNA mouth swab samples inside. Each swab provider's information was detailed on a labelled bar-code on the side of the cartridge that held their sample. This information was further contained in a master bar-code on the side of each box and when uploaded into the computer, the general information details of every mouth swab provider became available for analysis and research. It was a clever software programme that Das Volker Syndicate had designed and seriously minimised the need for a lot of man hours and unnecessary paperwork. Efficient, simple to use and informative and greatly reduced the risk of filing error or contamination of test results.

Just as everyone has their own fingerprint, everyone also has their own DNA patterns, and through DNA profiling and genetic fingerprinting, an individual's patterns can be uncovered. Each person has roughly 3 billion base pairs of DNA and 99.99% of human DNA is exactly the same in one person as it is in another, but, by looking at "junk DNA", the extra DNA that all humans have and doesn't seem to serve any purpose, scientific research discovered that short stretches of junk DNA vary between individuals. Short tandem repeats are sections of DNA arranged in back-to-back repetitions and the number of these repeats varies from one person to another. These variations are called alleles and distinguish one person from another so the possibility of people having identical alleles is slim to none. The comparison test for identical alleles is normally 12, 25 or 37 markers, but the Das Volker Syndicate also wanted a 100 marker test made of the mouth swab samples it collected.

Identical allele comparison was a secondary test that the Das Volker Syndicate wanted to be made when the genetic fingerprinting tests were being carried out. Harry didn't know any details about who the comparison DNA sample originally belonged to, but he did know that he had to make sure that all the tests he ever made were definitely compared with it. His own professional experience and personal knowledge told him that the company was also searching for a particular mitochondrial related common ancestor or MRCA. If two individual's test results matched exactly (12/12) in the 12-

marker test, there would be a 99% probability that they are related. If two individuals match exactly (25/25) in the 25-marker test, their MRCA would have lived between 1 and 32 generations ago, with a 50% probability that the common ancestor lived 7 generations ago or less. In the 37-marker test, their MRCA would have lived between 1 and 20 generations ago but with a 100-marker test the most likely time frame to the MRCA would probably be from 1 to 4 generations ago, but more importantly, the subjects were directly related to each other. There would be a distinct genetic and genealogical pathway.

Harry started processing the samples he had just received by inserting the contents of each box of cartridges into four machines that were on a worktop at the far side of the laboratory. Each machine was a 'Surefire 500' DNA testing machine originally developed by the American military for the Department of Homeland Security's U.S. Citizenship and Immigration Service and the collecting of DNA from would-be immigrants or criminal and terrorist suspects. Each machine cost £250,000.00 and was about the size of a standard desktop printer. All four machines conducted polymerase chain reaction or PCR analysis to procure a genetic fingerprint of each sample. They were connected to the laboratory computer system and printers, and after running their tests, each machine would transmit the technical data to the laboratory server and print out the analysis results for every sample replete with individual bar-code and subject information. It took about 90 minutes for each machine to analyse 500 samples and then print out these results.

This whole system cost millions of pounds and Harry was proud that he was one of the very few allowed to use it. Although he had operated the system many times before, he reached into the drawer beside him and read the instruction manual and operational guidelines clipboard. It was a habit that had become part and parcel of his everyday job. The clipboard had a single piece of paper with Das Volker Syndicate letter headings. In bullet point format, it detailed how to use the machine, what to do with the results within the computer system and where to store the samples after testing. A final paragraph and further bullet points described what the operator was to do if certain scenarios occurred. To Harry, it seemed an unnecessary amount of fail-safe protocol to follow when all the information from the tests and the machines was available for extrapolation from the internal computer system, but hey-ho, the company paid him well and life was good so he wasn't going to argue or ignore the guidelines.

Attached at the back of the clip-board was an orange-coloured break-away plastic card. It was about the same size as a credit card and had instructions on how to use it printed on its front: 'If 100 identical allele markers are discovered on a sample, please snap card in half and contact the telephone number inside". You snapped the card in half and read the details inside. Simple enough instruction and no chance of that ever happening thought Harry.

Matt and Gerry were on-line with Harry as they were close to completing the latest stage of the fantasy computer game they were playing. Matt Matalia was from New Jersey and Gerry Santenez was from Mexico. The three of them had met the year before at the "Fantasy Quest" science-fiction, computer game and comic book convention in San Diego. They all shared common interests and had become good friends. They regularly e-mailed and Skyped each other with updates of what they were doing and regularly played as a team on-line in a computer game called 'Typhoon Falls', a cyber arena where they could act out their fantasies as kings, princes, heroes and villains and always get the girls, whose body forms were fantastical but the reality for these three was that the game was the closest that they would probably ever get to having a relationship with someone of the other sex.

"Harry! Harry! Throw the rock at the tiger and run to your left" screamed Matt through the head-phones.

"Sounds like a plan" piped up Gerry, but Harry had become distracted from the game.

There was now a continuous beeping coming from somewhere and it wasn't in the game. The beeping was getting louder and Harry realised it was coming from behind him somewhere in the laboratory. He cusped the microphone of his headset between his thumb and forefinger and speaks to his two friends.

"I've got a problem at work just now so I have to go. I'll give you a call later", switches off the game and removes his headset.

He stands up and starts trying to locate the source of the beeping. The laboratory is dimly lit due to energy saving motion sensor lighting and as Harry moves, parts of the laboratory explode into bright lighting as he triggers the sensors with his movement. He passes a couple of worktops and heads in the direction of the beeping. He can see a blue neon light continuously flashing on one of the 'Surefire 500'

DNA testing machines and he heads towards it. The overhead lights continue to trigger. Harry had never seen this malfunction before and thinks to himself that the machine has probably run out of paper of something.

He gets to the machine and while it is also continuously flashing its blue neon light, it is emitting a syncopated beeping noise, the same noise that had interrupted his game. He looks at the visual display unit on the front of the machine – a message is flashing '100 Marker Test – Mitochondrial Related Common Ancestor Confirmed'. "Jesus Christ" shouts Harry aloud and he runs over to his desk, pulls out the clip-board and reads the instructions again. He takes the orange-coloured break-away plastic card, snaps it in half and takes the bit of card inside out and reads it. He picks up a nearby telephone and nervously starts to dial the number on the card. It rings. It is a single ringing tone and Harry realises that he is calling abroad to someone outside of the United Kingdom. The single ringing tone continues and Harry is adamant that it has rung about 30 times and is about to hang up when the phone is finally answered.

"Who is this?" a voice demands at the other end of the phone.

"Hello? My name is Harry Shalestrick and I work at the Das Volker Syndicate Research Clinic in St. Albans, England. I was running some mouth swab tests earlier and I've just got a MRCA result that meant I had to phone your telephone number to tell you about it. Who are you, by the way?"

"My name is Doctor Torstein Lindemann, Director General of Das Volker Syndicate" says the voice. Before Harry could react to the fact that he was talking to the top man of the company, the voice demands of him.

"How many allele markers were there in the test? Who do the markers belong to and where are they from?"

"Hold on Sir" says Harry as he runs over to the 'Surefire 500' DNA machine to get the information. "It is a 100-marker test and the swab provider is a Freyja Fulton. She's 17 and she's at St. Kentigern's College in Glasgow, Scotland, Sir".

The voice says "Thank you" and hangs up.

The Stream

The current Director General of the Das Volker Syndicate was a Doctor Torstein Lindemann. He was a young looking 74 year old. Tall, slim and with a physique more commonly seen in men thirty years his junior. His complexion was tanned, not artificial, but natural from spending time at homes in the West Indies, Sri Lanka and Portugal and where his love of golf had helped keep him fit over the years. His hair was very dark and combed backwards from his brow. It didn't move due to the layers of pomade that held it sharply down and close to his scalp. His face was angular and his nose was aquiline but the most distinguishable feature of his face, however, were the eyes. They were catching eyes with a coruscating luminosity that was piercing in their blueness, almost like the ultramarine of lapis lazuli. These were eyes that missed nothing and their fulgurating intensity had made a many people uncomfortable in their presence.

They may have been bright and sharp, but they were also the eyes of an extremely cold, driven and ruthlessly determined individual.

His father had been Dr. Pelle Lindemann, a Swiss doctor originally from the city of La Chaux-de-Fonds, who had worked in Berlin before the Second World War. He had gone to university there to study medicine and at the commencement of hostilities, had been the Senior Doctor at the Rudolf Virchow Hospital in the city. For a young Pelle, he had been originally drawn to Berlin fascinated by the story of

Rudolf Virchow, a German doctor who is now regarded as "the father of modern pathology", a founder of social medicine and the advancement of public health as well as being a noted anthropologist, prehistorian and biologist. Virchow was the early creator of cell theory and cell biology, the first person to recognise leukaemia and the discoverer of thromboembolism. His early investigations paved the way for changes to German medical education and he coined such scientific terms as "chromatin", "agenesis", "parenchyma", "osteoid", "amyloid degeneration" and "spina bifida".

But Pelle's admiration of Rudolf Virchow had turned sour quite early on in his stay in Germany. Pelle had discovered that Virchow had been a fervent anti-Darwinist and in the mid 1880s, he had repeatedly spoken out against the theory of evolution and saw it as a part of a politically dangerous agenda of an emergent socialist movement in Germany that had grandiose ideas about cultural superiority and militarism. Virchow had also developed craniometry which produced conflicting and contradictory results to the contemporary scientific theories of the day about the Aryan race, and these results led him to denounce the theories as nothing more than "Nordic mysticism" and that the people of Europe, be they German, Italian, Danish, Norwegian, British or French, belonged to a "mixture of various races", furthermore declaring that the results of craniology and craniometry caused these beliefs to "struggle against any theory concerning the superiority of this or that European race" on others.

As the political landscape of Germany changed in the early 1930s, there was a rise in the interest and research of the archaeological and cultural history of the Aryan race. Founded on Monday 1st July 1935 by Heinrich Himmler, the Ahnenerbe was tasked with launching expeditions and conducting various experiments in attempts to prove beyond reasonable doubt that the mythological Nordic populations had once ruled the ancient world. Ahnenerbe came from a German word meaning "inherited from the forefathers" and was at the forefront of a quest to find new evidence of the racial heritage of the Germanic people.

Pelle had been quickly drawn into the excitement of the time, and as a Swiss national, albeit of Germanic extraction, he had been most enthusiastic in getting involved. A chance meeting with an Ahnenerbe founder, Herman Wirth, had led to Pelle enjoying a meteoric rise from being a junior doctor to becoming the Senior Doctor of the Rudolf Virchow Hospital and free access to its facilities to conduct research to prove the genetic claims of Aryan superiority. With the backing of the Ahnenerbe and its resources, Pelle had embarked on a number of expeditions to Nordic territories and had begun fledgling casework in what would become immunogenetics and biological and biochemical research of the human body's defence mechanisms against germs such as bacterial, viral and fungal infections as well as foreign agents such as biological toxins and environmental pollutants. The early research of genetics, DNA decoding and the collation of the human genome had been aspirations of Pelle and it was his firm belief that destiny was determined by one's blood.

Torstein closed the door of his office, walked over to his large desk, picked up the remote control and started to press a few buttons. The blinds beside the windows whirred silently into action as they closed, shutting out the panoramic view of the Jura Mountains from the institute in La Chaux-de-Fonds. The lighting in the room became soft and gentle and on the far wall adjacent to the desk, a large plasma television screen slides into view. Torstein walks over to a sideboard, opens it and retrieves a glass and a bottle of whisky and pours himself a large measure. He places the drink on his desk, throws himself into his reclining chair, puts his feet up on the desk and presses another button on the remote control. The television screen comes to life as the flickering start of a black and white film begins to play.

On the screen, a number of figures are seen shaking hands as they are introduced to each other while in the background, rows of uniformed men stand still with their right arms extended in salute. A bespectacled man approaches a plinth and stands in front of a lectern and receives the salute of the assembled men. The men are the officers of the SS-Leibstandarte "Adolf Hitler", Hitler's personal bodyguard. The bespectacled man, Reichsführer SS Himmler, addresses the men:

"The ultimate aim for those 11 years during which I have been the Reichsführer SS has been invariably the same: to create an order of good blood which is able to serve Germany; which unfailingly and without sparing itself can be made use of because the greatest losses can do no harm to the vitality of this order, the vitality of these men, because they will always be replaced; to create an order which will spread the idea of Nordic blood so far that we will attract all Nordic blood in the world, take away the blood from our adversaries, absorb it so that never again, looking at it from the viewpoint of grand

policy, Nordic blood, in great quantities and to an extent worth mentioning, will fight against us."

The film continues to play as it pans along the lines of assembled officers. Torstein uses the remote control to pause the film on the screen. There is a headshot of a man with combed back black hair staring back at him from the television and Torstein stands up from his chair.

He picks up his glass of whisky, raises it towards the screen in a toast and gulps down the fiery spirit in one mouthful. As the whisky burns the back of his throat, Torstein speaks to the frozen image on the screen. "I have found her Papa. I have found her at last."

The Stream

7.42am - Thursday 8th June, present day
Daniel Lauridsen's house, 16B Runebergs Allé, Søborg,
Copenhagen, Denmark.

Daniel Lauridsen suddenly awoke. He had a cold sweat and realised that he had drifted off into a deep, reflective sleep. He sat up, walked over to the sink and bathed his face in water. He looked at his image in the mirror and asked himself what he was doing. At the age of 43, he had led a varied and interesting life. He was a graduate of the University of Copenhagen's Faculty of Social Sciences. He had a Bachelor's degree, a BA in Management Studies and on graduation, had joined the Royal Danish Navy and gone to the Søværnets Officersskole, the oldest existing officers' academy in the world.

Whilst there, he had shown an aptitude for management and problem solving, and coupled with being a keen sportsman, it had been suggested that he apply to join the Frømandskorpset and its nine month long training course. 600 people apply to join the Frømandskorpset each year and less than a dozen complete the rigorous and intensive course. Daniel had been one of only nine that had finished the course. After graduation, he found himself deployed around the world, from freeing hostages held by pirates off the coast of Somalia to trudging through the mountains of Afghanistan working alongside allied Special Forces.

It had been a good life and he had enjoyed it, but like all good things, it had come to an end with his compulsory retirement from the Frømandskorpset at the age of 35. Daniel had opted to leave the Royal Danish Navy altogether as the prospect of a military desk job did not really appeal to him. He travelled extensively around Europe and having gathered a network of contacts and associates, Daniel decided to form his own business as a security management consultant and professional diver.

The business had taken off as a result of early successes with a number of security management training courses initially tailored for banking and financial institutions. In the current climate of terrorist activity around the world, Daniel had found that by hosting two day conferences with the senior staff of a company, the company would then go on and review its various security protocols, whether it be data management to building safety to staff vetting and security clearance. His simple courses had caught the eye of corporate business and word of mouth recommendation had been extremely profitable. Daniel didn't really need to work as he had made sufficient money to fund at least three lifetimes. But Daniel needed the cut and thrust of working on a project. He couldn't sit on his hands and watch the world go by. He would get bored. He needed to be doing something.

When not providing security management training courses, he would take on professional diving contracts. Laying of cables to checking the structural competency of stanchion legs of a North Sea oil platform, they were all the same to him. Working, doing something that he enjoyed and being paid handsomely for it.

He had received a call out of the blue from a former colleague in the Frømandskorpset, Ingi Mortensen. Ingi had left the service a few years before Daniel and had started up a reasonably successful salvage diving company. Ingi had recently won the contract to search the wreck of the SS Sauternes, a British merchant vessel that had sunk off the Faroe Islands in December 1941. The wreck of the ship was lying at a depth of 100 metres and Ingi needed to have professional divers that he could rely on to do a decent job, but he also needed men that he could trust. The salvage operation in question was to attempt the recovery of 26,000 Danish coins that were on board the vessel when it had gone down. Daniel had agreed to meet up with Ingi and discuss the project.

Daniel's interest was piqued as he could have the chance to go and visit the Faroe Islands again. He had been once before, albeit as part of a NATO exercise, but he hadn't had the chance to go ashore and explore the islands. He had wanted to do a bit of research about a family story that had passed down to him from his late grandmother and his elderly mother. It was an anecdotal story about some local woman called Dagny Poulsen being his mother's nanny in Berlin in 1939 and how his grandmother had helped this woman escape back to the Faroe Islands as the Second World War broke out.

Today was the departure date for going to the Faroe Islands to help his friend Ingi attempt to salvage some coins. As he packed his bags, he wondered if he would be able to find out anything about this Dagny Poulsen while he was there. At the very least, he could always truthfully tell his mother that he tried to find her but the passage of time was too great and it had proved difficult to track down any information for her.

Daniel just viewed this as another trip, another place, another job with the possibility of doing some private research for his mother. He carefully packed away the documentation his mother had given him and called for a taxi to take him to the airport. As he waited outside his flat for the taxi, he hoped the weather in the Faroes was better than the last time he was there. But he prayed that it was much better than the weather of Sunday 7th December 1941.

The Christmas Ship

On Sunday 7th December 1941, a horrendous storm raged in the middle of the North Atlantic. Two vessels, the SS Sauternes and its escort, the Royal Navy armed trawler HMT Kerrara, had tried to seek shelter in the sea channel between two of the Faroe Islands, Svínoy and Fugloy. Both vessels had dropped their anchors and grimly tried to ride out the severity of the storm.

On the shores of the islands on either side of the ships, villagers watched the plight of the vessels in mountainous waves and hurricane force winds. Although familiar with the waters, the seas and winds made it impossible to lend any form of assistance to the stricken vessels.

The larger of the two ships, the cargo ship SS Sauternes, started to drag its anchor and drifted towards the shore of Svínoy. As it drifted closer to the island, it was caught in the swell of the sea and the anchor started to pull the ship down. It was swamped by three successive waves and started to sink, bow first. Two life-rafts were launched and people were seen boarding them, but the ferocity of the waves capsized the craft. There were no survivors and all 25 crew and passengers on the SS Sauternes were sadly lost.

The SS Sauternes had left the Port of Leith in Scotland on the 3rd December laden with supplies for the British garrison in the Faroe Islands. The cargo included some 250 tons of food, 3000 gallons of petrol, ammunition and various other military supplies. The SS Sauternes had also been provided with an escort to make her way to the Faroe Islands, a Royal Navy armed trawler, HMT Kerrara. The reason for the escort was that the SS Sauternes had an unusual cargo aboard. It was carrying 26,000 Danish coins that had been specially minted in Britain to address a shortage of coinage in the Faroe Islands. With Denmark under German occupation, an alternative source for currency had had to be sought. The coinage was inside a steel case that was bolted to the floor of the captain's cabin.

In the Faroe Islands, the sad story of the SS Sauternes became known as *Jólaskipið*, the Christmas Ship. The Faroese government gave permission for diving rights to be allowed and two expeditions made several dives to the wreck in July 2000 and May 2001. Some items were recovered such as the ship's bell, but the coins eluded the dive teams. Commercial diving salvage expeditions such as this were expensive exercises to operate and given the fact that the wreck of the SS Sauternes was at a depth of at least 100 metres in the very deep and treacherous waters of the North Atlantic Ocean, it was going to be a difficult task to achieve but Ingi Mortensen was confident that he could salvage the coins.

Daniel met up with Ingi Mortensen in Copenhagen in February. Ingi's salvage vessel, Nord Kaperen, was being fitted out with specialist equipment befitting a North Atlantic operation. Ingi had got financial backing for his expedition but he needed a specialist diver that had experience of working at extreme depths, and that's where Daniel came into the operational plan.

"Listen Daniel, the waters around these two islands are really dangerous. There are strong currents as the Gulf Stream circles the islands. The pull of the water is immense. This isn't a simple dive of laying a few charges and swimming away and waiting for them to go boom. This is hard diving in extreme conditions and you have only got about 20 minutes to do stuff when you are down on the wreck. You'll need your wits about you.".

Ingi sighed as he finished speaking.

"I'm too old, too fat and smoke too much to do a pressure dive like this. That's why I need you for this."

Daniel picked up his coffee cup, sipped the contents, placed it back on the saucer, looked Ingi in the eyes and said "When are you going? How long do you expect to be up there? Can you give me time off to go and check some personal things out and speak to some of the locals?"

Ingi was taken aback at what Daniel had said. His friend had technically agreed to join his trip but wanted dates and times of the expedition and leave to do some sort of business.

"Have you got family up there?" asked Ingi.

"Sort of." replied Daniel. "My mother has an aunt from up there that she hasn't heard a thing about since 1939. Well it's not an aunt like a relative or something. It's the woman that was her nanny in Berlin and she keeps nagging me to find out what happened to her. She's been biting my ear ever since I left the service and if I help you with this, I can kill two birds with the one stone and get Mama off my back at the same time."

Ingi's face went red and he roared with laughter.

"Same old Daniel. Always a planned method to the madness" and reached across the table to shake Daniel's hand.

"I am looking to go up in early June, spend a week or so doing some tests and then plan to have a two week window at diving to the wreck from about the 15th. We will have about

22 hours of daylight and the weather tends to be calm at that time of the year. The water visibility isn't the greatest from about March to October because of plankton blooms but at least the surface weather is reasonable. A winter month salvage attempt in the north Atlantic is not really something that's feasible. Don't you agree?"

Daniel shakes Ingi's hand and smiles.

"I will see you there round about the 13th June. I will make my own way up there, if you don't mind."

He stands up to leave and mock salutes his friend. Ingi returns the gesture.

"You never said anything about your fee and expenses Daniel?"

Daniel just looked at his friend with surprised indignation on his face.

"There's no fee or expenses. You are actually doing me a favour by asking me to come along and help you. I'm now looking forward to the trip. See you in June." and walks away.

The Stream

4.42pm - Thursday 8th June, present day
Edinburgh International Airport, Scotland.

Wendy and Freyja had become inseparable friends in just a short time. They both had similar interests; they liked the same type of music, television programmes, cinema and other such entertainments. The two girls had very distinct and idiosyncratic dress senses – Freyja's leaned to the rock and punk genres while Wendy's was slightly more bohemian. But both girls could adapt to the more expected style of fashion of short skirts, high heels and revealing tops when the occasion demanded such of them. It wasn't that they were embarrassed to dress like most other teenage girls around them, they simply chose not to. Freyja didn't want to be seen as some 'plastic wannabe' – false and artificial, while Wendy just couldn't be bothered with the 'bingo top' look – "eyes down for a full house" that many of her peers opted for. It was probably their own personal rebellion, that of not fulfilling the expectation of conformity that most others followed like lemmings. Both girls were comfortable with what they wore and how they looked and felt that people should take them for what they were as people and not some image that others wanted them to have.

But the important factor in their relationship as friends was that they had instantly bonded since meeting on their first day at college. They had helped each other through the first few weeks of learning the ropes of student life and the experiences that they faced. The naivety of adolescence and the journey into adult education and its obstacles they had agreed they were going to face together over the next four years. They were pleasant girls, gentle and considerate, articulate, well-mannered, courteous and respectful of others around them and polite. They weren't boorish, loud, spoiled, brash or offensive and didn't bring themselves to the critical attention of others by their actions or behaviour. They were both strong-willed and could become stubborn, determined and obdurate with others when required, but that would be as a result of experiencing some injustice, wrong-doing or bullying and being prepared to take a stand against the transgressors. Of course they intermixed with their fellow students and made friendships and associations, but the similarity of their character traits had meant that they had settled very quickly and trusted each other's company.

Their friendship was like that of close sisters, where they shared all their fears, hopes and secrets with each other. Of course they would argue and disagree over trite matters and opinions, but they wouldn't fall out about things.

They sat beside each other in the departure lounge and discussed their imminent trip while their university class-mates were off exploring the cafes, shops and entertainments, and the lecturers and course advisers were availing themselves with purchases in the Duty-Free area. Although nervous, the girls were excited that they were about to go on an end-of-year field trip to the Faroe Islands and both of them were bursting with expectance of what the next seven days would provide for them.

"What a great way to finish off our First Year at University. A wee trip abroad to somewhere neither of us has been to before. You must be really excited Freyja? You are technically going 'home' today. Do you think you'll meet some distant relations? I hope you do and some of them are single and handsome. I've always been quite partial to a bit of Viking." laughed Wendy and she pushed her friend back into her seat.

Freyja just laughed and told her to settle down. "I do have contact details for some relatives I've never met before but I don't know if I'm brave enough to cold call them with 'Hi. I'm Freyja, your long-lost Scottish cousin'. But I do want to find Dagny's house first though and I suppose we can take the finding of my relatives from there. The trip itinerary does give us a lot of spare time to go exploring and investigating."

The Stream

9.00pm - Thursday 8th June, present day
Vágar International Airport, Faroe Islands.

The BAe 146 Atlantic Airways aeroplane descended out of
the sunshine, through the clouds, and landed in light grey
drizzle at the near-deserted Vágar airport. Vágar Airport is the
only airport on the islands and was built by British Royal
Engineers during World War II. Flying to the Faroe Islands can
be difficult because of the weather conditions, the surrounding
mountainous terrain, and the fact that the airport runway is
relatively short at being only 1800 metres long. Perfect for
short take-off and landing aircraft such as the BAe 146 but
sometimes a challenge for larger planes such as Boeing 737s
and Airbus A319s that also have scheduled flights to the
islands. The British military originally chose the site mainly
because it was hard to see from the surrounding waters and
the threat of any potential German warship.

Although presently deserted on a damp Thursday evening
in early June, Vágar is a surprisingly very busy airport with
international destinations including Copenhagen, Aalborg and
Billund in Denmark, Reykjavík in Iceland, Aberdeen,
Edinburgh and London in the United Kingdom, Narsarsuaq in
Greenland, Oslo and Stavanger in Norway, Barcelona in Spain
and Milan in Italy.

As the plane taxied to the side of the main terminal
building, the passengers began to gather all their belongings
together from the overhead hatches and started to queue in the
central aisle, awaiting disembarkation. Daniel just sat back in
his seat and smiled at his fellow passengers, many of which
seemed to be young Scottish students, rushing and scrambling

to get in line to get off the plane. Why bother? They aren't going anywhere fast. They still have to go through passport control, collect their luggage, make their way through the terminal building and then go their separate ways. For most of the passengers, this looked like their first trip to the Faroe Islands and that there would presumably be some sort of transport arrangements in place to take them all to their various hotels and lodgings, Daniel had been here once before, albeit in a military operation capacity, and he was acutely aware that as a civilian, getting from A to B on an archipelago of 18 islands in the middle of the North Atlantic might have some difficulties.

Daniel was one of the last passengers off the plane. The two pretty Atlantic Airways stewardesses thanked him for travelling with them and they both hoped that he enjoyed his stay. What really struck Daniel about the stewardesses' comments was the conviction and sincerity that they had been said with. They were both Faroese women who were genuinely grateful for foreigners travelling to and visiting their islands. He thanked them both and said that he was really looking forward to his trip and walked down the exit gangway stairs onto the tarmac.

On the tarmac, Daniel put his luggage holdall down and surveyed the scenery around him. It had stopped drizzling and the sun had re-appeared from the clouds. Its brightness illuminated the starkness of the rugged, green mountains on two sides, the dark waters of the S–shaped lake, Leitisvatn, at one end of the runway and the expanse of the North Atlantic Ocean at the other end. It was just after 9.00pm but it felt like 5.00pm in the afternoon. A gentle breeze blew across the runway from the ocean and its air was crisp and clear, free from the pollutants that you associate with city dwelling. The scenery was breathtaking. High cliff faces sweeping to the sea interspersed with inlets that marked access to the land beyond.

As Daniel had travelled light with just a luggage holdall in his left hand, he quickly by-passed Passport Control and Customs. The Passport Control officers glanced at the Danish passport that Daniel presented and waved him through. Most of the passengers from the plane were being herded into a line for passport inspection. The Faroe Islands have been an autonomous, self-governing country within the Kingdom of Denmark since 1948 and have their own currency and control over most domestic matters. Denmark still determines important matters such as military defence, police, justice, and foreign affairs, but the Faroe Islands are not part of the European Union and are not covered by certain terms of the Schengen free movement agreement. However, they have been a part of the Nordic Passport Union since 1966 which allows most Scandinavian and United Kingdom citizens to be free from border checks.

Daniel had nothing to declare at Customs and walked through the terminal building with its shops, bistros and cafes. He had bought 200 Duty-Free cigarettes on the plane as a present for Ingi, but apart from some quick-change items of clothing, research material such as photographs, letters and addresses for tracing Dagny Poulsen and diving specification documents, he had nothing else with him apart from the clothes he wore. It was a hark-back to his military days. Only carry essential equipment and procure, which was nowadays buy, items such as clothing, as and when they are required. If he needed anything, he would just go and buy it.

He walked out onto the front apron of the terminal building. Three motor-coach passenger buses awaited the new arrivals. There were a handful of locals awaiting the return of loved ones and a few taxi and private hire vehicles parked near the main doors, the drivers holding cards denoting the names of their imminent passengers. A card held upside down caught Daniel's attention though. It must have been the way it was being held that caused him to look at it. 'Das Volker Syndicate' it read and Daniel tried to recollect why the name was familiar to him. He couldn't remember but knew that it would come back to him later. He looked around for the Avis Car Hire depot and spotted a portacabin type structure away to his left. An Avis flag flew from a flagpole on the roof. He walked over to the portacabin and an attractive woman in her late thirties emerged.

She was about 6 feet tall and although masked by the car-hire company's corporate business attire of skirt and jacket, it was obvious that she had an athletic body. Her face was framed with shoulder length dark hair and she smiled welcomingly at Daniel as she approached him.

"Mr. Lauridsen?" she enquired.

"Yes." replied Daniel, slightly taken aback at her guessing correctly his name.

"How did you know?"

He looked at her name badge and read that she was called Sólrun Jacobsen.

"Your friend, Ingi Mortensen, gave me a perfect description of you when he was booking a car for you to use."

Her hazel-green eyes twinkled as they shook hands and she escorted him back to the portacabin to sign for the vehicle.

"That was nice of Ingi. I never took him for getting descriptions right." he joked.

"His description never did you justice" said Sólrun.

Daniel noted a hint of mischief in the twinkling hazel-green eyes as she said it. Daniel handed over his passport and driving licence for Sólrun to check and she handed him the keys to a dark blue 4x4 Volkswagen Touareg automatic.

"It's a really nice car to drive and is very spacious inside. I think you'll like it. It has lots of room for all your diving equipment and gear. Do you think you will find the money aboard the SS Sauternes?" she asked.

Daniel's natural defence mechanisms kicked in when Sólrun mentioned the SS Sauternes and the planned dives for its cargo. Loose talk cost lives was Daniel's instant thought but he relaxed when he realised that Ingi's dive to the SS Sauternes would be fairly common knowledge in amongst a population of 50,000 islanders. The sad story of the Christmas Ship, the 'Jólaskipið' was part and parcel of the recent history of the Faroe Islands and still resonated with the locals.

"I hope so. Diving in those seas and at that depth will be very difficult and dangerous, but hopefully we can recover all of the coins." replied Daniel.

Sólrun walked Daniel over to the Touareg and as he got into the car, she gave him her business card.

"Give me a call if you need directions or help with anything. I have a few days off once I have finished here tonight. I have nothing really planned and I wouldn't mind showing you around Tórshavn, if you want."

Daniel thanked her and pocketed the card.

"I'll probably take you up on that. Keep your phone handy." he replied as he turned the ignition and drove out the parking lot and turned right, following the signs for Tórshavn, the capital of the Faroe Islands.

As he drove along the road, the stark and rugged beauty of this one island was struck home with its mountains and steep inclines versus the contrasting juxtaposition of the various hamlets and villages with their brightly coloured wooden and stone houses, most of which had grass roofs. 'How do you cut the grass on the roofs?' he mused to himself as he looked at the ominously black waters of the S–shaped lake, Leitisvatn, on his right.

Daniel had been researching the Faroe Islands and its recent history. The mountainous terrain surrounding the airport and this deep fresh water lake had seen a number of accidents over the years. During World War 2, a flight of Royal Canadian Air Force flying boats had attempted a number of test landings on the lake until there had been a fatal accident when one of the planes had hit submerged rocks and all aboard had been killed. These young Canadian flyers were of diasporic Scottish descent, and the British military garrison of the time, the Cameronians (Scottish Rifles), had insisted on affording them all a full military funeral in the capital, Tórshavn. As recently as August 1996, nine people, including the Danish Chief of Defence, Admiral Jørgen Garde and his wife, perished as the Danish Air Force aircraft they were travelling in collided with the high terrain surrounding the airport as a result of bad weather and poor visibility.

The Stream

When he reached Fútaklett, Daniel was not prepared for what he was about to drive into – Vágatunnilin (*the Vágar Tunnel*), a 4,900 metres long sub-sea road tunnel, 109 metres below sea level, through solid basalt rock under the Atlantic Ocean, that was going to take him from the island of Vágar to the neighbouring island of Streymoy and emerging at the village of Leynar.

He drove through the illuminated tunnel and what surprised him was that it was a two lane affair and that the carriageway was neither in a straight line or was flat. The road snaked through the various striations of the rock and rose and fell as it followed undulations in the geology. He felt he was travelling along on the wooden Rutschebanen roller-coaster ride back home in Copenhagen's Tivoli Gardens amusement park, only he was driving a motor vehicle underground. A hundred metres underground. A hundred metres below sea level. The same depth that he would be attempting to dive to in a few days time in search of some Danish coins lost in a shipwreck 75 years ago.

After exiting the tunnel and arriving on the island of Streymoy, Daniel had to pull the sun visor down. It was 10.00pm but the sun was still splitting the sky. The weather was going to take some time for him to adjust to. He continued with his journey towards Tórshavn following the road that seemed to cling to the sides of the steep inclines and cliff edges as it meandered around the southern part of the island. He drove up a rising gradient in the road, and at the crest of the hill, the ground levelled out. He parked the Touareg in a viewing area in a lay-by and got out of the vehicle to survey the panorama that now appeared before him.

The Stream

Below him lay the sprawl of the capital, but what made the vista even more so impressive to behold was the ability to view a number of the islands that form the archipelago stretching out as far as he could see. They were all bathed in this bizarre, sub-arctic, mid-summer's evening sunshine, and having checked his watch again, it was incredulous to think that it was 10.11pm and not mid-afternoon.

Back behind the wheel of the Touareg, he gunned the engine and made for the Hotel Havnar, situated in the heart of Tórshavn, within walking distance of the harbour and the historical part of the town. He parked the 4x4 in the car park at the rear of the hotel and walked up the hill to its front door in Aarvegur, a curving road that runs from the harbour, past the hotel and into the Vaglið Square, the setting for the Parliament buildings and the start of the commercial centre of the town. The Hotel Havnar is an oldy worldy type of hotel with its decoration, atmosphere and service reminiscent of times gone by, but the hotel's important secret for its continued popularity as a worthwhile temporary lodging establishment for travellers, tourists and even some permanent residents, is the centrality of its location within the town. It is conveniently placed to be handy for everything and anything one might require. Nightlife, restaurants, transport, tourism, business, the harbour and all of it within a 5 minute walk from its front door.

Daniel checked in, went to his room and freshened up. He had a shower, shaved and changed his clothes. He looked at Sólrun's business card and saw her mobile telephone number. He opened a side-door of the room that lead out onto a balcony with a glass balustrade and stepped outside. It was now 10.40pm but the still bright daylight made it feel like early evening. It was hard to believe that he had only taken the hire-car from her an hour earlier. He called her. On answering, Daniel spoke carefully.

"Hi Sólrun, it is Daniel Lauridsen here. You said I could call you. I know it's late, but can we meet up for a meal and a drink? I thought about what you said to me earlier and I could use your help researching something over the next couple of days if you don't mind. I really need a friendly resident who has good local knowledge to help me find the answers to some family matters I need to check up on while I am up here working. Is that OK?"

"Of course it is. I am glad you called. Where are you staying?"she asked. Daniel told her. "Good choice. Meet me at the Áarstova restaurant at midnight. The restaurant is near to the hotel. I will phone them just now and secure a booking for us. My cousin works there. If you go out the front door of the hotel, turn to your left and walk up to the square. I will see you there shortly." and hangs up.

As Daniel pockets his phone, he looks to his left in an attempt to see the restaurant or the square. His view is impeded by the rungs of a service ladder attached to the wall and running to the roof. He leaves the balcony, shuts the door over and takes a folder from his holdall and carefully slips it inside his jacket, leaves his room and goes down to the reception desk and asks for directions to the restaurant. He hands his room key over to the porter at the reception desk and walks out into Aarvegur, turns left and decides to have a wander round the town for a while.

He has an hour to kill before midnight.

The Stream

Daniel had slowly wandered around the periphery of Vaglið Square and had spent his time admiring the statues and works of art on show, staring in through a number of shop windows, looking at the fascinating old wooden and stone buildings with their grass roofs but also marvelling at how the proliferation of adjacent modern brick and concrete constructions did not seem to look out of place beside them.

Having located the whereabouts of the Áarstova restaurant, he had started to get his bearings on the locations of where some of the offices that he had to go and visit the following morning were. He ambled over to a bench seat beside the lush, green lawn in front of an impressive nineteenth-century building built of wood and dark-hued basalt. A plaque on its wall identified this building as the Raohus, or Town Hall.

It was now slowly beginning to get dark. He watched as growing numbers of locals of very differing ages started heading into the various cafes, bars and eateries that seemed to have suddenly appeared everywhere as the darkness began to fall. Everyone seemed to know each other and acknowledged one another in a friendly manner. It was a case of 'spot the tourist' as the odd singleton, couple or group entered or emerged from a hostelry and moved on to the next.

There was little road traffic, and what traffic there was appeared to be either tourists being dropped off or collected in taxis or local inhabitants going about their normal late evening routines. It was all very calm and pleasant to watch in the gathering darkness. It wasn't exactly darkness. It was an eerie and strange twilight type of darkness. Still light enough to see details and distinguish features, but dark enough to make you turn on the lights on your car or in your home. The street lights had just come on and all around the square, very cleverly and discreetly placed light bulbs threw their differently coloured hues onto buildings, walls, trees and bushes. The collective illumination gave the square and the surrounding roads and lanes a magical mystique that drew you into wishing to go and explore them further.

He reached into his jacket and took out the folder that he had placed inside it earlier. On opening it, he was immediately drawn to look at the slightly dog-eared sepia photograph of his grandmother Mille, his mother Petra, his Uncle Albert and the woman that he knew to be Dagny. All four of them were all standing in front of an ornate fountain. They had ice-creams in their hands and they were all smiling as they posed for the photographer. There was a slight distortion in the photograph. The sun was glinting off a brooch of a sailing ship that his grandmother was wearing. It didn't spoil the picture and it must have been a happy moment when the photograph was taken. He gently turned the photograph over. Handwritten in fading pencil in a corner was 'Viktoriapark. 13. August 1939'. Daniel realised that this picture must have been one of the last photographs taken before Dagny left Berlin.

He flicked through the rest of the folder and found a white, plain card postcard. On the front of the postcard, a handwritten address had been stamped over by the German postal censor of the time. The postcard had been addressed in Danish to a 'Dagny Poulsen, Funningstova, Torshavn,

Færøerne'. In bold black ink, the address field of the postcard had been stamped over in German with the stark legend 'Verbotene Postadresse. Auslandsterritorium unter dem britischen Beruf.'. 'Forbidden Postal Address. Foreign territory under British Occupation.'.

He read the message addressed to Dagny on the back of the postcard. It was from his mother and Uncle Albert. In a child's neat handwriting, the brief message to Dagny, again written in Danish and dated 20th May 1940, said *'Kære Moster Dagny. Vi savner dig meget. Kom tilbage til Berlin og være vores ven igen. Petra og Albert'*.

The English translation is simply *'Dear Aunt Dagny. We miss you very much. Please come back to Berlin and be our friend again. Petra and Albert'*. Just like the front of the postcard, the message had been overstamped by the German postal censors with the bold, black ink message 'Verbotene Postadresse. Auslandsterritorium unter dem britischen Beruf.'

The postcard had never ever left Berlin. The German postal censor had considered it, stamped it and returned it back to the sender. Daniel wondered whether his grandmother had been questioned about the writing and attempted sending of the postcard or had someone in the postal service simply realised that it was a child's message written in innocence, rejected it and returned it with the minimum of fuss. He would never know the answer to that question. But he did know that his grandmother had comforted her children, his mother and uncle, by keeping its return hidden from them until they were grown up. They had always believed that the postcard had indeed been sent to the Faroe Islands but Dagny had been unable to return back to Berlin to see them because of the ongoing war.

He had a photograph, an address and a verbal story to start searching for Dagny. He just hoped that Sólrun didn't mind helping him with his mother's demand.

He closed the folder over and put it back inside his jacket. He leaned back on the seat and spread his arms out along the back of its framework. He glanced at his watch. It was now 11.45pm. He should really be heading over to the restaurant and be waiting for Sólrun to arrive. It was like being on a first date. He laughed to himself and chuckled at the thought of him being slightly nervous about meeting an attractive woman for nothing more than the companionship of sharing a meal and a drink, and asking her for her help and assistance in finding out some information, if there was any to find, about this Dagny Poulsen, who she was and what happened to her.

A black Mercedes saloon car drove up the slight hill across from where he sat. Its headlights were on full beam and their dazzle had temporarily blinded Daniel.

He rubbed his eyes as the car entered into Vaglið Square while watching it slowly come to a standstill at the beginning of Aarvegur. The driver got out the front seat and walked briskly round to the back-passenger door on the pavement's edge. He opened the door and held it ajar to allow a tall, slim man with very dark brushed-back hair emerge from within. Daniel recognised the driver. He was the guy at the airport with the upside down card waiting for someone from the Das Volker Syndicate. "Das Volker Syndicate? I know them for some reason. What is it?" said Daniel quietly to himself. He remembered. One of the earliest two-day security conferences he had held had been at one of their research clinics in England. "Where was it? Ah! St. Albans." He looked over at the man who had got out of the back of the car. He was gathering his things about him as the driver was getting his luggage out of the boot. He watched the man fasten his light overcoat and studied the pointed face with the swept back hair.

"I know him. What's his name again? Lindt? Lindell? Lindemann? Fuck's sake! Lindemann? Torstein Lindemann? No Way?"

Daniel's mind was now racing and his mental cogs were turning very quickly. He reached back inside his jacket and pulled out the folder. He laid it on the seat beside him, threw open the cover and started searching through all the notes and papers inside. He had seen something in this folder that now alarmed him. He found it. A copy of a letter that his grandmother had written in apparent anger to Reichsführer SS Himmler complaining about her many concerns she had about the unhealthy interests that a Dr Pelle Lindemann seemed to have for her friend, Dagny Poulsen. He read the contents again and again. He watched Torstein Lindemann walk down the Aarvegur and go into the entrance of the Hotel Havnar.

"That's another bloody coincidence I don't like" muttered Daniel as he closed over the folder beside him and started to stare at the ground as he tried to gather his many thoughts together.

"If these two Lindemann's are related to each other in any way, the one that's just turned up here tonight and being here now is far too much of a coincidence for my liking.".

"What's too much of a coincidence?" said Sólrun as Daniel espied the black heeled shoes in front of him.

His eyes slowly rose up a pair of shapely legs that revealed the owner to be wearing a figure-hugging black frock. Her hair was different from earlier and to say that Sólrun was definitely attractive was an understatement. She was stunning. Daniel was pleased with the sudden distraction. He pocketed the folder.

"You and I meeting earlier today and now we are going for dinner. Pre-determined I think." he said.

Sólrun smiled and slipped her arm inside his. "Well Daniel Lauridsen. You called me and offered to take me to dinner. I'm starving and Áarstova is that way" as she gently pulled him across Vaglið Square towards the restaurant.

11.58pm - Thursday 8th June, present day
Áarstova Restaurant, Tórshavn, Faroe Islands.

Sólrun and Daniel pushed through the glass doorway and entered into the reception area of the restaurant. A smart young woman walks up to them and says "So Sólrun, who's the catch and why the late dinner booking?"

The two women hug and kiss each other on the cheek.

"Astrid, thanks for sorting out a booking for me. This is Daniel Lauridsen. He's one of the divers for the Jólaskipið, the SS Sauternes expedition. We know each other from way back and we are just catching up on old times. Daniel. Meet my cousin Astrid."

Astrid smiled and took his hand.

"Pleased to meet you Daniel. Is this your first time in the Faroes?"

Daniel thought about the reply and lied.

"Yes Astrid, it is. I like what I have seen so far and hopefully I'll get to see a bit more whilst I'm up here."

Astrid started leading them to a table in a corner by a window looking out across the square.

"Well I hope you have success with the Jólaskipið. I'll get you some menus. What would you like to drink?"

They gave their orders for drinks as Astrid sat them down at the table. She came back with the menus and their drinks.

"I'll be back in 5 minutes to take your order. It's really busy in here tonight and apparently there are a few late bookings about to come in." and departed through to the kitchen area at the side of the bar.

The Stream

The Áarstova is a popular restaurant, not only with the locals, but with the tourists. Having quickly gathered a reputation for producing fantastic meals from lunchtime onwards, it had tapped into the timing of the international flights and various cruise ship arrivals as well as getting an understanding of the habits of the Thursday to Sunday late licence clubbing scene. It had become a welcome venue for those wishing to be fed and watered from late evening to 4.00am. The differing types of patrons had the choice of sit-down meals until 2.00am or use of the premises as a café chill-out zone until 4.00am as well as providing a takeaway service for passing trade. It had been a superb piece of inspired business thinking by the owners and in doing so, they had established Áarstova as an important part of the Tórshavn entertainment and tourist scene.

Daniel looks at Sólrun. "We know each other from way back?" he teases her in mock disapproval.

She laughs. "It's a small place and what will the locals think? That Sólrun is a right hussy? She was in a restaurant with a man she had just met off a plane?"

They both laugh. Daniel studies the menu and looks at the offerings.

"I may have told a wee white lie to your cousin as well. I have been here before." Sólrun looks up from her menu at Daniel quizzically.

"I used to be in the Danish Royal Navy and I was up here a few years ago during a NATO exercise" he explained.

"Never set foot ashore though. Come to think of it, the weather was so bad you couldn't see any shores to set foot upon."

They both laughed again and Sólrun replies. "Well I'm glad you have this time" and sips her drink. "What is it you need my help with?" she utters in a tantalising tone.

Daniel almost blushes as he bats away the double entendre meaning. He goes on to briefly explain his situation about finding out about Dagny and retrieves the folder from his jacket and starts to show Sólrun some of the photographs and information. Sólrun picks up the postcard and studies it.

"The address, Funningstova, is a house in the old part of town. It's in Tinganes, about a 5 minute walk from here. It's down on the harbour. I can show you the house after we've finished here."

Astrid arrived back at the table to take their orders. No starters. Sólrun orders a 'Faroe Burger' with all the trimmings and looks over at Daniel. He seems to be struggling with the menu. Both she and Astrid start to giggle. He looks at them.

"What's so funny?" he asks.

Astrid laughingly tells him to just ignore the Faroese menu listing whale steak and deep fried blubber, wind-dried leg of mutton and the stuffed puffin in orange sauce and reaches over and turns a page in Daniels menu. She points at the top of the new page.

"That's the proper menu. The Faroese menu is really for the tourists and the resident traditionalists. They keep harking on about us younger generations having to remember our roots and where we come from. Well yeah, we do, but it's also the 21st Century and we also have to modernise and embrace changing society. We could be the richest country in the world with all the oil and gas we're sitting on but we have to change this perception that we are nothing else than whale killers and puffin eaters first of all."

Daniel looked at Astrid and was impressed with her honesty about the situation that the Faroese people have to deal with. They live on 18 islands that sit on the edge of the world but that same world was watching them with disapproval and envy at the same time. As a Dane, his own opinion was one imbued by what he had read in the papers or seen on television. Having been on the islands for less than three hours, he was starting to change that opinion to one of respect and admiration for what he had seen so far.

Daniel asked for the 'Faroe Burger' as well and handed back the menu. "Thanks Astrid"

Astrid takes the menu from him, and as she does, she gives a sharp intake of breath and gently nudges Sólrun while nodding her head towards the door. She whispers to her cousin in Faroese.

"Hygg, har er Heri, hann er so ræðuliga keðiligur" and walks away back to the kitchen.

Sólrun looks round in the direction indicated, shakes her head and says to Daniel.

"Astrid was telling me to look round as a dreadful bore of a man called Heri has just walked in. Heri Jorgensen is one of the traditionalists she was talking about. He would have us women gutting fish all day and the men climbing cliffs catching sea birds, out at sea fishing or hunting whales if he had his way. He would have us all living as if it was the 1820s all over again. Struggling to survive and living in abject poverty. He's a blinkered and misguided fool but Heri is also a dangerous man. People listen to him. He's the government's

Heritage Minister and I don't like him or trust him. I never have. He wants us all to go back to living in the past as long as he can still make lots of money for himself in keeping us repressed. He made a name for himself in the 80s and 90s by writing a few books and making a couple of television documentaries and became something of a celebrity. But it is all about him and he likes telling everyone about how really important he is to the Faroe Islands. I don't know who the man is that is with him but rest assured, Heri will be boasting about something and trying to impress him."

Daniel casually glanced over at the door and looked at Heri and the man with him. "I know who the man is." and closes the folder and puts it back inside his jacket.

He had noticed the contempt for Heri both women had demonstrated. It was clear that they did not like him at all. He slyly watched Heri making a fuss and a show of himself to the seated patrons at their respective tables. He went past each table greeting those sat around with an air of false importance, the real purpose for doing so was to introduce his guest to all and sundry and anyone that couldn't get away.

The two men are heading in the general direction of their own table. "Sólrun. If they come over to us, please don't tell them about Dagny? I will tell you why later but I cannot let that man with Heri know who I am, why I am here or anything at all about Dagny. Please? This is really important to me."

"Relax Daniel. Trust me on this. The man is an arse and I'm telling him nothing. He would bore the fleece off a black faced sheep"

The Stream

Daniel pictured in his mind the phrase that Sólrun had just used. It must be an ultimate Faroese insult of sorts. He looked over at Heri and imagined him doing just that. He smiled to himself at that mental image and relaxed. He was beginning to really like Sólrun. She was something of a feisty enigma who fascinated him. She can hold her own and she probably gives as good as she gets in an argument.

This might be quite entertaining if this Heri bloke came over and annoyed her.

12.31am – Friday 9th June, present day
Áarstova Restaurant, Tórshavn, Faroe Islands.

Heri Jorgensen was a strange looking man. Daniel's first impression of him was that someone had stuffed a pig into human clothes and taught it how to walk upright. He had really small feet, a middle-age paunch that was partially hidden by the traditional Faroese cardigan that he wearing, a pink, fat, round jowly face topped with dishevelled grey hair. His pig-like appearance was made complete with the affectation of pince-nez spectacles hanging on a cord around his neck. Heri approached the table. He spoke to them in heavily accentuated English.

"Ah Sólrun, what brings you here into Áarstova on a Thursday evening?" he asked.

Daniel could see the hackles rising on Sólrun.

"It's Friday morning actually Heri. I'm here with a good friend from my university days in Copenhagen and catching up on old times. I'm surprised to see you in here with company as I hadn't imagined someone dying and leaving you a friend in their will." she retorted.

Daniel quickly sipped at his drink, not only to mask his surprise at the venomous reply but to stop himself from laughing.

"Come now Sólrun. There is no need to be rude and embarrass yourself in public." jousted back Heri.

Quick as a flash, Sólrun countered with "Heri, the only person being rude and embarrassing themselves in public is you and you do that every time you walk out of your front door."

The entire restaurant had now fallen silent as the diners had become transfixed on listening to the verbal exchange between the two of them. To Daniel, it had become apparent that Sólrun really despised this pig-like man, and to be fair to her, he could see why from the brief contact that he had had with him. Time to defuse the situation he thought. He stood up from the table and introduced himself to Heri and his guest.

"Hi, I'm Daniel. Please to meet you." and shook both men's hands.

Heri had not expected such a reaction and stammered

"Oh. Eh. Heri Jorgensen and and and, this is my friend, Torstein Lindemann."

Sólrun had turned away and was looking out the window to the square.

"What brings you to the Faroe Islands Torstein?" asked Daniel pleasantly. Torstein Lindemann released Daniel's hand.

"I am here for a conference being held over the weekend here in Tórshavn. It's the European Viking Researcher's Conference. I am giving a lecture at it tomorrow. And you?"
Daniel glibly replied to the question.

"Just a bit of sightseeing, catching up with some old friends and doing a bit of commercial diving. Nothing really exciting. It's a working holiday really."

Astrid arrived back at the table and interrupted the exchange.

"Sorry to barge in. There's your order Sólrun. Sorry that you had to wait so long but we are dreadfully busy tonight. I hope you enjoy it." and handed over a canvas bag with 'Áarstova' emblazoned on the sides.

Sólrun accepted the bag from her cousin and took Daniel's hand and guided him towards the front door. The diners had returned to eating and the noise level of conversation had returned to normal as the prospect of a public confrontation had dissipated. As they were leaving, Astrid winked at Sólrun.

"I'll give you a call tomorrow. You shouldn't let Heri rile you like that. He goes out of his way to bait you, you know."

Sólrun sighs. "I know Astrid. I know. Takk Fyri." and leads Daniel back out into Vaglið Square.

She holds open the bag and looks inside. Astrid had put their orders into takeaway containers and had put a six-pack of Föroya Bjór Black Sheep Export lager in with the food. "Come on Daniel. Let's go and find this Dagny Poulsen of yours" and headed off down Aarvegur.

Sólrun was ahead of Daniel as they both started walking down Aarvegur. He jogged a few steps to catch up with her.

"Are you OK?" he asked but by looking at her, he could tell that she wasn't.

"I'm sorry for that scene back there, but I cannot stand that man. I find it very hard to be even pleasant to him at the best of times but tonight he just set my blood boiling."

Daniel slipped his arm inside hers and said "Well you can calm down now. Thanks for the distraction. Where are you taking me and what did you mean when you said that we should go and find Dagny Poulsen?"

They had walked down Aarvegur, past the front door of the Hotel Havnar and had stopped at the harbour. To the left was a rising sharp-faced escarpment with buildings below it. There was a ferry port and a long quay behind it. In front of them, many multi-coloured small boats were moored beside each other and to the right, a wide peninsula tapering to a point. All along this peninsula were wooden and stone houses of differing sizes and shapes, huddled together, so much so, they looked as if they had just been planted beside each other in a hurry. The buildings were either irregularly spaced apart or hard up against one another. Some were painted reddish-brown, others were painted black. Some of the buildings had grass roofs while others did not. The haphazard appearance of their location was both captivating and confusing at the same time.

Sólrun pointed at the mixture of houses and started to explain them to Daniel.

"Your search for Dagny Poulsen starts there. This is Tinganes, which means 'parliament jetty" or "parliament point'. This is the oldest part of town and where some of the parliament is based. Dagny's address, Funningstova, is just off Gongin, the main street. We'll go to the point at the far end and grab a seat. We can eat the food Astrid gave us" she holds up the bag "and we can wander back along Gongin and find Funnigstova. Deal?" she smiled.

Daniel was glad she was smiling and had become herself again. "Deal." he replied.

She slipped off her shoes and held them in her right hand along with the canvas bag. She reached over and grabbed his hand and moved forward towards Tinganes. Away to his right, a passenger bus had stopped a short distance away and a group of youngsters were alighting. Daniel recognised them as the group of Scottish students who had been on the plane with him. They were being herded together and lined up to enter the Hotel Tinganes, set back from the quayside. He was distracted back to Sólrun who was now skipping in her bare feet, the soles of which were making a slapping noise each time they landed on the smooth surfaces of the rocks.

They reached the outermost point of the Tinganes peninsula and sat down on a bench in front of a large reddish-brown building. Sólrun explained that it was called Skansapakkhusið and was the main parliament building. She opened the bag and passed him his Faroe Burger. She reached back inside the bag and retrieved the six-pack of Föroya Bjór, ripped the cardboard packaging apart, grabbed a bottle and placed its top against the edge of the bench. She slapped the palm of her free hand down hard on the bottle and removed the top. She passed the opened bottle to Daniel and then repeated the action with another bottle.

She toasted him. "To the finding of Dagny Poulsen" and clinked the side of his bottle then progressed to half-drain the contents of her own bottle. Daniel studied the picture of a black faced sheep on the label of the bottle. He thought of Heri talking to one and its fleece falling off. He looked at the 5.8% alcohol content marking and hoped that this wasn't rocket fuel.

He raised his bottle in reply. "To finding Dagny Poulsen" and swigged from his bottle. To his surprise, the lager had a soft taste of caramel and malt and was actually very nice to drink. It wasn't the only thing that was very nice, he thought, but he wasn't here for self-indulgent fraternisation with the locals. He was here to try and find clues to the mystery that seemed to be unfolding around him the more he pried.

The Stream

They finished their burgers and Sólrun opened another two bottles. She wandered across the rocks and sat down near the water's edge. The strange twilight darkness was slowly receding as the sun started to rise on the horizon. Sólrun called him over to join her. He lifted the remaining two bottles of lager and walked over and sat down. She went on to explain that Tinganes had been the site of the Løgting, or parliament, of the Faroe Islands since the arrival of the Norse settlers in the early 9th century. Christianity had been accepted here in 998 and that the Løgmaður, the lawman, or prime minister, had his office on Tinganes. She knew him well. He was a childhood friend of her father and when her father had suddenly died, he had been very helpful to her family over the years. He would definitely know something about this Dagny Poulsen and they should go and speak to him in the morning.

She walked over to some rocks and said to Daniel to come and look at the carvings and runes that had been there for a thousand years.

Daniel made his way over and watched Sólrun run a finger along the grooves of an intricate sundial carved into the rock. Beside it were some runes that were deeply etched into the stone.

ᛏᛁᛑᛁᚾ ᚱᛖᚾᚾᚢᚱ ᛋᚢᛗ ᛋᛏᚱᛖᛗᛋᛗᚢᚱ ᛁ ᚨ

"What does this mean?" asked Daniel and pointed at the carvings.

"Tíðin rennur sum streymur í á'." she explained. "Time runs like the current of a stream"

The Stream

Tinganes is a fairly compact area situated on a peninsula that divides the Tórshavn harbour into two parts, the Eystaravág and Vesteravág, the east and west harbours. Strolling down the Gongin main street, Daniel was fascinated by the fact that the parliament buildings and offices were side by side with private dwelling houses. Wandering around the well-preserved historical houses, the majority of which were built in the 16th and 17th centuries, it amused him to see residents' laundry hung out to dry alongside official and private offices. The charm of the whole area was the premise that you could probably enter any of the buildings and be made to feel welcome. He found a wooden door with a glass window pane. Written on the glass was 'Løgmaður' and below it in English was the translation of 'Prime Minister'. This was government that the local population had ready and available access to. That fact hadn't changed for a thousand years, the same thousand years where everything elsewhere in the world had changed, but the centre of decision making and administration of these 18 islands had been continuously constant by remaining where it had always been, located at the end of a narrow rocky peninsula in Thor's Harbour, Tórshavn.

Walking along a cobbled street, Daniel stumbled upon Funningstova. It was a painted black wooden and stone building with a grass roof and its house name displayed on an enamel plaque beside the front door. He peered in through a window. It was obviously still a dwelling house going by the seats and coffee table making up a sitting room. The vestiges of modern living were to be seen all around the room, such as the remote control for the television, a newspaper and some mugs on the table.

He stepped back and looked at the house. The first part of his search had been completed by locating the address. All he had to do now was to make some enquiries with the inhabitants inside to see if they had information about previous occupants. It was now 3.00am and waking the current occupiers inside up for a chat was not an option. He would come back later on in the day if Sólrun was able to arrange a meeting with her friend, the Løgmaður.

"I see you found Funningstova then?" said Sólrun as she came and stood beside him.

"What does Funningstova mean?" he asked.

"The living room." was the reply.

"Very apt." said Daniel and suggested that she had a quick look inside the window.

Sólrun peeked in through the glass. "It is, isn't it?"

"Well now that the first part of my search is complete by me finding the address mentioned on the postcard, I just need to go and find out some information about this Dagny Poulsen." replied Daniel.

"Well that should be easy to do in the morning." suggested Sólrun.

"We can go to the Raohus, the Town Hall, and ask to have a look at some of the census records and historical town archives that are stored there. Most of the information that you need will be kept there, and if you are looking for any human interest aspects and some family information, we should be able to get that from Jo-Jo."

"Jo-Jo?" asked Daniel. Sólrun laughed as she realised what she had just said.

"Sorry about that. Jo-Jo is the pet nickname that I have for Jógvan Johannesen. He's the Løgmaður, the prime minister. I have called him that since I was little girl. I'm probably the only person in the world that gets away with calling him that.

They had reached the end of the harbour and were at the junction at the start of Aarvegur. Daniel looked at his watch and realised it was now 3.17am. He had been on the islands for 6 hours but it felt like a week.

"Sólrun. Thanks for all your help tonight and I really appreciate you showing me around, but I'm fairly bushed as I have been on the go now for nearly 24 hours. Would you mind if I could go back to my hotel just now and get some sleep? We can meet up tomorrow, I mean later on this morning if you like?"

He points at a building across from them. A long wooden building painted reddish brown. It had a grass roof and at one end of the building, there was a conservatory type eating area and a patio beer garden.

"Café Natur serves the best all day breakfast on the islands. Do you want to meet up in there about 10.00am?" suggested Sólrun.

"Sure." Said Daniel and leaned forward and kissed her gently on the cheek.

"Thanks for tonight. It certainly was an interesting evening."

Sólrun just looked at him yearnfully.

"The best is yet to come, I think. I will see you at 10.00am. Takk Fyri Daniel Lauridsen." and she walked across the road and started to climb the stairs of a path that ran between some buildings.

Daniel watched her disappear out of sight. Not a single backward glance was made in his direction. He hoped that he hadn't upset her. He turned to his left and walked up Aarvegur to the hotel, collected the room key from reception and went to his room. Having collapsed on the soft bed, he quickly fell asleep.

The Stream

10.00am – Friday 9th June, present day
Café Natur, Tórshavn, Faroe Islands.

Daniel crossed over the Aarvegur and walked in through the front door of the Café Natur. Sólrun was already seated inside at a window and was pouring herself a coffee from a pot on the table. He sat down opposite her and asked if she had slept well. She poured him a coffee.

"Of course I did. Did you?"

Daniel went on to explain that the bed in his hotel room was the softest he had ever lain in and that he was probably asleep before his head had touched the pillow. Sólrun snorted and her hazel-green eyes sparkled with a mixture of disappointment and pleasure.

"Well I'm glad you did sailor boy, because you have a very busy day ahead of you and I don't want you getting all tired on me again too early." she uttered mischievously.

Daniel acknowledged the friendly rebuke and mentally noted that this was probably going to be an interesting day, and night, by the sounds of it.

"What's the plan then?" he asked.

Sólrun explained that she had already made a number of telephone calls on his behalf and had arranged for him to have a meeting with the Town Hall records keeper at 11.00am and after that, she had arranged a further meeting with her family friend, Jo-Jo, at 2.00pm. Daniel thanked her for arranging the two meetings. He was really impressed with her organisational skills and that she seemed very keen to help him.

"Why are you doing all of this? You hardly know me but you have gone out of your way to assist me with a personal matter."

Sólrun put her coffee down, met his gaze and said "When your friend Ingi was booking the car for you, we got into casual conversation and he explained that you were the closest thing to a best friend that he had. He told me that he totally trusted you and that he would put his life in your hands, whatever the situation. He had mentioned that you were also going to be doing some local research looking for someone while you were here for the Jólaskipið salvage attempt. I offered to help you on your quest because Ingi had said that you were diving for him, free of charge. For someone to go commercial diving in those seas, free of charge, is either completely mad or someone I would like to get to know a bit better. I know you probably have all sorts of history and personal secrets that you will never share with me, but then again, getting to spend some time with you is exciting and going by last night, maybe what you are searching for is all part of a far bigger mystery that you have uncovered. It's exciting. You are looking for lots of answers and maybe I can help you find some of them."

Daniel began to realise that Sólrun was not just a pretty face with an overtly friendly personality. She was one very perceptive woman who had quickly grasped that his investigations were not just a simple person tracing exercise.

"What did you go and study when you were at Copenhagen University, by the way? You never told me."

"Forensic psychology." was the reply.

"That explains an awful lot. If you have a degree in forensic psychology, why aren't you now using it? No offence, but hiring cars out at the airport does seem to be a serious waste of your talents?"

In between sips of coffee, Sólrun explained that it was a long story. She had been working as a very busy court based forensic psychologist back in Denmark but her mother had suddenly died six years ago. She hadn't been home for nearly a decade and had returned to bury her mother and settle all her affairs, sell up the family property with the full intention to then return back to Denmark. But on her return back to the Faroes, she had found that Heri Jorgensen had, over time, cajoled and manipulated her mother into signing over into his possession a number of title deeds to some plots of land that had traditionally been in the Jacobsen family for generations. Given Heri's many business interests and positions, he had astutely realised that the Faroese economy was recovering. He could financially profit from owning numerous plots of land that he could then sell on for potential development by foreign businesses and investors wishing to establish offices and facilities on the islands. When Sólrun had discovered what had happened, she had tried to recover back the land, or the financial equivalent, through the legal system and the various court procedures that were open to her.

Unfortunately for Sólrun, Heri had been clever enough to close all the loop-holes while ensuring that whatever transactions and agreements he had ever made when acquiring any land, they were all above board, legally binding and beyond recall. He had financially profited from operating deceitful and underhand practices and in doing so, he had denied Sólrun, and her cousin, Astrid, out of their rightful inheritance. She despised the man for what he had done, and what grated her more than anything else, was the smug air of superiority that he always portrayed towards her and Astrid whenever they were unfortunate enough to be in his presence. He knew that they knew that he had defrauded them out of their inheritances and he revelled in rubbing their noses in the fact that there was nothing that either of them could do about it, at least legally.

Instead of returning back to Denmark and resuming her career, as the Faroe Islands are relatively crime-free and there's not really a demand for her professional talents, she had opted to remain in the Faroes and find out as much dirt as she could on Heri Jorgensen. If she couldn't retrieve her rightful inheritance back, she would eke out some form of retributive justice on the man, by destroying his reputation and the various business ventures that he had accrued through unfair, immoral and illegal practices.

She just needed an opportunity to start her new career as a retributivist to make Heri Jorgensen suffer for all the crimes that he had committed. Six years had passed and she was now getting frustrated at the lack of success she had had in trying to achieve her objectives. With a small population and nearly everyone knowing one another, secrets could be easily kept or revealed. Heri was aware of that fact and had been extremely smart in all of his numerous dealings. He always targeted the weak, the vulnerable and the elderly who wouldn't, or in most cases, couldn't resist his plans.

She refilled her mug with more coffee and exhaled deeply.

"Well Daniel Lauridsen, you weren't expecting that, were you?"

Daniel didn't need to say anything. He knew that he had drawn out of Sólrun her innermost feelings and anxieties and for her to have shared them with him was both cathartic and traumatic at the same time. She had been able to finally purge herself of the emotional build up within her from the last six years but by discussing them with a complete stranger, she now had the trauma that she may have exposed her vulnerability to someone that she didn't know if she could trust. Daniel looked across the table and took hold of both her hands inside his own.

"Relax. You have nothing to fear from me. You can trust me, and believe me, when I have finished with this Dagny business, I can help you deal with Heri in ways that will really surprise you."

"Thank you." she said as a tear formed at the corner of her left eye.

Daniel passed over his napkin for her to use. He decided to change the subject. "Shall we go over to the town hall now?"

As they were leaving the café, Daniel stopped to look at something at the door. On a notice-board on the inner wall, a poster was on display advertising the European Viking Researcher's Conference in Tórshavn. The poster had the obligatory pictures of Vikings with swords raised and of longboats. There were photographs of various venues and locations and a picture of Torstein Lindemann addressing an audience. Daniel started to point at the centre of the poster. It listed the itinerary for the next two days:

- 9th/10th June - 1700 and 1830
- Spor í Tinganes. A guided tour on Tinganes, the site of an early Viking parliament, runes and rock carvings
- 9th/10th June - 1730 and 2215
- Viking DNA, genetics and other tests at the new Environmental Welfare Agency research laboratory
- 10th June - 1930
- Epigenetics – 'Reprogramming the code'. A lecture by Doctor Torstein Lindemann, Director General of Das Volker Syndicate, in the Town Hall
- 9th/10th June - 1800 and 2230
- Goymt, the men ikki gloymt. A display and discussion session on old lawbooks, minutes and other documents from the parliament archives.
- 10th June - 2330
- Kaga upp í himmalin. Learn about the stars to be seen overhead (weather permitting).

"Looks like we might be joining one of those tours and I think our Saturday night entertainment might be starting in the Town Hall." suggested Daniel to Sólrun.

They reached the Town Hall and entered inside. Sólrun was chatting to the receptionist. She knew her from school and they were catching up on girly gossip. Daniel looked around the foyer. There was a poster advertising the European Viking Researcher's Conference and the lecture the following evening. There were leaflets lying about detailing the various business interests of the Das Volker Syndicate. Daniel picked one up and slipped it inside his jacket. Might come in handy at a later date he thought. There were promotional flyers and posters advertising some university scheme with the slogan 'Reprogramming the Code' that Das Volker Syndicate seemed to have some involvement with. He pocketed one of the flyers.

Sólrun came over and said that the Records Keeper would be with them shortly. He was showing a group of Nordic Studies students from Scotland some of the records and archives that are kept here and in the Føroya Fornminnissavn, the Historical Museum, over in Hoyvík, which was in walking distance from where they were.

The foyer suddenly became full of people as a couple of swing doorways opened and a horde flooded out from what must be the auditorium. Daniel recognised the young faces as the Scottish students that he had shared the flight with last night. He stood to the side to let them past. A couple of girls flagged behind the main group. They were in deep conversation. Although Daniel's English was perfect, sometimes it took him a while to adjust to the regional dialects of the United Kingdom, and from experience, he had found the Scots the hardest to adjust to. They spoke very quickly and they also had regional brogues that at times were incomprehensible.

The two girls stopped just short of the exit doors. They were scanning a map of Tórshavn that they shared between them. Typical students, thought Daniel, with their strange dress senses and the requisite rucksack on their backs. They were pretty girls, about 17 or 18. They were both about 5 foot 6 and one had long brown hair and the other had a frizz of long black curly hair. He listened to their conversation. The black haired girl pointed to the map and Daniel picked up the word "Tinganes" from what she was saying. The brown haired girl had replied to her friend, but the only words that he could hear were "Dagny", "Funningstova" and "Tinganes."

Daniel's senses went on full alert. He walked over towards the door with the pretence of uplifting a leaflet from a table. He wanted to be able to get closer to hear more of what they were discussing. He picked up a leaflet and started reading it whilst trying to listen to the girls' conversation. From his new position, he was facing them with his back to the door. He looked up at them both but his eyes were drawn to the brooch that the brown haired girl had pinned to the right lapel of her jacket. It was a small pewter and silver brooch of a sailing ship, a larger version of the unofficial insignia of the Frømandskorpset, but if he didn't know better, it was a replica of the one his grandmother was wearing in the photograph with Dagny Poulsen that was taken in the Viktoriapark in Berlin in 1939.

The two girls smiled at him and the brown haired girl said "Excuse me? Can we get past please?"

Daniel saw that he was impeding their exit. "Sorry." and moved out of their way.

The black haired girl replied "Thanks." and Daniel watched them both leave to catch up with their fellow students.

He sat down in a nearby chair. "What the bloody hell is going on?" he muttered aloud and rubbed his face with the palms of his hands. Sólrun sat down beside him and put an arm around him.

"What's wrong? You look as if you have had a major fright. What's happened?"

He stopped rubbing his face and composed himself.

"After we have seen the record keeper, we need to have a discussion. I need to speak to someone about why I am really here. The more information I find, the more coincidences occur and I am getting more and more confused with it all, and concerned, that I may have walked into something far more sinister than I could have ever imagined. There is something happening and me being here, just now in the Faroes, seems to be pre-ordained. I know it sounds silly, but I have the feeling I am supposed to be here and it is for a reason I do not yet know."

Sólrun patted his shoulder. "We'll go and see the record keeper and then we'll go back to my house and get some lunch. We can discuss it then."

11.00am – Friday 9th June, present day
Raohus (Town Hall) Tórshavn, Faroe Islands.

The record keeper appeared behind the reception desk.

"Daniel Lauridsen?" he enquired. Daniel got up from his seat and went over and introduced himself. The record keeper identified himself as Ole Patturson and smiled at Sólrun.

"Hi Sólrun. Nice to see you again. It's been a while." Sólrun apologetically admitted it had been a while and asked him how the family was.

"Anna is expecting again and Trondur and Elise are so excited that they are getting a wee brother or sister, more so Elise."

He opened a ledger in front of him. Sólrun offered her congratulations and said she would come round and see them all soon.

Ole asked Daniel what information he was looking for. Daniel reached inside his jacket and brought out his folder. He laid it on the counter, opened it and retrieved the photograph from the park in Berlin in 1939. He showed it to Ole and tapped at Dagny in the picture.

"I am trying to trace this young Faroese woman, Dagny Poulsen. She was my mother's nanny in Berlin until the Second World War broke out."

He indicated his mother in the photograph. He drew his attention to Mille.

"My grandmother helped her flee from Berlin and paid for her return back here. My mother has asked me to find out what happened to her. I have an address. It's...?. Ole finished the rest of the sentence for him.

"Dagny I Funningstova. She's a popular woman today."

Daniel stiffened when he heard Ole's last words. Before he could enquire further, Sólrun launched into a fast and frenetic inquisition in Faroese. Ole couldn't get a word in reply, such was the ferocity of her outburst, and stepped back with his hands in the air.

"Sólrun." he shouted. "Stop it. Can you let me explain?"

Daniel looked at Sólrun. Her hazel-green eyes were burning with an intensity he hadn't witnessed before. Her demeanour had changed and she wanted answers and she wanted them now. She had gone on the offensive and wanted information. Daniel suddenly had the thought of the valkyrie shield-maidens of Norse mythology and them slaughtering everything around them. He moved between Sólrun and the desk.

"What did you mean by saying that Dagny Poulsen was popular today?"

He grabbed Sólrun by the arm, turned her towards him.

"Enough. Let him explain." and released her. She quietened down to muttering under her breath and stomped away over to the seats by the front door.

"Sorry about that Ole. You were saying?"

Ole came forward to the desk. He quickly flicked a glance over at Sólrun and started to explain how he was aware of Dagny. He had just finished a tour of the building with a group of Scottish students that were in the Faroes for the European Viking Researcher's Conference. During the tour, he had described to them the operation of the archive and the operation of record keeping that was kept at the town hall and over at the heritage museum. He had shown the students various documents and record books as examples. One of these examples displayed how huge parts of Faroese social history were recorded for posterity in special ledgers by detailing all the 'hatches, matches and dispatches' - births, marriages and deaths, in the islands over the years.

He paused and turned the ledger around to show Daniel. Daniel nodded at him to continue. The ledger he had in front of him was dated from 1909 to 1919.

Ole went on to say that two of the young students had expressed a real interest in this particular ledger and had gone on to ask him a number of questions on how they would be able to get further information and details about one of the entries. Ole opened the ledger and carefully turned the pages to September 1919. He ran his finger down the list of entries to find what he was looking for and then shifted the ledger around to allow Daniel to read the hand-written in Danish record of registration. The columns read as follows:

Fødsel (birth)
Fødested (place of birth) Tórshavn
Fødselsdato (date of birth) Mandag 15 September 1919
Køn barn (sex of child) Kvinde (female)
Far (father) Peder Poulsen
Beskæftigelse (occupation) Bogholder (book keeper)
Mor (mother) Lisbita Poulsen
Beskæftigelse (occupation) Kok (cook)
Navn på barn (name of child) Dagny
Registreringsdato (registration date) Onsdag 17 September 1919
Adresse (address) Funningstova

Daniel asked if he could get a photocopy of the page and Ole scooped the ledger up, tucked it under his arm and disappeared through a door behind him, presumably to copy the page for him. He walked over to Sólrun.

"What the hell was that all about Sólrun? Ole was just telling us that other people had asked about Dagny this morning and you suddenly get all aggressive on him. I hope you are going to apologise to him when he comes back, because it looks as if I need more of his help here. Other people are looking for Dagny and I want to know why."

She looked at him. There was genuine remorse etched in her face. "Sorry Daniel. I don't know what came over me. I'm intrigued with all of this and the more I get involved, the more I want to find out. My clash with Heri Jacobsen last night in the restaurant and my telling you my life story half an hour ago has made me a bit ratty. I'm sorry. Those two girls talking about Dagny got me really worked up. I am only trying to help you."

Ole came back through the door and handed Daniel a photocopy of the ledger of the book.

"Sometimes the old fashioned ways are better. Back in 2007, the Government started a project to create an electronic databank of the genealogical data of the inhabitants of the islands, drawing on all the records from the past 200 years. These are the remaining ledgers that haven't been digitalised for the national archive. Digitalisation is the current high priority for the powers that be because of our topography as an archipelago. The emphasis on the ten permanent staff here, and elsewhere, is of extreme urgency to get everything on-line and readily available to those wanting access to information,

24-7. I'd rather have people coming in and looking for it themselves or asking the staff questions or for assistance, and from my own experience, that type of personal contact often reveals a lot more information that can be ever found by scrolling through electronic archives, don't you think?"

Sólrun walked up to him and threw her arms around him in an embrace and started to cry and make her apologies to him. There was now an awful lot of Faroese being spoken, mainly by Sólrun, and Daniel was glad that he couldn't understand any of it. He decided to leave them alone for a few minutes and wandered into the auditorium. It was a small venue but none the less, an impressive one.

State of the art display screens and lighting rigs were mounted on and around the wide stage. The stage itself was elevated from the rows of seating in front of it and Daniel slowly walked down the slight decline in the floor towards it. His footfalls on the wooden flooring echoed around the auditorium. This hall has good acoustics and would be a great venue for a concert or musical show, he thought.

A display screen started to play a promotional piece about the Faroe Islands, its places of learning, museums, culture and history. Daniel sat down and started to watch the film. Daniel was taken aback with the stunning scenery on show and took a mental note of some of the tourist attractions that he might want to go and visit before heading to the town of Klaksvík and finalising the dive attempts with Ingi. The Heritage Museum, the Nordic House and the Art Gallery were three venues that he definitely wanted to go and see before he went diving.

He didn't notice Sólrun and Ole entering the hall and sitting behind him, and as the film finished, he was slightly startled when Ole mentioned that he had just shown the film to the Scottish students. Ole walked up on to the stage and switched off the film. He removed the DVD from a machine and placed it in his pocket. Sólrun came and stood beside Daniel.

"I have kissed and made up with Ole and he wants to show you something that I think you will be really interested in."

He stood up and both of them met Ole as he came down off the stage.

"Sólrun explained to me that you are diving to the wreck of the SS Sauternes? Over at the Heritage Museum, we have some articles on display that were recovered from the dives to it previously. There is a small exhibition about the Jólaskipið and it is quite popular with the tourists. Not everything is on display and I think you might be interested in something that we have through in the Records Department."

Ole led them through a side door and along a passage. He used a swipe card to open a door and then led them along a short corridor to a heavy, steel-framed door. He withdrew a long key from his pocket and inserted it into a lock in the door. He turned the key and then punched a code into a button lock system above it on the door. A series of clicks could be heard and Ole depressed the door handle and opened it inwards. They stepped into a long room with shelving racks that ran from the floor to the ceiling. The shelves were on moveable tracks and could be opened and closed by the turning of a handle at the end of each rack. Notices mounted on the gable ends identified what was stored on the shelves of each rack.

Ole locked the door of the room behind them and started to explain that this room contained many of the most treasured records of the Faroes. A state of the art storage facility was to be found over at the Heritage Museum containing the majority of the records and this was all that remained at the Raohus. He pointed out some of the preservation features such as a carbon dioxide gas sprinkler system in case of fire, humidity and temperature sensors on the walls and ceilings, venting ports to remove carbon dioxide if deployed and that the room was effectively air and water tight.

"Until they finally digitise all of this and get it uploaded into the national archive database, this has to remain here. It has taken a long time to manually record everything for the database, but we are getting there, slowly, but we are getting there."

He walked over to one of the racks and turned the handle to open up the shelving. Daniel looked at the notice on the end. 'Operation Valentine - British Occupation of the Faroe Islands, April 1940 to September 1945'. As the rack opened, the contents of the shelves came into view. They were packed with differently sized boxes, all containing records of the 'friendly occupation' by the British military during the Second World War. Photographs, aerial reconnaissance, Royal Navy charts, shipping lists, German Lufwaffe and submarine identification posters, letters, paperwork and various military documents detailing the occupation were stored all along the various shelves.

Ole remarked. "You could spend days looking at all of this. You open a box and start rummaging and before you know it, two, three, four hours have passed you by as you get caught up in looking at the past. It is amazing what you find in amongst all of this. Something that digitalisation cannot provide."

He escorted them down to the end of the rack and lifted up a roller shutter that sealed an end of the unit. Inside was a rotary binder case storage unit with alphabetically listed box binders inserted into the many levels. He spun the unit around and stopped at 'S' and removed a binder with 'SS Sauternes' written on its spine. Ole carried the binder and took Daniel and Sólrun back down the aisle towards a table. He laid the binder down, opened it, took the contents out and spread the various bits and pieces along the length of the table.

There were reports about the sinking, information about the 25 crew and passengers, the cargo it was carrying, Lloyds of London documents, press cuttings and details of the recovery of six bodies and their subsequent burial in Klaksvík. A number of photographs had been taken of the site as well as some of the villagers from the islands of Fugloy and Svínoy. These villagers had witnessed the sinking of the SS Sauternes as it was overcome by the treacherous seas in the sound between the two islands, Fugloyfjørður. The villagers had all been questioned at length by a British military garrison command-appointed investigation team and had provided vital witness statements concerning the last hours of the SS Sauternes.

These statements had been collated with those gathered from the crew of its escort vessel, the Royal Navy armed trawler HMT Kerrara, and the board of enquiry had apportioned blame to the human error of a simple spelling mistake by the omission of a single letter within a communication. The Captain of the Sauternes, a William Smith, had sent a telegraph to the Naval Headquarters based in Tórshavn giving the positions of both ships as being in Fugløfjord. Naval Headquarters personnel had misread this message and thought that both vessels were in Fuglefjord, a fairly safe anchorage off the coast of the island of Eysturoy. Both vessels were ordered to drop their anchors and ride out the worst of the storm. However, as a result of this unfortunate misunderstanding, the fateful destiny of the SS Sauternes had been sealed.

Ole handed Daniel an A4 size piece of paper. It had various stamps and identification marks and in bold letters at the top, it read:

Witness Statement – Sinking of the SS Sauternes. Sunday 7th December 1941. Time: 15.30.

Daniel scanned the document and very quickly understood that this was a contemporaneous witness statement that had been provided by Dagny Poulsen. It was hand-written in Danish, She had lovely hand-writing, he thought. The statement was fairly grim reading and Dagny had recounted that she had been staying on the island of Svínoy, and that she, and other residents had watched the last moments of the doomed ship. The seas were too rough for the locals to attempt a rescue. Dagny's statement explained the crew of the SS Sauternes frantically trying to break the anchor chain with axes. The anchor was pulling the ship down into the sea. Huge waves had swamped the vessel and she had watched two life-rafts being launched. One of the life-rafts had at least five men in it, but both rafts capsized and she could see the lights of life jackets bobbing about in the water as dusk fell. She could hear the screams of men trapped aboard the ship as it sank beneath the waves. The villagers of Kirkja on the island of Fugloy attempted to launch their boats but the rough seas beat them back. Dagny had also described the events of the following day when the storm had abated and the ocean waters were calm. All the menfolk of both islands had put out to sea in their small boats looking for survivors. There were none to be found. Six bodies had washed ashore in the following days and the seas had stripped them of their clothing. The bodies could only be identified by the weddings rings on their hands or by the dog-tags around their necks. The statement was signed and dated Dagny Poulsen, Tirsdag 15 December 1941.

Daniel handed the statement back to Ole. "They were brave men who died a terrible death. Not a pleasant way to go, I imagine."

Ole agreed with him and gave him another piece of paper. It was the details of the six men whose bodies had been recovered.

Captain George Albert Perris, 34 years, RASC.
Richard Smith, 35 years.
John Daniel McNicol, 21 years.
Robert Ross, 25 years.
Peter McKenzie Cormack, 21 years.
Unidentified man, approximately 35 years.

Ole explained that the bodies had been buried in the churchyard in Klaksvík. "Do you wish me to copy these for you as well?" he asked. Daniel nodded and Ole gathered all the other papers up into the binder and returned it to the rotary tower. He lowered the roller shutter and started to escort Daniel and Sólrun out of the room. He closed the racks over, unlocked the heavy steel-framed door, led them out into the corridor and locked the archive shut. He took them through the passage and back into the auditorium.

"If you wait at the reception desk, I will be back in a few minutes" and left by the side door.

Daniel was fairly sombre as he walked out of the auditorium with Sólrun by his side.

"It's a really dreadful way to die. As a sailor, it is your worst fear to be trapped inside a sinking ship." he said.

They walked out of the auditorium in silence and waited for Ole at the reception desk. He returned and handed Daniel a copy of Dagny's statement and the list of the drowned men.

"Is there anything else I can help you with?" he asked. Daniel indicated that Ole had done far more than he had expected and thanked him profusely for his time and assistance.

"You are most welcome. Good hunting with the Jólaskipið. I have other duties to attend to so forgive me if I take my leave of you just now. Takk Fyri."

Daniel shook his hand and Sólrun hugged and kissed him again. Ole went slightly red and Sólrun said she would come and see Anna and the children very soon. "Sorry about earlier." and smiled at him. He just nodded and smiled back.

Daniel stopped and shouted on Ole as he was walking away. "Ole. I forgot to ask you this earlier. Why were the Scottish girls so interested in Dagny Poulsen?"

Ole halted and moved back round to the desk. "Oh they were looking for where Funningstova could be found and I told them where it was. One of the Scottish girls was looking for her grandmother's house and that she was called Dagny Poulsen. Nice girl. She gave me the date of birth for this Dagny Poulsen and I looked up the ledger and showed her what I copied for you. The Scottish girl had a traditional Faroese name which I thought was a nice touch. She's called Freyja. You should go and talk to her if you see her again. She will be here tomorrow for the lecture with the other students. You'll find them easily though as they'll be on those tours, I should think." as he gestured at the poster on the wall.

"Thanks Ole. See you tomorrow maybe?" and left Ole to return to his business.

As Daniel and Sólrun left the building and stood outside in the midday sun, he mentioned to Sólrun

"There's another bloody coincidence to add to the growing list." Sólrun just nodded her agreement at him. Daniel looked at his watch.

"We've got a couple of hours before we go and meet your friend Jo-Jo. Are you going to verbally attack the Prime Minister as well when we meet him?" he joked with her. She slapped his arm and threatened to hit him again. He put his hands up in surrender. She laughed.

"We'll go this way. It's lunchtime and my house is not far from here. We can discuss everything while we grab something to eat." and they ambled up a lane towards Sólrun's house.

The Stream

The view from the living room of Heri Jorgensen's house was certainly arresting. With the house set amongst the rising slopes of the hills above the capital, the intensity of Tórshavn's setting was profound. The sea went on forever eastwards, interrupted in the middle of the view by the island of Nólsoy, five kilometres away across the waters of the Nólsoyarfjord. Nólsoy is a strange looking island. Starting off in the north as a long and thin strip of land, it tapers to a narrow isthmus where the small town of Nólsoy straddles either side of it. The island then spreads out southwards to a headland with two lighthouses situated at the capes on the southeastern and southwestern extremities, Øknastangi and Borðan. The main part of the island between the town and the lighthouses rises steeply to become a hump-back shaped mountain, Høgoyggj, its highest point being Eggjarklettur, standing at over 1200 feet. The midday sunlight emblazoned the whole of the island, and in doing so, it made the lush green colours of the grass to contrast sharply with the rocks, outcrops, crevices, escarpments and cliffs by creating shapes in the shadows that seemed to heighten and elongate the island even further.

Torstein Lindemann finished admiring the view and studied the paintings and photographs that adorned the walls of the room. He was drawn to one particular painting, an oil canvas by Frimod Joensen that replicated perfectly the view from the window. It was a genuine work of art in that its creator had wonderfully captured in oils, a singular moment in time that was very similar to the current aspect to be seen from the room. Beside the painting was hung a family photograph of a man, woman and a young child, presumably Heri with his mother and father pondered Torstein. The door of the room opened and Heri entered carrying a tray with assorted cutlery and crockery, a coffee pot and some breads and cheeses. He placed the tray on a coffee table, sat down in an armchair and invited Torstein to join him. Torstein sat down in another armchair and as Heri was pouring him a coffee, asked him "What did your father do for a living?" and nodded his head backwards to the family photograph. Heri, momentarily hesitated in mid-pour, looked at the photograph and then continued to fill the cup to its brim.

"He was a local historian. I thought you knew that Torstein?" he said nervously as he finished pouring. He put down the pot and lifted the cup and saucer and placed it in front of Torstein.

"I meant what did he really do for a living? Do you know Heri? Do you really know what he actually did?"
Heri was puzzled by this sudden and strange conversation about his father and had started to become somewhat flustered. The stare of Torstein's piercing blue eyes demanded an answer to a question he did not know and this was unsettling him. A solitary bead of sweat pooled above his left temple and trickled down his face. He reached for a napkin and mopped his brow and face.

"Do you want to know what your father really did for a living?" said Lindemann. Heri was now dumbfounded and was at a complete loss as to what the purpose of this discussion was really about.

The Stream

"Torstein. You obviously know something that I am totally unaware of. As far as I know, my father had been studying at the university in Copenhagen when Germany invaded Denmark and he couldn't come home until the war's end. He had stayed in Denmark until late 1944, where he had met your father and had gone to work for him in Switzerland until the mid 1950s. He came back to the Faroes, met my mother, I was born and he worked as a historian for the government and helped create what is now the national archive. That's all he did. That's all I know. What are you trying to tell me?"

Heri was now becoming extremely uncomfortable and agitated with the conversation and beginning to sweat profusely. He wiped his face and brow again with the napkin and loosened his tie and collar.

Torstein lifted the slim attache case beside his armchair and placed it on his knees. He opened it and removed a black and white photograph that he then placed, face upwards, on the coffee table. He slid the photograph across the table top towards Heri. Heri caught it before it fell on to the floor. He surveyed the photograph. It was a snapshot of his father in uniform. A soldier's uniform. Heri was puzzled by the image. His father hadn't been in the army. His father hadn't been in any military service as far he knew. There had to be some mistake. He reviewed the photograph again. It wasn't a Danish military uniform but there was a Dannebrog flashing, the Danish flag, on the left shoulder and on the cuff, a band had the lettering *Freikorp Danmark*. On the collar, were two symbols. One was the SS Schutzstaffel insignia and the other was a circular badge comprised of a rounded swastika flanked with a laurel wreath with a representation of 'Odin's pillar',

Yggdrasil, in the centre. It was a German uniform and a uniform of the SS. Heri's eyes bulge to the point of almost exploding as he looks at the photograph. His brain cannot process the ramifications of the image that is in his hands,

"What is this? What are you telling me here Torstein? What the fuck is this you are showing me?" he screamed.

He stood up and paced the room. The napkin was now being rubbed around his face at speed. His face had become puce. He threw the photograph at Torstein and held his head in his hands.

"What the fuck is this?" he shouts at Torstein and advances at him menacingly. Torstein stands up and swiftly kicks the approaching Heri just inside the left knee. Heri collapses downwards, and as he falls, Torstein kicks him very hard in the chest. Heri falls backwards and lands on the floor, his arms splayed out beside him. He is winded and starts to hyperventilate with short rasping breaths desperately searching for air. His red face has panic written all over and it quickly turns to one of distress as Torstein places his foot on Heri's throat. He exerts downward pressure on Heri's windpipe and the man starts to choke. He thrashes around on the floor and grabs Torstein's leg in a vain attempt to free himself. Torstein just leans forward and presses harder. Calmly and slowly, Torstein speaks down at Heri.

"I can kill you right now Heri or I can spare you if you will listen to what I am going to tell you. What's it to be Heri?"

Heri releases Torstein's foot from his grasp and lies passively on the floor. His breathing has now become fast-paced and extremely short. Torstein removes his foot from Heri's throat, picks up the discarded photograph and sits back down in his armchair. Heri lies floundering on his own living room floor like a beached whale, utterly helpless and struggling to survive. His breathing slowly returns to something resembling normal and he rolls over onto his front and attempts to get up from the floor. He finds the whole process very difficult as his throat and chest hurt and he is still short of breath. He eventually manages to stand up and shuffles over to his chair and collapses in a heap. Torstein passes the photograph back over to him and tells him to take it. A faltering hand accepts the photograph and Heri squints at it as he tries to compose himself.

"Your father, Thomas, was a respected member of the Ahnenerbe. You have heard of the Ahnenerbe?" Heri meekly shook his head.

"The Ahnenerbe was a branch of the glorious SS that sought to prove that the Aryan race were the descendants of a Nordic people, the Hyperboreans. Your father, as an idealistic student of Nordic history, had joined the DNSAP, the National Socialist Workers' Party of Denmark. Once within the ranks, Thomas had come to the attention of a distant cousin, Einar Jørgensen, a high profile leader of the DNSAP who was in the payroll of German spies who funded him to cause civic disruption. Einar Jørgensen passed your father's details on to his German handlers and informed them that Thomas could be useful to the cause. The handlers contacted Berlin and a young and enthusiastic Ahnenerbe officer, my father, Pelle Lindemann, recruited him with the task of finding the location of Ultima Thule, the sacred capital of ancient Hyperborea, the northern landmass that the Aryan race originally came from. Your father and my father were convinced that the Faroe

Islands were all that was left of the southern tip of Hyperborea, a lost continent that sank beneath the waves in ancient times. The continent started here and stretched northwards including Iceland and Greenland as it headed for the realm of eternal daylight."

Torstein Lindemann reached into his attaché case once more and brought out a piece of paper for Heri to study.

"Your father found this scrap of information in a poem by the classical Greek poet, Pindar. He painstakingly translated the passage and was able to place it into a modern context. This was a vital clue that triggered a number of the Ahnenerbe's various expeditions to Greenland, Iceland and Northern Norway that were mounted before the Second World War broke out."

Lindemann carefully watched Heri read the contents of the piece of paper.

"My father's three trips to Iceland in 1938 and 1939 were as a direct result of your father, Thomas, deciphering a short passage contained within an ancient Greek poem that had been written two and half thousand years ago." The paper had ancient Greek prose written in his father's hand. Beside each line was a translation in Danish. It read:

'They wreathe their hair with golden laurel branches and revel joyfully; No sickness or ruinous old age is mixed into the blood of that sacred race; Without toil or battles they live without fear;'

Heri finished reading the translation and handed the paper back to Torstein.

"What has this got to do me? I knew nothing about any of this and why are you bringing this up now? I thought we had become friends through our business dealings with each other?" he whined.

Torstein placed the translation back inside the attache case. He snapped his fingers and gesticulated at Heri to hand him the photograph. Heri gingerly returned the picture which Torstein snatched from him and put inside the case. He slammed the lid shut and Heri jumped at the suddenness of its closing.

"It has everything to do with you Heri. Come now. You are an intelligent man who has enjoyed being remarkably successful in the many aspects of your life. Television documentaries, a distinguished author with a number of published books, a pillar of Faroese society, a politician, a respected government minister, a creator of jobs for the community, a land owner, need I go on? In fact, one could say that you have had more than your fair share of good fortune, wouldn't you? What would happen if it came to light that your success has been as a result of your father's affiliations in the past? What would be the reaction of the Faroese population if they became aware that the sole reason for your ascendancy and accomplishments were because of your father's actions nearly 80 years ago? What's that biblical quote again? 'The son shall not suffer for the iniquity of the father, nor the father suffer for the iniquity of the son.'

That doesn't apply in this case. Your father made a solemn oath to the Ahnenerbe. 'Meine Ehre heißt Treue', 'My honour is called loyalty'. He benefitted for his contribution to the Ahnenerbe cause and the Ahnenerbe protected him. He was removed from Denmark into Switzerland where he worked for the Das Volker Syndicate. What do you think your father, Thomas, was doing in Switzerland? Do you think he was making watches or novelty chocolates to sell? He was recreating the Ahnenerbe's library in a special bunker in La Chaux-de-Fonds for my father. My father was Director of the Ahnenerbe. My father was the Director General of the Das Volker Syndicate. The Ahnenerbe lives on. It is the Das Volker Syndicate."

Lindemann had walked over to the window and was looking at a long white building on the far side of Tórshavn. Sunlight glinted off some of its reflective surfaces.

"Come over here and tell me what you see Heri. What's that building over there?" and points at the far side. Heri cautiously walks over to his own window and peers in the direction of the pointed finger.

"That's the new hospital, the research and development clinic and the new Environmental Welfare Agency research laboratory. What about it?" he asked.

Heri instantly regretted saying the last three words as he watched the fierce blueness of Lindemann's eyes harden and become cold like steel. Heri flinched as Lindemann grabbed him by the tie and dragged him to the window pane. He pressed his face hard up against the glass and tightened his grip of Heri's tie to that of a garrotte. Slowly and succinctly and without raising the intonation of his voice, Torstein Lindemann started to explain certain factual matters to Heri.

"The 200 bed hospital, research and development clinic and Environmental Welfare Agency building cost 400 million dollars to build. My 400 million dollars, Heri. I have created

523 jobs by investing 400 million dollars of my money into the Faroe Islands economy. I have spent my money creating those buildings and jobs on my land that you procured and sold to me at an over-inflated price Heri. How much was it you sold the land to me for Heri? Can you remember Heri?" and the grip of the tie got tighter as Lindemann twisted it further in his hand. Heri grunted and spluttered saliva down his window.

"Shall I remind you Heri? 742 thousand dollars. That's about 4.5 million Danish kroner, isn't it Heri? What was the name of that woman you were so rude to in the restaurant last night? Does she know how much you made on the sale of the land that you cheated her out of? I can't hear you Heri?"

He threw him down on the floor and kicked him hard in the side. Heri wheezed and coughed as he lay face down on the floor. Lindemann collected his attaché case and looked at the prostrate body of Heri Jorgensen lying on the floor below the picture window. A widening pool of clear liquid was emanating from Heri's midriff region. He had wet himself and the fluid was now flowing in rivulets along the joints of the wooden floor.

"Just remember that I own you Heri. Just like my father owned your father before me. Loyalty is everything and it will be honoured with financial reward. Cross me or compromise my work and I will destroy you."

"Clean yourself up. I will see myself out. Collect me at my hotel at 4.30pm this afternoon. I wish to visit the Raohus and also go on the guided tour around Tinganes. You will be escorting me to these places. Do not be late."

Lindemann gave Heri a final scornful glance and left him to sort himself out.

The Stream

Daniel and Sólrun emerged from the lane and turned right into Jónas Broncksgøta, a wide and long road with mainly residential properties on either side of it. They had only gone a few metres when Sólrun guided Daniel through a gateway into a garden. Set back slightly from the road, was a two storey wooden and stone house. With white stonework and the wood painted light blue, the building had a grass roof that complemented its traditional look of a Faroese house.

"Welcome to my house." said Sólrun as she led Daniel up some steps to the front door. The front door was set into one of the gable ends of the building, a feature that Daniel had noticed to be quite common with many of the houses. He was curious to see the insides. Sólrun opened the front door and removed her shoes and left them on a mat just inside. Daniel copied what she had done and entered into a spacious hallway with a staircase in front of him. On either side of the staircase was a door leading to unknown rooms. Sólrun took his jacket from him and hung it on a coat rack behind the front door.

"Do you want the guided tour then?" she asked and opened the left hand door. "This is the kitchen." It was a fair sized room with all the utilities, units and white goods featuring along two walls. On the right, an old fashioned kitchen table was against the wall with four chairs around it. Sólrun walked the length of the kitchen and went through another doorway at the end. "This is the living room" and took Daniel into a well furnished room that was in the shape of the letter 'r'. Daylight streamed in through net curtains that ran the length of a long window. There were a couple of armchairs, a long sofa in the main part of the room, and to his left and running behind him was the remainder of the room.

"This is my study area." proclaimed Sólrun and Daniel saw a roll top bureau with a computer screen and keyboard atop it on the writing surface. "This way." and she led him across the living room and through another doorway. "This is the dining room. I don't do much entertaining these days but it is nice to have a room by itself to share a meal with guests." A long dining table that could accommodate eight people to sit around it was the main feature of the room. The table was already set for two people and Daniel again was impressed with Sólrun's organisational skills and preparedness. They walked past the dining table and she opened a door at the far end of the room. It led them back out into the entrance hallway and Sólrun started to walk up the staircase. The wooden staircase creaked and groaned with every step they took. Sólrun laughed.

"When I was a teenager, I got to know where to step on the staircase so I could sneak in and out of the house without my mother hearing me. I think she could hear me, no matter how quiet I tried to be, but I believe she turned a blind eye to my illicit escapades with boys, cigarettes and alcohol and trusted me not to be stupid and get myself into any trouble."

She stopped at the landing at the top of the stairs. It was the width of the house. "The bathroom is over there" and she pointed to her left. "This is my bedroom" and opened a door to reveal her boudoir. Her room was situated at the opposite gable end from the front door. It was a bright room with the ceilings angled at either side where the roof sloped. She closed the door over and showed Daniel three other smaller bedrooms that were accessed from the landing area. She opened the bathroom door. It was an entirely tiled room that had the obligatory WC and sink fittings but featured a deep tiered seated bath and an enclosed wet-room shower area. Daniel looked at the bath and the shower area.

"I imagine you could spend a long time soaking yourself in here." he suggested to Sólrun. Her eyes lit up at his words.

"I suppose you could also be very naughty in here as well if you wanted to." she hinted and closed the door over. Daniel avoided looking at her and made his way back downstairs.

Daniel took the folder from his jacket and Sólrun seated him in the living room as she started to prepare a quick lunch for them both. They sat at the dining table and as they ate, Daniel started to show Sólrun all the folder's contents and began explaining all his rising concerns about the many coincidences that were now appearing the more he researched this Dagny Poulsen.

"Sólrun. Can you write down all the coincidences if I start reading them out to you?"

"Of course I can." and she left the table and returned with a notepad and a pen. "Shoot!"

Daniel sorted out the papers in front of him and started putting them into a running order. He mixed photographs and notes around in chronological order and took the two photocopies that Ole had given him and sorted them accordingly.

"First of all:

1. Dagny Poulsen, born 15th September 1919.
2. Travels to Copenhagen in the summer of 1938.

3. Moves to Berlin in September 1938 to work for my grandmother Mille.

4. My grandfather, Peter Bressler, takes this Dagny Poulsen as his guest to the opening of the Reich Chancellery in Berlin 1939.

5. Note from Mille to Reichsführer SS Himmler from July 1939 asking him to advise a Dr Pelle Lindemann to stop contacting Dagny.

6. Photograph of Dagny, Mille, my mother and uncle dated 13th August 1939, Viktoriapark, Berlin.

7. 1st September 1939. Dagny leaves Berlin and goes to Copenhagen and from there back to Tórshavn.

8. Undelivered postcard to Dagny from my mother, dated 20th May 1940.

9. 7th December 1941. Sinking of the SS Sauternes. Dagny witnesses the sinking.

10. Now. I'm here to salvage the wreck of the SS Sauternes.

11. Torstein Lindemann, head of Das Volker Syndicate, is in the Faroes for a conference.

12. Is Torstein Lindemann related to this Dr Pelle Lindemann that Mille complained about?

13. Some Scottish girl called Freyja looking for information about her grandmother, Dagny Poulsen, who lived in Funningstova.

14. Freyja wearing a brooch similar to the one Mille is wearing in a photograph from 1939.

15. Freyja and fellow students are in the Faroes for a conference that is funded by Das Volker Syndicate."

Daniels stops speaking and reaches over and takes the notepad from Sólrun. He reads over what she has written down for him and mentally checks that he has correctly thought through everything and had it committed to paper in the correct order. He counts the number of entries in the list.

"Sólrun. That's 15 different connections so far. There are too many coincidences here and I need to make further enquiries about some of them."

Sólrun looks at Daniel and looks at the list. "Maybe it is all just coincidental? These things do happen from time to time, but saying that, when you read them written out like that, there does seem to be some sort of connection with most of the events. What are you going to do about it? It's not like you are a proper investigator. You're just a former sailor enjoying the freedom of now being a self-employed businessman doing a bit of freelance commercial diving, are you not?"

Daniel decided that he should let Sólrun into his secret past. "I wasn't just in the Danish Royal Navy as a career officer. I was a trained specialist for the Danish Royal Navy. Ingi and myself did a few specialist operations together around the world as part of the 'war on terror' and we have certain skill-sets that few possess, if you know what I mean. Remember when I said I could help you with Heri Jorgensen earlier?" Sólrun nodded.

"Well I think it is time to call in the 7th Cavalry and deal with some of the restless natives. Can I use your computer please?" and he walked out of the dining room and went around the living room to the roll top bureau. Sólrun followed and switched the computer on for him.

"What are you going to do Daniel?"

"Gather information about a few people and have Ingi come and meet me here in Tórshavn. I think we are going to have to get what we really need to know surreptitiously." He winked at Sólrun as he reached into pocket for his mobile phone. He scrolled through the contact numbers and dialed Ingi. The phone rang a few times and Ingi answered.

"Daniel. How goes the travelling to the Faroes. Are you here yet?" he asked.

"I arrived last night and have been doing a bit of digging for Dagny. Have you still got your painting tool-bag with you?"

There was a brief silence at the other end before Ingi responded. Ingi was slightly taken aback at Daniel asking him if he still had some of his former Frømandskorpset surveillance equipment stowed away. This equipment had been given the nickname of 'painting tool bag' as the contents were kept in a tradesman's canvas holdall.

"Yes, I do. Why?" Ingi enquired.

"Sólrun has a bit of decorating that needs attended to and I said that you and I could help her fix her problem." Ingi knew not to ask further questions over an open line but he did reply.

"So you have met Sólrun then? I take it she gave you a decent car like I asked her to? Where are just now anyway?"

Daniel wished that he had a video link so he could see the look on Ingi's face when he told him the next bit of information.

"I am at Sólrun's house just now having lunch and then we are going out to meet the prime minister and then afterwards, we are going to do a bit of shopping. When can you get to Tórshavn?"

Ingi laughed and shook his head with what Daniel was telling him. "I can be in Tórshavn for about 6.00pm. I have a couple of things to do with the boat and I can give the crew some time off to go and enjoy themselves over the weekend, but I should be able to get through to Tórshavn from Klaksvík for about 6.00pm. Where will I meet you?"

Daniel considered this and said "Meet me at Sólrun's." and gave him her address.

"See you at 6.00pm." and hung up.

Sólrun stood with her arms folded and scowled at Daniel. "I don't have any decorating needing done. There is nothing wrong with my house."

Daniel grinned and explained that he had spoken to Ingi in code and asked him to bring some special equipment with him that they were going to use later that night and probably tomorrow. All would be revealed when Ingi arrived. "It'll be fun." he added.

Sólrun had started up her computer. "What do you want to go and do?"

Daniel pulled up a chair and joined her at the computer. "First thing we need to do is search for any information on this Dr Pelle Lindemann and see what comes up."

He typed the name into the search engine and hit the return button. Straight away a number of results came through. Most of the results related to articles concerning the success of the Das Volker Syndicate, its early beginnings as a pharmaceutical supply cooperative, how the war years had resulted in it becoming a global company and its involvement in the search for a cancer cure. A couple of biography articles dealt with Pelle Lindemann being a noted 'Oslerian', a dedicated follower of the respected medical historian, Sir William Osler, a Canadian physician who recommended that all medical education must revolve around the individual patient, and by following that ethic, doctors must have an open mind, rather than a set of theories when dealing with particular ailments. To understand the patient you had to research the patient and establish a historical timeline of their health.

Most of the biographical articles had mentioned that Pelle Lindemann was originally a Swiss national working at the Rudolf Virchow Hospital in Berlin before and during the war. He had some form of association with the Ahnenerbe as it tried to find mythological Nordic races, whereby, they had availed themselves of his expertise to try and confirm or justify their various researches. The majority of the internet articles explained that Pelle Lindemann had returned, or escaped, depending on the slanted viewpoint of the particular article, to Switzerland in late 1944. Lindemann had been subsequently exonerated from any associated Ahnenerbe wrong-doing or war crime activities during the many investigations that were made ahead of the Nuremberg trials in 1946.

Many of the articles continued with links about the Das Volker Syndicate and the great diversity of the work it was involved with in many differing scholarly and scientific fields. Its current Director General was Pelle Lindemann's son, Torstein, who had assumed control following his father's death, and was credited with taking the company from strength to strength from the 1980s onwards. Many great and life-changing medical advances had been made as a result of the dedicated work carried out by the various research and development laboratories belonging to the Das Volker Syndicate.

Daniel printed a few of the articles off and asked Sólrun if she had a highlighter pen he could use. She found one in a drawer of the bureau and handed it to him. Daniel starting highlighting, in bright pink, sentences, words, dates and names in the articles he had just run off the printer.

Sólrun asked him if they were connected to Dagny Poulsen. Daniel said he would have to look at them later as he had just noticed the time on a clock on the wall above the bureau. It was 1.40pm and should they not be making their way to see 'Jo-Jo', Jógvan Johannesen, the Løgmaður, in his office on Tinganes for the arranged 2.00pm meeting.

"Shit." shouted Sólrun as she dashed back and forth putting plates and cups in the kitchen sink and trying to do her hair and make-up at the same time.

The Stream

Sólrun had taken Daniel on some shortcuts from her house in Jónas Broncksgøta to eventually emerge at the bottom of a staircase close to the ferry terminal. Daniel was still trying to establish his bearings as he could see the reddish brown buildings of Tinganes in front of him. He eventually worked out where he was when he saw that Café Natur was up the road on his right. The café was currently packed with people sitting outside enjoying the sunshine and watching the world go by as they ate and drank. They crossed over the road and went along the quayside of the Eystaravág, the east harbour, and headed in the direction of the Løgmaður's office. Sólrun knocked on the glass panel on the door and opened it. A young woman greeted them, took their details and asked them to have a seat while she went and informed Jógvan Johannesen that his 2.00 o'clock meeting had arrived.

A smartly dressed man in a suit came out of a room and asked them to come through. They entered inside and the man closed the door behind them.

"Sólrun. It's so nice to see you again." and they both hugged and kissed each other. Sólrun introduced Daniel to the man.

"Daniel Lauridsen, meet Jógvan Johannesen." and they shook hands. It was a firm handshake and Daniel took stock of Jógvan. For a man he presumed to be in his 60s, he certainly didn't look it. He was about 5 foot 10, of average build but very fit looking, a look that would deceive most people into thinking he was in his late 40s. Daniel reckoned he would be able to handle himself in a difficult situation, and not just by using the quick thinking, sharp wit and the silver tongue of a politician that they seem to possess. This was a man who dealt with adversity head on, took its punches and moved on to the next challenge. He didn't strike Daniel as someone that would back away from a confrontation and would be a good asset to have as back-up if you got into difficulty. He could understand why Sólrun loved him so much. He had replaced her father when he had passed away and had filled the void of guidance and support that had been taken away from her at a young age. He had always been there for her as she had grown up and she truly valued everything he had done for her and her mother.

Jógvan asked them to take a seat and offered them some refreshments. Daniel and Sólrun politely declined and Jógvan asked them how he could help them.

Daniel explained that he was here for the dive to the SS Sauternes, a fact that really interested Jógvan and he wished him every success. Jógvan wrote on the back of a business card and passed it to Daniel.

"If you need any support or assistance from the Faroese government while you are here, just phone me on my private number and I will see what I can do for you. If you can recover the coins, it will be a great way to continue the story of the Jólaskipið and its importance to these islands."

Daniel thanked him for the offer and pocketed the card. He continued explaining the story of his search for Dagny Poulsen and gave a rough explanation of what he had discovered so far. He omitted to mention his concerns and growing suspicions about all the coincidences that he had uncovered but reiterated the fact that all he wanted to do was find out what had happened to this young Faroese woman that had been his mother's nanny in pre-war Berlin.

Jógvan sucked his breath in through his teeth and got up from his desk and started walking over to a row of filing cabinets near to his desk.

"We are talking about Dagny i Funningstova, aren't we? Correct?" he asked as he opened the drawer of a filing cabinet and started searching through the many folders inside. Daniel confirmed that was indeed the case. Jógvan closed the drawer he was in and opened another and started searching through its contents.

"I met her a few times when she came on holiday during the 1980s. She was a friend of my mother, Bjerga. She was an interesting woman." He closed the filing cabinet drawer and started a search of another. "Ah. Here it is. I knew I had something about Dagny in here."

He lifted a suspension file out from the drawer and brought it back over to his desk. He laid it out in front of him.

"I remember this." Daniel was now intrigued by what this suspension file contained and although it was upside down, he was still able to read the label on its cover. 'Dagny Fulton úr Glasgow, Skotland'.

"It is a fascinating story. She died just over 12 years ago in Scotland but her children wanted her cremated remains to be brought back to Tórshavn to be buried beside her father and mother in the town graveyard over on the Velbastaðvegur. I wasn't always the Boss man here, and at the time, I was a junior minister working in the Department of Health and Social Affairs. I remember this really well because it was such a strange request. I don't mean anything bad by that when I say strange, I just mean it was a type of request the department had never had to process before. We normally deal with bodies returning home for burial and we follow all the various internationally agreed guidelines and procedures, but the return of human ashes was a new challenge for us. We do not practice cremation in the Faroe Islands."

Jógvan refreshed his memory by reading some of the contents of the suspension file.

"There was initially a lot of communication with some of the United Kingdom authorities and the Procurator Fiscal's Office in Glasgow, Scotland. A joint minute of agreement allowed the release of Dagny's ashes to her children on the caveat that they were inside a specially sealed container. The joint minute provided the permission and lawful authority that enabled the sealed container to be allowed for international transport to the Faroe Islands. My department granted a licence for the internment of Dagny's ashes in the graveyard on the condition that a proper funeral service was held. Finalising everything at this end transpired to be a fairly simple task what with Dagny being a 'Daughter of the War' and she was finally coming home to rest.

Daniel interrupted Jógvan by asking him a question. "Daughter of the War? Why was she called that?"

Jógvan turned a couple of pages over in the suspension file and starting reading from a document.

"Because of her story. She had started a relationship with a young British officer from the Cameronians (Scottish Rifles) occupation force that was stationed here. They got married in Tórshavn and when her husband was posted back to Britain, she went with him. That was in 1943. It was a common event. About 170 Faroese women married Scottish soldiers and left the islands with them when the soldiers were ordered back to Britain. I suppose you can see why the time was called 'the friendly occupation'. Anyhow, Dagny ended up working in the Free Danish Embassy in London until the war's end. But while she was working in London, she got to meet some important people."

Jógvan passed over a press cutting from the Danish media giving an obituary notice for Dagny Poulsen. The notice included a photograph of Dagny from the war years. She was wearing a buttoned blouse underneath a pin-striped jacket. On the right lapel of the jacket was pinned a brooch of a sailing ship. Daniel recognised the brooch. It was the same as the one that his grandmother was wearing in the group photograph in Berlin 1939. It was the same brooch that he had seen being worn by the young Scottish girl only a few hours earlier, and now he was seeing it in for a third time in a photograph from the 1940s. His head was now spinning with all sorts of theories and suppositions, and as he read the obituary, many inferences as to the significance of the importance of this brooch raged around his thoughts.

He finished reading the obituary. Most of the details he had already gathered for himself but there were three further pieces of information gleaned from the article that he didn't know. Their inclusion only increased the mounting accrual that he had for Dagny. To further add to the story of Dagny, he now had to include the fact that she had met Niels Bohr, the Danish nuclear physicist who assisted with the Manhattan Project and the creation of the first atomic bomb. The two had met in the Embassy in early October 1943 before he was taken to the USA in December of the same year. Dagny had also met Crown Prince Olav of Norway, later King Olav V of Norway, in the Embassy in 1944 and the third piece of information was the fact that she had connected the Danish Ambassador to the Court of St. James with King Christian X of Denmark on the 7th May 1945, the purpose of which was for the Danish Ambassador to Britain to formally inform the King of Denmark, via a telephone conversation, that the war in Europe would end on 8th May 1945.

Daniel passed the article over for Sólrun to read. He noticed her exclaim "Oh!" as she read the contents. She handed the article back to Jógvan and he placed it back in the suspension file. Jógvan continued speaking and explained that after the war she had settled in the Glasgow area, raised a family and had returned to the Faroes on numerous occasions, often bringing her children with her on holiday. Old age and failing health had prevented her returning in her later years.

"She lived in interesting times. I was privileged to have some involvement in assisting her children organise the arrangements for her final journey home. Her story would make an interesting book, would it not?" suggested Jógvan. Daniel and Sólrun both agreed with him. Jógvan lifted the suspension file from his desk and went over to a photocopier in a corner. He scanned the press cutting and handed the copy to Daniel.

"Does this help you with your quest?" he asked. Daniel thanked him for the facsimile.

"Yes, it does. I can finally tell my mother what happened to her nanny. She can now take comfort from the knowledge that

Dagny did indeed make it home and went on to live, as you quite rightly said, a fascinating life in some interesting times."

Daniel thanked Jógvan profusely for affording him some valuable time and Jógvan had replied it had been his pleasure to assist him. He wished Daniel every success with his diving expedition and Daniel took his leave from the office. He left Sólrun behind to bid her farewells and he stepped back outside into Tinganes and found a seat. He looked around the harbour and watched how the small boats moored at the quaysides jostled against each other with the natural movement of the water. He casually looked to his right and watched a group of youngsters scrambling over the same rocks that he and Sólrun had investigated some 12 hours earlier.

He looked over at the youngsters and recognised them. They were the Scottish students and one of them, Freyja, had placed her forefinger in the centre of the carved sundial to form a gnomon, the part that casts the shadow to tell the time. Her black haired friend was helping her to work the sundial. They were laughing and enjoying themselves. He thought about going over and discussing Dagny with them but dismissed the thought almost as soon as he had considered it. He needed to establish that he wasn't becoming caught up in something sinister, and to do that, he had to make sure that all of these continuing coincidences and connections were nothing more than that.

But they were drawing together at the one moment in time. He remembered the runic inscription beside the sundial. What was it again? 'Time runs like the current of a stream'. But where is it flowing to though? He thought.

The Stream

2.27pm – Friday 9th June, present day
Tinganes Peninsula, Tórshavn, Faroe Islands.

Freyja and Wendy had wandered around Tinganes and had arrived at the end of the peninsula. They sat down on the rocks and Freyja passed Wendy a sandwich from the box inside her rucksack. They sat in silence as they ate. The early afternoon sun was high in the sky and it was getting rather warm. Their trip advisors had suggested that they take clothing for any eventuality and that the weather could turn at any time. 'Don't be fooled by what you see. Stormy weather engulfs these islands very quickly and you have to have appropriate clothing with you at all times.' was the warning that had been meted out to the touring party at breakfast. Wendy slipped off her jacket and laid it beside her then pulled her woolen jumper off. She folded it neatly and stuffed it into her rucksack. Sitting there in her jeans and t-shirt, she scoffed at the words of the trip advisors.

"I can't believe we were told to dress as if it was early March. It must be 20 degrees and the sun is splitting the sky. Not a cloud to be seen." She looked over at her friend. Freyja was going over the many photographs that she had taken with her phone while wandering around Tinganes. She had just texted her mother a photo of Funningstova. 'I found Funningstova. It's a really cool cottage.' read the message.
Freyja replied to Wendy's comment. "It's roasting here. The weather forecast said it was going to be horrendous this weekend. Just goes to show how badly they get it wrong."

Freyja suggested to Wendy that she pose for a photograph with the reddish brown of the building behind as the backdrop, and as she was getting Wendy into position, she noticed the sundial and runes carved in the rocks beside her. She took a couple of photos and indicated the location of the carvings to her friend.

"Have you seen these?" and Wendy strode over to investigate.

"Cool. I wonder what these runes mean? We should check our notes later." she remarked.

The two girls took some more photographs of the carvings and both of them sat beside the sundial. Freyja stuck her forefinger in its middle and watched the shadow fall on the face of the sundial. Wendy laughed.

"It's an hour slow. It's about 2.30 going by my watch."

The two girls thought this was hilarious and a couple of their fellow students came over to find out what was so funny. Freyja looked at the time. "Wendy, we've got three hours of free-time before the guided tour. Do you want to go and dump our stuff back at the hotel and have a wander round the town and the shops? We'll be back in time for the 5.30pm meet."

Wendy picked up her rucksack and jacket and the two girls started to walk along the Eystaravág. They passed a couple sitting on a bench. The couple seemed to be deep in conversation. Wendy joked with Freyja. "Lovers tiff, you think?" as they headed towards their hotel.

"Probably." said Freyja.

Daniel grabbed Sólrun close to him on the seat. "We need to go shopping for some stuff that I need for tonight and I think I also need a stiff drink. The information that your pal Jógvan has just given me has changed the parameters of the original search for Dagny. I now have to have a serious think about everything that we've found out so far today. I am going to have to use you and Ingi as sounding boards for all of this later and run some theories past you."

Sólrun put her hand over Daniel's mouth. "Shut up! Those Scottish girls are walking past you just now."

He watched them go past and along the quayside. "I really want to speak to that girl Freyja and tell her everything I know, but something is really niggling me about this whole situation. I don't know what it is yet, but I think the answer lies with your friend Heri and whatever he is mixed up in with Torstein Lindemann and the Das Volker Syndicate. It's probably just me being paranoid, but from experience, I tend to go with my first impressions and I have a fear that there might be something dark and dangerous going on behind the scenes. You heard Jógvan back there, didn't you? Dagny Poulsen was either a person who had an unbelievable knack of being in particular places during particularly important times and meeting some particularly famous people, or was she something else and we don't know what that is yet?"

He started walking along the quayside with a sense of purpose. Sólrun ran after him.

"Wait for me please?" she cried.

Daniel halted where he was and allowed her to catch up. "Sorry. I was too busy planning the next few hours in my head." He smiled reassuringly at her. "Let's go back to my hotel and collect the car. I want to do a bit of driving and go and check a few things out, if you don't mind. We can call it an advanced reconnaissance mission, if you like? I have a few suggestions for what I think should be tonight's proposed activities once Ingi has got here. Are you up for it sailor?"

Sólrun beamed a cheeky grin at him and stood to attention and saluted him.

"Sure thing Cap'n" she bellowed in a mock pirate voice.

Daniel just laughed. He had only known this woman for about a day but he felt like he had known her all his life. He suddenly realised that not only had he become dependent on her with finding stuff out about Dagny, he was beginning to have feelings for her and those feelings were something that were especially unusual for him to have. All through his adult life, he had always maintained a policy of not getting seriously involved with anyone. It might have been the rigours of his former military training and that he understood that each day could be his last, but he had always wanted to spare the anguish he had witnessed on peoples' faces all over the world when dealing with sudden and unexpected loss.

He didn't want to inflict that type of pain on anyone that truly cared for him. His family was different. They accepted the fact that he had chosen to pursue a career in the military, they knew that he would be exposed to danger and they understood the risks involved. They were prepared to hear bad news if something untoward ever happened to him. But Sólrun seemed to have got underneath his armour and penetrated his defences.

This wasn't just simple desire of lust that he was now experiencing; it was something more than that.

4.00pm – Friday 9th June, present day
The Hotel Havnar, Tórshavn, Faroe Islands.

Torstein Lindemann sat at the desk in his room in the Hotel Havnar. The hotel had given him their best suite, located on the top floor. From where he was sitting at the desk, he had a commanding panorama of the harbour and the old town on Tinganes. A roof-top terrace patio surrounded the room and Torstein unlocked the door, slid the panel across and stepped out on to it to admire the view. Slowly walking around the terraced patio, he observed the comings and goings of people below him on the surrounding streets of Tórshavn. It was a surprisingly busy place considering it was located in the middle of nowhere.

Torstein completed his 360 degree tour of the patio and returned to his room. He slid the door panel shut and returned to the desk. He was just finishing his speech for the conference tomorrow and had been flicking through the associated power-point presentation to ensure that the subject matter and all the images corresponded with each other. He had become distracted and had started to search through his personal folders and opened the folder with the header 'DAGNY', the real reason as to why he was in the Faroe Islands.

The contents had been sub-divided into separate folders, each one compartmented into different aspects of his research and the work of his father. With computerisation of the Ahnenerbe archive in La Chaux-de-Fonds, Torstein now had instant access to its data. He had created an electronic repository with state-of-the-art software that allowed him to input information and then search through the archive for cross-references and associations. This ability to extrapolate results from the cyber-vault had taken years off his search and had negated the need for manual and physical rummaging by hand to try and establish any connections and conclusions. He clicked on a sub-folder marked 'QADNA' and started to refresh his memory with the information stored inside. He murmured approval to himself as he recollected the contents of the folder.

The treasures contained within the Quedlinburg Abbey were irreplaceable. Its history as a national shrine for the Germanic people dated back to the first Saxon ruler of Germany, Henry I, crowned within the church in 919. King Henry I was the founder of the Ottonian dynasty of German rulers who would rule a unified Germany, and later the Holy Roman Empire, from 919 until 1024. Every other king of Germany for the next thousand years would be a descendant of this King Henry I. This was the historic birthplace of the German nation, its first capital, its point of origin. The treasury located within the Abbey contained gifts from King Henry I, and his successors, Otto I and Otto II. Amongst these gifts were items such as delicate reliquaries of rock crystal and gold, purported to contain some fragments of cloth and wood from the Virgin Mary's robes and the true Cross of the Crucifixion. Further items to be found inside the treasury were books and manuscripts including the ninth-century Gospel of Samuel, written entirely in gold ink.

Over the following centuries, the abbey continued to receive gifts of precious books, manuscripts and liturgical items, all of which were then stored in the treasury for safe-keeping. During the Nazi era of Germany, Reichsführer SS Himmler, who vainly considered that he was the embodiment of a modern day reincarnation of King Henry I, turned Quedlinburg Abbey into a 'Germanic sanctuary' and replaced Christian rituals with torch-light SS ceremonies. But during the course of 1943, to protect from both Himmler's SS and whatever conqueror might next arrive, local church and community officials secretly removed the contents of the treasury and hid them in a cave located in the mountains outside of the town.

US Army troops controlled the majority of the area in 1945, and during this period of occupation, US Army Lieutenant Joe Tom Meador was given the responsibility of being in charge for the security of the cave and the safety of its contents. Twelve of the most precious objects of the treasury disappeared during Meador's period of supervision. It was obvious that the contents had been looted by the American soldiers supposed to be guarding them, but the subsequent internal investigation by the US Army was dropped when Quedlinburg became part of the Soviet Zone of Occupation.

In 1987, various lost items from the Quedlinburg Abbey treasury started to appear as auction lots on the international art market. Investigations into the sudden re-appearance of these lost treasures revealed that Lieutenant Joe Tom Meador had committed the original looting. Meador had died in 1980 and the heirs to his estate had attempted to offload the treasures, piece by piece. A lengthy and diligent examination into the affairs of Meador revealed him to be a man possessed with a substantial knowledge and understanding of art. He had recognised and appreciated the importance of the differing artifacts, such as the Gospel of Samuel and the

Crystals of Constantinople, and had just stolen them for his own ends.

After a considerable amount of probing legwork by US Government investigators, researching the circumstances of the time and delving into whatever military records that still remained, it was discovered that by the implementation of an uncomplicated ploy, Meador had been able to bring about the theft of numerous articles un-noticed. He had just simply removed them from the cave, packaged them up and then posted them back to himself in his hometown of Whitewright, Texas, under the cover of US Army mail service. On arrival in the United States, the packages containing the stolen articles were placed in a safe at the First National Bank of Whitewright to await Meador's return.

After a lengthy judicial process, the artifacts were taken back to Germany in 1992 and finally returned to the Quedlinburg Abbey in 1993. In 1994, the town of Quedlinburg was placed on the UNESCO world heritage list. In the following year, a detailed report had been submitted to the World Heritage Committee to consider. This report was a periodic application that had been made previously to the world heritage convention by a delegation of German scholars, archaeologists and medieval historians. This delegation had applied for funding to repair the abbey of the extensive damage it had sustained in the years before, during and after World War II. The abbey's condition had deteriorated further due to neglect while it had been under the jurisdiction of the former country of East Germany.

Six years had passed before the UNESCO World Heritage Centre finally approved the original application and allocated funding for a full restorative and archeological investigative research project to be commenced. The subsequent funding allowed a joint operation to be conducted by two of the leading universities of the Saxony-Anhalt region, the Martin Luther University in Halle-Wittenberg and the Otto von Guericke University based in the town of Magdeburg. Their joint cooperation resulted in extensive research and repair work being carried out at Quedlinburg Abbey. This combined venture by two of Germany's leading universities had entailed detailed research to be carried out, primarily in the fields of archaeology, history, biological sciences, ethnology, environmental studies, medicine, cardiovascular diseases, oncology, social studies and agriculture. There had even been multidisciplinary cooperation between the subject areas of biology, biochemistry, pharmacy, medicine and agronomy with a considerable amount of assistance from non-university research institutions such as the Das Volker Syndicate.

Three long years had passed and Quedlinburg Abbey had been the welcome recipient of a 21st century makeover. Repairs had been made to the many buildings and edifices of the site. Detailed archaeological and historical researching had been completed and studies in many other fields had been concluded with interesting analysis and results that revealed a thousand years of human activity in and around the abbey and the local town. DNA profiling of a demographic of the local population had thrown up intriguing statistics that would make for further investigations, but the disseminated data yielded from the extensive and detailed scrutiny of both forensic anthropology and forensic archaeology, had created significant academic and scientific interest in the fields of pathology, toxicology, chemistry, biology, odontology and psychiatry. The DNA testing of the remains of Henry I himself had created a genetic profile of the first King of Germany. A thousand years of history was plain for all to see on a single piece of paper that detailed the composition of the hereditary of the country's first monarch.

Torstein closed the sub-folder down, returned to the main page and closed it down, and in doing so, he was brought back to his original speech and power-point presentation for the conference the next day. He recalled the significant importance of the Quedlinburg Abbey DNA retrieval exercise. Torstein Lindemann of the Das Volker Syndicate had acquired, through legitimate means, a copy of the singular DNA profile of King Henry I of Germany. He also had in his possession a singular DNA profile of a Dagny Poulsen from the Faroe Islands that his father had obtained. He had recently been in receipt of a singular DNA profile belonging to a Freyja Fulton from Glasgow, Scotland, and procured as a direct result of his company, the Das Volker Syndicate, sponsoring a 'Reprogramming the Code' DNA collection initiative in colleges and universities throughout Europe.

The three DNA profiles were almost identical to each other in that they shared a Mitochondrial Related Common Ancestor or MRCA. They were the proof of a familial lineage that transcended a thousand years of history. Dagny Poulsen was the 32nd great granddaughter of King Henry I of Germany and Freyja Fulton was the 34th great granddaughter of King Henry I of Germany, and more importantly for him, she was alive. In this young girl's bloodstream flowed the epigenetic history of the original Germanic people, the Aryan race, and the lost Nordic ancestors of the continent of Hyperborea.

To re-create the pure Nordic blood of the forefathers of Germany, her blood must be sought, by any means, foul or fair. He was, thought Torstein, very shortly going to be in a position to finish his father's life-long ambition. He closed the lid of the laptop and left the room to meet Heri Jorgensen in the hotel lobby. All he needed to do now was confirm Dagny's birth, visit her house to satisfy his curiosity and somehow dragoon this Freyja Fulton, presumably Dagny's granddaughter, into providing her blood to him.

Freely or under duress, he didn't really care. He was now so close to fulfilling his pursuit, how he went about acquiring it didn't really matter to him anymore.

The Stream

Daniel and Sólrun had parked the car at the rear of the hotel and were walking up the hill into the Vaglið Square. It has been a fruitful shopping expedition and Daniel had taken the chance to look around the capital. Sólrun had directed him to a shopping mall situated to the north of the town. Daniel had been surprised by the number of shops and the diversity of the stores and what they had to offer. He had remarked to Sólrun that he hadn't expected to find such a place in the Faroes and was taken aback that he had been able to purchase everything that he needed. Sólrun just laughed and explained that the shopping mall was often referred to by the locals as the 'SOS Shopping Centre' as you always got rescued by it in your time of need.

And Sólrun was right. He had been able to buy items such as clothes, shoes and toiletries, a hybrid laptop/tablet and a couple of SuperSpeed flash stick memory drives with relative ease. Daniel had simply used his Dankort, a Danish debit card, to make all the necessary purchases. Sólrun was impressed, but also appalled at how Daniel seemed to have no qualms when it came to using it. Daniel explained to her that he had got used to buying things, as and when he required them. Today he needed to buy these items and tomorrow he might just need to buy something else and when they had served their purpose, so be it.

They had passed a boutique on their way out of the shopping centre. Sólrun had stopped to look in the window and admire, longingly, at a pair of Vans ladies trainers. She tutted and turned away to leave. Daniel just stared at her.

"Go and get them. It'll be my treat for you helping me. On you go." and nodded at the shop door and for her to enter.

"No. No. No. I can't. They are far too expensive and I don't really need them. I have tons of shoes at home." she protested.

Daniel escorted her into the shop, sat her down and said to the sales assistant that his friend wanted to try on a pair of shoes that were on display in the window. The sales assistant spoke to Sólrun and ascertained the brand, size and colour that she wanted and went away to retrieve them from the store-room. Sólrun was annoyed with Daniel but also appreciative of his gesture.

"You shouldn't be doing this. I don't need them."

Daniel just looked at her. "Yes I should and yes you do. End of conversation."

The sales assistant returned and Sólrun tried them on. They fitted and the sales assistant led them to the cash desk. Daniel paid for them with his Dankort, took the carrier bag containing the shoes from the sales assistant and passed it to Sólrun.

"There you go Cinderella. Shall we leave now?" Sólrun kissed him on the cheek and thanked him.

They had just finished looking in through the windows of the fascinating bookshop located at the edge of the square, H. N. Jacobsen's Bokahandil, and were walking along the curve of the Aarvegur towards the hotel. Sólrun was on the outside and nearest the kerb. She suddenly pushed Daniel against the wall and then stood beside him with her back against it.

"Heri Jorgensen and that man Lindemann have just come out of the hotel. I don't want to speak to Heri after last night. I will not be able to control myself and I will do something I will regret." she told him. Daniel pushed off from the wall and cautiously peered along the curve.

"They are walking away from us and down towards the harbour."

He put his shopping bags down on the ground and started to search through them. He found the bag containing the flash stick memory drives and removed one from its packaging. He reached inside his jacket and pulled out his mobile phone and from within another jacket pocket, he took out a Bluetooth headset and inserted it into his right ear. He synced his mobile phone with the headset and picked up the shopping bags.

"We will head back to the hotel. You wait for me in the lobby and get yourself a coffee. I'm going up to my room with my shopping bags and I will put some stuff together while I'm up there that I have to take back to your house for tonight, but I need you to get a window seat and watch for Heri and Lindemann returning. If they return, call me immediately. It's crucial that I know if they return."

He pointed at the headset. Sólrun was completely non-plussed at this sudden change in Daniel and what he was asking her to do.

"What are you going to do? Why do you want me to keep a look-out for you? What's going on?" she pleaded.

"The less you know just now the better. We'll call it a 'need to know' directive. You don't need to know what I am about to do but I will explain to you later if my plan works. Are you ready for this? It is crucial that you let me know as soon as possible if they return." and he followed the curve to the hotel entrance.

He walked up to the reception desk and asked for his room key. As the porter turned around to get his fob, Daniel squinted at the bookings register to find out what room Lindemann was staying in. The roof suite, the svita, the best room in the hotel. The porter handed him his key and Daniel told Sólrun he would be about 10 minutes or so and left her in the comfy seats in the window alcove over by the door. He waved at her as the lift doors closed.

Daniel burst into his room and threw the shopping bags onto the bed. He opened the door out onto the balcony and stepped outside. "This is going to be interesting." he muttered to himself as he reached over the balcony's glass balustrade guard rail and heaved himself over its edge and clambered upon the service ladder than ran to the roof. He hoped that no-one had espied him leaving the balcony, but then again, he thought, no-one ever really looks up as he quickly shinned up the ladder and slipped over the wall and onto the roof-top terrace.

Peering in through the glass at first to ensure that the room was empty, Daniel then made for the sliding door. To his surprise, the door was unlocked and he slid the door open. On a desk in front of him lay a laptop and a mobile phone. He lifted the laptop's cover up to find that it was still switched on. On the screen, two items were on display. On the left was what looked like a speech and on the right was a power-point presentation frozen at a particular section with an image of scientists working in a laboratory.

The Stream

Daniel couldn't believe his luck when he saw that the laptop was still running. He took the flash stick memory drive from his pocket and inserted it into the port on the side of the laptop and clicked on the start icon at the bottom left of the screen. The menu list opened and he clicked on 'My Computer' that itemised the contents stored within. The local disk icon revealed that there was 117.4 GB of stored information on the laptop and Daniel was relieved that he had brought a flash stick with a capacity to hold a 128 GB of data. A pop-up screen asked him what he wished to do and he followed the instructions and started to copy the local disk to the flash drive. He just hoped that the 'SuperSpeed' branding on the flash stick lived up to its name. Another pop-up screen appeared to state that files were in transfer and it would take 7 minutes to complete.

He looked about the room and could see why Lindemann had taken it. It had a commanding view of the harbour area and from the roof-top terrace outside, you could observe the whole town. The room itself was opulent, from the furnishings to the large double-bed to the flat screen satellite television mounted on the wall to the Wi-Fi office system, replete with a printer, and with docking port facilities for hand-held devices. The minibar was well stocked and he resisted the temptation to help himself to a drink. The bathroom area was impressive with a private toilet, enclosed shower area and a wide, step-in bath. Daniel imagined businessmen and women reclining in the bath after a hard day's negotiating.

He returned to the laptop and the pop-up screen told him that files were still in transfer and that 3 minutes remained.

His headset started to ring. He answered it and Sólrun told him that Heri and Lindemann were about to re-enter the hotel.

"Sólrun. You'll have to stall them for me. Please? It's important. I need about 4 minutes to finish what I'm doing. Engage them in conversation about something or have another argument with Heri. I don't care how you do it but I need you to find me 4 minutes so I can complete what I'm doing." and rang off.

Just what he didn't want to happen was being caught red-handed in someone's room copying their personal computer files. The Faroes are relatively crime free, but I think they would throw the book at me, he mused.

"Come on Sólrun. Do this for me." he wished out loud.

Sólrun watched Heri Jorgensen hold open the door for Torstein Lindemann to enter into the foyer of the hotel. Heri looked on edge and Lindemann seemed to be irked for some reason. "Daniel better know what he is doing." said Sólrun to herself as she took a deep breath, stood up and walked over to the two men.

Sólrun faced Torstein Lindemann and introduced herself to him. "Hello. My name is Sólrun Jacobsen. Please accept my apologies for not introducing myself to you last night in the Áarstova restaurant but the company wasn't exactly conducive to me being my usual hospitable self." and glanced at Heri.

As Lindemann shook her hand, she noticed a glimmer of a smile appear on his lips as he acknowledged her cutting remarks about Heri.

"I am pleased to meet you, Miss Jacobsen. It was late and you can be forgiven as your evening was being interrupted by

Heri insisting on introducing me to everyone we met in Tórshavn."

Sólrun understood his sarcastic swipe at Heri, but at the same time, she was captivated by the blueness of Lindemann's eyes. They were sharp, attentive and disconcerting. Their blueness reminded her of the warm-watered swimming pools that you often saw in the holiday brochure adverts for far-off and exotic places. You wished you could dive into them and swim around, but at the same time, she reckoned these eyes could become very cold like the waters of the Antarctic, very quickly.

Daniel looked at the pop-up screen on the laptop. 90 seconds to finish the file transfer. "Come on. Come on. Come on." he directed at the laptop.

"So how have you found the Faroe Islands so far? Do they meet with your expectations?" Sólrun asked.

Lindemann replied straight away. "They are breathtaking. The scenery does make you think that you are on the edge of the world and I have found the people to be very welcoming and friendly. A hidden treasure awaits the passing tourist. I have been surprised at how many there are here just now."

Sólrun agreed with him that his sentiments were similar to the many tourists she encountered and that nearly all of them said that they would return.

"It has been a pleasure to meet you Miss Jacobsen, but I must leave you for now. I need to collect something from my room. I am sure Heri will be delighted to talk to you while I am away."

Lindemann collected his key from the porter at the reception desk and headed for the lift. The lift door opened and Daniel emerged into the foyer. Lindemann was standing right in front of him.

"Oh? Hello. How are you today? Did you have a nice meal in the restaurant last night? The takeaway we had was superb." said Daniel as he looked at Lindemann, then Sólrun, then Heri and back to Lindemann.

"The pan fried langoustine that I had was just simply exquisite. I would thoroughly recommend that to anyone to try. Good afternoon to you both." replied Lindemann and passed by him to enter the lift.

Daniel handed his key in at the reception desk and walked over to Sólrun and Heri. "Hi Heri. How are you doing?" Before he could reply, Daniel put his arm around Sólrun. "Let's go. See you later Heri." and escorted Sólrun outside.

They had walked a few metres down the Aarvegur before Sólrun stopped. "What the bloody hell were you up to in there? Why did you need me to stall those two for you?"

Daniel reached into his trouser pocket and removed the flash stick. He tossed it to Sólrun, and as she caught it, he remarked "I broke into Lindemann's hotel room and copied all the data on his computer. We can have a look at what's on it back at your house." and he continued down the Aarvegur leaving Sólrun behind him, staring at the flash stick and then at him as he nonchalantly slung a holdall over his right shoulder and started to whistle.

He stopped at the roadside and looked back at her and smiled. It then became a grin that turned to a laugh as he studied the picture of horror that was Sólrun. She ran after him.

"Are you some sort of mad bastard?" she demanded of him when she got close.

"No." he replied. "I'm just plain old Daniel Lauridsen." and walked her over the road towards Café Natur.

"Let's get a drink" and headed for the entrance. Sólrun just shook her head at the calmness of Daniel.

"I don't think they have enough booze in there for me just now." she quipped as she opened the door to the café.

The Stream

4.41pm - Friday 9th June, present day
Hotel Havnar, Tórshavn, Faroe Islands.

Heri watched Sólrun and Daniel leave the hotel. He really hated that bitch was his initial thought. He pondered what pain he could inflict on her if he ever got her on her own. He continued to fantasise about what tortures he would like to subject her to and hadn't noticed Lindemann appear on his shoulder.

"Now that I have collected my phone and laptop from my room, I need you to take me to the Raohus. I take it you being a government minister carries some weight with bureaucracy and I will be able to get what I want today?"

Heri flinched when Lindemann spoke to him. He had been startled by the silence of his approach and was now very afraid of this man. Four hours ago this man had attacked him in his own home, threatened to kill him and then made him piss himself all over his own living room floor.

"Yes. I will see that you get what you need. I will speak to the staff to make sure you are accommodated."

What did this man want from him? His world had been shattered earlier in the day when this lunatic had told him that his own father was some sort of SS soldier and was involved in some Nazi research mission that was still going on in the 21st Century. His father wasn't a Nazi, he was just a historian and fervent Faroese nationalist. All his father had wanted was the Faroes to govern themselves and be responsible for their own destiny. And as things had turned out, his father's hopes had been achieved in the main.

Lindemann spoke to him abruptly. "Are we going to this Raohus today?"

"Yes. Yes. Of course. It is this way." and Heri held the door ajar for Lindemann to exit the hotel. They walked up the Aarvegur in silence and entered into the Raohus. Ole Patturson was standing at the reception desk. He straightened up when he saw Heri Jorgensen walk in the front door with Torstein Lindemann beside him. He walked round from the desk and greeted them.

"Minister Jorgensen. Dr. Lindemann. So pleased to see you." and shook their hands. "I think you will find everything in order for your lecture tomorrow evening. A number of people have been making enquiries and I am expecting a packed auditorium."

Lindemann assured Ole that everything was in order, but he always liked to make sure things went smoothly.

"I have my laptop with me and I have a power-point presentation that I wish to use when delivering my speech tomorrow. Can you show me the auditorium and the lectern please? I just need to make sure everything is compatible. While I am here, I would also like to trace some information about someone that may be in your records. I have all her details with me."

"Come this way Dr. Lindemann and I can show the stage and the display screens. We will be able to test your power-point presentation for you and make sure that everything works. We cannot have any glitches tomorrow night, can we?" and Ole opened the door into the auditorium.

Ole and Lindemann were on the stage and Heri had been relegated to the role of the audience. Lindemann was enjoying ushering him around the auditorium and testing the acoustics and that Heri could properly view the power-point presentation from wherever he was sat. Ole, in the meantime, was relishing assisting Lindemann set up for the following evening. It was a prestigious honour for the auditorium to have someone of Lindemann's standing delivering a key-note speech. Ole casually asked Lindemann about the search he wished to make. Lindemann opened up his laptop and went through some files. He flicked a photograph as an image onto the display screens.

"I am looking for details about this young woman that I believe came from the Faroe Islands."

Ole looked at the black and white image that was on the screens. He asked Lindemann who she was and did he have a name for her.

"Her name was Dagny Poulsen and I believe she lived somewhere called Funningstova. Can you assist me with tracing her if I provide you with more details?"

Ole inwardly stiffened with shock but did not display it outwardly. This was the third time today he had been asked about this woman. He recalled the famous quote from Ian Fleming's James Bond novel, Goldfinger. 'Once is happenstance. Twice is coincidence. Three times is enemy action'.

He watched Heri Jorgensen milling about in the aisle of the auditorium and he remembered Sólrun apologising for her earlier outburst. She had explained her shortness with him was because that 'arse' Heri had upset her again last night. He knew, in fact everyone knew, that Heri had swindled Sólrun and a lot of other people out of land, but it had all been done legally. He had a responsibility, an obligation to her as an old friend, if Heri was involved with this Lindemann who was now also asking about this Dagny woman, he sure as hell wasn't going to give Heri Jorgensen, the arse, or his friend, any information apart from what was in the public domain and that was the ledger book.

"Do you have a date of birth that I could use? I should be able to find this woman from the records ledger." he asked. Lindemann continued looking at his laptop.

"I do. September 15th 1919. Is that enough for you?" Ole said it was and explained that he would go and get a records ledger. He would be back momentarily and left the auditorium through the side door.

Ole ran along the corridor and went into his office. He shut the door over and lifted up the ledger that he had shown the Scottish girls and to Sólrun and her diver friend. He hesitated as he thought about what he should do. He pulled a telephone directory from a bookcase and looked up Sólrun's home telephone number. He picked up his desk phone and dialed the listed number.

Sólrun was helping Daniel set up his new toy, the hybrid laptop/tablet, on the dining room table. Her house telephone was ringing and she walked through to the study area of her sitting room to answer it. Daniel heard her mention Ole's name a couple of times and then 'Takk Fyri' before she placed the handset back in its cradle. She came back into the dining room and Daniel could tell by her body language and demeanour, all was not well.

"Everything OK?" he asked.

Sólrun sat in a chair across from him. "That was Ole on the phone. He has Heri and that guy Lindemann with him just now. Lindemann has been asking him about Dagny Poulsen and that he was trying to trace her details."

Daniel showed no reaction and calmly asked if she knew what Ole had said or done with the request. Sólrun continued. "Ole said that he hadn't mentioned you or me asking about Dagny or those Scottish girls doing the same. He said he wasn't going to tell them anything apart from show them the ledger. I trust Ole and he wouldn't have phoned me if he didn't think it odd, especially with Heri sniffing about. Ole cannot stand the man either."

Daniel just nodded his head. "If you trust Ole to say nothing, then so do I. This is just getting better, isn't it?"

"Better? What do you possibly mean by better? How's it better?" exclaimed Sólrun.

"I mean by better, I mean that we are definitely up to our ears in a mystery and we are going to find out what it's about." He switched on the hybrid laptop/tablet and inserted the flash stick with Lindemanns' files.

Ole returned to the auditorium with the ledger. Heri and Lindemann were positioning the lectern so that it was to the side of the main screen set up on the stage. He got up onto the stage.

"I have a ledger that you might be interested in, Dr. Lindemann." and laid it on the lectern in front of him. Ole had opened it at the page that detailed Dagny's registry of birth. Lindemann scanned the entry and gently ran his fingertips along the grooves and swirls of the hand-written details.

"Excellent. May I be so bold to ask if I could have a photocopy of this page? I would be nice to have something to finish off my search."

"Your search?" asked Ole. Lindemann looked up from the ledger.

"My late father knew this woman, many, many years ago. From reading my father's diary, I think he was rather smitten with her but the war years intervened and they lost touch. It is cathartic to be finally able to see where she came from and where she once lived."

Ole lifted the ledger up. "I will be back in a few minutes with a photocopy for you." and left the two men on the stage.

When Ole returned with the photocopy inside an envelope, Lindemann was especially grateful for his assistance and thanked him for spending the time finding the ledger and copying it when he should be going home to his family on a Friday afternoon. Ole said it had been no trouble at all and it had been his pleasure to assist. He asked if everything was prepared for tomorrow, and if so, he would like to close the Raohus for the day but it would be open at 9.00am in the morning and that he would be here all day should Mr. Lindemann need anything else ahead of his speech.

Heri seized upon a chance to be important again.

"Torstein, can I take you to Tinganes and show you Funningstova?"

Lindemann's blue eyes narrowed on Heri and then relaxed. "Yes Heri. That sounds like a good idea. Take me to this Funningstova. Good evening Ole and thanks again." and exited the Raohus.

Ole closed the doors over and locked them. He pulled the window screens down and rested his arms on the door-frame. "What the hell has Sólrun got herself mixed up in this time?" he said aloud as he retreated back to his office. "She better explain it all to Anna when she comes round to see her."

The Stream

Daniel was engrossed with sifting through the contents of the data that he had copied from Torstein Lindemann's computer. Although he was a fluent speaker of German, it had been a while since he had to concentrate to mentally translate the language into his native Danish. A lot of the information he had read so far had been medical notation and gibberish that he was struggling to decipher, let alone comprehend, but thankfully, the majority of the stored files had been compressed into headed folders and appeared to run in some sort of chronological order. He had become increasingly impatient with his random sifting, and having viewed a fair number of photographic images and video clips so far, Daniel had come to the conclusion that for him to properly investigate all of the information in its entirety, would take a lifetime.

He opened up the control panel on his hybrid laptop/tablet and located the 'search' function. He typed in 'Dagny Poulsen' and hit the return button. His newly bought machine whirred as it started its task. There was a knocking sound coming from the front door and he listened to Sólrun answer the noise, greet Ingi and welcome him into her home. There was some general conversation going on and Daniel could hear the sound of boots being taken off and clothing being hung up on the coat rack in the hall.

The dining room door opened and Ingi and Daniel hugged each other in the way that only good friends do when they are pleased to see each other. Ingi had an excited look on his face.

"What have you been up to Daniel? You've only been here 24 hours and it looks like you're getting me embroiled in some sort of mischief. I've brought the painting tool bag that you asked for. What do you need that for? We're here to do a bit of salvaging but you seem to be keen on us to going on some sort of covert op or something?"

Daniel just looked at him in a hopeful way. "Promise not to laugh when I tell you this?"

Ingi nodded his agreement. "I promise. What is it? You've found an underground Al-Qaeda sleeper cell operating here in downtown Tórshavn? There are some cruise-ship tourists in disguise on-shore who are really Russian separatists wanting to declare the Faroe Islands as their sovereign territory? Someone has gone and kidnapped a couple of sheep and we have to rescue them from the PLO, the puffin lovers organisation?"

Daniel smiled at Ingi's sarcasm but Ingi realised that although his friend was smiling, his face wasn't as it still held a serious countenance.

"When you have quite finished being facetious, I will tell you Ingi. And trust me when I tell you this, you might want to take a seat first before I do."

Ingi nervously laughed, looked at Sólrun and then back at Daniel, saw that they were both being deadly serious and pulled a chair out from the table and sat down.

"Ready?" asked Daniel.

Ingi nodded that he was and Daniel turned the tablet/hybrid around to show his friend what was on the screen.

"Nazis, Ingi. Nazis. Proper Nazis, not the wannabe pretend Nazis and extreme right-wing skinhead boot boys that we've dealt with a few times before. These are real ones."

Ingi's face was transfixed at the screen as he studied the black and white image of Himmler, Heydrich and others he recognised from history lessons saluting over a tomb festooned with funereal wreaths. Ingi continued to stare at the screen and then at his friend.

"You are having a laugh here, aren't you? You two are playing a joke on me for some reason?" Both Sólrun and Daniel shook their heads. "Bugger off. What's the story then?"

Daniel reached into the holdall lying on the floor beside him. He removed a sleeve of 200 cigarettes from inside and passed them to Ingi. "I think you might be needing these." and started to tell his friend everything he knew. From what had started out as just a simple search on behalf of his mother to find out what had happened to Dagny Poulsen had got more and more complicated the more he found out about her, and what he had found out so far, was a mysterious story full of chance connections and coincidences that were becoming increasingly disturbing and sinister.

Forty minutes had passed and Daniel had brought his friend up to speed with all the information he had and what he had found out over the last 24 hours. He explained he had seen an opportune moment to break into Lindemann's room for a snoop and hadn't expected to find what he had copied. The reason for originally bringing him and the painting tool bag to Tórshavn was to find out some dirt on Heri Jorgensen that Sólrun could then use against him.

"But things just kept on getting more interesting." He passed Ingi the copy of Dagny's witness statement concerning the sinking of the SS Sauternes.

"We've come up here to recover coins from a ship that sank in 1941. While I'm here, I've promised my mother that I will find out what happened to Dagny Poulsen and then I go and discover she bloody witnessed the sinking. I then meet the Prime Minister after lunch and he tells me that she was known as a 'Daughter of the War'." and handed Ingi the obituary notice from the press.

"This photograph from Berlin has my grandmother wearing a sailing ship brooch. Look at the obituary article. What's Dagny wearing? The same brooch. Then, purely by chance, I bump into, here in the Faroe Islands of all places, the apparent Scottish granddaughter of this Dagny Poulsen, and she's now wearing the same bloody brooch. I then go and find a copy of a letter that my grandmother wrote to Himmler complaining about some guy called Lindemann, and as I finish reading it, his son draws up in a car, gets out and checks into the same hotel I'm staying at. You tell me Ingi. What do you think is going on? You've been about the blocks as much as me and have you ever come across so many cross-over coincidences in a story like this? Have we hell. We need to find out what is going on."

Ingi lit yet another cigarette and exhaled the smoke in a long, drawn out manner. "No, I haven't. Something is flashing at the bottom of your laptop, by the way." Daniel turns the screen towards him and clicks on the flashing icon on the tool bar. His 'Dagny Poulsen' search has finished and he opens the results page. There are 174 different documents listed and 15 topic folders are highlighted. Most of the documents seem to belong to the one folder. 'DAGNY'.

He quickly opens the folder to see what it contains. There are photographs, facsimile reproductions of medical reports, medical assessments, x-rays, notes, and DNA analysis data. A substantial amount of the documentation relates to comparison profiles with skeletal remains and complicated sentences about racial profiles.

It is has now become an information overload for Daniel with far too much detail to process at the one time. He leans over the keyboard to switch off the laptop but pauses at the last moment as his curiosity causes him to open one final document. At first, he cannot fathom out the image in front of him. At first glance, it appears to be some sort of flow chart that starts in the top left-hand corner of the page and finishes down at the bottom right, and his initial impression is that it is simply a jumble of names and arrows. With his forefinger on the screen, he starts to trace the direction of the arrows.

Dagny Poulsen - Lisbita Poulsen - Frederik Johansson - Hanna Justinusdóttir - Justinus Persson - Per Justinusson - Justinus Persson - Per Justinusson - Lisbita Sámalsdóttir - Samuel Michelsen - Michael Joensen - Herborg Guttormsdatter - Guttorm Arnbjørnsen - Arnbjørn Guttormsen - Guttorm Nilsson - Nicolaus Ragnvaldsson - Ragnvald Hákonson - Ónefnd Hákonardóttir - Haakon Jonsson - Birgitta Knutsdotter - Knut Magnusson - Magnus Knutsson - Hafrid Sigtrygsdotter - Kristina Magnusdotter - Magnus Bengtsson - Bengt Folkesson - Ingegerd Knudsdatter - Adela de Flandre - Robert

I "de Fries" - Adèle de France - Robert II le Pieux - Hugues Capet - Hedwige of Saxony - Heinrich I von Sachsen.

Daniel stops finger-tracing and scrolls down onto the next page of the document. It was a joint report from the Martin Luther University in Halle-Wittenberg and the Otto von Guericke University detailing both universities findings in their acquisition of a sample and the subsequent DNA profiling from the remains of Henry I, the first King of Germany.

A following page listed the genetic profile and the actual DNA analysis. A Das Volker Syndicate logo was at the bottom of the analysis report indicating that it was being signed off as a true and accurate record of the original profile test. The universities had obtained their own profile information and had forwarded it on for a secondary confirmation of the results.

Ingi was sitting beside Daniel and like his friend, had become fascinated with what he was reading on the computer screen.

"Daniel. Maybe this is all just coincidental and you are reading far too much into this. Admittedly, there does seem to be a lot of Nazi stuff from way back going by what we've looked at, but maybe this Lindemann bloke is just looking for some sort of closure by finding out the answers to some unsolved questions he's got as well? It's like he's doing what you are doing. Comes up here for a job, and while he's here, takes the opportunity to go and investigate some family history. Remember why you're really here in the first place. You've come to help me recover coins from a shipwreck. I think you're reading far more in to this than you should and you're looking for something that doesn't actually exist?"

"I know Ingi, but every time I do a bit of innocent research, I chance upon another connection to some story from nearly 80 years ago with events of now that are related to back then. The same two names of Lindemann and Dagny keep on appearing."

He moved onto the next page and it was an analysis addressed to Pelle Lindemann, dated from 1976 and from the Institut Pasteur in Paris. It was concerning a blood sample that Lindemann has sent to them for investigation and they had been able to provide an abbreviated summary of their findings. There were hand-written notes and equations in the margins of the report, and although Daniel was reading a digital scan of an original document, the scribbles were still legible to read, but to Daniel, they were indecipherable.

The following pages contained a modern day Das Volker Syndicate analysis of this 1976 sample. Far more detailed than the original with colour graphics and highlighted areas. There was even a comparison page of the results of this test with the results of another.

Mitochondrial Related Common Ancestor (MRCA)
12-marker test - 12/12 – MRCA ✓
25-marker test – 25/25 – MRCA ✓
37-marker test – 50/50 – MRCA ✓
100-marker test – 100/100 – MRCA ✓

Ingi started to get impatient. "Come on Daniel. I've just driven over from Klaksvík to Tórshavn, at your request I hasten to add, to help you with something that you need my assistance with. I'm happy about driving here to have an opportunity to discuss all the angles for the salvage attempt next week, but I'm getting a bit pissed off with looking at a computer screen and stuff that's got nothing to do with me, and to be perfectly honest with you, I have no real interest in." Daniel looked at his friend and agreed with him.

"I'm sorry Ingi. I've got carried away with myself. I will just finish this last document and then I'm all yours. Going by the sounds in the kitchen, I think Sólrun is making dinner for us. Do you want to give her a hand and I will finish up in here and clear the table for her?"

Ingi's eyes smiled at the prospect of food. He left the table and went through to the kitchen to help Sólrun. Daniel returned to the screen. He moved on to the final part of the document. It was a brief e-mail from a Harry Shalestrick to Torstein Lindemann. Daniel noted the date stamp of the e-mail and where it had been sent from. 10th November, Das Volker Syndicate Research Clinic, St. Albans.

Mitochondrial Related Common Ancestor (MRCA)
12-marker test - 12/12 – MRCA ✓
25-marker test – 25/25 – MRCA ✓
37-marker test – 50/50 – MRCA ✓
100-marker test – 100/100 – MRCA ✓

DNA mouth-swab test subject - Freyja Fulton - Age 17.
St. Kentigern's College, Glasgow, Scotland.

Daniel re-read the e-mail again out loud. "Freyja Fulton from Scotland? Another coincidence?" He moved to the final page of the file. It was another flow chart similar to the first one but with added names. The first and last names were in bold print.

Freyja Fulton - James Fulton - Dagny Poulsen - Lisbita Poulsen - Frederik Johansson - Hanna Justinusdóttir - Justinus Persson - Per Justinusson - Justinus Persson - Per Justinusson - Lisbita Sámalsdóttir - Samuel Michelsen - Michael Joensen - Herborg Guttormsdatter - Guttorm Arnbjørnsen - Arnbjørn Guttormsen - Guttorm Nilsson - Nicolaus Ragnvaldsson - Ragnvald Hákonson - Ónefnd Hákonardóttir - Haakon Jonsson - Birgitta Knutsdotter - Knut Magnusson - Magnus Knutsson - Hafrid Sigtrygsdotter - Kristina Magnusdotter - Magnus Bengtsson - Bengt Folkesson - Ingegerd Knudsdatter - Adela De Flandre - Robert I "De Fries" - Adèle De France - Robert II Le Pieux - Hugues Capet - Hedwige of Saxony - **Heinrich I Von Sachsen**.

At the bottom of this final flow chart, there was a handwritten note, scribbled in German. Daniel quickly translated it into Danish and considered the intent of its contents. Whatever context he tried to place the translation in, there was always a suggestion of something pernicious about it. An icy chill of iniquitous fear passed down Daniel's spine.

'Ihr Blut ist der Schlüssel. König Henry wird wieder regieren. Seine Soldaten wird auferstehen.'

'Her blood is the key. King Henry shall rule again. His soldiers will rise.'

Daniel comprehends the implications explained in the document's methodical detail. This was the proof, via DNA profiling, of a genetic and genealogical connection between King Henry I, the first monarch of Germany, to Dagny Poulsen and then through to her granddaughter, Freyja Fulton. Freyja Fulton was the direct-lineage descendant of the first ruler of Germany, and Torstein Lindemann was out for her blood, literally. For some reason he wants the blood of Dagny's granddaughter, Freyja.

Daniel now has to find out why.

The Stream

Sólrun started to clear the plates away from the dining table and came back through with a large pot of coffee. She fussed over Ingi and Daniel and poured them both large mugs for them to quaff. Sólrun was glad to have guests in her house again and she secretly enjoyed having some company to talk to. The last 24 hours had been exciting and for some unknown reason, she had been drawn into a completely different world of intrigue, mystery and probably danger. She was enjoying this unexpected change to her normal routine. She had marvelled at the discussions that the two of them were having about ocean depths, the Norway Current, the long-range weather forecast, water visibility, the type of specialist diving gear they were going to be using, such as rebreathers, underwater lifting bags and the use of underwater plasma cutting equipment that was required for cutting the steel of the SS Sauternes.

She passed the two men plates with slices of her home-made lemon cake. Ingi scoffed his slices and remarked that the cake was exquisite. She thanked him for his kind words.

"Do you want some more?" as she placed another slice on his plate. Daniel couldn't resist teasing Ingi.

"Careful now Ingi. We don't want your wetsuit being a tight fit for you next week, do we?"

Ingi simply replied with "Shut up!" as he crammed the latest slice into his mouth. All three of them started to laugh and it was the welcome release of humour that they all needed.

The Stream

Sólrun asked them both what the plans were for the evening and Ingi followed up her enquiry by directly asking Daniel what it actually was that he wanted to do tonight. Daniel looked at them both as he thought out his reply.

"First of all, we cannot do anything with this Heri Jorgensen until darkness falls. It only gets truly dark for about two hours and that's from about 1.00am to 3.00am. If we 'paint' his property then, we could find out if he has anything Sólrun can use against him to recover her inheritance. He comes across as such a pompous fool, he's probably got it all stored on a computer and if so, we just hack it and retrieve what we need. But we need to be discreet with this. It wouldn't surprise me if Heri's involvement with Lindemann is under some type of duress and that he's also got something to hide. What that is, I don't know yet, but having gone through a fraction of some of Lindemann's files, Lindemann strikes me as a man who gets what he wants by any means possible."

Ingi left the table and went through to the hall and quickly returned and placed a bag on the table. He slid the zip fastening open and removed a rolled-up canvas tool bag that was tied in the middle with a neat bow. After untying the bow, Ingi spread the tool bag open across the table. It was a series of pockets containing various pieces of electrical and mechanical hardware. Sólrun just stared at the contents and tried to understand what she was looking at. Daniel and Ingi started removing items from the various pockets and began assembling pieces together. She watched the dexterity of their finger work and realised that both men had completed this task many times before. The assembly of whatever apparatus they were completing was second nature to them and was an automatic action. Daniel had just finished assembling a piece together and had noticed Sólrun's fascinated expression.

"Sólrun? Could you close all the doors upstairs and draw the window curtains over please? Switch the landing light on and wait for me outside the bathroom door. I'll show you what this is if you go and do that."

Sólrun left the room and Daniel and Ingi could hear her climbing the stairs. Ingi chuckled and spoke to Daniel.

"What do you think her reaction will be when she tries it on?" Daniel shrugged his shoulders.

Sólrun called down to them that she had done as he had asked and Daniel and Ingi went out into the hall. Ingi closed the dining room and kitchen doors over and pulled the curtains at a small window shut. Daniel walked up the stairs and joined Sólrun. He placed the apparatus on Sólrun's head and adjusted it over her eyes.

"Can you see alright?" She nodded that she could. "Ingi. Will you stand out of sight just now?" and Daniel watched his friend move out of vision. He gently moved Sólrun into position near the top of the stairs and said to her "I am going to turn off the lights. We will be in near darkness. Don't panic and don't touch the headset. Tell me what you can see and then I will press a button just to the side of your right eye. OK?"

Daniel turned off the lights and felt Sólrun tremble. "Relax." he reassured her. "What can you see?" Sólrun grabbed at Daniel's side.

"Nothing." she shouted.

Daniel pressed the button beside her right eye and asked her to look around. Her vision had become green and white infused. She could make out the features of the upstairs landing such as the banister, the door-frames and the pictures on the walls. Daniel asked her to look down the stairs.

"What can you see?" he asked her.

"Nothing apart from the staircase, the front door and the coat rack. What am I looking for?" she blurted out.

"Ingi?" called Daniel and his friend moved out of hiding and stood at the bottom of the stairs.

"Jesus!" shouted Sólrun as Ingi suddenly appeared below her in white and green illumination. It was like looking at a negative of a photograph. Daniel placed his hand on her left shoulder and explained to her what she was viewing.

"These are night vision goggles that allow you to see in the dark. Wait till you've seen this though" and he pressed another button beside her right eye. "Christ!" was the reaction as Ingi had suddenly gone from green and white to a mixture of red, yellow and orange colours.

"Watch this now." and Daniel asked Ingi to move out of sight. Sólrun watched Ingi's colouration dissipate as he moved. Her view changed as she watched the shapes and outlines appearing before her eyes begin to re-adjust and she was now able to make out the figure of Ingi standing in front of the kitchen door.

"This is thermal imaging that looks for heat and body signatures." Sólrun removed the headset and started to blink repeatedly as Daniel switched on the lights upstairs and drew back the curtains. "It does take you a few minutes to get used to having normal vision again after you've been wearing this."

He led Sólrun back downstairs and into the dining room. She sat back at the table and watched them assemble more items from the tool bag.

"Why do you have this stuff? What do you need it for? Are you two burglars or spies or something?"

Before Daniel could say anything, Ingi replied. "Danish Special Forces, retired."

Sólrun mouthed silently. "Danish Special Forces, retired." She lifted what looked like a fat pen and examined it. "What's this for?"

Ingi took it from her and pointed it at the far wall of the sitting room. Daniel placed the headset back over her eyes and switched it on. Sólrun could see an 'X' on her wall. She moved the headset away from her eyes and looked at the wall. There was nothing there. She moved the headset back and the 'X' reappeared.

"What's that all about?"

Ingi started to explain that the pen was a laser guidance tool that could be used by ground troops for air-to-surface missiles to home in on. Dropped from a military plane at altitude, a missile would find a designated target guided by the 'X' that had been 'painted' on it.

"X marks the spot. Boom!" remarked Daniel. "It has other uses such as leaving a temporary invisible marker on a target or an individual that we can only see though the night vision goggles. Ingi could be on the other side of a field and I could 'paint' him to then be able to see where he was located through these night vision goggles. Sometimes we have had to do that so we didn't shoot each other in the dark."

Sólrun had become silent and obviously concerned that the two men in her dining room were not what she had thought them to be. They weren't just a couple of former sailors doing salvage operations or business security advice, they was a lot more to them than they had revealed to her previously. Daniel gave Ingi a knowing look and raised his eyebrows at him and the direction of Sólrun. Ingi put down the piece of equipment that he had in his hands.

"Sólrun. We are good guys. Remember the hostage rescue of the four kidnapped nurses in Afghanistan at Christmas time a few years ago? That was us." and moved a pointed finger back and forth in the direction of himself and Daniel.

"We have served our Queen and country and are now retired. I kept all of this stuff as you never know when it'll come in handy. Just as well I did." He laughed and looked skywards. "We are still on the reservist list and occasionally we are both asked to come and do a bit of 'consultancy' work, if you get my drift. Nothing too outlandish, but we can be classed as expendable if something goes wrong with whatever mission we are on. 'Accountable deniability' is the current phrase and we would just be referred to as private contractors. However, if the mission turns out to be a success, we are always claimed to be members of a Special Forces unit."

Daniel had taken a CD case from the tool bag and inserted a disk drive into his laptop/tablet hybrid. He was installing a programme.

"The reason I bought this earlier was to be able to have all of this equipment formatted for use." He waved his hand over in the direction of the tool bag. "The plan was to have all the information that we get from Heri's house remotely uploaded into this laptop and then downloaded onto a USB for you to then search for the dirt to expose him as the charlatan that you say he is."

The programme had finished its installation and Daniel removed the disk and returned it to its case. He placed the CD case back in a pocket and then removed a final item from another.

"This is a dongle that enables us to have additional functions and sychronises all of our equipment into a specific wavelength frequency that only we can access. It allows us to record, copy, remove or operate any electronic data that we are targeting by 'painting'. Remove the dongle from the laptop and no information is transmittable. Yet another piece of military technology that is now freely available for commercial use. Kids all over the world just now are synching their phones and computers with flat screen televisions to display and play games or go on the internet."

Inge finished what he was assembling and then started to gather everything together and return to the tool bag. "I need to check into the hotel, freshen up and then I will go for a drive around town and check out this Heri's address. I need to get a decent idea of the location and where to set everything up from. Have you got an address for Heri and I can use the satnav in the car and go over and have a look-see?"

Sólrun wrote the address down on a piece of paper and handed it to Ingi. "Thanks. When do you want to rendezvous then?"

Daniel suggested that they meet about 1.00am at the car park at the rear of the hotel.

"I will see you both then." and Ingi headed through for the front door. Sólrun accompanied him into the hallway.

"Thanks for doing all of this for me. Are you sure you want to do this though?" she asked him as he was standing outside the front door.

"Listen Sólrun. If Daniel says you need a hand with a problem, that's enough for me. You'll get all the help you need, and then some. Sorry if what you've found out about us tonight has come as a bit of a shock to you, but I'm also being selfish here. I need to have Daniel's head on straight for him to go diving for me, and if that requires him to solve this Dagny mystery, once and for all, and any other associated matters, such as your situation, so be it. I will help him, and you, to do all of that. I will catch you later. And thanks for dinner. The lemon slices topped it off for me."

He kissed her on the cheek and left.

Sólrun watched him go down the steps and get into his car and drive away down Jónas Broncksgøta. She closed her front door over and returned to the dining room. Daniel had tidied everything away and was now sitting in one of the armchairs in the sitting room and playing with his laptop/tablet hybrid.

"What do you want to do now?" he asked her. Sólrun looked at the clock on the wall. It was just after 9.30pm.

"Well I'm going to mow the lawn just now. The grass needs cut and I may as well do that while we wait for meeting up with Ingi later." and left him where he was sat.

Daniel continued going through some of the Lindemann files that were on the laptop. Distracted by the sound of the grass being cut outside, he got up and looked out of the sitting room window to watch Sólrun pushing the mower up and down the lawn. It was 9.45pm, there was still bright daylight, the sun was shining overhead and he was watching a woman mowing her garden lawn. He thought about what his neighbours would say to him back in Denmark if he thought about mowing the lawn at such an hour. He would be lynched for upsetting the peace of a Friday night, but then again, he wasn't back home in Denmark. He laid the laptop down on the armchair and went out to help Sólrun in the garden.

She laughed at him when she saw he had appeared in the garden. "You wanted to know how the grass gets cut on the roofs of the houses?" as she placed a step-ladder against a house wall and handed him a strimmer to use. "You do that and I will finish mowing the lawn. I normally use a sheep to do the roof, but you're here now and I may as well make some use of you." she taunted him.

Daniel climbed onto the roof and started about his task. He probably deserved the badgering that he had just received and smiled at himself as he started to cut the grass on the roof of a house at nearly 10.00pm on a Friday night.

His task was completed fairly quickly and Daniel was surprised at the briefness of the chore. He asked Sólrun if she was happy with his handiwork and when she agreed that she was, he came back down off the roof and helped her put the mower and strimmer away in the cellar at the back of the house.

They returned to the house and Sólrun gave him a chilled Föroya Bjór from the fridge. He took a swig from the bottle and then looked at the black faced sheep on the front label. "I now know how he feels" and laughed as she showed Sólrun the picture. She agreed and joined in with his laughter. He set the bottle down on a kitchen worktop.

"Can I take a shower please, if you don't mind?" he asked her.

"Off course you can. There are towels inside the unit that you can use."

Daniel left her in the kitchen as he went upstairs. She could hear him in the bathroom above her running the shower, removing his clothes and stepping under the water. She placed her bottle down beside his on the worktop and sneaked up the stairs. The bathroom door was slightly ajar and she peaked in the room. Daniel had his back to her and was inside the enclosed wet-room shower area.

She quickly slipped off her own clothes and tiptoed in her nakedness across the bathroom floor, silently slid the wet-room door open and entered inside. She grabbed a bar of soap from a holder on the wall and started to rub his back with it. Daniel turned around in initial alarm and was met with hazel-green eyes that stared longingly into his. He pulled Sólrun's body close to his and they embraced.

The Stream

6.01pm – Friday 9th June, present day
Argjaboðagøta, Tórshavn, Faroe Islands.

At the end of the long Argjaboðagøta, a main road that runs through the sprawling suburb of Argir on the southern edge of Tórshavn, lies the Faroe Islands state-of-the-art Environmental Welfare Agency building. It was a Das Volker Syndicate private finance partnership initiative in conjunction with the Faroese government that had also created the adjacent brand new 200 bed hospital with all the associated medical clinics and departments, together with this bespoke research and development unit.

A welcome business investment of over 400 million dollars into the islands had brought advanced, state-of-the-art, 21st Century technological and medical services to the capital and had led to the creation of guaranteed employment for over 500 people.

The complex, consisting of the hospital, research and development clinics, laboratories and the Environmental Welfare Agency buildings, had received many plaudits from around the world. The ingenuity of the Faroese government had been acclaimed for having engaged with private business to deliver a neoteric, pioneering and leading-edge facility that brought many social and economic benefits to a small community of 50,000 souls. This type of avant-garde partnership was nothing new for the Das Volker Syndicate, and its reputation as a world leader had been further enhanced with its continued promulgation of this type of revolutionary financial partnership investment with associated agencies, companies and governments.

Heri Jorgensen, of course, had financially benefitted from this relationship that his government had entered into with a multi-national company. He had personally sourced the required land by various questionable means, absolved himself of any malfeasance from its acquisition, legally removed himself of any accusations of impropriety and had amassed considerable wealth for himself along the way. But he hadn't factored in for the unforeseen, the small matter that all of his calculated and deceitful scheming had been observed and monitored by Torstein Lindemann, Director General of the Das Volker Syndicate. Heri hadn't appreciated, until only a few hours previously, that all of his actions had been surveilled from the outset. His world had been ripped apart when he now understood that he had been unwittingly coerced into procuring land for a foreign company to build upon, and while he had seized upon this unexpected opportunity to make a considerable amount of money for himself by being creative, Torstein Lindemann, somehow, had been completely aware of all of his subterfuge. Lindemann could destroy him and his reputation in an instant. He could destroy everything that his family stood for, and the work of his father, by the simple release of a photograph depicting his own flesh and blood in the uniform of the despised Schutzstaffel, the elite paramilitary bodyguard of the most hated man in history, Adolf Hitler.

Heri placed his right hand on the door frame of the research room. With his left, he mopped his face with an already soaked handkerchief. He was still sore from the injuries that Lindemann had inflicted upon him during the earlier attack. With a mixture of fear, contempt and hate, he watched

Lindemann being shown around the research room by the facility's lead scientist, Dr. Mette Bundgaard.

Standing in front of Heri, a large group of teenage students from Scotland attentively listened to every word that was coming from the mouth of Dr. Mette Bundgaard. Most of what she was saying, Heri didn't understand, but he reckoned that it must be of some importance as Lindemann appeared to be enthralled by what she was explaining to him, and the group, about the 'open doors' policy of the new Environmental Welfare Agency research laboratory as part of the European Viking Researcher's Conference weekend. Dr. Bundgaard kept repeating that, for her, it was a great opportunity to showcase the work being undertaken here concerning Viking DNA, genetics and other tests.

Heri jumped as Jógvan Johannesen placed a hand on his back and asked how things were going. "Hi Heri. Is our guest enjoying what he has seen so far? It is awfully good of you to show him around this weekend. I know he didn't want a fuss made of him, but it is not every day that you get to meet the man that has invested so much money into our society, do you?"

Heri agreed. "Hello Jógvan. Have you met him yet? I can introduce you to him if you want?"

Jógvan indicated that he would just as a tapping sound was ringing out around the room with a woman banging a glass beaker on a worktop.

"Ladies and Gentlemen. Can I have your attention please? My name is Dr. Mette Bundgaard and I am the Senior Administrator for the Environmental Welfare Agency of the Faroe Islands. I would like to thank you all for coming on the tour today and I will try to explain what it is we do here. This agency oversees the general health and well-being of these islands and the issues that affect the quality of everyday life. We aim to promote or enforce standards that preserve public health, public safety and protect the environment, such as food safety and food hygiene, environmental protection, workplace health and safety, public health and housing, social care and health matters, planning and building standards, animal welfare, environmental health licensing and many others including agriculture, fisheries, tourism, sport and leisure all the way through to the removal and disposal of everyday refuse.

But we also carry out tests and clinical studies in a vast array of scientific fields. The Research and Development laboratory here has conducted ground-breaking investigations into genetics and Viking DNA, and the results that we have collected so far are proving to be encouraging as the world of medicine attempts to eradicate many of the illnesses that affect the human population. I am especially privileged to be in the company of Dr. Torstein Lindemann of the Das Volker Syndicate. I am sure that he is known to you all and why he is here in the Faroe Islands just now, but I have asked him if he could say a few words. Ladies and Gentlemen. I give you Dr. Torstein Lindemann."

Applause greeted Lindemann as he stepped forward to speak to the room.

"Thank you Dr. Bundgaard. I will be brief. The importance of this research facility, and others like it around the world, is that they are the front-line battlegrounds in the war against the many illnesses that affect the human race. But to be able to find the cures, we must also trace the history. The answers to the future lie in our past, within our own DNA and genetic profiles, and hopefully, we can start to 'reprogramme the code' by removing the bad bits as we go along.

We can plot the early movement of Europeans by genetic markers, and the most travelled of them all were the Vikings. Recent scientific studies of modern humans have helped to determine some of the genetic impacts that the Vikings have had on present day countries, but this research has also led to the discovery of the origins of some genetic diseases and also their cures. Take Dupuytren's contracture or 'Viking disease' as an example of a terribly handicapping affliction where fingers contract inwards to the palm. There is no cure and most sufferers have to undergo surgery in attempts to re-straighten the fingers. However, by extensive genetic researching, a demographic profile identified that Dupuytren's contracture was prevalent among people of Nordic ancestry, mainly in men over the age of 40, and with those afflicted, nearly 70% of them had a family history of diabetes, epilepsy and liver disease.

Through modern science, a genetic predisposition to Dupuytren's contracture has been identified. By further study and diligent perseverance by scientists in facilities such as this, the DNA code of the human race can be reprogrammed over generations to eradicate the faults that currently exist amongst every one of us.

Forgive me for rambling and interrupting your tour of this facility, but thank you for your time and I hope that I will see many of you tomorrow night at the Raohus when I give my lecture about 'Reprogramming the code'."

The Stream

Dr. Mette Bundgaard thanked Lindemann for his words and continued to show a number of the visitors around the laboratory. Some of the students were talking to Lindemann and he seemed to be relishing the opportunity to have a discussion with them. Heri asked Jógvan if he wanted to go and meet Lindemann just now and both men joined the edge of the group of students that he was talking to. Jógvan stood patiently and listened to the current conversation. A Scottish girl with a frizz of black curly hair was explaining that she had found the first year of her Nordic Studies university course to be fascinating and that she was glad to have taken the course.

"I have to commend you Dr. Lindemann for having the business acumen to invest significantly in adult education and afford students like myself and Freyja here, the opportunity to come to places like the Faroe Islands and see for ourselves the many aspects of Nordic society that we are studying."

Lindemann thanked the girl for her kind words and turned to her companion. "Your friend" and he stopped briefly to read to read her name badge, "Wendy was telling me that your name is Freyja. Can I ask you if there is a reason why your parents gave you such a Nordic sounding name?"

The girl beside Wendy smiled. "My grandmother was originally from the Faroe Islands and I suppose it was my parent's way of keeping the Viking connections going. In Norse mythology, Freyja was the guardian deity of these islands and the goddess for the month of February and I was born in February."

Lindemann smiled and agreed with her that it was nice to keep connections alive with family names. "Is your grandmother still alive?" he asked.

Freyja explained that her grandmother had died a number of years ago and this was Freyja's first trip to the Faroe Islands and she had gone to her grandmother's childhood house earlier in the day.

"What was your grandmother's name, if you don't mind me asking?"

Jógvan watched Lindemann's eyes explode in a flash of blue delight when the girl gave her reply.

"Her name was Dagny Poulsen.".

Lindemann looked astonishedly at Freyja. His blue eyes now had a luminosity that had not been there before. He held out his hand towards her for a handshake, and as she took hold of his hand, he spoke in a gentle manner.

"I believe this is what you could call fate Freyja. I believe my father and your grandmother were friends many, many years ago in Berlin. After all this time, his son and her granddaughter meet in the Faroe Islands. It is quite bizarre, is it not?"

Before she could reply, Jógvan broke into the conversation. "Apologies for my rude interruption Dr. Lindemann. Ladies. My name is Jógvan Johannesen, I am the Prime Minister and I unfortunately have to leave just now, but I thought it would be rude of me not to introduce myself to you before tomorrow evening. Thank you for coming to the islands. Please contact me at some point tomorrow so I can properly welcome your arrival, if that does not interfere too much with your plans." and passed Lindemann a business card.

Lindemann studied the card and pocketed it and stated to Jógvan that he would be delighted to meet with him at some point the following day. The two Scottish girls had left the group and had re-joined their fellow students on the tour of the facility.

"I hope Heri has been looking after you and displaying traditional Faroese hospitality towards you?" asked Jógvan.

Lindemann smiled. "Heri has been a perfect host. He has been so kind so far."

"Glad to hear it. Sorry about this, but I have to leave you once more in Heri's capable hands. Until tomorrow? Have a good evening." and Jógvan left Lindemann and Heri alone in the now deserted laboratory.

Jógvan paced down the corridor and found the exit door. Once outside, he leaned against a wall and tried to take stock of what he had just witnessed.

At any other time, he wouldn't have thought twice about the last ten minutes or so, but having met Sólrun Jakobsen and her friend, Daniel, only a few hours ago and given the subject matter of their discussion, what he had just seen with his own eyes was too much of a coincidence. He would have to talk to Sólrun tomorrow and give her a heads up on what he had just witnessed. It was probably nothing but coincidence, but Sólrun always did seem to have a habit of somehow getting involved with matters that had nothing to do with her, innocently or not.

The Stream

Daniel drove the Touareg into the car park of a viewing area off the Oyggjarvegur, a winding route with scenic views that leads in the direction of Kollafjørður, a small fishing village to the north of Tórshavn, and the main road that takes you to the Vágatunnilin, the island of Vágar and the airport.

The car park was deserted, making it a perfect place to observe Heri Jorgensen's house. Ingi got out the front passenger seat and walked to the rear of the car and opened the back door. He lifted the painting tool bag out and laid it on the ground. Daniel exited the vehicle and opened the rear passenger door for Sólrun. She looked out across Tórshavn and although it was dark, she was able to ascertain landmarks by the streetlights of the town. In the distance, the hump-backed mountain of Høgoyggj on the island of Nólsoy loomed large in the darkness. The lights of the houses on the island twinkled like fairy lights, and from the southern end of the island, with a frequency of every 43 seconds, a probing beam of light from the Øknastangi lighthouse cut a swathe through the darkness as it completed a rotation.

Sólrun broke the silence as she watched Daniel and Ingi prepare themselves with items from the painting tool bag. "What do you want me to do while you are away?" she asked. Daniel was fairly blunt with her. "We need you to sit in the front seat and ensure that the feed we send to you is downloaded into the laptop" and he passed her the hybrid laptop/tablet.

He plugged something into the cigarette lighter and placed what looked to her like a wide tea cup on the dashboard. He then ran a cable from it and into the side of the laptop. He inserted a disk into the drive tray of the laptop, typed a message into a pop-up screen and pressed the return button. He took from his jacket pocket the dongle that he had shown her back at the house and plugged it into another port on the side of the laptop.

"Once the dongle is up and running, the equipment we are using will transmit data that will be recorded onto the laptop by the programme I installed earlier. Ingi is going to be my look-out and I will try and get into Heri's house. We will keep in touch with each other with these." and he passed her an earpiece with a microphone attachment.

Going by the expression on Sólrun's face, Daniel appreciated that the last few minutes' activity hadn't been explained to her properly. "Sólrun, I have placed a miniature military satellite dish on the dashboard and tuned it in to the laptop. The satellite dish is now synching to a global positioning satellite overhead and when Ingi and I switch our kit on, we will appear as icons on the laptop screen. We are just tapping into the same technology used for satellite navigation that nearly every car has and what every mobile phone has installed. Relax. It's fine."

Daniel looked around the car park and then placed one of the night vision goggles over his eyes. He took the marker laser pen and pointed it at targets in the distance. He pressed the return button on the laptop and the screen came to life with satellite coordinates and positioning information. She looked at the screen in mock horror as she suddenly realised that she was looking at a real-time electronic mapping overlay of her current situation. There were two blinking dots on the screen, both of which were side by side. Daniel stabbed a finger at the screen.

"That's me and Ingi." and he quickly typed in details for each of the blinking dots.

"I'm Puffin 1 and Ingi is Puffin 2. You're Puffin Control." and smiled at her.

Three red crosses had started flashing on the overlay upon the laptop's screen and Daniel studied the information pop-up that was appearing beside them.

"The Nordic House is 1100 metres northeast of here. The Listasavn Museum is 800 metres to the east and Heri's house is 643 metres to our north. It will take about 12 minutes for Ingi and I to set up a safe observation point. I need you to press the return button at precisely 1.30am. Are you ready for that?"

Sólrun stated that she was and Daniel pressed the return button and the screen went blank.

"We're off. Any problems, contact us on the headset. Just press the earpiece to transmit a message." and he leaned inside the car and kissed her on the forehead.

"We won't be long and remember to hit the return button at 1.30am."

She watched both men disappear out of the car park and across the moorland towards Heri's house. They were quickly out of sight in the darkness.

Sólrun was excited with this adventure, but at the same time, she was experiencing pangs of anxiety. She was now a part of something that was probably highly illegal and would have dire consequences for her should Daniel and Ingi get caught, but she was also exhilarated by the thrill of it all. She dismissed the panic that she was feeling. They were apparently highly trained professionals and they knew what they were doing, she thought. She hoped. She prayed.

Her eyes were glued to the clock at the bottom right hand corner of the laptop's screen as time seemed to slow inexorably in its march towards 1.30am. She wondered how close they were to Heri's house and pressed the return button at the allotted time. The screen burst into life with a raft of differing information pop-ups appearing and disappearing. At the top right corner of the screen, a long 'download in progress' icon denoted work in progress. Sólrun stared at the map overlay and ascertained where Daniel and Ingi were by the blinking dots. Ingi's dot 'Puffin 2' was stationary and she watched Daniel, 'Puffin 1', slowly approach Heri's house. This was better than what you see in a Hollywood film, thought Sólrun, except this was for real and happening a few hundred metres from where she was sitting.

Sólrun's earpiece crackled with Daniel and Ingi discussing Daniel's approach to the house.

"Daniel, there are no hot spots showing with the thermal imaging, so I think it is safe to assume the house is empty. There are two 'warm' spots coming from a room on the ground floor. I think it is electronic and one of them is probably the computer. You might want to have a look in there first."

There was a brief silence.

"Thanks. Just approaching the downstairs door just now. Keep alert for any movement above me." came the reply.

The Stream

Sólrun was glued to the laptop screen. 'Puffin 1' was blinking at the side of the house and she gasped as the blink stopped then started again as she realised Daniel had entered the house.

Daniel had tried the door handle and for the second time in 24 hours was shocked to find that the Faroese seemed to be care-free about security. He entered the house, and with his night vision, he was able to find his way around in the dark. He was in what seemed to be a man's play-room. DVDs and CDs filled shelving on two walls. In the corner was a bar type counter area with four bar stools in front of it. Behind the counter was a well stocked fridge with various beer bottles. An ice machine chinked away as it produced a fresh batch of cubes. Inserted into the corner walls were bar-butlers that held a number of different wines and spirits. Heri liked his den, thought Daniel. A third wall had a massive flat screen cinema-type television and the fourth wall had a full-length bookcase from the floor to the ceiling. Two large angled sofas filled the floor space, and built into a recess of the bookcase was a computer workstation. Daniel picked his way across the room in the darkness and investigated the computer. He found a USB port on the cowling of the system unit casing and inserted a dongle. A light on the dongle turned green and Daniel tapped his earpiece.

"Puffin 1 to Puffin Control. Over".

Sólrun became all excited by this sudden request and tapped her earpiece.

"Puffin Control" she giggled.

"Press the F2 button on the keyboard and tell me if the download icon on the screen is starting to chunter along?" replied Daniel.

"Puffin 2 to Puffin 1 and Puffin Control. A car is driving along the road towards the house. It will be there in about 5 minutes, and as it is a dead-end, you might want to get a move on."

Daniel stepped back outside and looked along the roadway. Away in the distance, he could see the headlights of an approaching vehicle rising and falling in the darkness as it followed the undulations of the road. He went back into the house and back to the computer.

"Puffin Control. What's happening?"
Sólrun glanced at the download icon. It was halfway through completion.

"56% complete." she said.

"Thanks Puffin Control. Give me an update as it progresses. This could be tight if that car is Heri coming home."

The car continued to get closer. "Puffin 1 from Puffin 2. The car is definitely headed your way."

"Puffin 1 from Puffin Control. 80% complete."

Daniel stood beside the computer with his right hand hovering over the dongle. He heard the car pull up on the forecourt outside and above him. Two car doors slammed shut and there was a conversation in progress. He could hear the front door being opened but there was laughter and banging sounds rebounding down the stairwell towards him.

"Puffin 1 from Puffin Control. 90%."

"Puffin 1 from Puffin 2. Target has female company and they are snogging at the front door."

Sólrun gasped in shock that Heri had convinced a woman to go back to his house with him. She must be blind or drunk or both, she nastily conjectured.

Daniel waited poised to snatch the dongle and make his escape. He could hear a man's heavy footsteps on the wooden floor above him and the clippity-clip of high heels. There was laughter, giggling and grunting sounds and then what was obviously the impact of two bodies collapsing on some seating furniture.

"Puffin Control to Puffin 1. 95%."

His hand is still poised to snatch the dongle from the computer as he becomes aware of footsteps coming down the wooden stairwell into the room. He throws himself flat on the floor, and by lying prone, he is hidden from view by one of the angled sofas. The room is in complete darkness until a light turns on over in the far corner at the bar counter and Heri stumbles into the room. Daniel's vision is temporarily affected by the sudden illumination and he slips the night vision goggles up onto his forehead. He peeks round the side of the sofa and watches Heri shuffle over to the bar and open the fridge to remove some bottles. Heri then starts tinkering around with glasses and starts to fill a large wine glass to its brim from a wine box on the counter. If Heri sees him, Daniel will have to incapacitate him there and then. He is coiled to spring into attack mode to do so but he realises that Heri is very drunk and is more focused on procuring some beverage and then returning to his female companion upstairs. Heri suddenly shouts

"Mette, I'm coming."

A female voice from above shouts back. "You bloody better not be. It's far too early for that."

Heri starts to laugh and he drunkenly makes his way towards the stairs with a glass of wine in one hand and three beer bottles intertwined in the fingers of the other.

"Puffin Control to Puffin 1. Download complete."

Heri stops just short of the first step as he thinks he has heard something in the room. He staggers around as he looks about him. In the darkness and behind a sofa, the harbinger of his imminent attack and probable death waits to pounce. The ice machine chinks another batch of cubes into its internal tray and Heri looks at the machine, shakes his head and goes back to climbing up the stairs. Daniel relaxes and takes a deep breath to let the pent up adrenalin coursing throughout the sinews of his body dissipate. He can hear Heri and this 'Mette' canoodling above him and the sounds of the obvious drunken precursors to intercourse. He snatches the dongle from the USB port, pockets it and exits the room to the garden outside. He closes the door over ever so gently and calls Ingi on his headset.

"Puffin 1 to Puffin 2. I'm outside and awaiting all-clear." He stands in the shadows waiting on Ingi's response.

"Puffin 1. We may have another problem. A car is coming along the Oyggjarvegur very, very slowly. I think the occupants are looking for something. Hold on a moment and I'll check it out for you."

Ingi had spotted a car moving slowly along the main road and it was heading in the general direction of the car park. He adjusted the night vision goggles and zoomed in on the vehicle. It was a white saloon car with two passengers inside.

Along the side of the vehicle, the legend 'POLITI' was emblazoned in neon-blue reflective lettering.

"Puffin 2 to Puffin 1 and Puffin Control. We have a police car approaching. They seem to be looking for something or someone. I would suggest that Puffin 1 ditches his equipment in a safe place and return to Puffin Control. Puffin Control? This might be the right time to start to disconnect the laptop and hide some of the apparatus on show, and you better start preparing a cover story in case our approaching friends come and speak to you."

Daniel had started running across the moorland towards the car park. He could see the lights of the police car heading towards him. As he continued running, he was putting all the tools that he had taken with him, the goggles and other equipment into the red rucksack that he had had on his back.

"Puffin 1 to Puffin Control. Press F5 on the keyboard to save all the data, then press F7 to clear the screen. Press F8 to return the laptop to its normal settings and get on the internet and start looking at anything. I'll be with you in the car park shortly. If the police come and speak to you, tell them I am looking for my wallet that I may have dropped earlier this evening. We were here looking at the stars or something."

He continued running towards the car park. The police car was turning into the far entrance about 300 metres away from him and about 100 metres from Sólrun. He hurdled a low fence and ran onto the road towards the near entrance. As he got closer, he saw a rubbish bin beside a viewing bench on the roadside verge and he shoved the red rucksack inside it and started to walk towards the opening into the car park.

The police car slowly drove around the car park and then crawled up parallel to the parked Touareg. Sólrun was studying the laptop screen and its glow lit up her face.

"Puffin 1 to Puffin 2. I'm about to go dark. Stay put until safe to move. My kit is inside the bin at this end of the car park."

In his earpiece, Ingi responded. "Copy Puffin 1. I'll stay back here awhile and watch this free sex show though my goggles. I'll pick your kit up for you and meet you back at the hotel later."

Daniel smirked at Ingi's comments about the sex show. He could mentally picture him watching the steamy action in the house unfold in glorious night vision and thermal imaging.

Sólrun was trembling with fear inside the car. She had followed all of Daniel's instructions and was now searching for shoes on the internet. Having removed the miniature satellite dish from the dashboard and stuffed it and its cables into the glove-box, she pretended not to have noticed the police car stop and the occupants get out and approach her own car. The window was rapped by one of the policemen and she pressed the button on the door frame to lower the glass.

"Can I help you, officers?" she calmly asked. The two policemen stood close to the car, and one of them asked her to get out of the car. She did. A torch beam was shone in her face and she lifted her right hand to shield her eyes from its glare.

"Is that really necessary?" she demanded. The police officer holding the torch replied bluntly.

"It is. What are you doing in this car park at this time in the morning?"

Before she could reply, she heard Daniel's voice come from behind her.

"It's ok Sólrun. I found it on the grass behind the bench. It must have fallen out of my pocket when we were sitting there."

The police officer with the torch turned its beam on Daniel. He also tried to shield his eyes.

"Is there a problem?" he asked.

The other police officer spoke. "Sólrun Jakobsen! Long time no see. It's Tommy. Tommy Carlsen. We were at school together." and beamed a wide grin at her.

"It's ok Jens. You can switch the torch off. It's Sólrun Jacobsen. I know her from my school days."

The other police officer, Jens, did as he was told. Daniel came round the side of the car.

"I found it Sólrun. It was on the grass." and waved his wallet at her and at the policemen.

"Hi. We were here earlier. Been for a drive as Sólrun was showing me around and we had stopped to see the stars. Look. There's Jupiter over there, just above that mountain top." and pointed to his north. The two police men followed his arm in the direction of an orange dot in the distance.

"You don't often get to see it so clearly with the naked eye, but with there being no light pollution up here in the Faroes, it's a great place to see the heavens."

The two officers just looked at him, back at Jupiter and then at Sólrun.

"Hi Tommy. It's been a while." and Sólrun then started having a conversation with Tommy.

Jens shuffled uncomfortably and then began asking Daniel who he was. Daniel was only too pleased to explain who he was and why he was in the Faroes. The mention of the Jólaskipið seemed to defuse the situation and Jens became extremely interested in the planned expedition and the dive details.

The separate conversations lasted for about 5 minutes and Tommy suggested that he and Jens better resume their futile search for the 'vagabonds' that old Mrs Fredericksen had seen from her living room window.

"She calls the police about three times a month and claims to have seen people wandering around in the dark on the moors up here and demands that we come up immediately and investigate." Tommy pointed at a house a short distance away.

"We come up here and no-one is to be found apart from youngsters having a few drinks and a laugh on a Friday night or adult couples having an extra marital conversation, if you know what I mean." and snorted as he raised his eyebrows and looked upwards in mock disdain.

Both Daniel and Sólrun laughed at the latter inference. "I'm not married." said Sólrun and "I'm not a youngster." joked Daniel and all four of them laughed at the unintended puns.

The policemen bade them farewell and got back into the patrol car and left to resume their search.

"Jesus Christ!" exclaimed Sólrun.

"I don't know if I can take much more of this. I need to go home and have a drink or three at least."

Daniel got into the driver's seat and started the engine. "Coming?" and invited her to get in the car. Once inside, he turned around to speak to Sólrun.

"Well done. We'll go back to your house, copy all the data over to your computer and I'll head back to the hotel and meet Ingi."

"Are we not waiting for him?" she asked.

Daniel drove out of the car park and onto the Oyggjarvegur and turned right to head back to the town centre. "No. Something came up back at the house and Ingi decided to stay and watch for a while."

He smirked again as he continued to drive along the road and then began explaining what he thought was possibly currently happening inside Heri's house.

The Stream

5.25pm – Saturday 10ᵗʰ June, present day
Jónas Broncksgøta, Tórshavn, Faroe Islands.

Sólrun and Daniel were sitting around the table in the kitchen eating a light meal that she had just prepared. It had been an eventful day for them both and he quietly reflected on its passage and the various contexts that had been thrown up.

The day had started off with Daniel coming round to her house about 10.00am, and on arrival, Sólrun instantly informing him of the telephone call she had just received from Jo-Jo, Jógvan Johannesen. Having digested the information that Sólrun had received, Daniel had begun to consider the implications and inferences to be drawn from the brief conversation that Jo-Jo had witnessed the night before with Lindemann and Freyja Fulton. He was grateful that Jo-Jo had used his politician's depth of perception and had recognised that there was more to this Dagny story than just seeking closure and a simple 'track and trace' exercise.

Jo-Jo had questioned Sólrun about what was she was involved in and he was troubled by the fact that three separate parties, all seemingly unconnected to each other, were now keenly expressing an interest into the background and life story of one Dagny Poulsen. Sólrun had re-assured Jógvan that it was just coincidental and that she wasn't involved in anything that was questionable or for that matter, illegal.

Jógvan had taken Sólrun at her word but advised her that if she got herself into any trouble, there was only so much that he could do for her. Sólrun had thanked him for his telephone call and had finished the conversation by telling him that he could breathe easy and he had nothing to worry about. But both of them knew that wasn't the case and Sólrun was feeling guilty that she could be compromising her father's lifelong friend and his official standing if matters went awry.

She poured her heart out to Daniel about the situation she now found herself in, and to be fair to Daniel, he had comforted her by remarking that intriguing coincidences were leading them all to have vivifying imaginings of some hidden story that didn't actually exist. It was all just chance and that these types of things do happen occasionally. But privately, Daniel was having none of it. He knew, and Jógvan Johannesen knew, there was far more to all of these supposed innocent coincidences and occurrences than what simply met the eye. There was a hidden story, a furtive and concealed narrative, shrouded by the passage of time and camouflaged with the many unfolding events and happenings of an 80 year period.

Daniel had helped Sólrun finish the copying of Heri's computer files onto her own system and had instructed her on how to search for details and information that she could use at a later date.

"Most of the stuff from his computer will be personal material, photographs, videos and music files etc, so be prepared for a lot of it to be rubbish. You need to explore all of the information and establish what is business and work orientated material, isolate it into folders and then spend your time going through it all. It's going to take you a while, but you can probably save yourself a lot of hassle by using the search functions."

He opened up the control panel and selected the search function. "What was the name of the piece of land that used to belong to your family?"

Sólrun typed the word 'Sandáfløttur' into the search field and Daniel hit the return button for the search to commence.

"Sólrun. I had a long chat with Ingi earlier over breakfast, and it looks as if we are going to head over to Klaksvik tomorrow and start the preparations for me to go diving to the SS Sauternes. You are welcome to come along and spend some time with us and continue as our local guide, but I should really be getting ready for the reason why I'm up here just now. I think I should be concentrating on that. What do you want to do today? No Dagny stuff. No break-ins. No spying missions. I'm all yours." and raised both his arms in a parody of meek surrender.

Sólrun had suggested that they both go to some of the museums in Tórshavn and she explained that there were three that they must visit. The Listasavn Føroya, the national art museum that permanently exhibits a substantial amount of Faroese art. She had said it was a good place to understand the Faroese psyche by studying the artistic depictions within.

She had also suggested that they go and visit the Norðurlandahúsið, the Nordic House, a purpose built institution that supported and promoted Nordic and Faroese culture, both locally and throughout the Nordic regions. Her final suggestion was the Føroya Fornminnissavn, the National Museum of the Faroe Islands. She hinted that the Føroya Fornminnissavn had some great exhibitions on the maritime history of the islands, including one concerning the SS

Sauternes, the Jólaskipið, and that the restaurant was also a very good place to have lunch.

Daniel had laughed at her subtle mentioning of a suitable luncheon venue and lifted his car keys up from the kitchen table. A pinging noise was coming from Sólrun's computer and he went over to investigate. The toolbar was flashing to indicate that the search for documents and files referencing 'Sandáfløttur' was complete. He opened the search field and discovered that a considerable amount of information had been found, mainly documents, but there were a few PDF files, photographs and videos. He copied the entirety of the search and then pasted it all over into a new folder that he had created on the computer's desktop, 'Justice 1'. He explained to Sólrun what he had done and asked her to close down her computer.

"Your search for justice starts with that folder. Go through it all and decide what is relevant and what is not. Keep a note of what you find and then start another search by typing in the name or title of whatever you hope to find. If you keep doing that, you will eventually start to create a spider's web of information that you can use to connect unrelated matters with each other. It is time consuming and laborious, but believe me, it will be a worthwhile process for you to do. By establishing all the contact points of the spider's web through their connections with each other, you will unravel the mystery and the underlying deceit that you are adamant that Heri has committed"

She shut down the computer. "Well I'm not doing it today, or any time soon for that matter. I'll make a start on it next week

when you're away. Come on, let's go and see some culture."
and she pulled him towards the front door.

They had spent an enjoyable day at the three museums and
Sólrun had even got to have her lunch in the Føroya
Fornminnissavn. For Daniel, the Heritage Museum had been a
revelation and had provided him with an authorative
appreciation of the tragic circumstances of the sinking of the
SS Sauternes and the effect that its story had placed in the
minds of the Faroese. He now fully understood that his
forthcoming salvage attempt was of huge importance to this
small community, and any successful recovery of the coins
was going to further embolden the story.

The return journey back to Sólrun's house had seen them
both discuss what was happening over the next week or so.
Sólrun still had a few days leave to take and would initially go
with Daniel and Ingi to Klaksvik to collect some equipment
and then go on to Viðareiði, the proposed base of operations
for the salvage attempt. Ingi's ship, the Nord Kaperen, was
berthed nearby in a small village called Hvannasund. She was
available until Wednesday and then she had to return to work.
She was looking forward to being involved with the salvage
expedition. Daniel was also glad of her involvement and told
her so.

They had just finished their meal and were washing the
dishes and tidying things up when there was a knock at the
door. Ingi had arrived. Sólrun welcomed him in to the house
and led him through to the sitting room. He joined Daniel on
the sofa and Sólrun returned from the kitchen, passed them
some bottles of beer and sat in the armchair facing them.

"So what's the plan of action for tonight then sailor boys?" she teased them both as she drank from her own bottle of beer. Daniel shot her a stern look of rebuke and then lightened his countenance.

"I was hoping that our good friend Ingi would go on a special solo reconnaissance mission tonight and give us both the night off." suggested Daniel. Ingi almost choked in mid gulp of his beer and spluttered "What?"

Daniel and Sólrun could not contain their laughter at the sight of a red-faced and indignant Ingi. He joined in with their laughter.

"Very funny. You've had your joke but what's the plan?" he asked. Daniel waited for Ingi's face to return to its normal colour and allowed him to finish quaffing his beer.

"Sólrun and I have to go and meet someone and we were both wondering if you could do us a wee favour tonight and go to Lindemann's lecture in the Raohus. You aren't known to anyone up here and you will be able to give us both a full de-brief of his lecture tomorrow when we are driving to Klaksvik. If you can go to the lecture and be anonymous, but watchful of the evening's events, you might pick up on some things that we have missed."

Ingi opened another beer and toasted them both. "Thanks for your planning of my Saturday evening entertainment for me." he scorned.

"I take it you want me to assess what's going on then? I can tell you for a start that Lindemann is leaving tomorrow because he was ordering a car to take him to the airport. I was down at the reception getting some directions and he was settling his bill in advance and sorting out his ride to Vágar.

We had a brief conversation and he was very pleasant and seemed awfully pleased with himself."

Daniel rounded on Ingi. "You spoke to Lindemann? What were the two of you discussing?" he demanded. Ingi took another swig of his beer.

"Nothing of any consequence Daniel, so enough of the attitude. We just remarked that the Faroes were not what we had both expected, he told me what he was up here for and I told him what I was doing. It was just passing the time of day as we waited to get attended to. He knew all about us and said that he had met you and wished that our expedition was a success. I returned the sentiment and wished him all the best with his lecture tonight." Ingi reached into a pocket and pulled out a business card.

"He even gave me his business contact details and invited me along tonight if I was available. I said I might pop along". Daniel laughed and slapped Ingi's knee.

"Sorry Ingi. I should have known you would have been sociable with him. Apologies to you my old friend for ever doubting you. What were you getting directions for anyway?"

Ingi reached into his jacket and pulled out long range weather reports and satellite images of the Faroes and the North Atlantic. "I wanted to find the best route to Sornfelli, a mountain not far from here. The mountain top is a plateau and has a military radar installation and a meteorological station sited there. I drove up and spoke to guys at both places and said who I was and they gave me all these printouts."

Daniel studied the printouts. He was impressed. Ingi had managed to obtain TAFS (terminal aerodrome forecast) and METAR weather reports for the next 7 days. These types of reports are predominantly used by pilots and meteorologists to assist in their weather forecasting. But the satellite images that Ingi had been given were high definition screenshots of real-time coverage from three earth orbiting satellites.

Daniel exclaimed. "How did you get these Ingi? These are better than what we used to get on the job."

Ingi simply replied. "It's amazing what you can get with a bit of charm Daniel. You should try it someday."

Sólrun giggled at the banterish exchange between the two men and understood that they were really close friends who delighted in gently ribbing each other. They reminded her of an old married couple who constantly sniped at each other but loved one another deeply.

Ingi started to explain the images. "These are from the NOAA-19 satellite, the National Oceanic and Atmospheric Administration polar orbiter. It does about 14 orbits a day and the fifth one is directly over the Faroes, so I was able to get these quite easily. These three images are from MetOp B, a polar orbiting meteorological satellite operated by the European Organisation for the Exploitation of Meteorological Satellites (EUMETSAT). But the piece de resistance are these images." and handed Daniel four sheets of paper. Daniel was struggling to understand what they detailed.

"What's this?" he asked.

"Ah! Daniel my boy, these are simply the dog's bollocks. Ooops! Sorry Sólrun. The guys up in the meteorological station made a telephone call to a bloke at Dundee University in Scotland for me. I spoke to someone called Andy Robertson and explained to him what I was after. This Andy Robertson told me that he managed the University's relaying station for the NERC Satellite, the Natural Earth Research Centre's Earth Observation satellite that does all sort of fancy monitoring of climate and environmental change in the North Atlantic region."

Ingi lit a cigarette before continuing. He felt that he needed to have one to hand before he carried on explaining matters. "Andy has given me access to SeaWiFs, the Sea-viewing Wide Field-of-view Sensor, and we now have access to an up-to-the-minute live feed of the North Atlantic Drift, the Norwegian Current and the waters around the islands of Borðoy, Viðoy, Fugloy and Svínoy. We need this type of information." Ingi started to point at a number of locations on the images and then continued speaking.

"The Norway Current enters the Norwegian Sea north of Scotland and flows northeastward along the coast of Norway before flowing into the Barents Sea. The current exerts a moderating influence on the climate of Norway and the rest of northern Europe. The main flow of the water reaches a velocity of about 0.5 knots and is dispersed westwards in eddies that meet those of the southwest-flowing East Greenland Current. The meeting point of these two currents is Svínoy, where the North Atlantic joins the Norwegian Sea. The pull of the water is tremendous, and if you make a mistake while down at the ship, these currents are going to take you with them at speed. We won't be able to rescue you in time. Just look what happened to the sailors of the Sauternes. There were 25 men on board when it started to sink and only 6 of their bodies were ever recovered. You're going to be at a depth of 100 metres and there's no chance of me saving you if you go and make an arse of it."

Sólrun left the room and went into the kitchen. Daniel and Ingi could hear her running up the stairs. Ingi looked at Daniel. "Sorry. I think I may have said something that Sólrun didn't like the sound of. If I was you I would go and see that she's alright."

He looked at his watch. It was almost 6.00pm. "Daniel. I'll go just now and get something to eat and then I'll head over to the Raohus for this lecture for you. It better be good and there better be drink and nibbles on the go. I need suitable sustenance to do these boring jobs, by the way." and he patted his stomach. Daniel laughed.

"I don't think there is enough food or alcohol on the islands to keep you suitably sustained." and put his arm around Ingi's shoulder as they made for the front door.

"See you at breakfast tomorrow with looking to leave for Klaksvik about 10.00am?" Daniel asked Ingi.

"Yep. That's a date. I think you might want to deal with more pressing matters though." and he casted his eyes up the stairs.

"Yeah. I know." replied Daniel as he closed the front door.

Daniel walked slowly up the stairs and chapped politely on Sólrun's bedroom door. There was no answer and he entered the room. She was lying face down on her bed with her head in a pillow. Daniel sat on the bed beside her and asked her what was wrong. She lifted her head and turned to face to him. Her hazel-green eyes were filled with tears and her make-up had become blotchy.

"You never told me that your dive was so dangerous and that you could die if you made a mistake." she sobbed. Daniel cuddled her and re-assured her that Ingi was only giving worst case scenarios and that she had nothing to worry about.

"Sorry you had to hear that Sólrun, but we were trained to deal with negative situations and that there may not be a happy ending. It's second nature to us and we've become impervious to it, but I can see why you got upset. You have nothing to worry about. I'll be fine."

Sólrun's face brightened at his last words. "Who are we supposed to be meeting tonight anyway? You never said anything about that earlier and I'll need to get changed and sort myself out."

As she tried to get off the bed, he pulled her back onto its covers. "There is no meeting anyone tonight. I just said that to Ingi to get him out the way for the evening."

Sólrun started to say something but was stopped as Daniel kissed her.

The Stream

Daniel and Ingi both parked up outside Sólrun's house and ran up the steps to the front door. She had already opened it for them and seemed pleased to see them.

"I have packed a picnic for us to have on the way. I've made a couple of flasks of coffee as well." and led them through to the sitting room. She had been busy as bags were packed and ready to go. All of Daniel's paraphernalia such as his laptop/tablet hybrid, notes, folders and documents had been neatly placed inside his red rucksack. His black holdall lay beside it. A pot of coffee awaited them on the small table in the middle of the floor and she poured them both a mugful that she passed to them.

"Thanks." said Ingi and Daniel in unison. Daniel handed Sólrun the car-keys to the Touareg.

"Is it alright if I leave the car here? I was thinking that we could all go in Ingi's and you could then drive his back on Wednesday. I don't know how long we are going to be involved for the dive and we don't really need them once we get to Viðareiði." Sólrun took the keys and hung them on a peg on the kitchen door.

"No problem. I'll sort out the return of the car when I'm back at work."

Ingi had all the car doors open and was fastidiously packing everything away. First to go in was the painting tool bag and he took great care in stowing it away safely. He placed his own travel bag alongside Daniel's holdall and then put Sólrun's weekend bag and the picnic hamper to the front. He flung coats and shoes into the spaces and slammed the boot door shut.

"Are you two ready?" shouted Ingi and Daniel and Sólrun came down the steps to join him. Sólrun jumped in the front passenger seat.

"I'll give you directions. I know a few shortcuts." Daniel went in the backseat and humphed his disapproval. Sólrun turned round and wagged a finger at him. "You said we should all go in Ingi's car. He's driving, I'm the navigator, so why don't you just settle down and be a good little tailgunner and keep an eye out for bandits?"

Ingi had to put the back of his hand over his mouth to stifle a laugh. He thought that the Second World War bomber reference was hilarious. He had always liked Sólrun even though he had only known her for about a week. He looked in his rear-view mirror and could see that Daniel was sulking.

Ingi followed Sólrun's directions and they went through the suburb of Hoyvík and along the coastal road, the Kaldbaksvegur, past the pretty village of Hvítanes. Sólrun explained that the Faroese government was planning to build a 6km long tunnel under the sea from the village over to the island of Eysturoy and Skálafjørður. They had just driven past the village of Kaldbaksbotnur when the inside of the car was suddenly plunged into darkness. Daniel sat forward and asked what was happening. Sólrun was surprised at Daniel's reaction, but presumed that he had started to drift off to sleep and had got a fright.

"You are currently underneath a mountain range valley called Mjørkadalur. There used to be a Danish Naval base here until about 10 years ago. Ingi was at all that remains of it yesterday when he was up Sornfelli at the meteorological station and the radar installation." She went on to explain that they had just entered a 3km long tunnel called the Kollfjarðartunnilin that connected the small village of Kaldbaksbotnur with Kollafjørður at the other end.

"What is it with the Faroese and tunnels? It seems to be a national pastime." blurted Daniel.

"It is." replied Sólrun. "The building of them creates employment, connects villages and towns, reduces national expenditure with ferry upkeep and ensures that our population will survive on these islands. If you want to see a tunnel, wait until we get to Leirvík and the Norðoyatunnilin. It's over 6km long and runs between the islands of Eysturoy and Borðoy. It connects Leirvík on Eysturoy with Klaksvík over on the island of Borðoy. It's another sub-sea tunnel like the Vágar one that's also 150 metres below sea level, goes through the solid basalt rock and under the Leirvíksfjørður strait and the Atlantic Ocean."

They passed through the village of Kollafjørður and Daniel leaned forward and laid his elbows on the backs of the front-seat chairs.

"So Ingi? How did it go last night with Lindemann and his lecture?"

Ingi continued focusing on the road ahead. "It was very good actually. I was really impressed with what Lindemann had to say and show and he's got a sense of humour. Some of his speech was very funny. I now know more about genetics, DNA profiles and this new science of epigenetics than I did this time yesterday. If what Lindemann says is happening just now in tests becomes fully developed and put to use, most of the debilitating diseases and cancers that are currently afflicting mankind could be eradicated by the end of this century. It was quite scary listening to what he had to say and some of the examples that he used were quite thought provoking."

"Are you taking the piss now Ingi? What really happened? Were the Scottish students there and was Lindemann talking to any of them?" gasped Daniel.

Ingi looked at his friend in the rear-view mirror. He could see that Daniel was rattled and wanted to know explicit details of the night's events.

"Daniel, it was a bit of a damp squib to be honest. Lindemann rocked up, spoke to a few dignitaries, shook a few hands, had a glass of wine or two, ate a few canapés, did his presentation, held a question and answer session for about 20 minutes, thanked everyone for attending, mingled for a while afterwards and then left for the hotel. The Scottish students were there. They were sitting in a group right in front of me but they left right after Lindemann had finished his piece. Their group leaders were keen to get them all out of the Raohus and on to the next items on their itinerary. I picked up on some conversations about going over to the parliament and then star gazing. I spoke to a few people afterwards while keeping an eye on Lindemann until he left with some guy that looked like a pig and a Danish woman that seemed to be in charge of the evening. I know that because I left when they did and followed them. Lindemann went into the hotel and the other two went into the Café Natur for a drink. So did I. They were still there when I left at 2.00am."

Daniel patted Ingi on the shoulder.

The Stream

"Ingi Mortensen, may I present to you Heri Jorgensen and Dr. Mette Bundgaard, the frolicking couple that you watched in glorious night vision and thermal imagery the other night. Sounds like you had a fun evening."

They had just driven on to the island of Streymoy, having crossed the Oyrarbakki Bridge, and swiftly through the village of the same name when Ingi suddenly pulled the car over into a parking bay and turned off the engine. He looked over his right shoulder at the grinning face of Daniel behind him.

"Are you seriously telling me that that fat, specky pig of a man was having" he looked at Sólrun and chose his words carefully "a drink-fuelled sexual rampage with that Danish doctor woman the other night and I watched it all unfold?".
Daniel nodded in the affirmative. Sólrun suddenly piped up in a voice of disbelief.

"Heri was shagging Dr. Mette Bundgaard? Get away with yourself. No Way?"

Daniel continued nodding. All three of them erupted with laughter hued with embarrassment. Sólrun asked if they wanted a coffee and got out the car to rescue the hamper from the boot. Ingi got out and leaned on the bonnet of the car and lit a cigarette. He was still shaking his head in disbelief when Sólrun handed him a coffee.

"I can't understand what that woman sees in pig-boy? I just can't."

Daniel had wandered down the road and was taking in the scenery when Sólrun approached him with a coffee. He took hold of the mug and sipped gently at the warm contents.

"These islands of yours are stunning. The scenery is breathtaking. Every time you think it cannot get any better, it does. You cannot get bored with this." and waved his free hand around at the surrounding geography. Sólrun agreed with him but countered his reasoning with a stark statement.

"If you are born and bred here, you get used to it all and get bored with it at the same time. All the way through your teenage years you become desperate to do well at school and go on to university in Denmark, Germany or the UK or to get a job anywhere but the Faroes. Most of the late teenage population leaves on finishing school and less than a third of them ever return permanently. There is the fear of becoming trapped on some islands in the middle of nowhere and under-achieving and not fulfilling your dreams. There is also considerable parental pressure on you to escape and not make the mistakes that their generation did. I'm guilty of it. I had left, gone to Denmark, got myself a degree and a decent job and I was never returning. Like so many Faroese, they leave and never return. Family bereavement brought me back here and circumstances made me remain. I have lived a full life and I have achieved what I always wanted as a youngster, but it is only really now that I fully appreciate where I am from and what I can decide to do, or not do."

Daniel put an arm round her. "Well I'm glad that you are right here, right now." She hugged him and kissed him.

"Ahem." coughed Ingi. "I think we should be making tracks."

They uncoupled and headed back to the car. Sólrun tidied the hamper back in the boot and they continued on their journey to Klaksvík.

"We are over half way there. We are not far from Leirvík." she told them both.

The Stream

Ingi carried on driving and was now driving along the Skipanesvegur, a road that seemed to cling to the sharp slopes of the steep mountains that fall into the dark blue waters of the Skálafjørður. The Skipanesvegur arrives at the village of Skipanes and just beyond the village is the left-fork junction to go inland to head for Leirvík, through the Norðoyatunnilin and into Klaksvík.

He followed the signs and maneuvered the vehicle around a flock of black faced sheep at the junction. Daniel tapped Sólrun's shoulder and pointed at the sheep.

"Are they related to Heri?" he asked her and she smiled back at him. Daniel continued to marvel at the scenery of stark green mountains that seemed to rise straight up from the sea and towards the sky and coloured by the blur of the brightly painted churches and houses of the villages that they drove through.

At Leirvík, Ingi drove through the town towards the dark entrance of the Norðoyatunnilin. Differently coloured boathouses lined the shore of the sea-fjord and the water was like the flat glass of a mirror, reflecting back images of all that was around to be seen. Whoosh! They had entered the tunnel and it was a marked descent into the bowels of the earth. All three occupants of the car could feel their ears popping as they drove 150 metres below sea-level and under the Atlantic Ocean. The tunnel itself is two lanes blasted through solid basalt and brightly lit with coloured bulbs and images. Sólrun explained that a local artist had designed the colouration effect and that it was classified as a work of art. The eventual ascent and emergence from the tunnel caused their ears to pop again and they had to adjust their vision to being back in daylight. The town of Klaksvík lay before them.

Ingi drove down into the town and parked at the cemetery.

"Daniel, you need to see this" and walked through the gate into the grounds. He had stopped at six graves and waited for Daniel to join him. Side by side, the gravestones bore the details of the six bodies that had been recovered from the sinking of the SS Sauternes.

Captain George Albert Perris, 34 years, RASC.
Richard Smith, 35 years.
John Daniel McNicol, 21 years.
Robert Ross, 25 years.
Peter McKenzie Cormack, 21 years.
Unidentified man, approximately 35 years.

Daniel knelt down to read an inscription on one of the gravestones. 'He would not have you weep nor idly pray for him who gave his yet young life'. A tear formed in his eye as he stood up and took a pace backwards to stand beside Ingi. In unison, they saluted the graves and both men began to sing the Navy Hymn.

'Eternal Father, strong to save,
Whose arm hath bound the restless wave,
Who bidd'st the mighty ocean deep,
Its own appointed limits keep;
Oh, hear us when we cry to Thee,
For those in peril upon the sea!'

They finished the verse, bowed their heads and retired back on to the path.

"Thanks Ingi. I am glad you brought me here and I have been able to pay my respects to those brave men. With what I have learned over the last few days about the sinking of the ship, that simple and emotive display of respect towards those men was the least that I could do."

Ingi walked slowly beside Daniel. "As men of the sea ourselves, they deserve that we remember them."

Sólrun stood by the gate of the graveyard and watched them walking back towards her. She knew where they had just been and had witnessed their act of remembrance at the sides of the six graves. She returned to the car and poured them both some coffee and brought out some sandwiches for them to eat. Both Ingi and Daniel thanked her for the gesture and she left them alone to gather their thoughts and wandered into the graveyard.

She had studied the gravestones for herself and had discovered that these six perished sailors had all been younger than she was. These men had lived in the tumultuous times of a global conflict that had changed the modern world forever. The comforts of present day living had all been achieved as a result of the unnecessary loss of numerous lives, like these six sailors, and millions of other people around the world, in an era that had borne unheralded cruelty, brutality, bloodshed and savagery upon the human race. Their sacrifice must never be forgotten.

She came back over to the car and Ingi had stated that he needed to go to the post office, the Posta, and find out if his parcels had arrived. They all got back in the car and Sólrun directed him to the post office. On arrival at the Posta, Ingi and Daniel left Sólrun in the car as they went in to collect Ingi's parcel. About ten minutes had passed before they slowly came back to the car weighed down with the carrying of what looked like heavy packages. She got out the car and opened the boot and the back passenger doors for them to place the parcels.

"What's in the packages, Ingi?" she asked.

"Daniel's early birthday present. He's costing me a fortune. Seriously though, this is the specialist re-breather diving equipment that he needs to have if we want to successfully locate the coins. The other package arrives tomorrow, and Daniel will definitely need that to recover the coins. It's a bespoke underwater plasma torch that he can use to cut through the metal of the ship. The coins are in a steel box bolted to the floor of the Captain's cabin. Find the cabin, you find the coins, but getting the steel box out and to the surface is the tricky bit, hence why I ordered up the re-breather and the torch.

With the re- breather unit, Daniel can work at depth, he'll be less laden down with bulky breathing tanks as he'll only need conventional SCUBA breathing equipment to return to the surface in the event of a problem with the rebreather. This will make him much more stream-lined and moving around the wreck will be easier for him. He's using a fully closed circuit re-breather apparatus. You see the two small bottles. He'll only need a fraction of those for the entire dive! The one on the left, the trimix, allows him to work at depth with a clear head and the one on the right, the oxygen, is what his body is actually burning and will also optimise his decompression.

Both are essential on a dive to this depth! Daniel's going to be on the edge of the capacity of the re-breather, but he's using a Danish naval unit that has been tested to a depth of 120 metres by the Frømandskorpset.

There are no air bubbles released from a re-breather as everything the diver exhales is internally scrubbed and re-used. And air bubbles in an enclosed space underwater can cause all manner of problems such as unsettling materials off the ceilings and walls and obscuring visibility to work in. The plasma torch also doesn't generate air bubbles when in use and somewhat reduces the need of elbow grease by the operator. You just light it up and point and it'll start to cut."

Ingi shut the doors of the car and got in behind the steering wheel.

"Let's get this show back on the road and dump this stuff at the boat moored over at Hvannasund and then we can head to the hotel and relax for a bit. I want to go for a walk and show you both something."

Daniel and Sólrun fastened their seat belts and sat back as Ingi drove the last part of their journey to Viðareiði and the Hotel Nord, the northernmost point of the Faroe Islands.

Driving northwards out of Klaksvík along the Stangavegur, the road suddenly forks at the village of Ánir. Ánir lies about 3 km north of Klaksvík on the west coast of Borðoy and faces the southern tip of the island of Kunoy. The left-hand fork takes you through the village and on to Strond, where the road crosses a causeway to the island of Kunoy to connect with the villages of Haraldssund and Kunoy. Ingi took the right-hand fork and started to drive up the side of the steep mountain slope. Daniel whistled as he espied the smart modern villas that had been built between the fork of the road.

"They must cost a packet to buy" he mused out loud as they continued to climb.

Sólrun began to explain that Ánir had been annexed to Klaksvík and a lot of money had been invested locally with building a new harbour and container port for the village. Luxury villas had been built about 10 years previously and there were more planned as the economy was improving and the population was increasing. She turned round and smiled at Daniel.

"I know how you like tunnels, so be prepared for the next 5 kilometres or so. We're about to enter the Borðoyartunlarnir, a pair of unlit, single lane tunnels that connect Klaksvík with the eastern side of Borðoy and allows you to cross over to the island of Viðoy. This is called the Árnafjarðartunnilin."

The car was plunged once more into the darkness of a tunnel and Ingi put the car's headlights on full beam.

"This tunnel comes out above the small town of Árnafjørður. It lies way below us on the right at the bottom of a deep inlet called the Árnfjarðarvík, 'corner fjord's bay'."

Daniel could see the opening of the tunnel looming towards him in the dark.

"We drive about 100 metres and then we will be entering into the Hvannasundstunnilin."

The car emerged into bright sunlight and as Daniel looked to his right to view the town of Árnafjørður below him, Ingi chicaned the roadway and entered into the 2 kilometre long Hvannasundstunnilin and more darkness.

The Stream

"This tunnel will take us to the village of Norðdepil which lies on the east coast of Borðoy and is directly across from the village of Hvannasund over the water on the island of Viðoy. Norðdepil has been connected with Hvannasund by means of a road dam since about 1963. A large cracked rock rests just north of Hvannasund and there is an old Faroese legend that claims that this rock, Skrudhettan, split and cracked at the very moment of the birth of Jesus Christ."

Daniel sat back and stared straight ahead and focused on the widening horseshoe of daylight at the end of the tunnel. It wasn't that he was scared, it was just that, as a passenger in a car, he found tunnels disorientating when you went from near darkness into daylight. If he was driving, the tunnels wouldn't have been an issue as they would have been all part of the concentration process that one requires while in charge of a moving vehicle.

The horseshoe in the distance got closer and closer and finally, after what seemed an eternity, they spurted clear of the innards of the mountain and out into the light. Norðdepil was about a kilometre below them to the left and Hvannasund was directly across a narrow strip of water spanned by a dam. Daniel gasped as he took in the view that instantly hit him outwith the enclosed darkness of the tunnel. The road meandered along the steep incline of the mountains on the eastern side of Borðoy towards Norðdepil, but what transfixed his attention was that Hvannasund appeared to lie at the foot of an almost obliquely vertical sloped mountain range that disappeared into the distance. He could see the Nord Kaperen berthed in the small harbour on the other side of the fjord. Although it was a large marine salvage vessel, its size was dwarfed by the menacing pitch of the rock above and all around it.

They quickly crossed the dam and turned right towards the harbour. A couple of deck-hands waved from the Nord Kaperen as they realised that Ingi had returned. A reception committee met them as they parked beside the ship. There was a lot of excited conversation and Daniel was introduced to the crew who all shook his hand and treated him like some all-conquering hero. He was getting slightly embarrassed by the adulation and made a mental note to ask Ingi what he had been telling these men. Their attention was thankfully diverted when Sólrun stepped out of the car. The reaction of the men was comical and both Ingi and Daniel chortled as they studied the collective ogling of the crew towards Sólrun. It was as if they had never seen a woman before, let alone someone as alluring as she. Daniel reckoned she milked the moment by nonchalantly shaking her hair to the side to catch their attention. The crew's faces were glued to the mesmeric direction that her flowing locks followed. To be fair to the crew, it wasn't everyday you encountered a bewitching black haired beauty that was almost 6 feet tall.

Ingi shouted at the crew.

"Right you lot, this is Sólrun and she will be working with us for a few days. She's a Faroese government representative that will be monitoring our work, so she has to be treated with the upmost respect if you want to get paid. There are some packages in the car that are to be stowed away in my cabin, so get on with it. Chop, chop!"

The crew swarmed around the car and emptied it of the packages and took them aboard the Nord Kaperen. Daniel watched the last of the crew disappear onboard and he noticed a small Jolly Roger and a raven banner flying above the ship's bridge. Catching sight of the two pennants brought a smile to Daniel's face as he remembered that Ingi always thought of himself as something of a modern-day buccaneer, hence the pirate flag, and the raven banner symbolised the weather vanes used aboard Viking long ships on their voyages of discovery and plunder.

Sólrun walked over the quayside towards him and leaned against the door frame of the car.

"You enjoyed teasing the men back there, didn't you?" he asked her. She feigned ignorance of what he meant.

"Jealous are we, Mr. Lauridsen?" and got back into the car.

Daniel took his place in the back seat and Ingi jogged down the gangway from the ship and joined them in the car.

"The restaurant of the Hotel Norð is calling my stomach. I'm starving and I need to be fed." proclaimed Ingi as he turned the car out of the harbour and began to head towards Viðareiði.

They had been driving in silence for about 5 minutes until Sólrun asked why she had been referred to as a Faroese government representative. Ingi just laughed and replied to her.

"Sólrun my dear, it is not often that a working maritime ship has female company onboard, and the crew can get, em, distracted if you know what I mean. They are all scared of me, in complete awe of Daniel, and with me saying that you were there in an official capacity was to quell whatever stirrings there may be dwelling amongst them. You saw how they all gaped at you when you got out of the car back there. It was for your own personal protection. Nothing would happen to you anyway, but I'm not taking any chances."

Sólrun thanked him for his thoughtfulness towards her safety. Daniel couldn't resist the moment.

"So Ingi, what is it that you have gone and told your crew about me then? They treated me if I was some sort of superstar."

Ingi looked in his rear-view mirror and caught his good friend's gaze. "Oh that's simple Daniel. I told them about your rescue mission in Afghanistan and the four nurses. To them, you are a living legend that's also going to find the money aboard the SS Sauternes."

Daniel just sighed and looked out the window at the passing scenery. "Nothing like putting a bit of pressure on me, eh Ingi?" and both men laughed. Sólrun was perplexed though. "What's this rescue mission in Afghanistan?" she asked.

Daniel just looked at Ingi looking back at him in the rear-view mirror. "You better spill the beans Ingi. Everyone else seems to know the story apart from Sólrun." Ingi told Sólrun the story about the rescue of the four nurses.

They shortly arrived at Viðareiði, the northernmost village of the Faroe Islands that straddles an isthmus with high mountains located to both the north and south. After checking in at the Hotel Norð and visiting the restaurant, Ingi was most insistent that the three of them should go for a walk. He was desperate to show something to them. They had walked a few hundred metres when Ingi suddenly stopped and started to point out aspects to be seen from where they stood.

"To the west, we have the three islands of Borðoy, Kunoy and Kalsoy. To the north here, we have Cape Enniberg, which at 754 metres tall makes it the highest sea-cliff in Europe. And to the east we have the islands of Fugloy and Svínoy." Ingi was excited and pointed at the island of Fugloy.

"That's the open North Atlantic from here to Fugloy. There's the village of Kirkja about 10km distant on the island. The water between Fugloy and Svínoy is called Fugloyfjørður. The SS Sauternes went down somewhere in that stretch of water between the two islands. We are going to find it this week Daniel and recover the coins. Yes we are." and he skipped a little dance.

Daniel watched his friend and then looked at the open water and the calmness on the surface. It looks peaceful enough but what lies below was what worried Daniel.

One single mistake by him while doing the dive attempt and his dead body would probably be found somewhere to the north of Norway.

The Stream

The waitress had just cleared away the breakfast plates from the table and refilled their coffee mugs for them. Ingi was excited and had the air of expectation of a small child about to open birthday presents. It was a mixture of contentment and anticipation as the many months of planning, preparation and investigation for his expedition were about to be realised as today was the day that the search for the coins onboard the SS Sauternes commenced.

Sólrun and Daniel were discussing how recovered items from the ship would be transported to the surface. Daniel explained that there were various types of underwater salvage lifting bags that could be used.

"The type Ingi has on board are like parachutes in reverse. You fill the parachute with air to give it buoyancy and it will then float upwards to the surface carrying its payload. Once it surfaces, divers will secure the attached payload and one of the ship's cranes will then lift the payload onto the deck. Depending on the payload weight and shape of the 'items of treasure', different types of bag are used to get recovered salvage to the surface. Ingi, how many coins are there supposed to be in the steel box aboard the Sauternes?"

Ingi went into his jacket pocket and extracted a small notebook and leafed through the pages. "I have a note of the details of the coins and the rough dimensions of the steel box that they are in. It's all in British imperial measurement scales and I haven't got around to working out the metric conversion but the guys at the Royal Mints in Denmark and London both said the steel box and coins would weigh about 180 kilograms all in. The London Royal Mint guy joked with me and said the steel box would be about the size of a microwave oven with the weight of two dead men."

Ingi passed over his notebook to Sólrun and Daniel opened up his laptop/tablet hybrid and sourced an imperial measurement to metric conversion site.

"Sólrun, start reading out to me those British dimensions please? Will you write down the metric conversion beside Ingi's notes as well?"

She nodded.

"Each coin weighs 0.23 ounces."

Daniel replied with "6.5 grams."

Sólrun noted the figure down and moved on with

"The thickness is 0.07 inches."

Daniel did the conversion and said

"1.85 millimetres. Next."

"The diameter is 1 inch."

Again Daniel tapped the details in and replied with the conversion. "24.55 millimetres."

Daniel asked for the notebook and started to work out some figures. He wrote various numerical details down in Ingi's notebook as he retrieved answers from his computer screen. He then started to doodle a three dimensional box in the notebook and passed his artwork around for both Sólrun and Ingi to admire.

"Going by the British records, the coins were packed in paper tubes that each contained 200 coins. The paper tubes were laid in rows of 15. Using the dimensions of the coins as a guide, each paper tube is about 40 centimetres long and about

2.5 centimetres wide which is a width of 37.5 centimetres."
Daniel drew their attention to his drawing of the steel box.

"That's 3000 coins per row, so there'll be nearly 9 vertical
columns of coins packed 15 across giving us 26,000 coins in
total. The height of the box will be about 20 centimetres. If
each coin weighs 6.5 grams, multiply that by 26,000 gives us a
weight of 169 kilograms, and if we factor in the construction of
the steel box, the total weight is going to be about 175
kilograms. Yeah, your pal in London was right Ingi. The steel
box is about the size of a microwave oven and will be about
your weight."

Daniel winked at Sólrun and waited on his friend's reaction.
"I'm not that fat yet, so enough of the weight jokes if you don't
mind?" was Ingi's calm reply. He lifted his coffee cup to take a
sip and burst out laughing.

"That's what I miss about the old days Daniel. The repartee,
the banter, the camaraderie and that's why I am so glad you
are here with me for this trip." and leaned over and slapped
his thigh.

"Me too, Ingi. Me too. They were good times. We will
probably need to use an M5 lifting bag to get the coins up to
the surface. Hopefully there'll be no obstructions on the ship
and the box will slide out of the cabin when I inflate the
buoyancy parachute to take them upwards."

Sólrun finished her coffee and set the mug back down on the
table. "What are we going to do today then boys? Do you not
have a plasma thingme to pick up from the Posta in
Klaksvík?"

Ingi returned his mug to the table, pocketed his notebook
and fumbled around for his car keys.

"I do, Sólrun, I do. I was planning to drop you two off at the ship in Hvannasund and I would head over to Klaksvík to get the torch. I was my intention to take the ship out for a recce over the SS Sauternes and take a few measurements and the like of the water conditions and the weather. Daniel will need to do a bit of arithmetic to use the re-breather set and the depth of the wreck and using a plasma torch."

"That's a good shout Ingi." replied Daniel. "It'll give me a chance to correctly gauge what mixes I need for the re-breather and also work out the descent time, how long I realistically have to find the steel box, cut it free and get it topside with the lifting bag, stow the cutter away and then start the long journey back to the surface."

He opened up the laptop/tablet hybrid and began to type in some equations. The machine whirred as it computed a table format. He turned the laptop around to show Sólrun who just stared blankly at what seemed like gobbledy-gook to her untrained eyes. Daniel spotted her expression and began to explain what each of the four vertical columns of figures and instructions in the table meant.

"Going by the specifications of the re-breather, I need to work out how long it's going to take me to dive to the wreck, how long I have down there and how long it's going to take to get me back up to the surface. I can then have the re-breather correctly calibrated to function properly for the depth I will be going to and what I will be attempting to carry out while I'm down at the wreck. There are a couple of additional things that I need to work out as well, but I have to do this one first. Here's another good reason for me buying this laptop the other day."

The Stream

Action	Depth	Duration	Dive Time
Descent	100m		(4)
Level	100m	16:00	(20)
Ascent	69m		(24)
Stop at	69m	0:34	(25)
Stop at	66m	1:00	(26)
Stop at	63m	1:00	(27)
Stop at	60m	1:00	(28)
Stop at	57m	1:00	(29)
Stop at	54m	1:00	(30)
Stop at	51m	1:00	(31)
Stop at	48m	1:00	(32)
Stop at	45m	1:00	(33)
Stop at	42m	2:00	(35)
Stop at	39m	2:00	(37)
Stop at	36m	2:00	(39)
Stop at	33m	4:00	(43)
Stop at	30m	3:00	(46)
Stop at	27m	4:00	(50)
Stop at	24m	6:00	(56)
Stop at	21m	6:00	(62)
Stop at	18m	8:00	(70)
Stop at	15m	10:00	(80)
Stop at	12m	13:00	(93)
Stop at	9m	18:00	(111)
Stop at	6m	76:00	(187)
Surface			(187)

The Stream

Ingi was keen to leave and get the day started. "If you two can gather all your stuff together, I'll get you at the car in 5 minutes." and left for the hotel foyer. Sólrun stood up from the table and suggested to Daniel that he do the same.

"I think that was a subtle hint from Ingi that he's keen to get 'Operation Coin Recovery' started. Shall we go?"

Daniel tucked the laptop under his right arm and intertwined his left arm with Sólrun's right.

"A day of arithmetical equations is before me.". The sun was splitting the sky and its warmth could be felt when they stepped outside the hotel.

"You could always tease the men on the ship by doing a bit of sun-bathing." he suggested. She broke free and slapped him on the shoulder.

"Maybe I should and maybe I could be provocative as hell just to make sure that I grab their attention?"
He just laughed at her remark. "As Ingi said, your just being on the ship has grabbed their attention."

Ingi was already in the car and had the engine running. He was certainly focused on his day ahead and had even put on his sun-glasses. Daniel and Sólrun joined him in the car and they had hardly closed their respective doors as it sped away towards Hvannasund and Klaksvík. Daniel looked out his passenger window and again studied the landscape around him. The sharp cruelty of the surrounding mountain tops seemed to be in contrast to the stillness of the fjord waters. The intensity of the green grass slopes was certainly in contraposition to the slate grey-blue of the water, the same slate grey-blue waters that he would soon be submersing himself in.

The Stream

On arrival at Hvannasund, Ingi parked the car on the quayside beside the Nord Kaperen. Daniel and Sólrun had followed him aboard the vessel and watched him speak to the crew and bark a series of orders at others in the engine-room via an intercom. The whole ship started to shudder as the engines came to life as the power generation reverberated throughout the hull. The low hum of a powered vessel was music to Ingi's ears.

"Daniel. I'll go just now to the Posta and collect the plasma torch. Can you get the crew to get everything up and running and operational while I am away? It's 9.15am just now. I should be back about 10.30am and we could put out to sea by 11.00am. I want to take you and Sólrun over the site of the SS Sauternes and if the weather is fair, we can deploy and moor the floating jetties in anticipation of sending the first dive teams down tomorrow."

"No probs Ingi. I'll do that for you." said Daniel as Ingi left to drive to Klaksvík. He shouted more orders at various crew members and laughed and joked with them at their cutting and sarcastic replies.

Daniel explained to Sólrun that the mood of the crew would change as they were about to start the mission to recover the coins. The intensity of months of planning and preparation were about to be realised with actually commencing the salvage operation. Just getting to the shipwreck site and securing the floating jetties would be enough to release the pent up expectation and the crew would now focus on the tasks that lay ahead. A successful mission means bonuses in their pay-packets and increases their re-hiring opportunities for other adventures.

The Stream

Daniel spoke to some of the crew and asked them to unpackage the floating jetties, check the air tanks and prepare the rib boats for launching. The men went about their duties and Sólrun watched them from above from the bridge. The flurry of activity on the deck below her made her appreciate that she was possibly going to be a part of Faroese history if the coinage aboard the SS Sauternes was recovered.

When Daniel came back into the bridge, she asked him. "Do you think you'll be able to recover the coins?"

Daniel just walked over to his holdall and removed his laptop. "I wouldn't be here if I didn't think we could do it, but the pressure is all on me though. I need to get it right."

He switched on his laptop and started to work out some more of the re-breather calibrations. He looked at her and suggested that she might want to make some coffee. He led her to a small galley behind the bridge that was really a basic kitchen with running water, tea and coffee making facilities, a small fridge and a microwave.

"Sometimes we don't have time to go down to the mess-hall and we eat and drink on the go up here."

Daniel returned to his laptop and left Sólrun in the small galley. He could hear her opening cupboards and placing mugs and cutlery on the small work-top. He pressed the intercom button twice and asked if the helmsman could come to the bridge. A few minutes passed and a man in his late 20s entered into the bridge.

"Hi. I'm Neils Rothe, the helmsman. You were looking for me?" Daniel extended his hand out for a handshake which was accepted.

"Thanks for coming up. Ingi asked me to get everything started to be ready for leaving for the dive site as soon as he arrives back. Have you been out over the site at all?"

Neils shook his head. "We only arrived a few days ago and Ingi was waiting for your arrival before sailing over to the site. He also wanted to get some navigational and satellite information before venturing out into the Fugløfjord."

Daniel reached into his holdall and brought out the charts, images and satellite relays that Ingi had procured from the Sornfelli meteorological station.

"Ingi has been able to get us access onto the real-time TAFS and METAR weather reports. He has also arranged for us to be connected to the various satellites overhead and we can use Sea-WiFs while we are here."

Neils rushed forward and took the data sheets from Daniel. "How did he get access to Sea-Wifs? This makes this trip a whole lot easier."

Neils started switching on overhead monitors and began to type in access codes on the keyboard in front of him. One by one, the monitors came to life with different information being relayed on the various screens. Neils beamed a huge smile.

"I knew Ingi had a reputation of being able to get what he wanted, but to get access to this stuff is incredible. These are really military and scientific feeds that ordinary merchant vessels don't really get to see."

He looked at Daniel who had his index finger in front of his mouth and said. "Sssssshhhh!"

Both of them laughed and Daniel left Neils to continue with his preparations and checked in on Sólrun. She had made a pot of coffee and some sandwiches for them to eat. She brushed past Daniel and handed Neils a mug of coffee and a plate of sandwiches.

"Thanks very much. That's really nice of you to do that. I'm Neils. I'm the helmsman."

Sólrun smiled at him. "I'm Sólrun, the ship's distraction apparently and the monitor of this expedition for the Faroese Government."

Neils just replied with a simple "Oh!" and started to eat a sandwich.

Daniel followed Sólrun back into the galley and closed the door. "Play nice Sólrun. He's doing his job and was trying to be pleasant."

Sólrun shook her head at Daniel. "You really don't understand women much, do you? With me coming across as pleasant enough but slightly frosty with a point of view, Neils will now go and tell the rest of the crew that I am a bit of an ice-maiden and they should leave me alone and concentrate on their jobs and not me."

Daniel just nodded at her and left her alone in the galley. He crossed over to the port side of the bridge and looked out of one of the wide viewing windows.

Ingi had just pulled up on the quayside and was opening the rear of the car. He whistled at some of the crew who came over to help him unload some cumbersome packages. Daniel watched as crew-members came back aboard laden with the packages that he knew were the various components of an underwater plasma torch but he was fascinated as to what Ingi had in his hands. Ingi held a circular package that was about a metre wide in diameter in his left and a long cardboard tube in his right. He watched him come aboard and told Sólrun to get a coffee ready for Ingi. Ingi entered the bridge and placed his two packages on the pilot's seat and pressed the all-ship intercom button.

"Get everything ship-shape and in order. We set sail in 10 minutes."

He switched off the intercom and leaned over and gave the ship's horn three short blasts. The blasts echoed back off the surrounding mountains and appeared to be one long interrupted tone. He was grateful for the coffee and sandwiches that Sólrun handed him and he grunted acknowledgement of Neils at his station as he ate.

"What's in the parcels, Ingi?" asked Sólrun as she pointed at the two packages in the pilot's chair.

Ingi put his plate down and grabbed the long cardboard tube, removed a plastic stopper at one end and slowly withdrew the contents. It was a flag. A Faroe Islands flag, the Merkið, an azure blue-fimbriated red Nordic cross, offset to the left, on a white field background.

"Come with me Sólrun. We will do this together." and he opened a door and walked out onto the platform around the outside of the bridge.

"Flag etiquette and Danish Maritime regulations dictate that all merchant vessels must fly the courtesy ensign of the nation in whose territorial waters they are sailing in. These regulations also state that the ensign must be flown from the starboard yard-arm."

He gathered the halyard rope and attached the toggles to the eyelets at the end of the Merkið.

"Right Sólrun, you can hoist away now." and he watched her pull on the halyard rope to raise the flag. Once it was in position, he secured and fastened the halyard to the clip located on the side of the bridge.

"Thanks Sólrun. We can now officially leave port and go a-searching for treasure."

He guided her back into the bridge and pressed the ship's horn twice. The crew was now aware that the ship was about to get underway. Ingi spoke in the intercom to the engine room and the ship trembled as the engines began to turn over. Crew members unslung the mooring ropes from the bollards on the quayside and Ingi asked Neils to take the ship out and down the Hvannasund Fjord and towards the wreck of the SS Sauternes. A final and long blast of the ship's horn denoted the departure of the Nord Kaperen towards the open sea.

The sea looked fairly calm but when the Nord Kaperen ventured out of the protection of the Hvannasund Fjord to pass through the narrow stretch of water, Svínoyarsund, and into the open waters of the Atlantic between the islands of Fugloy and Svínoy, those aboard the bridge of the Nord Kaperen had to brace themselves against the doors, consoles and bulkheads as the vessel tipped and rolled out to sea.

The ship had ploughed through the calmish waters for about fifteen minutes when Ingi suddenly left the bridge and started to talk to the crew below him. He returned to the bridge and asked Neils to stop the vessel. Ingi flipped on the echo sounder and its pings reveal an image that is displayed on the screen of an overhead monitor – lying 100 metres below the Nord Kaperen, the final resting place of the SS Sauternes can be seen. Ingi pressed the ship's intercom and picked up the hand-set.

"Attention all crew. We are currently above the wreck of the SS Sauternes and with the weather being fair, we will shortly deploy the floating jetties in preparation for attempting the first dives in the morning. I want all crew members on the aft deck in 5 minutes. Ingi out."

Ingi replaced the hand-set and walked over to the circular package he had brought aboard at Hvannasund. He carefully unfastened its wrappings and revealed an ornate floral wreath. He turned around and said to Sólrun, Daniel and Neils.

"We are all here to do a job, but we must have respect for the memory of the 25 souls who perished when the ship sank. I want the crew and everyone involved with this expedition to remember the tragic circumstances that has led to us embarking on this expedition."

Sólrun, Daniel and Neils said nothing but the expressions on their faces confirmed to Ingi that he was correct in his thinking and they followed him as he left the bridge and headed towards the aft deck where the ship's crew was now gathering. Ingi called them over to the port side and pointed at the calm waters below.

"Crew. Below us lies the wreck of the SS Sauternes. We have come here to salvage part of its cargo, but before we do so, we, as men of the sea, must pay our respects to the 25 brave men that perished when the ship sank in December 1941. Please join me in a minute's silence in honour of the crew and passengers of the SS Sauternes."

Ingi carefully threw the floral wreath onto the surface waters above the wreck. Behind him, Daniel and Sólrun joined with the crew of the Nord Kaperen as they remembered those that had perished all those years ago. The minute passed and Ingi thanked everyone for their time to remember. He started to bark orders at them to go about their business and prepare to launch the rib boats, man the cranes and ready the floating jets for launching. The crew all began to head off towards their respective duties, but Daniel noticed that every single one of them looked over the port side guard rail and stared momentarily at the slate-grey water and the bobbing wreath before departing off to their respective tasks. He imagined that they were all saying a personal prayer or message to themselves in lieu of the SS Sauternes, but more importantly, he realised that Ingi had gathered together a crew of decent individuals that understood what it was to be a sailor and to have respect for the cruelness of the sea and its victims.

The AK34 HE3 hydraulic crane effortlessly lifted and lowered the floating jetties from the aft deck onto the sea. Crew members on the rib boats secured the jetties and towed them into position. The inflatable air bags for the jetties were filled and the ballast supports for the sides were attached. The mooring buoys were tethered to the corners of the jetties and the warning lights were switched on. Ingi watched all the activity from the bridge's gangway and pointed out the vastness of the cleared aft deck to Sólrun.

"Look how much room there is now we have started. We could have a five-a-side football match down there later." and smiled contentedly and went back inside the bridge.

Sólrun walked over to Daniel who was carefully assembling what she took to be the underwater plasma torch. She placed a hand on his shoulder. "Do you need a hand with this?"

Daniel grunted and asked her to pass him over the instruction manual lying on the seat beside her. He flicked through a few pages and then studied one in particular, returned to assembling the torch, clicked two pieces together and then attached the piece to what looked to Sólrun like a shower head fitting for a bath. Daniel caught her attentive watch of what he was doing.

"I thought this underwater plasma torch thing was going to be really impressive and look like a gun or something. I wasn't expecting it to be so small and looking like a shower head with some cable running out the back." she remarked.

Daniel explained that the cutting aspect of the tool, the torch, was relatively small and had to be versatile and maneuverable at the depth he would be using it at.

"I've got the torch and 6 metres of feed hose that connects to the plasma cutter. The plasma cutter is that blue box." Daniel pointed at a square blue box beside him on the floor. It had surface mounted handles on its top, and at one end, dials, knobs, switches and input/output ports. The opposite end had input valve ports for cabling.

"It weighs about 22 kilograms on dry land, but underwater, it's relatively lighter. So all I have to do is find the Captain's room and then locate the money box bolted to the floor. I'll then have to get the torch and the plasma cutter down to the ship to use, but I need to work out how much space I have to operate in. The plasma cutter itself is powered by a bobcat generator that we'll install on one of the floating jetties. 6000 watts of generator power needs to be sent down by cable to that blue box to give me enough juice to cut through steel for about 15 minutes. But because I'm working at depth and using a re-breather unit, I need to gauge how it all works as well as being aware of the water conditions and any changes that could occur. There isn't a lot of light at that depth and visibility will be really poor so we're going to have to use special lighting units to illuminate the area."

He stood up and walked out onto the bridge gangway. Down on the aft deck, some of the crew was beginning to assemble remote-controlled submersible lighting rigs that would be operated from the bridge controls. Other crew members were carefully preparing lifting bags and measuring the length of supply cable required. He watched as Ingi supervised the installation of the bobcat generator on one of the jetties. The hydraulic crane held it suspended over the floating platform as four men gently lowered it downwards. A fifth man waited, primed with a bolt gun to secure and tether it to the jetty. The preparation for the first dives was almost complete. He looked at his watch. They had been at sea for nearly four hours now, and as he gazed over at the islands of Fugloy and Svínoy, he spotted villagers watching their every move. A sudden sea-chill hit him, and as he shuddered, Daniel wondered if any of those villagers could have witnessed the sinking of the Sauternes. It was nearly 80 years ago and he very much doubted it, but he had the feeling of a presence close by that had.

He turned to Sólrun and suggested that they go and speak to Ingi and mention dinner.

"I'm sure that rumbling we can feel is Ingi's stomach and not the ship's engines." he joked with her and led her down the stairs onto the aft deck and over to Ingi for a chat.

09.05am – Monday 12th June, present day
Das Volker Syndicate Institute Headquarters, La Chaux-de-Fonds, Switzerland.

Torstein Lindemann sat in front of his computer at his desk and assessed his trip to the Faroe Islands. From a business perspective, the weekend's public relations exercise had been a worthwhile opportunity to showcase some of the many facets of a global company and its involvement in a number of projects. His Saturday night lecture had trended on social media and the established German newspapers, such as Die Zeit, Süddeutsche Zeitung, Frankfurter Allgemeine Zeitung, Die Welt and Der Tagesspiegel, all had reviews and articles about him, Das Volker Syndicate, the Faroe Islands and the various aspects of involvement that his company had. The Das Volker Syndicate funded paper, Die Flamme, waxed lyrically about Lindemann's visit, the lecture, the business ventures, the research initiatives and that the 'company's astute entrepreneurial alertness was at the forefront of cutting edge 21st Century business model design and marketing strategies that fully utilised the fields of technology and business networks.'.

He casually surfed around the internet and read a number of on-line reviews before turning to the company's profile on the share markets. There was considerable interest in the company today. He smiled to himself, clicked open the 'DAGNY' folder and refreshed himself with the details of the 'QADNA' file.

The chain of coincidences had continued with the unexpected meeting with Freyja Fulton in the Faroes at the weekend. He had known she was going to be in the islands as part of her university course, but he hadn't expected to actually meet her. To casually meet the person that held the answers to an 80 year old search had been a profound moment for him. Torstein looked at the photograph of his father on the desk. "I'm close Papa. I'm close."

He picked up his telephone and asked his secretary, Yvette, to locate Phil Harris in the United Kingdom and advise him that he had to make contact with Torstein immediately.

He replaced the handset in its cradle and resumed reading his computer files. This girl's blood was to be retrieved as soon as was humanly possible and Phil Harris's little indiscretion of a few months ago was going to ensure that it was. The telephone rang and Lindemann answered it.

"Dr. Lindemann. I have Phil Harris on the line for you. I'm just putting the call through to you now."

"Thanks Yvette." and Lindemann listened as the connection was made.

"Dr. Lindemann? It is Phil Harris here. I believe you wished me to contact you?"

Lindemann paused before speaking and opened a folder on his screen and started to play a video. He watches Phil Harris cavorting around with two women in a bedroom and then becomes embroiled in various sex acts with them.

"Ah Philip. I have a task for you. I need you to locate a young woman, escort her to a secure facility and take a sizeable amount of blood from her. It's for research purposes and I need as much of her blood as possible. Once you have collected all of her blood and stored it, just dispose of her body."

The Stream

There was a brief silence at the other end of the telephone conversation before Phil Harris spoke. "I'm sorry Dr. Lindemann. I may have picked you up wrongly there. You wish me to find a young woman, take her for a blood sample, i.e. take all of it and then dispose of her body? I think I've misunderstood what you meant there."

Lindemann sucked in his breath. "Philip. You will do exactly what I told you to do. You will retrieve as much blood as humanly possible, have it stored correctly and properly for future use and you will then dispose of the young woman's body. It is a simple instruction and you will do what I want you to do and what is necessary. You have associates that you can employ to do the dirty work for you but you will be gathering that blood for me and soon. Do you wish me to release the interesting video footage that I have of you with the young ladies in Glasgow of a few months ago? You are aware that one of them you had fun with was only 15 years old? How will you explain that to your wife and family as you get sentenced to a lengthy term in prison? I am led to believe Scottish prisons are not exactly the most welcoming of places for sex offenders."

Phil realised that he had been conned and then coerced into what this old bastard wanted and there was nothing he could do about it. Lindemann had used him as a man on the ground to deliver the 'Reprogramming the Code' initiative, and in doing so, he had stupidly gone and got himself caught up in a moment of silliness with some lap-dancers in Glasgow, and that indiscretion was now going to be used against him if he didn't comply. The two guys that he had been given as help were obviously all part of some devious game and he had been caught with the bait, hook, line and sinker. "Sneaky old bastard" he thought to himself.

"OK Dr. Lindemann. Send me the details of this young woman and where she will be and I will collect the blood for you." He hung up before Lindemann could respond and sat back in his chair and mulled over everything in his head. He needed to get to the Glasgow office by Friday at the latest and to try and sort out his mess.

Lindemann replaced the telephone in its cradle and walked over to the window to surveill the view. Things were happening quickly and he was glad that they were. After all these years, he was now close to finally having in his possession the true blood of the Aryan race. The direct lineage blood of the first German king, Henry I, and this blood was the starting point of restoring a new world order of pure Nordic types that would rule, this time around, for at least a thousand years.

The Stream

Having spent the night out in the open water of the Fugloyarfjørður, the passage of sea between the islands of Svínoy and Fugloy, the anchored Nord Kaperen, quite literally, bobs like a cork. The ship rises and falls up to 3 metres on the swell of the Atlantic Ocean as Daniel watches the waters cause the tied rib boats to ricochet off the sides of the floating jetties and catapult themselves back towards him in the strain against the moorings.

The floating jetties themselves, although secured to the ocean floor and weighted down with the likes of generators, lifting gear and lighting rigs, hem and haw in the surge of the Atlantic waters. Although the sea was calm, Daniel could only wonder what the conditions were like all those years ago when the SS Sauternes was pulled down beneath the waves.

He gave Sólrun a final kiss and padded across the deck to the waiting rib boat. He could see the fear and concern in her face as he departed towards the floating jetties. Ingi placed his arm around her in a comforting manner and Daniel acknowledged them both with a wave of his hand as he got closer to the dive platform floating jetty.

Other rib boats zipped about all around the jetties and the first of the scuba divers hit the water as they commenced providing the needed support for this mission. On board the dive platform, Daniel performed the final checks on the re-breather and patted his suit pouch to make sure he had the plasma cutter torch head. He watched as the blue box plasma cutter unit had its power cabling connected to the bob-cat generator and then slowly winched into the sea. Divers secured the box to a tethered remotely operated underwater vehicle, an ROV, secure the power cabling with those attached to the ROV and switch on the lights of the locator beacons. The flashing neon lights slowly disappear from view as the ROV and its payload makes its downward journey to the wreck.

On board the bridge of the Nord Kaperen, Neils Rothe watches the camera monitor for the ROV as he controls it via a joystick mounting. The transmitted pictures on the monitor screen displays the ROV's lights illuminating the darkness in its descent to the wreck. Ingi and Sólrun stare at the screen as Neils explains that the ROV has a load-carrying umbilical cable powering it and has a tether management system (TMS) attached. The TMS lengthens or shortens the tether to minimize the effects of cable drag with the underwater currents. The umbilical cable is an armoured cable containing electrical conductors and fibre optics carrying electrical power, video, and data signals between the operator and the ROV. Sitting on the edge of the jetty, Daniel watches the ROV's descent and the cabling paying out behind it. He switches on his intercom. "Hi Neils. Can you hear me?"

"Yes Daniel. Loud and clear."

"Tell Ingi that I'm ready to go and that I'll get his coins for him."

Ingi smiled as he heard Daniel's voice over the loudspeaker. He leaned past Neils and depressed the speaker button. "Just make sure you do and be careful down there."

Daniel nodded in the direction of the Nord Kaperen and waved as he checked the time. 06.13am. "No probs Ingi. I will. Niels? Start the clock, will you?" as he pressed the timer button on his LCD digital depth timer and slipped into the water, grabbed hold of the TMS cable and started to pull himself downwards through the ever darkening waters towards the SS Sauternes.

Niels started the timer within the graphic on his computer screen and watched the minute clock start. Ingi sighed, put his hand around Sólrun's shoulders and pulled her close to him. "This is going to be a long 3 hours."

The Stream

The dive down to the SS Sauternes had been an uneventful 4 minutes. Daniel checked the LCD digital depth timer on his left wrist to confirm his position. 87 metres down and 3 minutes 28 seconds elapsed so far. He scanned below for the flashing lights of the ROV. Visibility was only about 15 metres but Daniel could just make out the blinking beacons and a large shape underneath being opaquely illuminated by the submersible.

The ROV hovered above the stern of the wreck, its arc-lights confirming the final resting place of the SS Sauternes. It was lying on its starboard side and the passage of 80 years underwater had taken its toll on the vessel. The superstructure of the ship, such as the masts and funnel had been stripped away during its descent to the bottom, and its hulk was eerily coated in a combination of rusting decay and sea-bed materials. The arc-lights of the ROV captured ocean-borne particles in its beams and Daniel could just make out sea cucumbers frolicking on the side of the ship, looking impressive with their long tentacles displayed around them.

He stood on the side of the ship and used his torch to scan the area for an entrance. He was aware of the pull of the currents as he manouevred the ROV and its lights over the stern of the vessel. The SS Sauternes had been 65 metres long with, at the time of her construction, an uncommon amidships-based bridge between the fore and aft cargo holds with the crew and passenger cabins, along with the engine room and ship's stores and facilities located at the stern. The previous salvage attempts had concentrated on the bridge area and the search for the coins had been fruitless. The Captain's cabin was to be found on the port side at the stern of the ship, just below where the funnel had been.

Using his torch with his left hand to survey the area around him, he tugged at the ROV with his right to concentrate its lights on the hull. Daniel spotted a dark opening in front of him and flicked his torch light around its edges. It was a doorway with rusted hinges denoting that there had once been a timber covering. He peered into the hole and established that it was an enclosed space, a cabin. Daniel searched around the doorway and brushed away at the detritus on the metal work above the door. A square shape, as in a brass name plaque, started to emerge and lettering upon it appeared as his hand wiped away at the coating. He rubbed vigourously at the square and the lettering revealed what he was hoping for. 'William Smith, Captain'.

Ingi stared at the monitors and watched Daniel brush the plaque. As the letters of the ship's captain appeared, Ingi thrust a clenched fist upwards in triumph. He reached for the microphone.

"Well done Daniel. You've found the cabin. It's exactly where we thought it would be. Can you see anything? Can you see the box?" he gasped excitedly.

"Neils? I need you to hover the ROV almost over the doorway. I need as much light as possible to be shone inside. If I go in and find the box, I then need you to get the ROV as close as possible for me to connect the plasma cutter. How long have I got on the clock?"

Neils looked at his computer screen. The time was 06:19 hours. "You've got 14 minutes to find it, cut it free and get it into the airbag."

"Call it 15 minutes and give me a countdown every 3 minutes."

Daniel pulled himself carefully into the cabin. The darkness was swiftly removed as the ROV was guided overhead and its lights were concentrated into the aperture.

The cabin was about 8 feet by 10 feet, and with the ship lying at a 40 degree angle on the sea bed, it was initially disconcerting for Daniel to work out the layout of the room. The rusted remains of what had been a bed-frame were disintegrating on the far wall. To his right, the captain's roller desk bureau was just a crumbling mound. To his left, the shelving that had contained books, letters, maps and ship's papers, had collapsed and their contents had spilled onto the floor and then perished into sludge.

Daniel focused his attention on the floor. Sand and sludge had formed at an angle in the room and made the cabin seem smaller than it actually was. He shone his torch around looking for the steel box and feared that it was under the sludge. It would take about 20 minutes to find it under it all and then at least another 20 minutes for the water to clear before even attempting to start cutting.

A shape on the floor on the left, just inside the door, caught his eye. He swam over to it and banged it with his knuckles. It had a solid feel to it and Daniel started to wipe away the marine decay from its surfaces. It was box-shaped and about the size of a microwave oven. He scooped at the sludge on the floor around the shape looking for bolts. Sure enough, this box was bolted to the floor. Daniel checked the four corners and steel bolts anchored it to the floor of the cabin. Three heavy padlocks were still affixed to the box.

"3 minutes" rang in his ear-piece. Daniel exited the cabin and headed for the ROV. He unhooked the air-bag from the submersible and took it back into the cabin and placed it on the floor. He returned to the submersible and attached the plasma cutter hose-feed to the blue box.

"Neils. Get the bob-cat generator started. I've found the box."

Daniel returned to the cabin and started to unfold the lifting bag net and placed it at the steel box. He connected the tether line for the parachute and its air bottle to the lifting bag and then placed them on the outside of the cabin. He reached into his pocket and attached the plasma-cutter to the hose-feed, flicked the switches on the blue box and smiled as all the dials sparked to life.

Daniel started to cut at the bolts furthest away from the wall. If he could cut the front ones off first, he could slip the lifting bag under the edges to catch the box when he started on the bolts nearer the wall.

"6 minutes" rang in his earpiece.

The front bolts were quickly cut and Daniel slipped a side of the lifting bag under the box and draped the rest over and around the remainder of the frame. He cut the third bolt and pulled at the box to ensure more of it was caught by the bag. He turned his attention to the fourth bolt.

"9 minutes."

The fourth bolt was taking longer than the other three to cut. Daniel gathered more of the bag under and around the box.

The Stream

Back on the Nord Kaperen, Ingi, Sólrun and Niels stared transfixed by the camera feed from the ROV in silence. On the monitor they watched a flickering silhouette of Daniel's body caught by the plasma-cutter's flame dance across the screen in front of them.

The bolt fell away and Daniel tugged at the box. It slid inexorably into the lifting bag and then started to slide across the floor towards the mound of sludge. Daniel dropped the cutter and sped towards the doorway. He grabbed at the air-tank and turned the valve on its side. The release of air started to fill the canopy of the parachute and in doing so, caused it to start to float towards the surface. The rise of the parachute tightened the tether on the slack of the straps of the bag and halted its slide towards the sludge. The strain on the straps was visible as the weight of the box was greater than the parachute was able to lift. Daniel turned the air-valve to full pelt and watched the accelerated inflation. Slowly the bag started to rise from the floor and the box settled into its netting.

"12 minutes."

The bag floated upwards through the doorway and Daniel helped to guide its passage past the framework and then on its way to the surface. He grabbed for the plasma-cutter and disconnected it from its hosepipe. He turned off the switches on the blue box and removed the feed hose from its side.

"Neils. The bag is on its way and I'm preparing to come back up. Is there any chance of giving me a tow with the ROV to 69 metres so I can start the decompression procedure?"

"Certainly Daniel. Grab a hold and I'll take you up."

The Stream

Rib boats zipped about the ocean waves near to the floating jetties and some scuba-divers surfaced close by. On board the Nord Kaperen, some of the crew members were leaning over the ship's side and calling to the scuba-divers for information while others joined Ingi and Sólrun in a circle around the M5 lifting bag that had just been winched aboard the vessel.

One of the crew, Martin, relayed to Ingi that Daniel was at the final decompression stop 6 metres below and that the scuba-divers had indicated that he was in good shape and ready to surface. Ingi blew out a long sigh of relief.

Ingi guided Sólrun over to the rails to watch for Daniel's emergence above the waves. "This has been the longest 3 hours of my life." said Sólrun.

He squeezed her shoulder in comfort as they both looked for Daniel to appear. As his head and shoulders surfaced and he bobbed about in the water, a cacophony of sound greeted him as cheers and shouts of jubilation from the crew were drowned out as the Nord Kaperen's horn gave a long and continuous blast. On the islands of Fugloy and Svínoy, watching villagers started to clap as the realisation that the salvage mission had been successful. Ingi noticed the celebrations and mentally noted that the airwaves and internet were about to become very busy as news of a successful recovery bounced around the Faroes and beyond. He could feel the release of emotion in Sólrun's body as the pent-up anxiety and concern gave way to joy and relief at seeing Daniel safe and sound.

"Bloody typical. Gets the job done and gets the girl as well. My training's been far too good." he uttered under his breath as it became apparent to him that Sólrun was very fond of him.

"What did you say Ingi?" asked Sólrun.

"Nothing Sólrun. I'm just glad to see Daniel's made it." and embraced her.

Scuba-divers helped Daniel into a rib boat and ferried him over to the Nord Kaperen. As he clambered up onto the deck, he was greeted with cheers and back slaps by the crew as he made his way over to Ingi and Sólrun. Ingi shook his hand and hugged him and stepped aside for Sólrun who threw herself at him.

As he caught her, he remarked "You'll get wet Sólrun..." but was stopped from saying anything more as she passionately kissed him. After about 20 seconds, Ingi interrupted the embrace with a polite "Ahem! Shall we?" and pointed at the lifting bag and the steel box.

Daniel, Sólrun and the crew gathered round as Ingi picked up a set of bolt-cutters and approached the box. He snipped off the three padlocks and with an air of suspense, grabbed at the lid and when he went to open it, he stopped and looked around at all the eager and expectant faces surrounding him.

"There better be coins in this." he jocularly roared as he forced the box open. Through a ripple of laughter at Ingi's comment, the gathered crowd got closer, keen to see the contents for themselves. Inside the box, although still full of discoloured water that was a mixture of grime, rust and disintegrated packaging and paper tubing, rows upon rows of coins could be seen.

Ingi gingerly extracted a solitary coin from one of the rows, wiped it on the sleeve of his jumper and inspected it. On one side of the coin, the obverse, was the year of mintage, 1941, stamped around the seal of King Christian X surrounded with capital lettering 'KONGE AF DANMARK' – King of Denmark. He turned the coin over to see what was on the reverse. Ingi put his hand to his forehead and then drew it back through his hair and exclaimed "Jesus Christ!"

He turned to face the crowd and Daniel recognised that his friend had just experienced a shock. Ingi held the coin out for Daniel to inspect. Daniel checked the same obverse side first as had Ingi and then turned it over to view the other.

Daniel staggered back and was caught by Sólrun before he fell over. "What is it? What's wrong?" she shouted as Daniel showed her the coin in the palm of his hand. The reverse of the coin had an engraved sailing ship on it surrounded by the lettering 'FÆRØERNE' – Faroe Islands. The design was the same sailing ship that Dagny Poulsen had worn as a brooch in Germany, 1939.

The Stream

Sólrun, Ingi and Daniel sat around the table in Ingi's cabin. The air was thick with fumes as Ingi chain-smoked one cigarette after the other. Sólrun thought the fumes were beginning to resemble cirrostratus cloud formations and asked if she could open the port-hole to let some fresh air into the room. The opening of the aperture dispersed the nicotine-infused storm that was gathering over the table.

On the table lay a selection of some of the recovered coins. Daniel picked one up and examined it on both sides.

"Ingi. I need to go to the Royal Mint in London and speak to your pal there and make some enquiries about the coins. I'll also need to go to the Danish Embassy in Sloane Street and get some information about Dagny Poulsen from the archives there. There's something not sitting right with her story, these coins, my grandmother in Berlin, the brooch of the sailing ship, this Scottish girl, Freyja Fulton and whatever this guy Lindemann is up to. There are now far too many coincidences and circumstances that I need, in fact, we need the answers to. We have to start joining all the dots together to get the real picture of what we have discovered. I also think this Freyja Fulton is now in some sort of danger. I don't know from what or why yet, but I have a genuine concern that this Lindemann and his Das Volker Syndicate is involved in something disturbing and nasty."

Daniel looked over at Sólrun who was typing away at the laptop in front of her.

The Stream

"There's a flight to London tomorrow morning at 10.00am. If we can get back over to Hvannasund, we could drive to Vágar tonight and stay over at the rented flat in Miðvágur that I use during the week so you can catch the flight tomorrow."

Ingi rubbed his face with his hand and suggested that they take a rib-boat back to Hvannasund and use his car parked at the harbour. "I'm going to be here, out in the open sea, for at least the next few days anyway, so I don't need the car. I've no intention of going ashore just yet. I want to finish the exploration survey of the wreck with the ROV and I also want to avoid the media circus that'll be going on now that word is out we've recovered the coins. "

"Are you sure Ingi? I don't want to leave you in a lurch here. You still have a lot of work to do and I'll feel guilty about leaving you to deal with matters."

"Just go Daniel. You've recovered the coins for me and done what I wanted you to do. But this adventure of yours is far more important than just me and some bloody coins. Here. Take these coins and show them to Tommy Caldwell, he's the guy at the Royal Mint that I know. I'm sure he'll help you with information that you need if you have some of the recovered coins to show him. Give him some to keep for their records. That'll sweeten him up for you." and he scooped a pile up and placed the contents in a transparent plastic tube container. He scooped up another pile and repeated the action.

"That's your cut of the treasure for now." and winked. They both laughed and Daniel embraced him in a man-hug.

"Thanks Ingi. I need to get to the finish line of this saga and find out what it's all about."

"Oh you will Daniel. You always do."

The Stream

London Mint Office, Harmsworth House, 13-15 Bouverie Street, London EC4Y 8DP.

The London Mint Office is situated in Harmsworth House, 13-15 Bouverie Street, London EC4Y 8DP, and a brisk five minute walk from Blackfriars Underground Station on the Circle Line. Daniel was grateful for the fact that the London Mint office was so conveniently located to the same underground system that he could use to get to the Danish Embassy in Sloane Street after he had spoken to Ingi's contact there, Tommy Caldwell.

The London Mint Office is an unassuming building, and after having introduced himself to the receptionist and presented her with a business card, asked if it would be possible to speak to Tommy Caldwell and sat down in one of the many empty seats in the waiting area.

There were a few other people waiting around and most of them were fairly anonymous looking. Daniel mused to himself that they must be numismatists, coin collectors, and if they were, they could all be aptly described as nondescript. He was probably doing the gentlemen seated around him a huge dis-service but Daniel mentally noted that if he ever had to provide a disguise for himself in the future, he would take into consideration the look of his fellow man currently within this waiting room. Everyone was just a perfect stranger to each other.

A middle-aged stocky man appeared at the side of the receptionist and started to ask her some questions. Daniel observed the conversation and quickly realised that he was the topic of discussion. The receptionist pointed in his direction and showed the stocky man the business card Daniel had left with her minutes earlier.

"Daniel Lauridsen?" said a gruff Scottish voice and Daniel looked up to see the stocky man standing at the edge of the waiting area. Daniel stood up and identified himself.

The stocky man came forward and shook his hand.

"Tommy Caldwell. How can I help you today Mr. Lauridsen?"

"We have a mutual friend in Ingi Mortensen. He spoke to you last year about a possible salvage attempt to recover some coins from a shipwreck, the SS Sauternes." Tommy's eyes lit up at the mention of Ingi and the SS Sauternes.

"Oh I remember Ingi. Of course I do. He came in to see me about the specially made Danish coinage for the Faroe Islands during World War II. The ship, the Sauternes, sank during a storm and the coins have never been found. Ingi came to see me here looking for the specifications and dimensions of the coins as he was planning to do a salvage mission for them. How can I help you?"

Daniel handed him the transparent plastic tube container that Ingi had given him. "There are 26,000 more of them if you are interested?"

"Ingi's recovered the coins?" barked Tommy in a loud voice that caused the perfect strangers in the waiting room to look up to see where the noise was coming from.

Daniel nodded the affirmative and was becoming slightly concerned at the changing demeanour of the man that he had just met.

"He's recovered the coins? All of them? The full steel box load?" demanded Tommy. Again Daniel nodded confirmation of same towards him.

Tommy ran by the edge of the reception desk, his right hand tightly clenching the tube of coins, and like a footballer celebrating the scoring of a goal, punched the air in delight and shouted "Ya dancer!!"

Daniel was bemused by this sudden and unexpected acclamation from Tommy Caldwell. The receptionist just looked up at Tommy, raised an eyebrow, shook her head and continued with her work. Daniel was now completely confused. He hadn't anticipated such an expressive reaction to occur when giving someone a plastic tube of coins but he definitely hadn't expected the receptionist not to bat an eyelid with her colleague having such an emotional outburst in public, especially in front of potential customers, even if they themselves looked perfectly strange to the casual onlooker.

"I take it you are pleased that Ingi has managed to salvage the coins then?" quipped Daniel in an attempt to try and restore some sort of normality to his visit to the London Mint.

Tommy had calmed down and rushed over to Daniel and shook his hand furiously. He started to guide Daniel over to a doorway.

"Come through to my office and tell me everything" and pass-keyed the door and held it open for Daniel to pass through.

Once seated inside Tommy's office, Daniel proceeded to explain his association with Ingi, the invitation to help with the salvage attempt, the dive and the subsequent recovery. Daniel didn't explain anything about all the other matters that were running parallel with his trip to the Faroes but, having gauged Tommy's joy at having a plastic tube of coins salvaged from the SS Sauternes, he decided now was as good a time as any to press the man for some information.

"I take it that the successful salvage of these coins is important to you and the London mint then? I can understand all the historical aspects associated with the coins being minted and the subsequent shipwreck and recent recovery, but what's their significance? Going by your …err…outburst back there in the lobby, is there something I should maybe know about these coins?"

Tommy stopped examining the coins in the tube and stared at Daniel.

"You don't know the importance of these coins? Do you how much one of these coins would fetch if up for sale in the current collectors markets? A starting price would be at least £90.00 per coin. We are talking about £2.5 million at the very least for the whole lot but because of their story, their provenance and place in war-time mintage history, the value is going to sky-rocket. A conservative estimate for the purchase cost of a solitary coin will quadruple at auction. These are 'Holy Grail' coins in that they have become the stuff of myth and legend and will now turn out to be really sought after items. This was a special mintage for a one-off order and the moulds were broken on the instructions of the War Office. We've only got the original obverse side test cast samples and they are locked up as reference items in the mint museum. We don't actually have any specimens of the final castings. Did Ingi not tell you any of this?"

"No, he didn't. It must have slipped his mind or I wasn't paying attention to him when he was telling me about them."

Daniel racked his memory to see if Ingi had told him about the value of the coins if recovered. He couldn't remember being told anything about how much they would be worth. "You said that they were a special mintage. I notice that the coins don't have the face of Christian X stamped on them but there is a sailing ship and 'FÆRØERNE' on the reverse side."

"Aye, there's a story or two about why the King's face isn't on the coins. I don't know which one is true but they both seem plausible reasons enough.

Denmark fell to German occupation in May 1940 and the Faroe Islands had to immediately begin counter measures to protect themselves from rampant inflation since they used Danish currency. By authority of the Faero Amt, the local government administration, all of the paper currency on the islands was stamped 'Kun gyldig paa Færøerne Færo Amt, Juni 1940' - Only valid on the Faroes/Faroe County, June 1940.

A series of emergency local issues were dated November 1940 with an inscription in the centre to signify that these notes were issued in place of the National Bank series and were restricted in validity to the islands. This series was printed in Britain by Bradbury, Wilkinson & Co. and were somewhat more elaborate in design than previous issues by including a sailing ship and a ram's head in the upper right corner of the notes. This issue remained in use throughout the British occupation and circulated until new Danish banknotes arrived in the Faroe Islands in November 1948.

On 4th April 1941, Britain established a protectorate over the Faroes, and as it turns out, just in the nick of time as a German naval fleet had been spotted nearby. A battle between the German battleship Bismarck and Royal Navy vessels took place near the Faroes a few weeks later.

One of the stories is about the fact that with Denmark being under German occupation, the British didn't want to issue coinage in the Faroes with the King's head on them, just in case he turned out to be a Nazi sympathizer or a puppet-king doing the bidding of an occupying force. I can see the British point of view where they have themselves occupied Danish territory for the duration of the war and are faced with a serious coinage shortage in the local currency. They need to get some coins minted but can't have the chance of King Christian X suddenly going all Nazi on them and the British garrison possibly having some un-rest in the Faroe Islands with the locals as a result of their King turning in favour of the enemy. It would have been embarrassing enough to issue new coins with the face of an enemy collaborator monarch on them and then have to deal with a local rebellion breaking out in support of their King, so it was decided that the reverse side would be faceless and have a sailing ship stamped on them instead.

Tommy took a mouthful of cold tea from a mug on his desk and continued speaking.

"The other story is a strange one and seems a bit far-fetched but given the events of the time and what I've found out whilst I've been working here, doesn't actually surprise me anymore and is probably the closer tale to the true facts. Apparently some German big-wig industrialist had had some jewelry made for his Danish wife, two brooches, a pendant necklace and a pair of matching earrings in the design of a sailing ship. The brooches and pendant could contain a picture, a lock of hair or some other keep-sake in a hidden compartment. The wife really liked the jewelry and wore it a lot. Her husband was something to do with the design and build of the new Reichstag and she had come across some paperwork that she wasn't supposed to see or know of. The paperwork was about some pre-war hypothesis for the proposed construction of a coastal defensive wall that would run from Spain all the way to the top of Norway, if and when the Germans had secured all of mainland Europe through military action and then occupation of these captured territories. It was to be a barrier against invasion from the west and the Atlantic. It had a funny name. Hold on a moment…"

Tommy started tapping on his computer and looking at pages on the internet.

"Here it is. 'Das Schild', the shield. It seems to have been the embryonic idea that was suggested a few years before the building of the 'Atlantikwall' was started in 1942. Anyhow, the story goes that the wifey copies the rough details down in note form and hides them in amongst her jewelry. She's become really angry and disappointed with her husband because he is somehow involved with the possible construction of an enormous concrete wall fortification to be built along the shores of her beloved mother country, Denmark.

She goes home to Copenhagen to see her family in 1938 and meets some Scottish chap there called Ronald Turnbull. He's a student at the university there and also working part-time as a press attaché at the British Embassy. It turns out that he's actually an undercover British agent tasked with the setting up of a resistance movement should war break out. He's working for a section that would eventually become the covert Special Operations Executive. She passes him the plans of 'Das Schild' that she had noted down and hidden inside one of the brooches of a sailing ship.

Ronald Turnbull apparently hadn't given the plans much thought at the time, and it was only when the Germans invaded Denmark and he had returned back to London that things really took off. The Germans had now overrun most of mainland Europe and intelligence sources had hinted that an Atlantic Wall, with heavily defended and fortified naval and submarine bases, was going to be built along the coast of continental Europe and Scandinavia as a defence against an anticipated Allied invasion of Nazi-occupied Europe being launched from the shores of Britain.

The Free Danish Embassy was in Sloane Square which isn't all that far from here and that's where the War Department conceived the Operation Valentine plan, the occupation of the Faroe Islands by British forces. The intelligence that this Turnbull fellow had passed over inside the brooch had been enough to convince the powers that be in Whitehall that the Faroes had to be taken as soon as possible. If the Germans got there first, they would have secured control of the North Atlantic by being able to build perfect bases for their submarines and aircraft to operate from and would have complete control of the air and seas to the north of Britain. Britain would fall quite quickly to the Germans with relentless attacks from there, Scandinavia and western Europe.

With what I've heard in rumours in here over the years, Turnbull suggested that the image of the sailing ship, already on the notes issued by Bradbury, Wilkinson & Co., should be used on the reverse side of the coinage as a 'get it right up you' gesture at the Germans. Typical Scottish defiance and confrontation by noising up the Germans with issuing coins to a territory that Britain now occupied as a result of information contained inside the brooch of a sailing ship. There's also an ironic aspect with some German industrialist commissioning some bespoke jewelry for his wife and the wife then using it to shaft his Nazi overlord plans.

It's a brilliant story and I'd love it to be true, and the coins that you've recovered now give it some credence with the sailing ship on them, don't you think? I do like the stuff about Ronald Turnbull though. He seems to have been a bit of a doer of things during the war. He ended up being based in Sweden running a Special Operations outpost that was in contact with the Danish Resistance. He's the guy that persuades the Nobel Peace Prize winner, Niels Bohr, to escape Denmark and join the British and American scientists working on the Manhattan Project and the building of the first atomic bomb. He also obtained, with the help of the Danish Resistance, drawings of the V-1 rocket flying bomb about ten months before the V-1 attacks began on London."

Daniel sat back in his chair and thought about the two versions that Tommy had just told him. He reached into the inside pocket of his jacket and pulled out the sepia photograph of his grandmother Mille, his mother Petra, his Uncle Albert and Dagny taken in the Viktoriapark in Berlin in 1939. He passed the photograph over to Tommy to study.

"The second story is true. How much would the coins now be worth if I told you that the Danish wife you mention is for real, she is in that photograph wearing the original sailing ship brooch and that the woman that welcomed Niels Bohr into the Free Danish Embassy in London is also in the picture? The photograph is dated 13th August 1939." Daniel then pointed out the two women to Tommy.

Tommy's eyes almost exploded out of their sockets and he grabbed for a magnifying glass to inspect the detail of the photograph further.

"The Danish wife was my grandmother and the other woman was Faroese and she was my mother's nanny in Berlin until the war broke out. She was given the brooch as a leaving gift and I saw that very same brooch on her grand-daughter's lapel just last week up in the Faroe Islands. This same sailing ship appears on the banknotes and coins that were issued by Britain."

Daniel just watched Tommy's face contort with various movements and expressions as he began to piece together the consequences, costs and provenance that the photograph and Daniel's information now gave to the whole story of the minting of the coins that had been previously considered lost forever with the sinking of the SS Sauternes.

The Stream

12.13pm – Thursday 15th June, present day
Danish Embassy, 55 Sloane Street, London SW1X 9SR.

Denmark's bold, modern embassy building sits on the west side of Sloane Street in Belgravia, facing onto the gardens of Cadogan Place. The embassy stands six storeys high and is a striking, metal-faced building made up of glazed boxes, cantilevered out from concrete walls. The entrance on the ground floor is flanked with painted metal cladding complemented by an abstract, geometric concrete mural by the famous Danish painter and sculptor, Ole Schwalbe.

Although it is a modernist building in a Scandinavian style, it bizarrely does not look out of place amongst the more traditional mansion housing to be found elsewhere along Sloane Street and its design pays formal respect to the general appearance of the adjacent buildings.

Daniel jogged up the steps at the front door and made his way across the brightly lit entrance hall to the Queries desk. After a short conversation with the woman behind the counter about what he was visiting the embassy for, he passed over his Danish passport and his Personal Identification number, his 'personnummer', a national identification number, which accesses an individual's personal information that is stored in a computerised Civil Registration System,. The possession of a 'personnummer' is an integral part of Danish society, and it is virtually impossible for anyone to receive any form of government service without one. Even in the private sector, one would be hard pressed to receive services without such a number, unless it is minor daily business.

The woman swiped his card into the CRS terminal beside her and his details appeared on the computer screen in front of her.

"Have a seat Mr. Lauridsen. One of my colleagues will be with you shortly."

A tall man with bleached blonde hair and wearing spectacles that seemed to enlarge his rounded face, approached Daniel and introduced himself as Michael Pederson.

"How can I help you Mr. Lauridsen? I believe you are looking for some information about a Danish national that may have worked in the Free Danish Embassy here in London during World War 2. Is that correct?"

Daniel confirmed the position and gave him Dagny Fulton, nee Poulsen's details. Michael Pederson asked Daniel to follow him and he was taken through to a large library room with tables and chairs set in the middle of the floor space.

"Have a seat Mr. Lauridsen. I will go and see if I can retrieve some details for you. This may take about 30 minutes or so. Do you have time to wait?"

Daniel just smiled and confirmed that he was in no rush. He would just use the opportunity to do some paperwork that he needed to catch up on. Michael Pederson left and Daniel got his laptop out and started to flick through all the details he had gathered so far about this Dagny Poulsen. He refreshed himself with the information that Jógvan Johannesen, the Løgmaður, the Faroese prime minister had given him and started to mentally mull over the story that Tommy Caldwell had given him.

The Stream

He opened a new word document and began to input all the details that Tommy had given him this morning in a bullet point format for later reference – the coins, the paper currency, Operation Valentine, Ronald Turnbull and SOE activities, the sailing ship jewelry, his grandmother Mille and the Berlin 1939 photograph. He had just finished typing in the last details when Michael Pederson suddenly ghosted into the seat beside him.

"Mr. Lauridsen. Thank you for your patience. I have some documentation that you might be interested in reading, however, while I was away retrieving the file from the basement, I made some enquiries about you. I see from the details contained in the Civil Registration System that you possess some interesting....employment skill sets and that your security clearance is very high, a lot higher that mine, I hasten to add. But, before I let you read this file, I just have to remind you that some of the contents are still sensitive, nearly 80 years after the events and that I need you to exercise the upmost discretion while utilising any information in the future. You can take notes but if you need copies or scans of anything, I will need to check with my superiors."

Daniel nodded and Pederson passed over the table a file tied with white cotton ribbon. It had a serial number stamped in the top left corner and below it, in bold lettering, was:

Dagny Poulsen
Fødested: (place of birth) Tórshavn
Fødselsdato: (date of birth) Mandag 15 September 1919
The file cover had a large red ink legend stamped on it:
Begrænset Adgang (Restricted Access)

"If you need any assistance, I'll be over at the desk by the door. Take your time though. You have until 4.30pm." and Michael Pedersen left Daniel alone with the file.

He undid the ribbon fastening of the file and started to read the contents. He looked at his watch. It was 1.00pm.

An engrossing three hours passed with Daniel reading the file and its contents twice. He had made a number of notes on his laptop and identified a couple of pages in the file that he would like to have copied. He shut down the laptop and attracted Pederson's attention and asked if he could have copies made of the pages that had captured his interest.

Pederson gathered up the file and left Daniel at the table. Pederson said that he would need to check if the pages could be copied.

In Pederson's absence, Daniel began to try and mentally piece together the on-going puzzle that now had got even more complicated with the reading of this restricted file and the information that Tommy Caldwell had given him this morning.

As he thought about where all the pieces of this jig-saw of intrigue fitted with each other, the more Daniel became convinced that a series of events, situations, circumstances and opportunities had all collided with each other, and that Dagny Poulsen had unwittingly become involved with how some things transpired and then played out over some very important years in 20th century history.

A chance meeting with his own grandmother, Mille, in Copenhagen in 1938 had led to a young Faroese girl becoming embroiled in international espionage and covert communications between a Danish national, who was married to someone high up in the Nazi elite, and British intelligence. This young Faroese girl, Dagny Poulsen was completely unaware of what was happening around about her and that the brooch that she had worn as a decoration to the opening of the Reichstag was in fact a signal to alert British intelligence of further information that was now available to them, courtesy of Mille.

What had complicated matters though, was that Dagny Poulsen had become a person of interest to the Ahnenerbe, and that its Director, a Dr. Pelle Lindemann, had become particularly smitten with her and was eager to have further involvement, professionally and socially. Dagny Poulsen had inadvertently been thrust in amongst the elite Nazi hierarchy at a level that British intelligence could only dream about, but Mille had become appalled at what she had got her children's nanny involved in. Mille had realised that Dagny was in danger of possibly being accused of involvement in crimes against the German state, and that of spying for a foreign power. There would only be one outcome, and a tragic one, if that ever happened.

Mille's complaint to Himmler accusing Lindemann of *'harbouring un-natural desires bordering on the realms of moral turpitude'* had been a smoke-screen to extricate Dagny out of the situation that Mille had inadvertently placed her in.

There was no doubt that Mille was especially fond of Dagny and that Daniel's own mother had missed her terribly when she had escaped from Berlin back to the Faroe Islands, but Dagny continued to have some influence in matters not of her own making. The sailing ship brooch design appeared on banknotes and coinage made by the British for the Faroe

Islands. She had met a British soldier, got married and returned with him when he was posted back to Britain. She had worked in the Free Danish Embassy in Sloane Square for the remainder of the war and had gone on to meet important people and witness events that re-shaped the outcome of the conflict. As stated in the obituary notice that Jógvan Johannesen had shown him back in Tórshavn, she truly was a 'Daughter of the War'. Dagny's unexpected return to Britain in 1943 had afforded British and Danish intelligence direct contact with a person who had unprecedented knowledge of people, contacts and connections in pre-war Berlin and general information that would be advantageous for them to have.

A large area of the mental jig-saw puzzle had been completed but there were still a few pressing matters that he was going to have to research further. Daniel also realised that the unofficial Frømandskorpset badge of a sailing ship was a thank you to his own grandmother for the service she had provided for her country. He would never be able to have that confirmed but he knew in his heart that it was indeed the case.

But the real concern that was looming large in his head was this fascination that Torstein Lindemann, the son of Dr. Pelle Lindemann, Director of the Ahnenerbe, had for Dagny Poulsen's grand-daughter, Freyja Fulton.

He knew from reading some of the files that he had procured from Torstein Lindemann's computer, Freyja Fulton was now in grave and mortal danger, and like his grandmother before him in protecting Dagny, he was going to have to do the same for Freyja. The city of Glasgow was his next port of call and hopefully Michael Pederson had been given clearence for copying the documentation that he needed from the file.

"There you are Mr Lauridsen. I have copied the two pages that you requested. Here is your passport and your Personal Identification number. Is there anything else that I can assist you with today?"

"No Michael, there isn't. What you've copied for me is brilliant and just what I need. Thanks.".

Daniel exited the building and began the 20 minute walk towards South Kensington Underground Station. From there he could get on the District Line and catch a train to London Heathrow Airport. It didn't matter what flights were available or what the cost would be. What did matter was him getting to Glasgow as soon as possible and locating the whereabouts of Freyja Fulton and putting a stop to whatever Torstein Lindemann and Das Volker Syndicate had planned for the girl.

But putting a stop to something he didn't fully understand in a city he didn't know might be difficult. He needed to get local help. Lindemann's computer files must have something that he could use.

The Stream

12.02pm – Friday 16th June, present day
Buchanan Street, Glasgow.

Daniel stood with his back to the entrance of the Buchanan Street Underground station on the corner of Buchanan Street and West George Street. He was looking southwards down the length of Buchanan Street and its pedestrianised precinct lined with its endless offices, shops, cafes and bars, all busy with shoppers, office workers, ordinary Glaswegians and many tourists. The centre of the city seemed to be heaving with people all going about their lunchtime business in a polite and orderly fashion.

Banners hung from street lights proclaiming 'People Make Glasgow' and having only been in the city since 10.00pm the night before, his impression was that the banner was indeed correct. From his conversational taxi driver on his journey from the airport to the pleasant manner of the hotel staff, he was surprised at the friendliness of the people.

He had dumped his gear in his hotel room and gone for a wander around the city centre. What fascinated him was how Glaswegians inter-acted with one another and guests to their city. They smiled at each other in the street. The holding open of doors to let others pass by, the zig-zagging by the pedestrians to avoid collision, and if contact made, profuse apologies made to one another in passing. The queues at bus-stops, taxi ranks and shops were all conducted in a 'first come, first serve' method. No jostling for position or jumping ahead of others but all aware of the elderly, couples with young children, tourists and the lost stranger. The Glaswegians seemed to go out of their way to talk to each other while waiting, would freely give up places in line to others whose need seemed more urgent than their own, the offering of help and assistance to those who might need it. It was these little courtesies that you often don't see in major cities around the world that made Glasgow and its people seem refreshing to him, especially when he had been on foot and also using public transport in London the day before.

He had never been in the city before and the only Glaswegians he had ever come into contact with previously was while he had been on military missions in Iraq and Afghanistan. His recollection was of hard, wiry, extremely professional and disciplined soldiers who got the job, no matter how difficult, done. They liked to socialise with others and he recalled a commanding officer suggesting to Danish troops to go and enjoy a night out with them and make some friends but with a warning - don't talk about football or religion as it'll start an argument or two.

He remembered the former and being in the mess-hall in Kandahar and a group of Scottish troops watching a Rangers v Celtic football match on the television. Some American soldiers came into the mess, ordered up some beers and started to antagonise the Scots watching the football. The constant jeering, name-calling and the throwing of peanuts at them had all been ignored until one of the Americans foolishly changed the channel and refused to switch it back over to the football game. It was the sudden ferocity of the attack to retrieve the remote control for the television that was the graphic image in his mind. In a flash, five or six American soldiers had been felled by men half their size. There was teeth, blood and snot everywhere, and when the MPs rushed in to quell a reported riot, all they found were a group of American soldiers licking their wounds and some seated Scots, with their backs to them, supping beers and watching a football match on the television screen. There were no witnesses, unsurprisingly, and the Americans quickly left making excuses about tripping over cables and the like.

When Daniel was going through the terminal building at the airport the night before and he passed a sign at the entrance denoting the site of the foiled terrorist attack there in June 2007, he remembered the deeply ingrained mentality that all the Glaswegians he had ever met seem to possess – gregarious, garrulous, amicable, sociable and hospitable are the traits that they openly portray, but impinge or invade their air-space, well, that's another matter and there's hell to pay.

They will defend the weak and the put upon, take umbrage at injustice, and react, more often than not, with threatening and aggressive behaviour and, if required, take matters into their own hands to deal with the situation that has presented itself, sometimes described as "inspiring others to take personal initiative and act decisively in a crisis".

A perfect example was this attempted terrorist outrage at Glasgow Airport. It is Saturday 30th June 2007, the school summer holidays have started the day before and many families of the Glasgow area are at Glasgow Airport to depart on their annual two weeks holidays abroad. These holiday-makers witness the ineptitude of the attackers, but also their foolhardy choice of Glasgow as a target, a city whose citizens are considered by the rest of the United Kingdom to be amongst the toughest, and perhaps, the last that one would want to pick a fight with.

The Stream

As the terrorist incident unfolds, instead of the terminal buildings being evacuated in a mass panic, hundreds of Glaswegians stream into the buildings to intervene or lend assistance. The hero of the hour, John Smeaton, a baggage handler, had his forever immortal line of "fuckin' mon, then" beamed around the world by CNN and the humour of the day's events displayed by the comedian, Frankie Boyle, and his famous quip of the time - "I just love the naïveté of someone trying to bring religious war to Glasgow."

From South Kensington Underground Station to Heathrow Airport to Glasgow Airport, Daniel had immersed himself in the Lindemann files stored on his laptop. He had searched for names or places with a Glasgow area locale that he could use to get some leverage into the workings of what was going on. A name, Philip Harris, had popped up along with some interesting files and video footage.

In the past 24 hours or so, the parts of the mental jig-saw puzzle inside his head were fitting together to complete the final picture, but the nefarious elements concerning this young girl called Freyja Fulton still eluded him. He needed to get some answers, and pretty fast by the looks of it, to some questions that he was afraid wouldn't be given pleasantly. He hoped that this Phillip Harris could be an approachable man, failing which, a man he could negotiate with considering the salacious content of a video he had just watched.

An internet search of the Das Volker Syndicate's many Scottish holdings and properties had yielded a few Glasgow area addresses. The company had a sizeable research and development laboratory to the north of the city, a pharmaceutical repository on the south side of the River Clyde and a city-centre based regional office devoted to the administration, management and distribution of a global company's numerous interests.

His waiter at breakfast earlier had been extremely helpful in providing him with directions and advice on how to get around the city. A local tourist information leaflet, available from the reception desk, had provided a simplified map of the city, on which, Bobby the waiter, had marked out how to get to various locations and destinations.

He was trying to get his bearings with the map while admiring the buildings around him. Glasgow's city centre lies to the north of the River Clyde and adheres to a grid system layout of streets mainly lined by grand Victorian-era buildings. The details and intricacies ornately contained in the red and blond sandstone edifices impressed him as he walked along West George Street towards George Square. On entering into the square, Daniel had to stop to fully survey an unexpected vista of a 19th century municipal showpiece augmented at its eastern side with a near-palatial City Chambers. This building, with its war memorial cenotaph before it and dominating a spacious, pedestrian-friendly square flanked with trees, seats and numerous statues, was more than just a statement of a city, it was a declaration. 'This is Glasgow'.

Heading diagonally across the square, he quickly spotted the Das Volker Syndicate corporate logo above a doorway on the corner of Cochrane Street and South Frederick Street. Its entrance, flanked with ionic columns replete with their ornately carved volutes and scrolls, were an architectural misnomer to what lay inside. The ground floor was an open-plan office layout straddling a staircase to the upper floors. Staff busied themselves in what can only be described as a lounge-like work-space, more suitable for short-term activities that demand constant collaboration with colleagues while allowing for impromptu interaction with visitors. He made enquiries with one of the staff members and was pointed to the first floor area.

On the first floor, there were opaque glass-fronted meeting rooms, shared offices and study booth areas complemented with modern 'touch down' stations, open work spaces for one person to use. There were a number of private meeting rooms and offices set back into the walls, and Daniel surmised that the more confidential affairs of a global pharmaceutical business, or those that required concentration and privacy, took place behind their doors. He passed his business card to a member of staff and asked if it could be possible to see Philip Harris. The staff member departed and Daniel leaned on a balcony and surveilled the area around and below him. His security management consultant experience made him start to assess the layout of the office, the closed-circuit camera placing, entrance, exit and escape points and the vulnerability of the building should an 'incident' occur. There wasn't as much foot traffic on this floor as there was on the floor below. That could be to his advantage.

The staff member returned and informed him that Philip Harris would see him now and followed her into one of the private offices. She closed the door and a man got up from behind his desk to greet Daniel. He was dressed in a smart suit, albeit slightly dishevelled looking, and his facial features were strained in that his eyes were tired and he had the haggard stubble of a full day's growth that needed an urgent shave.

"Hi. Philip Harris. What can I do for you today Mr. Lauridsen? Please excuse my appearance but I've just had a long drive up from St. Albans to deal with a couple of pressing matters this weekend."

Daniel lied that he was in Glasgow for a few days and was just touting for some security consultant business. He mentioned that he had done a security assessment at the St. Albans facility a few years back, and with him recently meeting Lindemann, he thought he would chance his arm with the Glasgow office. The mention of Lindemann's name had triggered a pained look and the man's body language changed to something Daniel recognised as anxiety. Daniel quickly analysed that Phillip Harris was a frightened man. Daniel asked Phillip if he could show something of interest stored on his laptop. He took the laptop from his rucksack, opened it and started to play the video footage. He turned the screen around for Phillip to watch. Philip's face caved and he slumped at his desk with his head in his hands.

"What do you want from me? I've already told that bastard Lindemann I would get the girl grabbed and taken to the research facility. What the fuck does he need all her blood for and why does she have to die once I've got it?" sobbed Phillip.

Daniel seized Philip's right hand and twisted it backwards, propelled him from the seat and forced him downwards into a corner of the office. He squealed in anguish at the intensity of sudden pain coursing through his arm and body.

"What about her blood and what's this about her dying?" growled Daniel menacingly while still exerting pressure on the hand. He could tell that this man, Phillip Harris, was close to breaking-point and that the answers he wanted to so many questions were about to be revealed unexpectedly quickly.

"Listen mate. I'm just a guy who submitted an idea and the next thing I know I'm promoted, a crazy salary and told to deliver a project, no matter the cost. I didn't know that it was all about finding some girl. Please...?" he whined through the tears running down his face. "I'll tell you everything I know. Please?" he cried.

Daniel came to quickly realise that this man Harris was genuinely scared and utterly out of his depth with whatever was going on concerning the girl. He released the pressure on his hand, pulled him upwards and sat him back down in his chair. Daniel opened a door within the office and found a small toilet area inside. He grabbed the towel beside the sink and passed it to Harris to wipe away his tears and sort himself out. As Harris was doing so, Daniel sat down opposite, pulled his laptop towards him, pressed a few buttons on the keyboard and started an audio recording session on the machine.

"Spill the story. I'll help you and get you out of the trouble you've got yourself into, but you need to tell me everything about the girl, Lindemann, his plans, what's going on, what this is all about – everything! Lie to me, and I won't help you and I won't be so forgiving."

Philip Harris explained his involvement with Das Volker Syndicate and the 'Reprogramming the Code' initiative. Daniel just listened intently to the man's story and started to place snippets of it into the mental jig-saw puzzle.

The Stream

Daniel loitered on the street corner of Cochrane Street and South Frederick Street across from the entrance into the Das Volker Syndicate offices. He had just finished having a coffee in the Brown's Hotel opposite the office and was now awaiting the arrival of Phil Harris. He gazed at the imposing edifice of the City Chambers to his right and the impressive Cenotaph in front of it, and recalled some surprising facts he had discovered when reading a tourist information pamphlet while he was drinking his coffee. The Cenotaph commemorated the sacrifice of the 200,000 Glaswegians who served in the Great War and that the City Chambers contained the world's longest marble staircase, larger than anything to be found in the Vatican.

Having repeatedly listened to Phil's freely given utterances during the recorded meeting on Friday afternoon, Daniel had spent most of his time since then going through a lot of Lindemann's files and folders stored on his laptop. As much as he despised the man, Daniel couldn't help himself from having a modicum of respect at how Lindemann operated his business, cut corners here and there to steal an edge on competitors and used local situations and circumstances as beneficial resources in making the Das Volker Syndicate the global company it had become. The meticulous record keeping of meetings, conversations, business concerns, interests, projects and research archives for not only the pharmaceutical aspects but for the Ahnenerbe activities was certainly impressive. Daniel reckoned Lindemann must have inherited some sort of Nazi gene from his father whereby he tracked and recorded the progress of every single endeavour.

But this type of methodical record-keeping had been the downfall of leading Nazis at the Nuremberg trials at the end of World War 2. Their need for identifying, classifying, storing, securing, retrieving, tracking and permanently preserving records of their activities and atrocities committed throughout the genocide of the Holocaust, had effectively placed nooses around their necks. Daniel hoped that the same would be the case with Lindemann's files.

Lindemann's many compressed computer folders would take years for someone to process and catalogue, even though simple advances by the computer industry allowed for ease of access to sift through data storage of electronic files and documents. But Daniel didn't have that length of time to spare and hoped for, even prayed for a bit of luck.

He found a folder with the title 'COR-Glasgow' and was going to ignore it but he saw that it was 1GB in size and decided to have a casual glimpse at the contents. He wasn't expecting to find much but he certainly wasn't prepared for the documentation it contained and footage of deeply distressing CCTV recording concerning a business meeting. The folder's files were in a chronological order and explained how the Das Volker Syndicate had sourced facilities in Glasgow and how Lindemann had personally dealt with a few operational issues. It was grim reading.

The expansion of the business into Scotland had been very attractive to the company as a result of the Scottish government's various international trade and business investment initiatives. Through these initiatives, as part of the devolution agreements with the UK parliament at Westminster, Scotland had become a major European location for global companies and attracted more international investors than any other United Kingdom region outside of London. Significant financial incentives and assistance had helped establish a proven track record of companies succeeding in business in and around the Glasgow area with having lower operating costs, 30% lower than London, and in a business friendly environment with the lowest tax rates to be found in the G20 economic area.

With a strong transport-link infrastructure and easy local connections to global markets, including the rest of the United Kingdom, Europe and America, the creation of a research and development laboratory to the north of the city, a pharmaceutical repository on the city's south side and a city-centre based regional office had resulted in having access to a skilled workforce that excelled itself in terms of research, innovation and creativity.

But Daniel's investigations through the copious files and records that had been originally stored in Lindemann's computer, had given him an insight into how Torstein Lindemann operated his business concerns, and if they weren't by fair means, they tended to be administered by foul actions. The Glasgow area operations had witnessed some particularly foul ways of operating to ensure that the 'squeaky clean' business side aspect was maintained at all times.

In late 2012, the company's in-house pharmaceutical stock auditors noticed alarming discrepancies in what was being produced, supplied and stored at the Glasgow repository. E-mails, replete with spreadsheets and reports detailing the concerns of the auditors, made their way through the various chains of command, but bypassing the Scottish administrational hierarchy along the way. These audit concerns had reached the Das Volker Syndicate headquarters in Switzerland along with recommendations for possible police involvement and for detailed investigations to be made in respect of fraud, false accounting and the continual theft of sizeable amounts of particular pharmaceutical products.

Lindemann had been keen to avoid any public negativity about the operational aspects of his company and was reluctant to have police or government agency investigations made into what appeared to be an in-house problem and local to the area. The economies of the western world were on the up after a global recession and the Scottish facilities received direct financial capital investment from a devolved parliament. To call in the authorities, who would then conduct some probing work-place inspections based on the findings of investigative scrutiny by company auditors, was not something Lindemann wanted to be carried out.

He out-sourced an investigation to be made by a German firm, Fernenstiche, a licensed independent pursuance company with consultative connections to the Bundesanstalt für Finanzdienstleistungsaufsicht, or BaFin, the German Federal Financial Supervisory Authority, specialising in the research of the possibility of a business losing money due to a fraud or theft being perpetrated by one or more of its employees. Forensic accounting investigations were to be conducted in a confidential and prudent way in order not to alert the guilty parties of the real reason for their being there.

Lindemann was worried that the fraud was larger than was originally thought and he was acutely aware that investigations often show that it has been going on for a number of years. He wanted a forensic accountancy report that focused on the extent of any criminality and identified the weakness in the system that allowed the fraud to take place, and Fernenstiche were to report directly to himself and him alone, but with a caveat. He wasn't really interested in the names of the staff involved perpetrating the loss to his company, as they could be dealt with through legitimate channels, but through covert surveillance and intelligence gathering, he wanted identities - the names of the men that were masterminding the fraud in the first place. He wanted the ring-leaders.

After a six month investigation, Fernenstiche had completed their task and in late May 2013, submitted a detailed report for Lindemann to consider and then act upon.

The report identified that substantial amounts of local anaesthetic drugs, such as procaine, tetracaine and lidocaine had gone astray over an eighteenth month period as well as quantities of the analgesic phenacetin. It was suggested that the missing drugs were being used by drug dealers or 'distributors' in the process of cutting cocaine along with other additives, thus helping to thin out a narcotic batch and increase the profit margin for the supplier. By simply increasing the amount of available narcotic for sale by using low cost chemical additives to bulk out the weight, phenacetin had become one of the key chemicals that could be used because its properties and effects closely resembled pure cocaine.

Recreational drugs like cocaine were now responsible for a £16bn annual bill in social and economic costs with Britons consuming more cocaine than almost any other European Union nation. Although the price of cocaine was rising globally, its final street value was dropping in the United Kingdom. The suggested reason for the fall was because organised drugs gangs were using cutting agents, substances added to cocaine, to dilute its purity. The Glasgow area dealers were selling the drug with a purity as low as 30% and were making handsome profits in doing so.

The economics were breathtakingly massive. The source production costs were £1,000/kg. The cost to buy, after transportation to Europe was around £18,000/kg and the United Kingdom price was roughly £30,000/kg. Once in Glasgow and cut at about 30% purity, the price became £90,000/kg. And stolen Das Volker Syndicate products were being used by third parties to make illicit financial gains.

The report from Fernenstiche was able to identify how the drugs were being stolen and who they were being given to. A number of staff at the repository had been engaged through Calton Office Recruitment, an employment agency providing quality staffing solutions. This recruitment agency had established for itself a solid reputation for sourcing trained staff for production line industries, such as pharmaceuticals and electronics. The company had won many plaudits, however, it had also been under the watchful eye of the Scottish Crime and Drug Enforcement Agency (SCDEA), a specialist police force that was responsible for the disruption and dismantling of serious organised crime groups. The three partners of Calton Office Recruitment, Stuart McGregor, Colin

McCallum and Dunky Stevens, were believed to be heavily involved in prostitution, human-trafficking, loan sharking and drug dealing and used the company as a front for their activities. But repeated attempts by the police to bring them before the courts always seemed to fail.

With more and more economic migrants coming from the former Soviet Bloc countries that had joined the European Union in 2004 now enjoying freedom of movement throughout Europe, Glasgow had become a desirable destination. McGregor, McCallum and Stevens suddenly found themselves with an unexpected influx of flesh to populate some of their more seedy business concerns. Through the relatively simple action of creating an atmosphere of apprehensiveness by confiscating passports and identity papers, and the use of violence, intimidation and threats upon family members, a fear of McGregor, McCallum and Stevens had resulted in them having access to a conveyor belt of meek and frightened employees easily coerced into performing unsavoury acts for paying customers. And the rest of the 'employees' were distributed into proper employment but with percentages of their wages being withheld by the three partners. The threat of savage brutality and reprisal ensured that the 'employees' did as they were told and kept their mouths shut.

Some idle chatter about the stock levels of various Das Volker Syndicate pharmaceutical products had resulted in agency staff being forced to procure quantities of certain drugs from the repository and pass them over to be used as adulterant substitutes in a profitable cocaine empire. But greed and avarice had got the better of Calton Office Recruitment and the scale of the disappearing stock had been flagged up by the in-house auditors.

Fernenstiche had provided an exceptionally detailed report to Lindemann with the names, addresses, contacts, photographs and other items concerning the ring-leaders of a criminal gang profiteering from his company.

Lindemann bided his time and arranged a business meeting to be held at the nearly-finished research and development laboratory being built in the Possilpark Business Zone to the north of the city. The purpose of the meeting was for the three partners of Calton Office Recruitment to personally meet with Doctor Torstein Lindemann, Director General of Das Volker Syndicate and to discuss the supply of around 80 ancillary staff for this new complex.

McGregor, McCallum and Stevens had turned up and had been given a guided tour of the facility by the Project Manager. It had been explained to them that there was a need to have a certainly quality of staff that could be trusted and relied upon and that Dr. Lindemann wished to discuss matters with them at the end of their visit. The tour had gone well and the three men were taken through the animal vivisection unit. Rows upon rows of empty cages and tanks of different sizes had been placed in a brightly lit room about the size of a tennis court. The Project Manager introduced McGregor, McCallum and Stevens to Lindemann who was putting golf balls into a returnable cup and left the room. Two sharp-suited aides then stood over the door frame once the Project Manager had left.

"Do any of you play golf?" enquired Lindemann of the three men. They all said that they didn't.

"That's a pity. A round of golf keeps you fit while allowing you to discuss business matters with associates. You should consider taking up the game." as he flawlessly putted a ball into the cup and waited for its return.

He addressed the ball, paused and turned to the three men and used the putter to point in the direction of the corner behind the returnable cup.

"Do you see that machine there? It is a state-of-the-art animal carcass disposal machine. Once the animals that will soon be occupying the cages in this room" and pointed at the rows behind the men, "have served their purpose for the clinical tests that this facility will be carrying out, they are euthanised and placed into that machine. The machine grinds the body parts into mulch which is then incinerated and the subsequent ashes are then blown into vacuum packs that are stored in sterile boxes for removal. It costs around £275,000.00. The same amount as the cost of the drugs that your employees have stolen from my pharmaceutical repository.

He turned and bludgeoned Dunky Stevens' skull with the putter. The putter head had inserted itself into the poor man's head. His eyes rolled upwards as he collapsed on the ground, gargling as blood and brain matter gushed from the wound. Lindemann struggled with removing the putter from the man's head and had to put his foot on a lifeless shoulder to provide some purchase to set it free. The aides, who were in fact personal bodyguards, had appeared beside Lindemann and had automatic weapons drawn on both McGregor and McCallum.

Lindemann reached down towards Stevens' body and wiped the putter head clean with the dead man's jacket. He tucked the handle of the putter through a belt loop on his trousers and it hung by his side like a sword. He walked over to the disposal machine and switched it on.

"You may wish to bring your friend's body over here." he callously suggested to McGregor and McCallum. The aides waved their guns at the two men and suggested that they better do what Lindemann said. They were both traumatised by what they had just witnessed. Their friend had just been murdered in front of them and they were now being asked to dispose of his body.

"Pick him up and bring him over here. Now!" shouted Lindemann. They grabbed an arm each and dragged Stevens across the floor to the machine.

"Put him in there." as Lindemann pointed at the entrance hopper and started to press some buttons on a console. The body moved along a metallic sliding floor and through opaque rubberised fronds. A rhythmic whine increased in speed while a grating scrunching noise could he heard from inside the contraption.

"Your late friend is now being mulched by 200 angled blades and the resultant residue remains of his body will be passed along a heated metallic sliding floor into the incinerator."

McGregor and McCallum were somewhat uneasy with the calmness of Lindemann and both of them were completely frightened at what they were encountering. They could hear the liquefied remains of their friend slopping into another part of the machine and suddenly the whirring and scrunching decreased in speed and all was silent.

Whoosh! A sudden roar erupted from within the machine. Lindemann laughed. "That'll be the cremation chamber kicking in. The average temperature is around 1650 Fahrenheit or 900 Celsius, depending on what you prefer. This intense heat reduces the mulched body matter to basic elements of ash and dried bone fragments."

The whooshing sound abated and a low hum started to sound. The metallic sliding floor started to move for a few seconds and then stopped. A beeping warning tone sounded and Lindemann walked round to the rear of the machine. He was briefly partly obscured from view and seemed to be busying himself with something.

Lindemann re-appeared holding a small wax-coated box. He slowly walked towards McGregor and McCallum and smiled at both of them as he presented the box to McGregor to take possession of.

"Here's your friend Mr. Stevens. He's not much of a conversationalist, is he?"

McCallum went to punch Lindemann and fell to the ground as one of the bodyguards pistol-whipped him across the back of the head and the other aide kicked him over. Lindemann withdrew the putter from his belt loop and jabbed McGregor under the chin with the club head.

"You and your associate are nothing more than pond life to me. In the grand scheme of things, you are both fairly insignificant to me, in fact, you are an unfortunate irritation that can be easily remedied. You run a number of ventures in the hope of amassing great fortunes. You profit from the poor and vulnerable, you prey on the stupid and you steal from the successful. People like me.

You want to be rich. But you don't understand, do you? Being rich is nothing. Power is the ultimate fortune and the secret to having great wealth. I have power! I control great wealth and fortune and have power over everything and everyone. I determine what happens to whom and to what. And that is what you'll never have. I now know you and own you and I have the power to decide what happens to you for the rest of your sorry little lives."

With the putter, he pushed McGregor backwards by the throat. McGregor stumbled and tripped over McCallum's unconscious body and landed on his bottom. He looked a pathetic figure with fear streaked across his face as he still held on to the box containing the ashes of his recently incinerated friend.

Lindemann opened a briefcase and lifted out a large brown envelope. He walked over to McGregor and emptied the contents out over him and McCallum lying by his side. McGregor blinked repeatedly as his eyes darted between the falling items around him. He gulped as he realised that the contents were documents, tickets, flyers and business cards for some of the various businesses he ran. There were photographs of him, McCallum and Stevens at events and clubs along with photographs of their family members and friends, employees, associates and clientele. As he frantically tried to comprehend what was happening to him and whatever fate now awaited him, he realised that this mad man in front of him had spent a considerable amount of time, effort and money to understand everything and anyone he was involved with. He was a scared man. Lindemann knelt down beside him and picked up some of the articles strewn around and threw them at McGregor's chest. Lindemann's blue eyes had become cold and fierce as he gazed into McGregor's face.

"I own you now. I have it in my power to decide how the rest of your pathetic life pans out from this day forth. You will do what I want, when I want and without question. You will not fail me otherwise you will be joining your friend here." and tapped the box with the putter.

Lindemann stood up and walked towards the exit door. A yellow coloured industrial mop and bucket set on wheels was beside the door. He pushed the mop and bucket across the floor towards McGregor and McCallum and barked instructions at the two bodyguards cum aides.

"Make sure this rubbish cleans up the mess they have made to my premises and kindly escort them off the property when they have finished." and left the room.

Daniel had all of this information in his head and he now understood how Phil Harris was merely an innocent party who had become ensnared into some particularly distasteful and reprehensible activities of an obviously psychotic individual in Lindemann and the malaise of Glasgow underworld figures who feared the power of Lindemann.

He had genuine pity for Phil Harris. He was just an ordinary family man who had made a poor mistake and was now being enforced to carry out the wishes of others against his will. He would help him sort out his mess while he saved this Freyja Fulton from these fuckers. A car pulled up beside Daniel and the driver's window lowered. Phil Harris motioned Daniel over to get in the vehicle.

"Sorry I'm late but I had Lindemann on the phone. He's flying in to Glasgow on Tuesday morning and he wants Freyja Fulton in his possession by then. She's just a girl, for Christ's sake! She's not a bit of property."

Daniel told him to calm down and explain what instructions he had been given by Lindemann. If he knew what Lindemann had ordered to happen he could then interfere and upset these plans while also rescuing Freyja Fulton from whatever fate awaited her. He would get Phil out of his situation as well, but he needed to know what was being considered, the time-frames and the locations. If he had advance knowledge of all of that, he would be able to take direct action. 'Preparatory reconnaissance' was the phrase he used.

As they drove off around the expanse of George Square and headed towards the north of the city, Phil explained that a couple of Lindemann's local underlings, basically thugs for hire, had been commissioned with the task of abducting Freyja Fulton by any means possible and then delivering her to a Das Volker Syndicate facility to the north of the city.

"Messrs. McGregor and McCallum and the Possilpark Business Zone? I know all I need to know about those two gentlemen but let's go and have a look at this facility and get the lie of the land."

Phil flinched as he realised that his passenger knew far more than he had previously let on. There was more to this Danish guy and his reasons for getting involved than had been mentioned previously. But Phil didn't really care anymore for the 'why" and 'how' aspects for this man's sudden arrival into his predicament. He was just glad that someone else, an outsider, had got involved and appeared to be committed to resolving certain situations while erasing all trace of his own indiscretions and impropriety that had originally been manipulated by Lindemann.

Harris turned the car into Castle Street to head towards Possilpark. "After the girl has been grabbed, they're going to take her up to this facility for whatever Lindemann wants. He said to me that he wanted her blood – all of it. I don't know why. Do you?"

Daniel ignored the question. "Where are they going to try to snatch her? Can you show me where?"

"Bridge Street Underground Station tomorrow during the morning rush hour."

The Stream

08.07am – Monday 19th June, present day
Bridge Street Underground Station, Glasgow.

It's the last week of college before the summer break and Freyja is looking forward to having a rest. The pressure of recent exams and then the class trip to the Faroe Islands had been particularly taxing for her. The days and nights of constant study followed by the excitement of a visit abroad had been a constant adrenalin surge. The last few days had been especially fraught with her having to compose an essay report about her recent trip away. She now just needed some time to chill, wind down and relax to enjoy a deserved care-free summer before going back to college in October.

Her double-decker bus pulled into the bus-stop in Bridge Street and Freyja alighted and waited patiently on the pavement for it to drive away into the morning rush-hour traffic and continue its journey into Glasgow City Centre. Packed with commuters all heading for another day of 9.00am to 5.00pm drudgery in the many offices of a commercial city, thought Freyja. "Thank God, I have a few years of being a student ahead of me" she said to herself as she started to cross the road over to Bridge Street Underground Station. Around her, people darted in and out of the traffic in their rush to cross the road while negotiating, and avoiding, the moving vehicles travelling in either direction.

Wendy was standing outside the underground station and waved in Freyja's direction as she crossed the busy road. Freyja smiled and waved back as she stepped onto the pavement in front of the station. Neither of them had noticed the white van that had stopped in the bus-stop to their left or were even aware of the two men inside that watched their every movement as they entered the station.

A third man appeared at the passenger door of the van and rapped on the window. The window rolled down and the third man, an unkempt and shockingly foul looking individual called Manus Neeson scowled in through the open window and addressed the occupants.

"Have you two bastarts got the gear 'n' that, by the way?"

McGregor, in the passenger seat, passes Neeson a polythene bag and tells him "Don't make an arse of this. Walk up to her as the tube arrives, stick that into her side and walk away. We'll deal with everything when she collapses on the platform."

"Where's ma money? Gi'es it here, ya fud" rebuked Neeson as he took the pen taser out of the polythene bag and put it in his jacket pocket. McGregor passes over an envelope that Neeson snatches, opens it and starts to count the reddish hued £50.00 notes inside.

"There's only a grand in here. Where's the rest?" demands Neeson.

McGregor suddenly jerks opens the passenger door and deliberately hits Neeson in the legs with it in doing so. As Neeson yelps with pain and rubs his knees, McGregor grabs him by the left ear and throws him inside the foot-well of the van.

"Don't ever threaten me and just remember I am doing you a favour, you wee trouser bandit. You'll get the rest of the cash when we have the girl. Now get on with what you're supposed to do."

The Stream

McGregor lets go of Neeson's ear and pulls him out of the foot-well and points him to go on his way. Neeson rubs his ear and trudges off into the underground station whilst harbouring murderous thoughts on what he would do to McGregor and his pal, McCallum.

"A couple of shite-bags if you got them on their own" mused Neeson as he purchases a ticket, puts it into the turnstyle and passes through and walks down the two flights of stairs to the platform.

The Bridge Street Underground Station platform is a long and narrow affair with a slight eliptical aspect to it. The single island platform is only about fifteen feet wide and passengers wait in the middle of it for the trains to arrive. The trains are three carriage appliances and are bright orange in appearance. It is the third oldest underground system in the world after London and Budapest and Glaswegians refer to their 15 station underground system as the "clockwork orange" and its two lines, the Inner and Outer circles, run clockwise and counter-clockwise respectively.

As Neeson starts to walk down the flight of stairs onto the platform, he looks to see where the two girls are. Right in front him and in the middle. The platform is crowded and there are probably about a hundred odd people waiting on trains coming in either direction. He looks at a digital notice board hanging from the ceiling above the platform. 'Outer Circle: 6 minutes/Inner Circle: 4 minutes'. "These two lassies are students heading for St. Georges Cross. They'll be waiting on the Outer Circle train coming. It's only 4 stops" thinks Neeson. "I'm going to have to get closer to them as the platform is mobbed. I need that extra grand and I'm no having that tadger McGregor having a go at me again."

He makes his way through the throng of commuters as the Inner Circle train arrives. Its automatic doors open and about 50 people disembark. The waiting commuters stand back to allow the passengers to get off the train and make their way to the exit stairs to the right. Neeson is pushed back by the disembarking passengers and curses loudly. He is still about 20 feet from his target and has less than 2 minutes to get beside her. The waiting commuters move forward into the space created by the departing passengers and the centre of the island platform fills once more with people. More and more passengers are coming down the stairs onto the platform and Neeson is now getting impeded by the volume of commuters and the obstructions of back-packs and sports bags slung over shoulders. He is about 10 feet away from the targets with less than a minute before the Outer Circle train arrives.

Wendy and Freyja are talking about the dreadful television programme they had watched the night before 'How Fat is My Bride', a reality show where a number of portly girls go to drastic measures to lose weight in the six months prior to their big day. The winner, the portly girl who loses the most weight and has a svelte figure to dream about, wins £100,000 and a two week, all expenses paid, 5 star honeymoon in Cancun, Mexico. It is cheap and tacky television at its best but utterly addictive viewing when watching the trials and tribulations of six women and their chasing of a fairytale. Last night's episode's winner, 19 year old Charmaine from Bedford, had discovered on her wedding night that her husband, Tony, had been having an affair with her own mother, Maria, for the previous 4 months.

The approach of the Outer Circle train is preceded by a warm wind that travels ahead of the vehicle. It tugs at trouser legs and skirts and causes coat-tails to flutter in its breeze. Hair is blown across faces by its sudden presence. A whine is emitted from the rails on the track signifying the coming of the train. Two lights, the train's headlights, appear in the tunnel like a pair of dragon's eyes, getting larger as the train approaches. Freyja's hair blows across her face and she unceremoniously barged by a large man with a red rucksack on his back. She stumbles, loses balance and falls to her hands and knees on the platform. The train emerges from the tunnel and the waiting commuters jostle into position on the platform. Neeson, who is about 3 feet away from Freyja, has a cylindrical implement in his right hand. It looks like an oversized pen but with two thick prongs where the pen nib should be. A compact taser powered by two 9 volt batteries delivering a high voltage shock which essentially short circuits a person's neurological system and incapacitates them. He moves forward to strike with the taser as Freyja is bundled to the ground. The man with the red rucksack turns to assist Freyja, and in doing so, his rucksack connects with Neeson in mid-lunge, hits him waist high and propels him past Freyja and into the path of the train.

It isn't pretty. A howling scream followed by a blinding blue flash as Neeson hits the electric rail and is then effectively diced and sliced by the slowing train. Sprays of blood are on the walls, the platform and the front panels and windows of the train. People are screaming and shouting in panic. Freyja, winded, and oblivious to the sudden carnage around her, pushes herself up, and watches the man with the red rucksack pick something up from the platform, pocket it and then bound up the exit stairs, two at a time. He's familiar to me and I don't know how Freyja thought to herself. Wendy is open-mouthed in shock at what she has just witnessed but is dumbfounded as to why there are now £50.00 notes fluttering about above her like butterflies on a summer's day.

Daniel Lauridsen bounded up the steps of the exit stairs, two at a time. His heart was pounding and his mind was all over the place. He had just saved someone from a particularly nasty assault, bundled another to their death in front of an underground train, picked up a pen taser off the platform concourse and now had to make his escape from the invasive questions of investigators, emergency services personnel and others. On their checking of the station CCTV Systems, he would probably be readily identifiable with the red rucksack on his back. He had to dump that as soon as possible.

He reached the first turn of the exit stairs. People were still going down the stairs to his right to get on the platform as the events of what had just happened were still unclear and confused. On the wall to his left, he sees a yellow emergency alarm box with the legend on its front housing 'Break Glass to Sound Alarm'. Daniel elbows the glass and triggers the alarm. Instantly, yellow flashing lights come to life on the walls and ceilings of the underground station. A three pulse alarm tone sounds and a recorded voice message plays through speakers throughout the entire complex "Please proceed to the nearest exit in a calm and orderly manner" followed by another three pulse alarm tone. The tone and message continuously repeats itself. Commuters suddenly stop going down to the platform and about turn while those on the platform start to stream towards the upwards exit stairs. Underground staff and personnel, instantly identifiable by their wearing of neon high-visibility blousons, begin to appear from side-doors and offices and try to assess the emerging situation. Some start marshalling commuters towards the exit, while others try to make their way through the on-coming hordes to the platform. The automatic ticket turn-style barriers have fallen away to allow unimpeded escape from the station.

Daniel strides purposely through one of the ticket barriers as two men with high visibility jackets approach him. Both of the men are holding evacuation chairs, lightweight devices to assist with the safe removal of people in the event of an evacuation situation, and as they pass beside each other at the barrier, McGregor says to Daniel.

"What's happening chief?"

Daniel replies. "Someone jumped in front of a train" and makes his way out into Bridge Street.

McGregor turns to the other man with him, McCallum. "Jesus Christ! I knew this was going to go pear-shaped."

McCallum grunts in agreement and both men head towards the platform stairs. At the top of the stairs, both men come face to face with an advancing mass of commuters attempting to get out of the station. McCallum opines "Bugger this" to McGregor and turns around and makes his way back out to the street. McGregor, looking at the situation, has to agree with him and follows suit.

They walk over to the parked van and throw their high-visibility jackets and the evacuation chairs into the back of the van, get in the front of it and drive off. As they drive off, flashing red and blue lights and different sounding sirens mark the arrival of police, ambulance and fire brigade vehicles around the underground station.

Daniel walks briskly to the junction of Bridge Street and Norfolk Street, crosses diagonally over the road and turns into South Portland Street. He spots a group of men queued up outside a Salvation Army establishment on the other side of the street. The men are unfortunate Glaswegian mendicants waiting for the soup kitchen to open and the chance of a meal and a hot beverage. Daniel stops, takes off his rucksack and opens it. He takes out a black rain jacket and puts it on. He rummages in the side pockets of the rucksack and gathers whatever personal effects there are together and places them in a carrier bag he has found. He takes a BlackBerry Z10 mobile phone device from another flap in the rucksack and sticks it inside his jacket and puts its USB cable and charger inside the carrier bag. Daniel takes his wallet out, opens it and removes some paper money and puts it in the various side pockets of the rucksack. He sorts through the remainder of the belongings inside the rucksack, grabs a black ski hat and places it on his head. Having decided that there is nothing remaining in the rucksack to identify him as the owner, he zips it up and puts it over his right shoulder, picks up the carrier bag in his left hand and walks over to the queue of men outside the Salvation Army. As he gets closer, he slips the rucksack off his shoulder into his right hand and gives it to the nearest man.

"There's some clothes and stuff for you boys. There's some cash as well in the side pockets. You've not seen me, have you?" and winks at the men.

The men look at him and one says "Seen who, Boss?" in a toothless grimace and Daniel walks away and smiles as the men start arguing and fighting with each other over the ownership of the bag and its contents.

Adjusting the ski hat on his head, Daniel moves a metal badge of a sailing ship to the front, and continues walking down South Portland Street into Carlton Place and goes across the pedestrian Suspension Bridge over the River Clyde to Clyde Street. Halfway across the bridge, he throws the pen taser into the river. Once over on the other side, he crosses Clyde Street and makes his way through St. Enoch Square and heads for Buchanan Street. Morning pedestrian rush hour in Glasgow's city centre as people are heading to work, college, university or are waiting for the many shops and businesses to open. "I'll be hard to track now" thinks Daniel as he walks up Buchanan Street and disappears into the heart of the city.

On the platform of the underground station, Freyja and Wendy are struggling coming to terms with what has just happened. Wendy, still in shock with what she has witnessed, has caught three £50.00 notes flapping beside her when Freyja, still winded and unaware of what has happened, grabs her friend by the arm and asks.

"What the hell is going on?"
Wendy, still watching butterflies in the air, says "I don't know. I don't really know."

The Stream

Yellow flashing lights have come on and a pulsating alarm sound rings everywhere with a message blasting "Please proceed to the nearest exit in a calm and orderly manner."

The two girls start to walk along the platform. The driver is at the front of the underground train and is shining a torch on the tracks below trying to see if the jumper is still alive. In front of the girls, people disembark from the train and follow other commuters making their way to the exit stairs. As Wendy catches another £50.00 note, she slips on a greasy substance on the platform, looks down and realises that she had just trodden on a spray of blood from the man that she saw fall in front of the train. But then she questions herself. He didn't fall. He was knocked into its path by some bloke who hit him with a red rucksack. The man was going to attack Freyja and red rucksack man stopped him by barging Freyja over and then hit him with his rucksack.

"Freyja. That guy was going for you" blurts Wendy.

"What are you talking about? What guy? And what's the story with the money Wendy?" snaps Freyja.

"The guy who fell in front of the train was going for you but someone with a red rucksack stopped him. And all of a sudden there was this money flying about."

Freyja remembers being barged, falling over and seeing someone with a red rucksack pick something up off the platform and then run up the stairs. Red rucksack man did seem familiar to her but she couldn't place him. It didn't make any sense to her and she couldn't fathom what possible connections there could be.

"Freyja, someone tried to kill you back there and some bloke intervened and saved you." blurts Wendy.

"Don't talk mince Wendy and will you stop grabbing bloody money please" barks Freyja. Wendy starts to laugh at Freyja's words.

"Bloody money. That's very good Freyja. Bloody money. Brilliant".

Police officers, paramedics, firemen and Underground staff are flooding onto the platform as the two girls get to the bottom of the stairs. There are still commuters attempting to make their escape from the platform. A police officer stops the girls and asks them if everything is ok. Freyja says it's not and starts to tell the officer what she thinks has just happened. The police officer calls over a female colleague to assist him and they start to take down details in their notebooks. The girls are now sat on the bottom steps of the stairs and a couple of paramedics come over and check them over. The girls give their details and versions of events to the two police officers and are told to stay where they are as the paramedics finish checking them over.

The first police officer, Constable Watson, turns and speaks to his female colleague, Constable Greig.

"There's something's not right with all of this. Something has definitely happened here and these two wee girls were targeted for some reason. I think we should go and check the CCTV footage."

Constable Greig goes over to the girls and asks them to stay where they are and that they'll be back in a few minutes to take further details. Constable Greig speaks to another police officer, explains the situation and asks him to stay with the girls and then joins her colleague as they both head to the station's control room.

Inside the station's control room, senior police officers, firemen and underground staff are already reviewing the recordings of the station's various CCTV cameras. The footage of the final moments of Manus Neeson is being replayed on two screens. The grainy images were recorded by two ceiling cameras placed at either end of the platform. On the left hand screen, the Inner Circle platform is displayed and at the top right of the picture, in amongst the figures of the passengers awaiting the arrival of the Outer Circle train, Manus Neeson can be seen getting accidentally barged in front of the train.

"Looks like an accident" say an underground official.

"Bollocks!" growls a female voice watching the right hand screen. "Play that bit back again, will you?" say the voice. "Look at that" as a forefinger jabs the screen.

On the screen, The Outer Circle platform is displayed and on the bottom left of footage, a teenage girl is seen being pushed to the ground by a man with a red rucksack who then turns and uses the rucksack to swipe another man into the path of the train. The footage then shows the rucksack man pick something up and then run out of frame.

"Replay that bit again please?" says the voice and the CCTV operator duly obliges.

"That's a deliberate course of action. Rucksack man saves that girl from some sort of attack and then blooters the guy in front of the train. The picture isn't great but that looks like that wee jakey toe-rag Manus Neeson and someone has just offed him. Just done society a favour, but that's still murder. Can we formally identify the guy that got hit by the train as Manus Neeson?"

The Stream

"Not yet" says Constable Watson while Constable Greig pipes up.

"We have the two girls down on the platform just now getting checked by paramedics. Do you want to speak to them?"

"Of course I do" growls back the female voice of Detective Inspector Chalmers.

"Fill me in with the details as we go" and the three police officers leave the control room and head down towards the platform.

The Stream

The platform is now deserted apart from police officers establishing the area as a crime scene and Underground staff trying to assist them.

At the foot of the stairs, paramedics are finishing their examinations of the two girls. Wendy is still clutching a handful of £50 notes as Freyja is approached by two police officers and a smartly dressed woman in her late forties. Freyja recognises the two police officers and smiles at them. Constable Greig asks her how she is doing and introduces the woman beside her.

"This is Detective Inspector Blair Chalmers and she would like to ask a few questions, if that's all right with you?"

Freyja nods in agreement and shakes the hand of the woman and scans the identification badge that has just been thrust in front of her face.

"Hi. I appreciate that you are still trying to come to terms with the situation just now, but I have to ask you some questions that'll help me with my enquiries. Do you know why someone was trying to attack you this morning? Do you know the guy that tried to attack you?"

Detective Inspector Blair points down the platform in the direction of the stationary train, the blood sprays on the platform, the carriages and the walls as scene of crime officers, cladded in white tyvek coveralls, are photographing and videoing the area, leaving numbered markers at particular points and sealing off sections with blue and white striped tape.

Freyja just blurts out "Err, no. I was just waiting to get on the tube and I was shoved to the ground and the next thing I know some guy tries to pick me up, then runs off, grabs something off the floor and then buggers off up the stairs."

Freyja puts her hand over her mouth and apologises for swearing. Detective Inspector Chalmers smiles and re-assures her that she's heard far worse.

"The man that knocked you to the ground, the man with the red rucksack, do you recognise him?"

"I know this might seem a bit stupid, but the rucksack guy I'm sure I've seen before, and the more I think about it, it becomes even sillier because it can't be true. It's not possible."

Chalmers presses Freyja for more information. "What do you mean by it's not possible?"

"I was up in the Faroe Islands recently and I think I bumped into that guy a couple of times when I was there."

"The where? The Faroe Islands? Where the hell are they?" asks Chalmers.

Freyja explains that she and Wendy had been on a recent field-trip to the Faroes with her college and as she does so, she becomes more and more adamant that she has seen the rucksack man before as she recollects the occurrences in her mind. As she replays her memories, she cuts off in mid-sentence with the detective.

"Wendy! Wendy! That rucksack guy spoke to us in the hallway of the conference place in Tórshavn. He was also sitting on a bench when we went to look at the sundial. I think he was also on our plane going up to the Faroes. I'm sure of it. I told you I had seen him before."

Wendy stops counting the £50 notes and thinks about what Freyja has just told her. She reaches into her pocket for her mobile phone and starts to scroll through recent photographs she had taken with it. She finds what she is looking for. A photograph of Freyja kneeling beside a sundial carved into some rocks. Freyja has placed her forefinger into the centre of the sundial to form a gnomon to tell the time. Wendy uses her thumb and forefinger to explore the background of the photograph behind Freyja. As she starts to enlarge aspects of the photograph, she suddenly stops, puts her hand to her hair and exclaims "For Christ's sake Freyja, you were right." and turns her phone around to display the photograph.

In the background of the image, behind Freyja, can be seen a couple sitting on a bench. A black haired woman is talking to a man looking towards the camera. He has a red rucksack beside his feet.

Chalmers snatches the telephone and stares at the photograph and turns to officers Greig and Watson.

"Get these two back to the office pronto and get that telephone to forensics ASAP. I want stills of all the photographs printed, the works, ready, and on the wall of the conference room by 1.00pm. We need to assemble MIT and start to piece things together. Move."

Officers Greig and Watson take the mobile telephone and ask the girls to accompany them back to the police station. Detective Inspector Chalmers looks at the girls, who by now are becoming frightened and alarmed with what is happening to them. She sympathetically speaks to them.

"I'm sorry girls, but there's no college for you today. With what you've just told and shown me, I believe that there's been a deliberate attempt to hurt you both this morning, so I am going to have to detain you for your own safety and make further enquiries, just to be on the safe side. I don't know where the rucksack man figures in all of this but he stopped you both being attacked but he murdered someone in doing so. These officers will take you back to the police station and get Family Liaison Officers to contact your parents and bring them to the station for you as support. I'm satisfied that there has been a serious crime committed this morning that I'm now duty bound to investigate, but you are both the principal witnesses. I now need you to speak to members of the MIT, the major incident team and tell them everything that you know and can think of that could be relevant to this investigation. It doesn't matter if you think something is silly, just tell them everything. Sometimes silly matters are the most crucial pieces of evidence."

The Stream

5.23pm – Monday 19th June, present day
The Centurion Hotel, Buchanan Street, Glasgow

Daniel Lauridsen lay back on the bed in his hotel room and went over the day in his head. This morning's events in the underground station had changed matters. Lindemann was definitely trying to do harm to the girl and he had reluctantly had to intervene. He didn't want to, but he had to. He hoped that the man that he bundled to his death didn't suffer. It was a terrible way to die, but Daniel knew from personal experience, there were far worse ways to go. And some of them were extremely painful, tortuous and prolonged. He slowly drifted off to sleep and flashbacked to Afghanistan and Task Force K-Bar.

Daniel had been in the Frømandskorpset, an elite commando frogman corps of the Royal Danish Navy. A secretive special forces unit skilled in conducting long range reconnaissance, direct assault on land and sea, sabotage of fixed installations, professional diving, counter terrorism and search and rescue missions. His unit had been part of a U.S. Army Special Forces led coalition special operations forces task force made up of about 3,000 troops from eight nations such as Canada, Norway, Denmark, Germany, Australia, New Zealand, Turkey and the USA. The task force was the first major ground deployment in the invasion of Afghanistan and it operated from October 2001 to April 2002. They had been based near to Kandahar.

Four female nurses from the military hospital outside of Kandahar had been kidnapped just before Christmas 2001. The nurses were two Danish and two Norwegian nationals, and intelligence reports suggested that they were being held by tribesmen in the foothills close to the Pakistan border and the town of Chaman. There was no political or terrorist agenda for the kidnappings by local tribesmen. The kidnappings had simply been opportunistic and that there was a ransom being demanded.

Captain O'Donnell, of the New Zealand Special Air Service, was a liaison officer for the different units serving under the K-Bar banner. He had called a special briefing meeting and had asked Denmark's Frømandskorpset and their land and air commando unit, the Jægerkorpset, to attend along with Norway's elite corp, the FSK, the ultra-secretive Forsvarets Spesialkommando. During the briefing, he explained the situation to the assembled men and asked for volunteers to search for and rescue the four nurses. A deadline had been given of 31st December 2001 for the ransoms to be paid or all four women would be brutalised then executed as a warning to other western women coming to Afghanistan. Captain O'Donnell went on to state that local informants had provided details as to the possible whereabouts of the women, and it seemed likely that they had been separated and were being held in four differing locations but in close proximity to each other. All of the assembled 170 men volunteered and Captain O'Donnell thanked them for their commitment, informed them that he would consult with their respective commanding officers and appoint four 6 man teams to rescue the women, two from Denmark and two from Norway, each tasked with rescuing their own nationals.

Daniel's six man Frømandskorpset team had been assigned to rescue an Anna Haroldsen, a 26 year old nurse from Esbjerg serving in the 4th Medical Battalion. A six man team from the Jægerkorpset was given the task of rescuing 31 year old Mariella Osternuit from Odense. It was the 21st of December.

Both teams relied on information given to them by two youths who had witnessed the original kidnappings. They were brothers, Hassan who was 14 and Wajid who was 17. Both orphans, they were street sellers of anything that they could get their hands on and they were enjoying a boom period with all the differing military personnel from all over the world now on their doorstep. There were rich pickings to be made. The brothers had quickly found a niche market to trade all the different cigarettes and confectionery that they procured from various military sources, and they had a particular penchant for Danish Prince cigarettes and Yankie chocolate bars, owing to their popularity amongst the locals. They had gotten to know the nurses as they kept giving the brothers cigarettes and chocolate to sell. They liked them because both women always talked to them and treated them as if they were adults. The brothers had just got a carton of cigarettes from the nurses when a covered truck suddenly stopped in the street, 5 men emerged and grabbed the women and threw them in the back of the truck and drove off. Hassan and Wajid had recognised the men as Wallabi tribesmen from the village of Alijakrit, just off the A75 Highway and close to the Pakistan border.

The four teams had covertly made their respective ways to the area around Alijakrit on the 23rd December. It was a sprawling village of about fifty buildings and outhouses spread out over a distance of half a mile. Most of the buildings were flat-roofed dwelling house affairs that had small outhouses beside them, surrounded by brick wall livestock pens. The village was located in the middle of a valley with rising foothills on either side of a dirt track road that ran through the village in an east/west direction. The Jægerkorpset had commenced reconnaissance of the village from the hills above and had accounted for 79 people coming and going in the village.

During this reconnaissance, the frequent movements of a covered truck arriving in the village from the east had been tracked. It would arrive and a group of armed men would get out, talk to the locals that greeted them and then the men would visit four separate outhouses. Each of these outhouses was guarded by a local tribesman armed with an AK-47 automatic rifle. The Jægerkorpset surveillance had established that these four guarded outhouses were the likely locations of where the missing nurses were being held. In communication with the FSK and Frømandskorpset teams, a plan for rescue was developed.

The Forsvarets Spesialkommando had compact, monocular thermal imaging cameras designed for long range observation by the detection of heat signatures in daylight or at night and could identify a man sized object at a range of up to 2 kilometres. The FSK had studied the four outhouses for heat signatures and had found that there were indeed signatures of prone figures lying on the floor of each of these buildings, presumably the nurses, bound and gagged. Under cover of darkness in the early evening of the 24th December, Daniel's Frømandskorpset team had stealthily entered the village and placed a multispectral covert target marker on each of the outhouses. Each marker emitted a signature only visible through night vision devices and they had been strategically placed to identify the locations of the hostages. It had been agreed that the Jægerkorpset and one of the FSK teams would cause a distraction at either end of the village, provide sniper fire and eliminate hostiles, and in the confusion, the other FSK team and the Frømandskorpset would split into 3 man cells and effect simultaneous rescue of the four nurses. The attack time was set for 2100 hours with an exit airlift by helicopter arranged for 2110 hours.

Explosions at either end of the village heralded the commencement of the rescue. Armed men flooded out of various buildings to investigate the disturbance. As they did, the sniper support from the hills above picked them off. The 3 man cells made their way to their designated outhouses, aided by night vision goggles that illuminated the flashing diodes of the target markers.

Many of the local tribesmen fled as they comprehended that they were under a concerted attack from professional soldiers. The armed guards at each of the outhouses had been eliminated by the sniper support and the nurses were quickly freed from their bindings and carried to the rendevous point to await helicopter extraction. Occasional gun-fire rang out and brief firefight exchanges occurred as the four special forces teams awaited uplift. The heavy chugging sound of rotor blades marked the approach of the two U.S.Army Huey rescue helicopters. Both Huey's M60C Flexible Machine Guns fired 7.62mm rounds, interspersed with tracer ammunition, in and around the village as they landed. It was enough to dispel any further attack from the locals that had the stomach for it. The Danish and Norwegian troops got on board the helicopters and they took off, heading for their base at Kandahar.

On Daniel's helicopter, he checked the condition of the two nurses they had rescued. One of them was Anna Haroldsen. She was distressed, dirty, hungry, thirsty and exhausted. She was still trying to process the fact that she had just been rescued and was extremely frightened for her safety. Daniel spoke to her gently to reassure her, brushed a lock of her hair to the side of her face and offered her a bottle of water. She snatched the bottle and gulped its contents ravenously. She drained the bottle, wiped her mouth with the back of her hand and said "Tusind tak", a thousand thanks.

Daniel smiled back at her and replied. "Du er velkommen. Glædelig jul." You are welcome. Merry Christmas.

The success of the rescue mission had been flagged up on the media all over the world. 'The Miracle at Christmas' was the major headline of the Nordic press, where the actions of two relatively small countries special forces were being praised. Most of the press coverage was about the four nurses, their kidnappings, their rescue, their recuperation and what they were going to do in the future. It died down after a few weeks and Daniel and his fellow soldiers had continued on their daily duties as part of the K-Bar Task Force. Intelligence gathering, reconnaisance, routine patrols.

After the nurses had been rescued, the two Danish women had been de-briefed on events and were to be repatriated back to Denmark for recuperation before the year's end. Both women had wanted to express their thanks to the brothers, Hassan and Wajid, for providing information that had been crucial to their saviour. They had met the lads, thanked them and had given them a significant supply of cigarettes and confectionery as a token of appreciation.

It had been noted that the brothers had not been seen around Kandahar since early January. They had achieved a wee bit of celebrity status for their actions and their business had become very successful. Around about the 20th January 2012, reports had come in that the body of one of the brothers had been found just outside of Kandahar. Daniel had gone to investigate whether it was or not. He had arrived at the scene and was met by the usual crowd of gaping onlookers and Afghani police trying to control the situation. He pushed through the crowd and was met with the scene of a kneeling body with its head face down on the ground. The body's hands were bound behind the back. The kneeling body was inside a dried pool of blood that surrounded it. There were empty cigarette packets and their contents strewn all around the body. An Australian Army doctor was attempting to establish the cause of death. He looked up at Daniel.

"This is a strange one, mate. This poor bugger has had his throat slit and has bled to death where he knelt. But by the looks of it, he's been beaten badly beforehand. What I can't understand is why someone would try to suffocate him first before slitting his throat."

Daniel looked at the doctor quizically. "What do you mean?" he asked.

The Australian Army doctor gently raised the head of the victim. Daniel immediately recognised the face of young Hassan and that his mouth and nostrils were full of crushed cigarettes. It was now clear that Hassan had been force-fed cigarettes to eat right up to the point of choking and he could swallow no more, and at that point, he had had his throat slit by assailants unknown. The cigarettes were a Danish brand and this was not just a pointless murder of a child. This was a symbolic warning message being issued out to the Afghan population that fraternistion with foreign nationals would not be tolerated. Daniel was appalled at the needless and barbaric slaughter of an innocent. He was just a child living in difficult times. He had to fend for himself as best he could and had been callously executed for no other reason than helping some foreign women get rescued from their captors.

Three days later, a Turkish patrol had found the body of Hassan's brother, Wajid. He had been staked out in a star shape with his hands and legs pinned to the ground with wooden pegs. His eyelids had been sewn onto his eyebrows and his torso had been cut open and he had been bleeding. The cutting of his torso and the scent of his blood had attracted animals to feast on him. Bearded Vultures had repeatedly pecked at his face and body during the day while caracal lynx had dined on him at night. It had been a horrendous way to die. Staked out in the beating sun, eyes sewn open and torso slit to attract wildlife to gorge upon you. The Turkish soldiers that had found him had reckoned that it had probably taken about 36 hours for Wajid to eventually die. An appalling form of torture.

Daniel sat up in bed, picked up his black ski hat from the bedside table and looked at the badge of the sailing ship on the front. There were far too many coincidences in amongst this mad situation that he was now in the middle of. The past few weeks had been crazy. Having gone from doing his own thing, care-free and answerable to no-one but himself, he had become drawn into a disturbing affair that seemed to have some very dark and worrying aspects to it.

Through no choice of his own, and whether he liked it or not, he was now the unseen guardian angel, the protector, of a young Glaswegian girl called Freyja Fulton from some sinister forces and the interests of a multi-national company. He didn't know all the reasons as to why he was protecting the girl as yet, but he was now determined to find them out as well as the many answers to all of the questions he had.

What had originally started out as an innocent investigation on behalf of his mother to find out some information about some woman called Dagny Poulsen, had turned into like being on a full-blown solo mission from his Frømandskorpset days: reconnaissance, sabotage, direct action, intervention and search and rescue.

Too many incidents, people, stories and events were bizarrely connected with each other but separated by the passage of time and 80 years. Then and now, and their coincidences, were inextricably linked with each other leaving Daniel piecing together a jigsaw puzzle that transcended time and a story that had never been told before or even understood.

He switched on the television and a local news channel came on. It ran a story about a man committing suicide in front of an underground train at Bridge Street Station during the morning rush-hour. There were interviews with emergency services and members of the public about how events had unfolded earlier in the day and the news story finished with a picture of a man wearing a red rucksack. It was him. The news story was asking for the public to assist in identifying the man and there was an appeal for the same man to contact Police Scotland to help them with their ongoing enquiries into the events of this tragic incident.

Daniel was impressed at the cleverness of the police and the appeal for information and identification. He thought of Sólrun, their time together in the Faroes and her showing him some runes carved into some rocks at Tinganes.

ᛏᛁᛘᛁᛏ ᚱᛖᛘᛏᚾᚱ ᛋᚾᛗ ᛋᛏᚱᛗᛃᛘᚾᚱ ᛁ ᚠ

Sólrun had converted the runes into Faroese, a variant of Old Norse. 'Tíðin rennur sum streymur í á'. She had explained that the runes had become a famous Faroese proverb. When translated into modern language, it read as 'Time runs like the current of a stream'.

For Daniel, time was flowing like a stream and he was riding the current in the middle of it, bobbing along in its many eddies, making a journey towards its unknown destiny.

But for Daniel, and obviously Freyja Fulton, time was also running out and he didn't have the luxury of delaying matters anymore.

It was time to revert to taking direct action and bringing this whole affair to a close, by whatever means possible.

The Stream

The sun was still shining and its beams made the red sandstone facades of the tenement buildings appear to be glowing in the warmth of the late evening sunshine.

Blair Chalmers unlocked the street-door entrance to the close, the connecting passage, stairs and landings within a tenement building that provide common access to two or more of the flats contained inside, and climbed the three flights of stairs to the top-floor where her apartment was located. It had been a long day and she was now glad to be home, to relax and have a think about the day's events and circumstances. She opened the door to her flat, kicked the mail lying on the floor out of the way, threw her bag and jacket down beside the hall table, slipped off her shoes and turned right into the kitchen/dining-room.

She made herself a large mug of coffee and padded across the hall into her living-room. She put down her mug on the coffee table, extracted a cigarette from a packet lying nearby, lit it and reached for the remote-control for the television. She switched on the television and sank backwards into the red leather armchair to watch whatever mind-numbing rubbish was on offer. As she relaxed into her seat and took the first draw of tobacco as if she was sucking a milkshake through a straw, she noticed the seated figure of a man on the two-seater settee in the darkness of the wall recess behind the television. She calmly exhaled the smoke towards the man and put the cigarette down in the ashtray in front of her. Leaning to her left, she flicked on the Ottoman ceiling light to illuminate the darker corners of the room. The dark mahogany wood panelling added an eerie glow to the room as DI Blair Chalmers studied the man seated less than 15 feet from her in the recess.

"Can I help you?" she asked in a quiet and passive manner.

The man threw a USB memory stick and a passport onto the coffee table, raised his hands upwards in a manner of surrender, and introduced himself to her.

"My name is Daniel Lauridsen. I believe you are looking for the man wearing the red rucksack at the underground station this morning. I am he, but you know that already. I mean you no harm but I cannot waste time in a police station answering questions. Time is of the essence and I would suggest that you hear me out, have a look at the information on that USB stick and check out my credentials from my passport details. I really need your help but I have to be at liberty to save someone. In return for my liberty, I'm giving you the opportunity to close down a huge criminal operation in the Glasgow area involving drugs, prostitution, human trafficking, money-laundering and corruption as well as taking out a multi-national company with links and associations going back to the horrors of Nazi Germany. The ramifications of the subsequent arrests through police involvement and investigations will reverberate around the world. Trust me when I tell you that this isn't just an investigation into someone's unfortunate death on a platform this morning. This is going to involve the major police and security services of the world."

Chalmers picked up the USB stick and inserted it into the side of her television. She used the remote control to bring up the contents on the screen. There were loads of document folders, images and video files on display. Before she could start studying anything, Daniel continued speaking.

"You might want to begin with the file marked 'COR-Glasgow' and watch the video footage. That's just a taster for starters. I'm sure you will recognise a few familiar faces and also discover why someone isn't around anymore."

She opened the folder and pressed play to watch the video. Her eyes widened as the last moments of Dunky Stevens played out on the screen before her. There was an expression of shock on her face as she comprehended why this person of criminal interest was no longer to be seen around the Glasgow crime scene. She paused the footage on her television screen and looked over at Daniel. "Before I agree to help you Mr. Lauridsen, I need to know a few details. You've broken into my flat, accosted me in my own home, suggested that I help you and given me a memory stick with information that you say that I might be interested in. How did you find me? How the fuck did you get in here and why should I fucking help you?" she snarled at him.

Daniel simply smiled at her. "I'm a former military specialist with high security clearance within my own country and NATO. Finding out your details was relatively easy if you make a few phone-calls, speak to the right people and call in a few favours of old. As I said, I need your help to save someone, a young Glasgow girl called Freyja Fulton, but to save her, I need back-up, assistance and resources that I do not have at my disposal. I've been told that you are a very determined individual with an extremely analytical mind and that you are a detective of high regard and reputation. I just thought that you might want to be the source and starting point of a thorough and systematic investigation of criminal activities that will ultimately cross many state borders and jurisdictions."

"So why is Freyja Fulton so important to you and why do you have to save her? Save her from what? Spill the beans and tell me why I should help you."

Daniel leaned back in the settee. "I hope you have a couple of hours to spare for me to give you the abridged version of what I know? The important thing to consider is that someone wants Freyja Fulton's blood, literally, and all of it and by any means possible."

"I'm listening" said Chalmers as she lit another cigarette. She glanced at the clock on the mantelpiece. It was 9.59pm.

The Stream

4.42am – Tuesday 20th June, present day
The Centurion Hotel, Buchanan Street, Glasgow

Fully clothed, Daniel lay on top of his hotel bed and contemplated whether this DI Blair Chalmers could be trusted or not. He had taken a gamble by breaking into her flat and waiting to confront her in her own home about recent events and circumstances. One thing that he did know for sure was that she was an exceedingly sharp-witted individual who grasped the enormity of all the information that he had told her. The USB stick had helped to confirm many aspects and he hoped that she would keep to her end of the bargain – he retained his liberty and that he was free to do his own thing, if and when required but on the proviso that he was only a phone-call or a text away. As a token of good faith on his part, he had allowed her to retain his passport.

The two of them had discussed matters until 4.00am when he had taken his leave and had flagged down a passing taxi in the street outside her flat. As he got in, he looked upwards to see her frame in the bay window of her living room. He couldn't be 100% sure if she had but he thought she'd waved at him as he got into the taxi.

He kept on rewinding the last few hours in his head and was positive that he hadn't left any salient details out. He'd probably told her more than she actually needed to know but, on reflection, his trip to the Faroes, the salvage dive, his grandmother's story, the promise to his own mother, how he had ended up in Glasgow in the first place and why he had intervened in a situation on an underground station the day before, probably made him, and his story, all the more plausible and believable. A provision of provenance to a bizarre chain of events and circumstances that had conspired to create his current predicament – he was now the unseen protector of Freyja Fulton.

To be fair to DI Blair Chalmers, he thought, she had listened to his story and indeed, it did appear to him that she seemed to be genuinely fascinated in how all the differing aspects and inter-locking pieces of information were creating, as he had described, a complicated jigsaw that portrayed an intriguing tale that transcended decades.

As their discussions had progressed, she had contacted some colleagues and had arranged for a briefing meeting to be convened at the Glasgow City Centre Police Office at 9.00am. She had invited him to come along and attend the briefing and that his attendance would be classified as a 'guest consultant' offering advice, explanations and information on what she was going to have to reveal to her superiors and then co-ordinate with other agencies and police forces in the execution of any subsequent investigations. When he baulked at the mention of him attending, she gave him an assurance that he would not be arrested and he would be free to provide whatever assistance as necessary, or demanded.

When he was leaving her flat, she had given him a business card with the police station's address. 50 Stewart Street, Glasgow, G4 0HY.

"See you tomorrow at 9.00am sharp. You'll find that the Stewart Street police station is a five minute walk from Cowcaddens Underground Station. Try not to bump anyone over on the platform though" and closed the door.

The Stream

The police station at Stewart Street in Glasgow will never win any prizes for its architectural design or presentation. Irrespective of how you looked at the building, it was just simply a stark, 3-storey high rectangular shaped office block, clad in blue and slate-grey coloured metal paneling that was interspersed with some small square windows. As Daniel passed through the entrance doors, he mused to himself that from the outside, the building looked like the side of a naval oil tanker with some square port-holes.

Once inside, the grimness of the exterior had been replicated with the interior. It didn't help that the police station was north facing with very little natural sunlight being able to penetrate through the square port-holes, but Daniel was surprised that no-one had considered the lux capacity, the strength of the artificial lighting, when designing the utilitarian aspects of the building as a working police station with modern office design to meet the needs of 21st Century policing. With low ceilings and neutral coloured decoration on the walls, the artificial illumination was simply depressing. The key elements of using utilitarian style is that it is supposed to be somewhat representative of function, edginess and unpretentiousness while providing its setting with a clean-lined, modern look with a very low maintenance design. The style works particularly well in large, open spaces with a bit of an industrial feel to them, but that certainly wasn't the case with this police station. What had probably started out as a well-intentioned design, with the focus concentrating on practical use rather than attractiveness, had failed pretty miserably, and the innards of the complex had a continuous blandness that made you feel claustrophobic.

At the reception area, he introduced himself and a police officer guided him into a conference room. He fully expected to be pounced upon and hand-cuffed by the people in the room, but DI Blair Chalmers smiled in his direction, shook his hand and asked him to sit down.

"Attention everyone. Take a seat. What I am about to explain to you is extremely detailed and is classified as restricted information. It is not to be discussed outside of this room unless in an operational context. There would be 'undesirable effects' if what I am about to detail to you became publicly available."

There were nods of agreement around the room and Daniel noticed that all eyes and ears were trained on DI Chalmers. She continued her introductory spiel.

"As you will probably now have gathered with you all being in this room together today, there is a major operation about to break in the Glasgow area in the next 24 hours or so. The Major Investigation Team will be leading the case, and I have been tasked by the Chief Constable with bringing other agencies and divisions up to speed with the situation we are about to face. Let me do the introductions.

We have officers from the SCD, the Specialist Crime Division, and they will provide us with the access to national investigative and intelligence resources we'll require to have as we go along. We need SCD assistance for matters relating to major crime, organised crime, counter terrorism, intelligence, covert policing and public protection.

The SCD officers will liaise directly with OCCTU, the Organised Crime and Counter Terrorism Unit and we can rely on having daily support from Box 500 aka MI5 and advice and updates from the Office for Security and Counter Terrorism at the Home Office.

On my right are officers from the NHTU, the new National Human Trafficking Unit, and Armed Response have provided us with four ARVs, armed response vehicle teams, to use, if and when necessary.

Finally, this gentleman here to my left, is Daniel Lauridsen, a security specialist and a former Danish Special Forces operative. In a consultant capacity, Daniel will be providing us with detailed information and an oversight of the complicated situation I am about to reveal."

There were muted conversations and murmurings from the people in the room and casual nods of acknowledgement and half-hearted smiles were thrown in Daniel's direction.

"Right. Settle down now and pay attention" barked Chalmers as she dimmed the lights and started to bring up images and documents on a large projector screen on the wall behind her. She explained who the various people were and gave brief descriptions of documents and the like. There was silence apart from a few gasps and inward sighs as she played the CCTV footage of the last moments of Dunky Stevens and then she suddenly placed Daniel in a difficult position with the rest of the room. She played the video footage of him bundling Manus Neeson in front of the train. Before he or anyone else could react or comment on what they had just watched, Chalmers calmly addressed the room with an explanation.

"I've spoken with analysts from the Accident Unit within the Procurator Fiscal's Office and they are satisfied that the tragic death of Manus Neeson was entirely accidental and was not an intentioned act of foul play by Mr. Lauridsen here. There will obviously be a Fatal Accident Inquiry held in due course, but the mitigating circumstances in the prevention of a serious assault being committed resulted in the thwarting of an attempted abduction then taking place thereafter, have convinced the PF's office that the death of Manus Neeson was an unfortunate accidental outcome of a potential criminal act being commissioned by him on a packed underground station platform during the morning rush-hour."

Daniel silently mouthed 'Thank you' at Chalmers. She nodded and continued on with her briefing. Chalmers then brought up photographs of Lindemann, Freyja Fulton, Phil Harris, McGregor and McCallum on the projector screen. "I'll pass you over to Daniel and he'll quickly explain who these people are and where we think they fit into the current investigations."

She beckoned him forward and whispered "Just tell them who's who and what you know about them and explain the jigsaw. They'll quickly grasp the importance of things."

For the next fifteen minutes, Daniel explained the connections and correlations between the five photographs and how Phil Harris was now essentially his 'inside man' who could and would provide much-needed information and intelligence when required. He detailed what he thought was Lindemann's true intention with his urgency to have Freyja

Fulton in his possession as quickly as possible, and that was to have access to every single drop of her blood. The room just hung on to his every word and he had to stifle a laugh when he heard a comment whispered aloud in broad Glaswegian. "Fucking Nazis? Ah fucking hate Nazis!" He almost stopped speaking to agree with the commentator but continued explaining his perception and comprehension of the many occurrences he had recently encountered in the past few weeks, and how, at first, their connections to each other had appeared to him to be nothing more than just coincidence and happenchance.

Daniel explained how he had quickly ascertained from going through Lindemann's files that the Das Volker Syndicate had fingers in many pies going all the way back to Nazi Germany. It was by going through these files that he had un-covered that Lindemann, and his father before him, had used the company, Das Volker Syndicate, to 'cloak' the many activities, history and concerns of the Ahnenerbe and its principle ambition - to find a source and then recreate the blood of the Aryan race, and to that, the 21st Century face of the Ahnenerbe required Freyja Fulton.

He noticed that his mobile phone was ringing by its flashing display screen and the vibration alert function was making the device move across the table top in front of him. A couple of people had entered the room and were having an intense discussion with DI Chalmers. Whatever that conversation entailed must be important as he observed that all three heads were very close to each other. There was some animated hand-waving and gesticulation punctuating the sentences that were being spoken. His phone started flashing and vibrating again and the distraction made him momentarily pause and squint to see who the caller was. It was Philip Harris.

DI Chalmers put two fingers in her mouth and blew a piercing whistle to attract everyone's attention.

"Gather round everyone. I've just been informed that two females have been snatched off the street outside St. Kentigern's College. The local uniforms state that the females, presumably students, were stopped in the street by some foreign women and a van pulled up, two men got out and bundled both females inside. The van sped off northwards. The police helicopter is up in the air looking for the van and uniforms are conducting enquiries, trying to find out who the two females are and taking statements from witnesses."

Daniel waved his left hand and caught the attention of Chalmers. He was finishing a telephone call. "That was Phil Harris. McGregor and McCallum have just rocked up at the Das Volker Syndicate place in Possilpark in a white van. They dragged two young females out of the van and then handed them over to Lindemann. He's apparently prepping them both for some medical procedure. Phil says that one of the girls is Freyja Fulton."

12.13pm – Tuesday 20th June, present day
The Das Volker Syndicate Research laboratory, Possilpark Business Zone, Glasgow.

DI Chalmers stepped out of her car and approached the group gathered around the side of a long removal lorry. Other vehicles were parked around it, and as the nearside canopy of the lorry was unhinged and lowered to the ground, Daniel recognised that the lorry was a covert control and communications centre with computers and television screens to co-ordinate matters. Chalmers noticed him studying the control centre.

"This was built as a mobile unit for deployment in case of a terrorist incident or serious situation unfolding during the Commonwealth Games here in Glasgow in 2014. It was the biggest security operation in Scotland's history and saw the co-operation of the police, emergency, security, military and intelligence services of 71 countries and territories. It was a logistical nightmare that needed a number of mobile command centres like this one to be readily available to co-ordinate the neutralisation of any terrorist threat. There were thousands of troops from army units such as the Black Watch, the Royal Dragoon Guards and the Ghurkhas deployed along with many RAF and Royal Navy personnel. There were Apache helicopter gunship landing pads throughout the city and anti-aircraft missile systems were placed on top of high-rise buildings protecting civilian flight paths. The RAF had Typhoon fighter jets on standby and flying restrictions were enforced over the whole of the greater Glasgow area to protect the city and all the sporting venues. Once the games were over, Police Scotland then allocated the mobile units around the country for the regional forces to have. They are three of them in the Glasgow area."

Daniel walked over to a grass verge and climbed up its banking to a hedge lining a copse of trees. From there, he could see that the laboratory building was about 400 metres away on the other side of the trees. The building sat in the middle of an expansive grass bowl-like field, the perimeter of which was bordered with a green trimesh security fence that ran parallel with the trees on all four sides. He looked back down the verge and realised that Chalmers had chosen well by locating the command centre at the bottom of a dead-end road that was obscured by trees and hedges. The heavy police presence would not be noticeable to anyone within the building. He strolled back down the banking and walked over to Chalmers who was talking to a group of officers. The Armed Response units were checking their Kevlar clothing and sorting out helmets and faceguards.

"You may have a slight problem or two if you try to approach the building un-noticed. There seems to be only a single entrance point with a gatehouse and a hydraulic ramp barrier blocking a roadway operating a one way system in and out for traffic. The road circles the laboratory with the staff and visitor car-parking area at the front of the building and the goods and services area at the back. Both can only be accessed by travelling along and around the one-way system. The perimeter area has a trimesh security fence topped with barbed wire, but behind it, rolls of concertina razor wire are stretched out along the ground. It would be extremely difficult to scale the fence and then cross through the razor wire without being spotted. There are also cameras on lighting pillars every 50 metres or so and I suspect that the fencing, going by the small yellow boxes situated along the top of it, has some sort of vibration detection system. I would go and have a look for yourself if you don't believe me."

Chalmers glared at him and went and spoke to the Armed Response Commander. The two of them climbed up the banking and walked backwards and forwards along the hedge looking through the trees to the laboratory. They stopped occasionally to study aspects of the layout and the fenced perimeter. The commander kept on looking through field glasses and then would pass them over for Chalmers use to confirm whatever he was pointing out to her.

Daniel was leaning against the side of the command centre vehicle when they returned. Chalmers asked him to come in and they sat at a central table. The Armed Response commander and a number of other men joined them.

On the table, a schematic plan of the laboratory building and the adjacent grounds confirmed what Daniel had said. There were various suggestions being made about getting into the facility and Daniel, through frustration, banged his hand on the table. Silence and stern stares greeted him.

"Why not go simple? Why not let me just go in myself, disable the gatehouse defences, isolate and switch off the cameras and the fence security and open the doors for you? I have a man on the inside that'll get me past the gatehouse and I can wing it from there."

The Armed Response commander just scoffed at him. "Why don't you just leave this to the professionals? We're trained to do this sort of thing."

Daniel just laughed at him. "Professionals? So you're going to ignore the advice of a security specialist who was in the Frømandskorpset, skilled in reconnaissance, direct assault, sabotage, counter terrorism and search and rescue missions who also trained a number of elite commandos of your SAS and SBS? Very good! By the time you come up with a plan these girls will be dead."

"Enough!" shouted Chalmers. "We'll go with your plan. Call Phil Harris and sort it." She turned to the Armed Response commander. "Give him a weapon and an ear-piece."

The commander unfastened the Velcro of his Kevlar body armour and passed Daniel a Glock 17 police issue 9mm pistol. "Do you know how to use it?" he sarcastically snapped.

Daniel just started to disassemble and then re-assemble the pistol. "It's most effective at a range of between 10 and 25 metres. It has three built-in safety catches, and the pistol can be kept fully loaded with 17 rounds, including one in the chamber, even when it's holstered. The pistol is standard issue as a secondary weapon for the Frømandskorpset to use whether it is in the icy wastes of the Arctic to the deserts of the middle-east. From temperatures ranging from -40C to over 50C. Yeah! I think I know how to use it in Glasgow."

"Will you two cut it out and concentrate on finalising a plan?" shouted Chalmers at them both. "Have you called Phil Harris yet?" she asked Daniel. Daniel picked up his phone and called Phil Harris.

"Phil. It's Daniel Lauridsen here. I'm about to arrive at the front gate and I need you to tell security that I have a meeting with you and Lindemann. I have the cavalry with me but I need to be inside the building first to disable the alarms and secure the girls. Can you manage that?"

"Eh. Eh. Err...leave it with me and I'll sort it out. When will you be here exactly?" queried Harris.

Daniel looked at his watch. "Ten minutes. I'll be at the front gate bang on 1.00pm. Are the girls safe?"

"They are for now but not for long. Hurry. I'll sort out the front gate for you."

Daniel killed the call and turned round to the Armed Response commander. "Can we start again? Level playing field? Could you pretend to be my chauffeur and drive me up to the gatehouse and we can play it by ear from then onwards? I don't even know your name." and held out his hand towards him.

"Peter Thompson. Sorry for the snash earlier. Let's do this." and shook Daniel's hand.

The Stream

Peter Thompson slowly drove the unmarked police car up to the gatehouse of the facility. He had changed into civilian clothing so as to not to draw suspicion to himself and had stowed his tactical gear and weaponry in the boot of the car. In the back seat, Daniel Lauridsen sat with the air of a disinterested passenger keen to get to his destination. Peter stopped the car in front of the hydraulic ramp barrier and lowered the driver window to speak to the approaching security guard.

"Can I help you?" asked the guard as he peered into the vehicle and studied the driver and his passenger.

"I have a Mr. Daniel Lauridsen here to see Phil Harris and Dr. Lindemann for a meeting at 1.00pm." said Peter as he passed over a business card for the guard to examine.

The guard checked his clipboard. "I'll need you to come in to the gatehouse to sign the Visitor book."

Peter got out of the car and opened the rear passenger door for Daniel and both men followed the guard into the gatehouse. Another guard was seated in front of a bank of screens that displayed differing camera angles inside the complex and the adjacent grounds and perimeters. As Daniel was signing the Visitor book, he nodded at Peter to indicate that the pre-agreed distraction was imminent. The seated guard suddenly spoke. "Tommy. There's a woman coming up to the gate with a dog. It looks like a walking fur coat with teeth. Goany go and tell her that this is not a park for dug walking?"

Daniel looked up to see DI Chalmers approaching the gatehouse with a tethered Alsatian dog straining at its leash and dragging her along. It was a brute of a beast and he liked the analogy of a 'walking fur coat with teeth'. Tommy the guard started to exit the gatehouse and Daniel grabbed him from behind and banged his head off the door-frame. The guard collapsed to the ground shouting in pain. Peter stood over the seated guard and told him to stand up slowly with his hands in the air. The seated guard did as he was told and was persuaded by the fact that a Glock 17 pistol was being waved in front of his face.

"Tweed's a bit of a handful" said Chalmers as the dog stepped over the body of Tommy and entered into the gatehouse. Both of the guards were then bound, hand and foot, with cable ties and dragged across the floor to a corner. Chalmers told the dog to sit and she walked over to the two guards. She pulled out her warrant card and showed it to them. "You two are going to sit here nice and quietly. Not a word from either of you. There's a wee situation going on inside just now that requires some Police involvement. I know you guys are probably innocent and just doing your jobs, but Tweed here" and she pointed at the Alsatian, "he's not been fed for a week now and he will eat you if either of you two bawbags move a muscle or make a sound. Don't even fart."

The sedentary Alsatian just stared at both guards. He licked his chops, wrinkled his nose and then bared his front teeth at them. A deep and worrying growl came from within the animal and both guards just lay there, petrified, staring at the dog. Chalmers walked past the dog and patted him on the head. "Good boy. Watch them."

Daniel and Peter got back into the car and Chalmers, now sitting on a raised swivel seat in the gatehouse, depressed the button for the ramp to lower. She waved at them as they drove off towards the car park at the front of the facility. She kept the ramp lowered and reached into her jacket for her Airwave handheld transceiver. "They are in. Move! Move! Move!"

Peter pulled the car up at the front of the car park and opened the rear passenger door for Daniel to get out. Daniel started to walk to the entrance door that Phil Harris was now holding open. Peter went round to the back of the car and opened up the boot. Masked by the raised boot lid, he put on his tactical gear, headset and checked his Heckler & Koch MP5 carbine and awaited developments and back-up to arrive.

Phil was jitterish as he let Daniel into the foyer of the complex. He was shaking and struggling to compose himself. Daniel told him to pull himself together and asked where the girls were. Phil pointed to a mezzanine floor and started to walk up a stairway. A door opened above them on the far end of the mezzanine and a man looked down as they were walking up the stairwell. The man stopped and about-turned back into the room and shut the door.

Colin McCallum confusedly shook his head and decided to seek his friend, Stuart McGregor, for some advice. He opened another door and passed through into a large labyrinthian laboratory unit area with offices and sealed individual workspace compartments with opaque one way glass. Inside a compartment, you could watch the world go by but no-one could see into the room. Passing into another room, he saw that Lindemann was attempting to rouse the young girls who were both still unconscious and were now strapped into triage chairs. Two personal body-guards were standing against the far wall and Lindemann was verbally berating McGregor and threateningly brandishing a golf putter in his friend's face.

Lindemann was incandescent with rage. His blue eyes flashed with anger and the grip on the putter was tightening. "What did you inject these girls with to subdue them? I need this one to be conscious to do what I have to perform. I need to know what you used as it may affect the purity of the blood I need. It was a simple task and yet you still managed to fuck it up."

"Amobarbital. We used Amobarbital on them. We injected it into their arms as soon as we got them in the van." blurted McGregor.

"Because you stupidly used an intramuscular injection of Amobarbital, it takes between 16 and 40 hours for the drug to metabolise out of an adult's system. That's a mean average of 25 hours. We now have to keep these girls alive for another day at least." Lindemann's annoyance was evident and fearful for his friend and remembering what happened to Dunky Stevens, McCallum interrupted Lindemann's rant at McGregor.

"Stuart. Remember that bloke that talked to us at the underground station yesterday? The guy that told us there had been a jumper on the platform? He's walking up the stairs the now with Phil Harris. Will you come and have a look?"

McGregor was glad of the sudden intrusion by his friend. Both he and Lindemann looked at McCallum and started to follow him back through the maze of offices and workstations. Lindemann ordered his bodyguards to take the girls to the containment and isolation room.

From behind the one-way glass of the office room, McGregor, McCallum and Lindemann could see Harris and Daniel walking along the mezzanine towards them. McGregor confirmed that Daniel was the man that spoke to them on stairs of the underground station the day before and Lindemann muttered "Daniel Lauridsen".

Lindemann glowered through the glass as Phil Harris went to open the door. As he entered, a shout of "Verräter", the German for traitor, met him and he caught sight of a metallic swish coming towards him at speed. From behind, Daniel had glimpsed the start of a downward arc of a golf club aimed head height at Phil and pushed him through the door. The golf club glanced a sickening sounding blow on the side of Phil's head and blood erupted from a wound and started to spray in all directions. A slight scuffle ensued with the advancing McGregor and McCallum as Daniel grabbed Phil by the collar and dragged him back out on to the floor of the mezzanine. Daniel pulled the door shut on the two Glaswegians and drew his Glock and shot at the door lock. The bullet shattered the mechanism and sealed the door. No-one could now open the door. He pressed a fire-alarm button on the wall and ripped at Phil's shirt to make an impromptu bandage to stem the head wound.

The sound of a solitary gun-shot and then the fire alarm had brought Peter Thompson running through the front door. He could see that Daniel was kneeling over someone on the mezzanine level and he sprinted up the stairs towards him. Doors were opening around him as various Das Volker

Syndicate staff made their respective ways toward the designated fire escape exits. They didn't seem to be at all nonplussed to see a man, dressed in black and carrying a machine gun, running past them. Outside, flashing blue lights signalled the arrival of the various police teams. The Armed Response officers approached the building exits in standard two by two formations and ordered the fleeing staff to lie face down on the ground with their hands upon their heads. Other police officers started to cable-tie the hands of the rescued behind their backs and led them away to the safety of the police vehicles.

Thompson skidded to a halt beside Daniel and the distressed Phil Harris. "It's just a bit of a flesh wound thankfully. It looks far worse than it is. Have you got a field first-aid kit on you?" Daniel asked Peter. Peter retrieved a box from his Kevlar flak-jacket and passed it to Daniel. Daniel applied a dressing to the wound and joked with Phil.

"Luckily for you it was putter he used and it's only a small divot. If it had been a wedge, we might be calling you Sandy now."

Phil just blinked in confusion. "Sandy? Oh! I get it now. Sandy as in sand-wedge. Ooooh! That's sore." he winced in pain as he laughed at the humour of the moment.

"Pete? Can you look after Phil while I go and get the girls? Can I also borrow your MP5 please?"

Peter Thompson handed over his MP5 and watched Daniel expertly cock and load the weapon and then pull Phil's door security pass lanyard free from around the man's neck. "Good luck." he shouted as he watched Daniel run off down the mezzanine and swipe open a door at the far end.

The Stream

The Das Volker Syndicate Research laboratory, Possilpark Business Zone, Glasgow.

The containment and isolation room within the Research Clinic laboratory was fairly Spartan. It was a retreat facility within the laboratory in case of spillage or contamination. It worked both ways. In case of an accident, staff could retreat inside it and call for assistance, or, if someone had been contaminated or infected with something nefarious, they could be contained and isolated within it. The room was basically an island cubicle and was about 6 metres square with wide viewing panels on all four sides. It was an airtight and sound-proof room. The door was hermetically sealed into the wall and was fitted with a Vistamatic window to allow for visual observation from outside. The windows were double-skinned and made with armoured glass clad polycarbonate laminates that had an automatic titanium blind between the inner and outer panels. If something, or someone, tried to break into the room, the titanium blinds would shoot upwards from the floor to the ceiling.

The ceiling was completely flat with no light fittings or inspection hatches. The walls were also flat with no fixtures or fittings. The floor was flat but had a continuous coved bunding where it met the walls. The room was illuminated by white panel lighting inset to the four curved corners of the room. There were no ledges or window sills and all the surfaces were completely smooth.

The only furnishing in the room was a long double-sided stainless steel tube frame seat that was in the centre of the floor and a plinth that had an angled touch-screen display unit with a key-card and key-pad terminal beside it.

Wendy and Freyja lay either side of the double-sided seat and both were still unconscious from the effects of the Amobarbital sedative that McGregor had injected them with.

A piercing alarm tone sounded inside the room. Its volume was excessively loud, but that was the whole point of it – a sound that would awaken the dead. In this instance, it was to rouse both girls from their drug-induced torpor and grab their attention. The touch-screen display unit was flashing. Wendy was the first to stir. She was lying face down on the seat with her long black curly hair sprawling over the end and onto the floor. As she began to come around, her senses were assaulted with the sonic blast emitting from all around her.

Her head was sore, her vision was blurred and she felt terrible. She was thirsty and wanted a drink, it didn't matter what it was as long as it was wet. She pushed herself up from the seat, staggered around and sat back down on the seat. She had her hands over her ears trying to shut out the noise that seemed to be liquidising her brain. "Will you shut the fuck up?" she yells and the alarm tone stops. Perfect timing or coincidence, Wendy didn't really care as the sound had stopped. But there was another noise in the room. Wendy groggily looks around the room and spots a flashing screen on an upright plinth. A bing-bong tone denotes that a video message is trying to connect. Wendy looks at Freyja lying on her back on the other side of the seat. Completely out for the count she hopes. A vein in Freyja's neck throbs and Wendy is relieved to see that her friend is still alive. She sidles around the seat towards the plinth. The bing-bong message tone is now beginning to grate almost as much as the alarm tones that had just stopped. A flashing icon on the screen is asking 'Accept' or 'Decline'. Wendy presses 'Accept'.

The face of Phil Harris appears on the screen. He looks dreadful. Blood is still seeping from the now-bandaged wound on his head where Lindemann hit him with the golf club.

"My name's Phil and I'm going to try to help you get out of the room there. Sorry about the sonic alarm but I had to wake you guys up. You've got about 5 minutes to get out of there. That lunatic Lindemann is on his way to you now. I can't come and get you out as I'm gubbed and too far away from you, but I can give you the code to get out of the room though. You have to type it in three times as you don't have a swipe card for the machine. Will you remember the code?" he asks.

"What's the code?" says Freyja.

Wendy turns round and looks at her. She looks like she has just eaten a stinging nettle. Freyja's face is all screwed up in pain and she is rubbing her right arm where she had been injected. She realises that her left arm is also sore and discovers that someone has inserted a cannula into her. "What the fuck is this?" she grunts as she pulls the cannula out of her arm and throws it across the room.

"It's a scramble code. The same three numbers jumbled up but followed by a letter. 187X and press enter. 781Y then press enter and 871Z and press enter. The door should un-seal. When it does un-seal, go to your right and head towards the double-doors about 10 metres in front of you. Go through those double-doors and head down the corridor to the end. There's a fire escape door that takes you out on to the lawn at the front of the building."

"Thanks Phil" says Wendy as she starts to type in the code.

The door un-seals and the girls exit the isolation cubicle. Having emerged from a sound-proof room, the first things they hear are warning klaxons sounding with a message playing "Please evacuate the building. This is not a drill. Please evacuate the building". What sounds like shouts and screams can be heard coming from other parts of the building and every so often 'Pop. Pop pop pop pop. Pop pop. Pop. Pop pop pop pop' sporadically rings out amongst the sounds of panic and alarms going off elsewhere in the complex.

Wendy runs towards the double-doors and realises she is alone. Freyja is not with her. She stops and looks around for Freyja and sees her friend bending down and picking something up from the floor. Wendy runs over to her. "C'mon you. This isn't the time for pissing about and reading stuff. We have to get out. C'mon. Let's go."

But Freyja just walks over and hugs Wendy strongly and then stands back. "You go Wendy. I have to go and do something. I need to know what this is all about. Look around you. Look at this security door key card. There are Das Volker Syndicate logos everywhere and that isn't coincidental. I have to do this. I have to get some answers." and runs over to another doorway, opens it, goes through and shuts it behind her.

Wendy runs after her friend. "Freyja. Don't be bloody stupid. Let's get out of here and get some help. C'mon Freyja"

Wendy tries the door. It's shut fast. She tries shouldering the door but nothing gives. Wendy realises that Freyja has locked the door from the other side to stop her following. "Silly wee cow" she mutters as she turns and continues with her own escape, just as Phil had suggested that the two of them should follow. She opens the door and runs into daylight and grass lawn. She runs about 5 metres and then is man-handled to the ground by armed police officers, her hands are cable-tied behind her and she is dragged unceremoniously to the back of a police van.

The Stream

1.24pm – Tuesday 20th June, present day
The Das Volker Syndicate Research laboratory, Possilpark
Business Zone, Glasgow.

Daniel's ear-piece had the voice of DI Chalmers giving him directions. From the gatehouse security cameras, she could watch how events were unfolding. She'd contacted Peter Thompson to get information from Phil Harris as to the whereabouts of the girls. She had just watched two men push the girls on chairs along some passageways and then tip them both out onto a bench inside a brightly lit room. From the cameras, she could see that the two men were now advancing on Daniel's position and that he was going to be flanked in a pincer movement.

"Daniel! Daniel! Can you see them? There's a guy about 10 metres away from you on your left and another one is about 15 metres away on your right."

"Negative. I can't see anything unless it is right in front of me in these corridors. The wall glass is opaque and it stops me seeing through it."

He took the butt of the MP5 and smashed it against the nearest glass panel. It cracked and started to splinter. He stood back against the wall and with the thumb of his shooting hand on the pistol grip, flicked through the three-position fire mode selector of 'S' or *Sicher* for weapon safe, 'E' or *Einzelfeuer* for single fire and 'F' or *Feuerstoß* for continuous fire. He selected 'E' and started to shoot at the glass panels to his left. The bullets caused the panels to shatter and broken glass started to cascade downwards inside the rooms and compartments around him. He barrel-rolled into the room directly in front of him and took some cover behind a desk. A figure suddenly stood up in the corridor outside and looked around the room through the broken panels. The man had a weapon in his right hand and Daniel, looking down the iron-sight of his carbine, depressed the trigger three times. Tap. Tap. Tap. The figure in the corridor jolted in different directions as the three rounds hit the man squarely in the chest. The weapon in man's hand fell out as he bounced off the wall behind him and then slumped to the ground.

Daniel could see a silhouette of another man through the broken glass on his left. He raised his weapon in readiness for firing. A door opened in the corridor away to his right and Freyja Fulton burst into the passageway. She screamed as the saw the dead body lying in the debris of the glass on the carpet in front of her. Daniel shouted for her to get down and the man to his left fired his weapon at him. Bullets thudded in and around the desk and he felt a sharp pain sting throughout his body. Blood is seeping from his waist and he realises he's been shot. He flicks the fire mode selector to 'F' and squeezes the trigger. The rapid fire shudder of his weapon causes even more pain to course through his body as 13 rounds leave the barrel and find their target. The man in the corridor convulses and jerks as each and every round finds their mark upon his body. The impacts cause him to fly backwards and scrunch into a lifeless heap on the floor.

"Freyja! Freyja! Get the hell out of here. Follow the exits signs and run for your life and don't stop for anyone. Head for the safety of the gatehouse outside. Run." shouts Daniel.

Freyja stands up and looks at the prone body of Daniel lying on the floor of the room. He's holding his side and winces in pain as he gesticulates at her to go. She turns and blindly runs down the corridor. Exit signs on the ceiling indicate her escape route. Pushing at doorways, she continues following the signs and emerges out into a loading bay area. A motorised roller-shutter doorway is opening and she heads towards it. She is halted in her progress as her right forearm is suddenly pulled backwards. Torstein Lindemann has grabbed a hold of her and she struggles against him as he tries to drag her into the back of a stationary car. Two men are in the front seats and Lindemann is screaming at her. "You will not evade me now like your grandmother did, you little bitch." as he continues trying to pull her into the car. She whirls her right hand around in a clockwork motion and breaks Lindemann's grip of her arm. With her left foot, she kicks in him the groin and shouts "Fuck off!" and runs towards the rising roller-shutter doorway.

Lindemann falls back into the vehicle and pulls himself back upwards and closes the door over. He shouts at McGregor and McCallum in the front seat.

"Run that bitch down now."

Freyja stoops under the rising roller-shutter and sees the gatehouse about 50 metres away from her across a lawn. She runs towards it. Behind her she can hear the car revving its engine impatiently as it waits for the roller-shutter to rise sufficiently high enough for it to pass through. Her heart is pounding and every sinew in her body is straining as she sprints towards the gatehouse. A horrible metallic screeching sound is now coming from behind her and she looks backwards to see the car roof scraping against the bottom of the roller-shutter door. The struggle of the vehicle against the mechanism is causing the roller-shutter to billow like a sail in the wind. The car breaks free of its restraint and surges forward as the shutter bursts from its trackings.

Freyja gets closer to the gatehouse and can see the banks of flashing blue lights beyond it and uniformed figures milling about. Safety, but the roar of a car engine is right behind her. Uniformed police officers run towards and past her in the direction of the chasing vehicle and she hears shouts of alarm followed by screams and crumps as the advancing car runs roughshod over the top of them. She passes the gatehouse and is conscious that the car is almost upon her. DI Chalmers watches in alarm from inside the gatehouse and presses the button for the hydraulic ramp. The ramp starts to rise and Freyja skips over it. The car is almost upon her.

Lindemann sits in the back seat of the car and is leaning through the space between the front seats. He is screaming and shouting at McGregor to drive faster.

"Kill that bitch. Kill her". The car is close to collision with the girl when it suddenly stops. The ramp has halted the car's progress and the vehicle's framework concertinas against the immoveable barrier and bounces backwards. The impact causes Lindemann to be propelled through the windscreen, out of the car and over the barrier. His body tumbles, bumps and slides across the tarmac roadway and comes to a halt.

Freyja is caught by a passing police woman and Chalmers runs out of the gatehouse, past the wreck of the car and stops at the body of Lindemann. His arms and legs are in distorted positions to his body. He is covered in cuts and scrapes and blood is seeping slowly from his ears, nostrils and mouth. Lying on his back, he pants breathlessly and his eyes are slowly blinking as he looks upwards in the sunlight. Chalmers watches the intensity of his blue eyes begin to dissipate as his life force expires. He aspirates blood from his mouth as he gargles "Meine Ehre heißt Treue" in his final breath. The blue eyes turn slate grey and Chalmers gently rolls her hand over them to close the eyelids.

A glint on the roadway catches her eye and she picks up what she thinks is a coin and puts it in her pocket. She looks behind her towards the laboratory complex and sees emergency service personnel dealing with staff and casualties. Paramedics are trying to resuscitate the police officers mown down by Lindemann's car and Fire Service and Rescue officers are beginning their attempts to cut McGregor and McCallum out of the wreckage remains. She walks towards the gatehouse and comforts a stricken Freyja Fulton as paramedics begin to attend to her. "It's over Freyja. It's over now."

The sight of Peter Thompson lugging an injured Daniel Lauridsen out of an exit made her jog over to them. Thompson lay Daniel down on the grass and shouted for medical assistance. Chalmers asked how serious the injury was. "It's a through and through bullet wound on his right-hand side. No internal organs affected but he'll have a lovely scar to remember his visit to Glasgow by." said Thompson.

"Lindemann has been killed in a car crash and Freyja Fulton and her friend are now both safe and well thanks to you. I found this on the ground beside Lindemann's body. Do you know what it is?" and she passed Daniel the coin she had picked up.

Daniel looked at the coin on both sides and handed it back to her. On one side of the coin was a motif of a rounded swastika flanked by a laurel wreath with a representation of 'Odin's pillar', *Yggdrasil,* in the centre. "It's the badge of the Ahnenerbe with its motto inscribed on the back, 'Meine Ehre heißt Treue'. Translated into English it means 'My honour is called loyalty'."

"Well I hope he's rewarded well for it in Hell and he burns for all of eternity." wished Chalmers.

Epilogue

11.42am – Thursday 9th November, present day
The McLennan Arch, north-west entrance to Glasgow Green, Glasgow.

The McLennan Arch, found at the north-west entrance to Glasgow's oldest park, Glasgow Green, faces the High Court building in the Saltmarket. On a bench seat near to the arch, DI Chalmers sits with Freyja Fulton and her friend, Wendy Russell. Two plainclothes officers are standing close, keeping a watchful eye on the various passers-by of the park. Arm in arm with each other, Sólrun Jacobsen and Daniel Lauridsen walk slowly under the archway and advance towards the bench. DI Chalmers stands up and greets them and introduces Freyja and Wendy.

"Thanks for agreeing to meet with us today. I can appreciate that it has been a difficult few months or so for you both." said Daniel. He asked Chalmers why she wasn't across the road at the High Court.

"Someone else can deal with the media circus in the aftermath of that sentencing today. I know Lord Dunderave is a bit of a heavy hitter but I didn't expect him to sentence both McGregor and McCallum to whole life prison terms and they're to be detained without limit of time. But I suppose when you have been indicted on a multitude of charges ranging from kidnap, abduction, robbery, human trafficking, extortion, prostitution, money laundering, assault, conspiracy, blackmail, drugs, fraud, theft, attempted murder, perverting the course of justice, attempting to defeat the ends of justice, lewd, indecent and libidinous practices, culpable and reckless injury and culpable and reckless endangerment of the public to name but a few and you get found guilty on all of those charges, unanimously, by a jury of 15 of your peers, you are not going to get a slap on the wrist and a bar of chocolate as a punishment. Anyhow, the streets of Glasgow are now a far safer place with those two doing serious time in the pokey". Daniel agreed with her and sat down beside Freyja.

Sólrun reached into her handbag and handed Daniel a large brown envelope. He opened it and took out a photograph and showed it to Freyja.

"You are probably wondering what the last few months have all been about. This photograph was taken in the Viktoriapark in Berlin on the 13th August 1939. That's my mother Petra, that's my Uncle Albert, that's my grandmother, Mille, and that's your grandmother, Dagny. Look at the brooch that my grandmother is wearing on her jacket lapel."

Freyja studied the photograph and felt for the brooch that she was wearing on the lapel of her own jacket. "Is that the same brooch?" she asked. Daniel nodded in the affirmative and reached into his pocket for a tube of coins from the SS Sauternes. He opened the tube and poured the coins into Freyja's hand. Freyja looked at the coins and turned them all over to check each side. She saw the image of the sailing ship on the coins and she unbuttoned the brooch from her jacket to compare it with what was on the coins.

"The brooch matches the ship on the coins but they are dated 1941. I don't understand. The photograph says 1939. What came first and why do they match each other? What's the connection? Your grandmother is wearing the brooch but I seem to have it now?" She was genuinely perplexed and her interest was certainly piqued.

Daniel laughed. "Forgive me for laughing Freyja, but as Sólrun will confirm, I probably had the same look of disbelief and confusion on my face back in June this year when I started to discover all sorts of connections and mysteries. My mother had asked me to find out what happened to her childhood nanny, Dagny, your grandmother, when I was up in the Faroes on business salvaging those coins and I started to make some enquiries. The more information that I discovered about Dagny, the enquiries just became even more complicated. And believe me when I tell you it got worse when I discovered that through Lindemann, we were connected to each other by coincidence, our grandmothers and by time."

"Yeah. Tell me about it. What a year I've had. I go to college to do a particular course with great job prospects post-degree, I give a mouth swab DNA sample for £30.00 and then end up with some mad Nazi chasing after me and wanting my blood. I'm now in a police protection programme while his business concerns around the world are being investigated for corruption and Nazi links, the educational institutes that he financed are either closed or have disassociated themselves with the Das Volker Syndicate and I've been told that I have to be 'protected' until all of the various international police investigations have been concluded. But thanks for saving me from Lindemann's clutches, and twice I believe." She said it all in a concise, matter of fact way and Daniel was impressed that someone so young was realistic about the circumstances that had befallen her, and that none of them were of her own making. She was accepting of her lot.

"Freyja, your grandmother's story is a fascinating one. This envelope contains all the research and evidence that I had or have found out about her, but I have also included a memory stick with all the information that Lindemann had about her as well. Dagny is referred to as a 'Daughter of the War' because of what she saw and who she met, but I think there was much more to her story than we will ever know. I've written an explanation of the significance of the coins and the brooch in my notes, but you should be really proud of Dagny. I am, because she was obviously someone very special to my own mother and grandmother, and I am glad to have that connection." He reached into the envelope and withdrew two pieces of paper.

"These are copies of documents that are within a restricted-access wartime file about Dagny and her employment at the Free Danish Embassy in London. This document here concerns the re-opening of the file a few years ago when there had been a consideration to award Dagny the Order of the Dannebrog for her meritorious service for Denmark during the wartime years. It is the highest possible honour that can be bestowed upon a Danish citizen or national, and although she was no longer a Danish national having remained in Britain after the war, exemption was going to be granted to make the award to her on the occasion of the 60th anniversary of the liberation of Denmark from the Germans on 5th May 1945. Unfortunately, Dagny had passed away just a few months beforehand and the consideration of the award was shelved and archived back in amongst the restricted file.

This other document is about the specifications of the sailing ship brooch. May I have a look at your brooch please?"

Freyja passed the brooch of the sailing ship to Daniel and she watched him twist and turn the clasp and pin mechanism sideways to reveal a hidden compartment. Daniel took Freyja's hand and gently tapped out the contents. A thin cellulose strip fell into her palm.

"Freyja, I believe that is a microfiche film, an analog copy of the original secret documents concerning the hypothetical construction of a defence barrier along the west coast of Europe that the Nazis were proposing to build during World War 2. It was called 'Das Schild', the shield. My grandmother, Mille, placed that microfiche inside the brooch and your grandmother took it with her when she escaped from Berlin as the war broke out."

Daniel took the microfiche and carefully inserted it back into the compartment of the brooch. He twisted and turned the mechanism shut and placed the brooch back into her palm and folded her hand into a tight fist around it. "Keep it safe."

He stood up and handed her the brown envelope. "We will take our leave of you now and good luck for the future." said Daniel as Sólrun kissed Freyja on the cheeks.

"Takk Fyri Freyja. If you are ever back in the Faroes, please come and see me and maybe we can go and find your relatives."

They started to walk away. Freyja shouted after them both.

"What do you want me to do with all of this? The coins? The brooch? All of this information about Dagny and the photographs and stuff you've given me?"

Daniel stopped walking and turned around to look back at her.

The Stream

"Remember that sundial on the rocks at Tinganes? You told the time when you placed your forefinger in the middle of it? The runes carved about it said 'Tíðin rennur sum streymur í á', 'Time runs like the current of a stream'. This past year and everything's that happened to you, to us, has all been about your blood, your DNA, your family history and how it flows, how it......, streams through time. You should go and write a book about it, about your grandmother and your own story.

You could use pictures of the coins and brooch for the cover and call the book 'The Stream'. I'm sure it will be a best-seller."